HIGH PRAISE FOR GRAHAM MASTERTON!

"One of the most consistently entertaining writers in the field."

—*Gauntlet*

"Graham Masterton is the living inheritor to the realm of Edgar Allan Poe."

—*San Francisco Chronicle*

"Graham Masterton is always a lot of fun and he rarely lets the reader down.... Horror's most consistent provider of chills."

—*Masters of Terror*

"Masterton is a crowd-pleaser, filling his pages with sparky, appealing dialogue and visceral grue."

—*Time Out* (UK)

"Masterton is one of those writers who can truly unnerve the reader with everyday events."

—Steve Gerlach, author of *Rage*

"Masterton has always been in the premier league of horror scribes."

News

KILLED BY NO ONE

George was soaping his chest when he felt something cold sliding down the inside of his left leg. Looking down, he saw that he was bleeding from a long thin cut that ran all the way from his testicles to the side of his knee. Blood was already running down his calf, mingled with foam and water, swirling down the drain.

How the hell...?

George reached out of the shower for his towel. He could tell that the cut must be deep as well as long, because the blood was a rich arterial color, and it was flowing out in thick surges.

"Jean!" he shouted. "Jean, I need some help here!"

He tugged his towel off the rail and wound it around his thigh as tightly as he could. All the same, it was soaked scarlet in a matter of seconds.

He lifted his right hand to turn off the water, but as he did so he felt an intense slice across his knuckles, and another cut appeared, so vicious that it almost severed his little finger. He cried out in bewilderment more than pain, and thrust his hand into his mouth, so that it was filled up with the metallic taste of fresh blood.

George staggered sideways. He slid down the wall until he was down on his knees. His back was cut in a series of diagonal slices that went right through to his shoulder-blades and his ribs. He actually felt the blade sliding against the bone. He flailed around with his bleeding hands, trying to stop his invisible assailant from cutting him any more, but there was nobody there....

Other *Leisure* books by Graham Masterton:

THE DOORKEEPERS
SPIRIT
THE HOUSE THAT JACK BUILT
PREY

GRAHAM MASTERTON

THE DEVIL IN GRAY

LEISURE BOOKS NEW YORK CITY

A LEISURE BOOK ®

October 2004

Published by

Dorchester Publishing Co., Inc.
200 Madison Avenue
New York, NY 10016

ISBN 0-8439-5361-6

Printed in the United States of America.

Visit us on the web at www.dorchesterpub.com.

THE DEVIL IN GRAY

CHAPTER ONE

Downstairs, the long-case clock in the hallway struck three. *One*, pause, *two*, pause, *three*, as if it were dolefully counting out how many lives would be lost before it struck again.

Jerry finished slapping paste onto the second-to-last roll of cornflower-patterned wallpaper and began to climb up the stepladder with it double folded over his arm. Three more lengths and the nursery would almost be ready for baby—just as soon as baby was ready for the nursery, anyhow.

He had been decorating the nursery for over a week and he had transformed it from the poky, neglected little box room it had been when they first moved in. Now the paintwork shone glossy and white, the pine door had been stripped and waxed and the doorknob polished. Once he had finished pasting up the wallpaper, there would be nothing more to do than hang the matching flowery drapes, lay the pale blue carpet, and move in the crib and the chest of drawers.

Jerry had never felt so buoyant in his life. Less than four months ago he had been promoted to full partner at Shockoe Realty, with a $17,500 hike in salary. At last he and Alison had been able to move out of their single-bedroom apartment on the second floor of Alison's parents' house south of the river and buy this tall, narrow Victorian house in the historic Church Hill district—a rare fixer-upper that hadn't come on the market for over forty-five years. Admittedly, "fixer-upper" was an understatement, because the elderly couple who had lived here since 1959 had let the rain soak into the left-hand side of the eaves since the closing days of the Nixon administration, and they hadn't changed the kitchen fittings since Buddy Holly died. But Jerry was a home-improvement buff who was in his element when he was sawing and painting and wiring and putting up shelves. Alison complained that he suffered from "fixamatosis."

He was a well-built young man of thirty-one, with cropped blond hair, a snub nose, and a cheery, obliging face—almost a natural-born Realtor. Apart from decorating he enjoyed football and hockey and white-water rafting on the James River rapids, and barbecues. He had a taste for khaki Dockers and red-checkered seersucker shirts.

As he climbed the stepladder he was singing to himself "Have I Told You Lately That I Love You?" It was Alison's favorite song. He had fallen for her the moment he first saw her that summer lunchtime three and a half years ago sitting alone on a bench by the Kanawha Canal, eating a ciabatta salad sandwich and reading a book. He thought she looked so darn *fresh*. She had bouncy blond hair and wide blue Doris Day eyes and she wore sleeveless blouses with turned-up collars and tight blue jeans so that she looked like the next-door sweetheart from a 1960s sitcom.

She wasn't dumb, though. The book she had been reading by the canal was *Ulysses*, by James Joyce. Jerry had sat down next to her and bent his head sideways so that he could read the spine. "Hey, *Ulysses*. I saw the movie of that, with Kirk Douglas." She had laughed; and they had started talking; and she had never found out that he hadn't been joking. He had found the book early last year and opened it, and read the words *"History," Stephen said, "is a nightmare from which I am trying to awake,"* and shook his head in a silent admission of bewilderment.

Alison called up the stairs, "Jerry, sweetheart, your chicken sandwich is ready. Do you want a beer with it?"

"Sure. Give me a minute, could you? I'm just—"

Balancing on top of the stepladder, he positioned the paper against the wall and butted the edge to the previous piece. He creased the top against the ceiling with the handle of his craft knife and started to cut it.

As he did so, blood welled out from under his left hand and started to slide down the wall. "*Shit*," he said. The cut didn't hurt but he didn't want to mess up the paper. He gripped the knife in his teeth and reached around for the damp cloth that was hanging from the back pocket of his jeans.

When he lifted his hand away from the wall to wipe it, he saw that he had somehow cut himself vertically all the way down from his wrist to his elbow—and cut himself deep. There was a bloody handprint on the paper, and now blood was starting to run down his arm and drip quickly from his elbow. Instead of trying to wipe the mess off the wall, he wound the cloth tightly around his arm and shouted out, "Alison! *Alison!*"

There was a pause, then: "What's wrong? Do you need any help with the wallpaper?"

"I've cut myself, can you bring me up a towel or something?"

He eased himself down the stepladder, holding his arm upright to relieve the pumping of his circulation. All the same the cloth was already soaked a dark crimson and drops of blood were pattering across the bare-boarded floor. The piece of wallpaper slid drunkenly sideways and then dropped down by his feet.

"*Alison!*"

"I'm coming!" she puffed. She reached the top of the stairs and crossed the landing, holding a checkered tea towel and a packet of Band-Aids. "My *God*," she said, when she saw the reddened cloth and the blood spattered all over the floor. "My God, Jerry, how did you *do* that?"

"I don't know . . . I was just trimming the top edge. I didn't even *feel* anything."

"My God, let me look at it."

She took hold of his hand and unwound the cloth. The cut in his arm was far more than an accidental nick—it was the kind of cut that a determined suicide would make, and blood was welling out of it relentlessly. Alison dabbed at it, but it was bleeding faster and faster, and in less than a minute her tea towel was drenched red, too. She took off her apron and bundled it into a pad.

"My belt," Jerry said, unfastening his buckle. "Tie it tight around here." He was already beginning to gulp with shock. "That's it, really tight."

Alison pulled out his brown leather belt and lashed it around his arm just below his bicep. She pulled it so tight that it squeaked. "Come downstairs, quick," she said. "I'll call 911."

She helped him to the door and down the two flights of stairs. He leaned against the wall as he went, leaving a bloody smear on the primrose-colored paint. When he reached the last three stairs he stumbled and staggered forward, and Alison had to pull at his shirt to stop him from falling over.

"Here," she said, as they went through to the kitchen. "Sit

down. Keep your arm up high and I'll call the paramedics."

Jerry kept swallowing and swallowing as if he were thirsty. The bundled-up apron was already soaked, and blood poured onto the kitchen table, running along the grain of the freshly stripped pine.

Alison picked up the phone. "Yes, ambulance, please. It's really urgent. My husband's cut his arm and he's bleeding so bad."

There was a blurting noise on the phone, and then the operator said, "I'm sorry, can you repeat that?"

"It's my husband! There's blood everywhere!"

"There seems to be a fault on the line, please say that again."

"For God's sake! My name is Alison Maitland, 4140 Davis Street, Church Hill! It's my husband!"

Jerry was sitting with his arm still raised, but his eyes were closed. Alison said, "Jerry! Jerry! Are you okay?"

His eyes flickered open and he nodded. "Feeling woozy, that's all."

"Please tell them to get here quick," Alison begged the operator. "I think he's going to pass out."

"Ma'am, can you repeat that address, please? I can hardly hear you."

"Forty-one forty Davis Street! You have to help me! There's so much blood! I've tied his belt around his arm, but he's cut himself all the way down from his wrist to his elbow. Hello? Hello? Can you hear me? There's so much blood!"

Jerry suddenly slumped forward, so that his forehead was pressed against the bloody tabletop. Alison dropped the phone and went over to lift him up again. "Jerry, you have to stay awake! I've called for the paramedics, they won't be long!"

Jerry stared at her with unfocused eyes. "I feel cold, Alison. Why am I feeling so goddamned *cold?*"

She bent over him and put her arms around him. "It's the shock, sweetheart. You have to hold on."

"What?"

"Think of our baby. Think of Jemima. Think of all the good times we're going to have together."

"Good times," he repeated, numbly, as if he couldn't understand what she meant.

She heard a tiny, diminished voice. It was coming from the phone that was dangling from the wall. "Hello? Hello? Are you still there, ma'am? Hello?"

She went over and scooped up the phone. "My husband looks just awful. He's shivering and he's very pale. How much longer is that ambulance going to take?"

"Hello? I'm sorry, you'll have to repeat that."

"My husband's dying! How much longer are you going to be?"

"Do you have another phone there? Maybe a cell phone?"

"Listen!" Alison screamed. "I just need to know when the paramedics are going to get here!"

"Only about a minute now. Hold on."

Alison turned back to Jerry. She was shaking so much that she could hardly speak. "They're almost here now, sweetheart. Hang on in there."

She opened the kitchen closet and pulled out five or six clean tea towels, dropping even more of them onto the floor. As she bent to pick them up, she heard Jerry say, "*Ah!*" as if something had surprised him. She turned around, and to her horror saw that he had a deep horizontal cut on his face, starting from a quarter of an inch beneath his left eye, across his cheek, and into his ear, so that his earlobe was dangling from a single shred of skin.

Blood was streaming down his chin and spattering his shirt-collar.

"Jerry! Oh my God, what's happened?"

He was so stunned that all he could do was shake his head from side to side, so that droplets of blood flew across the tabletop.

Alison folded up one of the tea towels and held it to his face. "The knife, Jerry . . . where's the knife? What have you done to yourself?"

She pried open his left hand, sticky with blood, but it was empty, and he wasn't holding anything in his right hand, either. She looked on the floor, but there was no sign of his knife anywhere. How could he have cut himself, without a knife? She lifted the tea towel away from his face for a moment and she could see that the cut under his eye was so deep that it had exposed the yellow fat of his cheek and his cheekbone.

"Oh, sweetheart, what have you done?" she sobbed. There was so much blood in the kitchen that it looked as if they had been having a paint fight. But now she could hear the *yip-yip-yipping* of the ambulance siren, only two or three blocks away.

"Hear that, Jerry? It's the paramedics. Hold on, sweetheart, please hold on."

Jerry rolled his eyes up and stared at her. He was shivering, and he had the numb, desperate expression of somebody who knows that they are not very far from death.

"Jerry, you're going to make it. You're going to be fine, sweetheart. The ambulance is right outside."

Jerry had never felt so cold in his life—a dead, terrible, all-pervasive cold that was creeping into his mind and into his body and gradually freezing his soul. A few minutes ago the kitchen had been dazzling with afternoon sunlight, but now it seemed to be dimming, and all the colors were fading to gray.

"It's getting so *dark*," he said, and his voice was thick with shock.

The door chimes rang. Alison said, "Hold on, sweetheart. The paramedics are here." She stood up and started to walk toward the hallway. Jerry thought, *Please, God, let me survive. I have to survive, for Alison's sake, for the baby's sake.* They already knew that she was going to be a girl, and they'd already chosen the name Jemima.

Alison reached the hallway, but as she did so she unexpectedly stopped. Jerry stared at her, willing her to move, willing her to answer the door, but she didn't. She stayed where she was, in the colorless gloom; and she was swaying, like a woman who has suddenly remembered something dreadful.

"Alison?" he croaked. "*Alison?*"

She tilted—and then, in a succession of impossibly choreographed movements, like a mad ballet dancer, arms waving, knees collapsing, she began to fall to the floor. As she did so, she pirouetted on one heel, so that she turned back to face him. Her eyes were staring at him in amazement.

For a moment Jerry couldn't understand what had happened to her. But then her head dropped back as if it were attached to her body on nothing but a hinge. Her throat had been cut so deeply that she had almost been beheaded, and blood suddenly jumped up from her carotid artery and sprayed against the ceiling.

A minute later, when the paramedics kicked the front door open, they found Alison lying on her back in a treacle-colored pool of blood, and Jerry crouched down next to her, whimpering and whispering and trying with sticky hands to fit her head back onto her neck.

CHAPTER TWO

Decker sat up in bed and peered shortsightedly at his wristwatch. "Holy shit! Two-thirty already. Time I wasn't here."

Maggie grinned at him from underneath a tent of sheets. "Can't you stay for dessert, lover?" She had a thick, husky voice, as if she had been smoking too many Havana cigars.

"Ex-squeeze me? What was *that*—what we just did? Wasn't *that* dessert?"

"That? That was only a little something to tickle your palate."

"My *palate?* You were trying to tickle my *palate?* I'll tell you something about you, sweet cheeks. You are in *serious* need of anatomy lessons." Decker swung his legs out of bed and retrieved his glasses from the carpet. "Listen, I have to be back at headquarters about forty minutes ago. What did you do with my shorts?"

"You've lost your appetite, Decker, that's your trouble. You're growing weary of me."

He leaned across the bed and kissed her smartly on the forehead. He wasn't growing weary of her at all, but, Jesus, she was almost inexhaustible. She was a handsome, ripe, huge-breasted woman with skin the color of burnished eggplants. Her eyes had a devilish glitter and her glossy red lips always looked as if they were about to say something outrageous, and mostly they did. She snatched back the sheets to give him a split-second glimpse of those tiny gold and silver beads she wove into her pubic dreadlocks. Then instantly she bundled herself up again and gave him a dirty laugh.

"Hey," Decker protested, tapping his forehead. "I'm not weary up here but I'm worn out down there. Give me a break, will you?"

"Just showing you what's on the bill of fare, lover. If you don't want it . . . well, that's your choice."

"Listen—I have to go or Cab will assassinate me."

"He'd assassinate you even more if he knew where you were."

Decker switched his cell phone back on. Then he found his shorts under the bed and hopped into them like a one-legged rain dancer. He lifted his scarlet necktie and his crumpled white short-sleeved shirt from the back of the chair and retrieved his black chinos from the other side of the room. Maggie lay back on the pillow watching him dress. "So when am I going to see you again? And don't give me that 'whenever' stuff."

"I don't know. Whenever. You know what my caseload's like."

"Oh, you mean Sandie in dispatch."

"Sandie and me, that was over months ago."

"What about Sheena?"

"Finished. *Kaput*. I haven't seen Sheena since Labor Day."

"Naomi?"

"What is this, the third degree?"

"More like every woman in the Metro Richmond telephone directory, lover man."

Decker went into the bathroom to comb his hair and straighten his necktie. He would have been the first to admit that he didn't exactly look like a love god. But he was lean and rangy, with thick black hair in a rather bombastic pompadour, sage-green eyes, and a kind of etched, half-starved look about him that seemed to appeal to practically every woman he met. He liked his nose, too. Narrow. Pointed. Very Clint Eastwood.

His cell phone played the opening bars of Beethoven's Fifth. Maggie mischievously reached across the bed and tried to snatch it off the nightstand, but Decker got there first. "Martin," he said, and touched his finger to his lips to tell Maggie to stop giggling.

"Martin, where the hell have you been?"

"Oh, hi, Cab." To Maggie, "It's Cab, for Christ's sake. Yeah, I'm sorry I'm running late, Cab. I had to swing by Oshen Street and talk to Freddie Wills. Well, he said he had something on that business on St. James Street. But listen, I'll be there in five."

"Forget coming back to headquarters. There's been a stabbing on Davis Street. I want your ass over here now."

"Anybody dead?"

"Unless you know of a cure for missing head, yes."

"Jesus. Give me fifteen minutes. I'll pick up Hicks on the way."

"Hicks is already here. Just haul your rear end down here as soon as you can."

Decker sat down on the end of the bed to pull on his loafers. Maggie rose out of the white sheets behind him like a gleaming black Venus rising from the foam and wrapped her arms so tightly around his neck that she almost throttled him.

"Cab's going *fishing* this weekend," she said, her breath thundering hot in his ear. She smelled like cinnamon and honey and sexual juices and sweat. "Maybe you'd be a dutiful fellow officer and come around for dinner on Saturday evening, keep me company."

"Dinner with dessert?"

"Of course dinner with dessert. Dinner with *three* desserts."

Decker unwound her arms and stood up. He buckled on his shoulder holster with its absurdly huge nickel-plated Colt Anaconda .45. He lifted the revolver out, opened the chamber, and emptied out all of the shells. Then he kissed the tips of them, one by one, and thumbed them back in again.

"You never told me why you do that," Maggie said.

"Hmm? Oh . . . superstition, that's all."

With an operatic chorus of tires, Decker pulled up outside 4140 Davis Street and climbed out of his shiny black Mercury Grand Marquis. This was an elegant, expensive district, with redbrick sidewalks and shady trees and nineteenth-century houses with white-pillared porches. Usually, at this time of day, it was soporific and almost completely deserted, with no sign of life except for sleeping cats and American flags stirring idly in the breeze, but this afternoon there were four squad cars parked diagonally across the street with their lights flashing, an ambulance, a van from the Richmond Coroner's Department, two TV crews, a crowd of uniforms and forensic investigators and reporters and all of those people who turn up at homicide scenes shouting on cell phones and looking harassed, even though Decker could never work out what most of them actually did. He even recognized Honey Blackwell from the mayor's office, all 235 pounds of her, in a daffodil-yellow suit and a daffodil-yellow bow in her hair.

"Afternoon, Ms. Blackwell."

"Afternoon, Lieutenant. Tragic business."

"Must be, if it took you away from Ma-Musu's." He was referring to her favorite restaurant, Ma-Musu's West African restaurant on Broad Street.

"You have a sharp tongue on you, Lieutenant. One of these days you're going to cut your own throat with it."

"Not a very tasteful remark to make, Ms. Blackwell, under the circumstances."

Captain Cab Jackson came down the front steps of 4140, closely followed by Sergeant Tim Hicks. "Come by way of the heritage trail, did you, Decker?" Cab demanded, checking his watch. Cab was huge, over six feet five inches, with a dented bald head like one of the bollards where the sternwheelers tied up by the James River. All the same, his face was chubby and his voice was unexpectedly high, so he had grown himself a Little Richard–style moustache in the hope of investing himself with some extra maturity. He wore a red-and-yellow-striped shirt with rows of pens and pencils clipped in the pocket, and his buttocks stuck out so far at the back that Detective Rudisill had famously described them as "Mount Buttmore."

Hicks himself was short, handsome, young, and bouncily fit, like a human basketball. He had been transferred to Richmond's Central Zone only three months ago, from Fredericksburg, upstate, and he was still pepped up about working in the city. "We the *elite*," he kept repeating, as they drove around town, slapping his hand rhythmically on the car door. Decker didn't have the heart to tell him that his transfer had probably had far less to do with the excellence of his service record than it did with the interim chief's urgent need to fill her quota of detectives of color.

"So what's the story?" Decker asked. "Pretty upscale neighborhood for a stabbing."

"You'd best come inside and see for yourself."

Decker followed Cab's buttocks up the front steps and in through the glossy, black-painted front door. He noticed that the frame was splintered, where the paramedics had kicked it open. Hicks bubbled, "I never saw anything like it. I mean, the *blood*, Lieutenant. It's like *all over.*"

"Well, remember that you can decorate an entire living room with the blood from a single person's circulatory system. Two coats, if you use a roller."

Alison's pregnant body was still lying in the hallway, one shoe on, one shoe off. She was staring at the skirting board, her blue eyes wide open. She looked more baffled than horrified, even though her head was three inches away from her neck. Hicks was right about the blood. It was all over the polished oak floor, in splashes and smears and handprints. It was up the walls, all over the doors, spattered all over the cream linen blind. There was even a fan-shaped spray of blood on the ceiling.

Decker knew from experience that blood had a way of getting everywhere. You could shoot somebody in an upstairs bedroom and tiny specks of blood would be found on the walls in the hall.

A sallow, acne-pitted police photographer called Dave Martinez was taking pictures, and the intermittent flash gave the optical illusion that Alison was still twitching. Decker hunkered down beside her and looked into her wide blue Doris Day eyes. She looked back at him, her expression pleading, *What's happened to me?*

Decker glanced at her blood-drenched smock. "How far gone?" he asked Cab.

"She was due on the twenty-first, according to her mother. But she was stabbed at least six times in the stomach. Baby didn't stand a frigging chance."

"Uncanny, don't you think?" Hicks said, breathing down Decker's neck. "She looks as if she's just about to say something."

"Oh yeah? You'd crap your pants if she did." Decker abruptly stood up again, so that Hicks had to step back out of his way. He collided with one of the kitchen chairs and almost lost his balance.

Cab sniffed and said, "Victim's name is Alison Maitland, aged twenty-eight, wife of Gerald Maitland, aged thirty-three, who's a junior partner with Shockoe Realty, 1818 East Cary Street."

"Where's Maitland now?"

"Still out in the ambulance. Arrested. Mirandized. They're giving him first aid for some serious lacerations to his arms and face. Don't worry . . . Wekelo and Saxman are with him."

"Talked to him yet?"

Cab shook his head. "I tried, but he's pretty shaken up. He said, 'It just kept cutting us.' I asked him what he was talking about, *what* kept cutting them, but he didn't give any response. Well, nothing that made any damn sense."

"I also heard him say, 'There was nobody there,'" Hicks put in. "He said it five or six times, 'There was nobody there, there was nobody there.' He was kind of muttering and mumbling, so you couldn't hardly hear him."

Hicks paused, and then he added, "Funny thing was, it wasn't like he was trying to convince *me* that there was nobody there. It was like he was trying to convince *himself*."

"I wouldn't read too much into that," Cab said. "Guy totally flipped, for whatever reason. Stress, business problems, domestic dispute, who knows? Every marriage is a mystery. Mine is, anyhow."

"Who called the cops?" Decker asked.

Hicks snapped the elastic band off his notebook. "Alison Maitland put in a 911 call at 13:56 screaming for an ambulance. She said something about blood and she called out her husband's name, but there was some kind of fault on the line and the rest of it was unintelligible. The paramedics arrived here at 14:14 but nobody answered the door and it took them a couple more minutes to gain access. When they broke in they found the victim lying right here in the hallway and her husband kneeling next to her, apparently attempting to replace her head."

"Looks like we're dealing with an optimist, then," Decker said.

"Gerald Maitland himself was very badly cut, especially his arms and face. In fact his injuries could have been life-threatening."

"Self-inflicted?"

"Must have been. When the paramedics broke down the door, the security chain was still fastened on the inside. Officers Wekelo and Saxman arrived a few minutes later at 14:28, and they found that all the back doors were securely locked and the only windows that were open were too small for anybody to have climbed in."

"Okay," Decker said, looking around. "What about the weapon?"

Cab said, "We haven't actually located it yet."

"We haven't located it? He would have needed a goddamned *sword* to cut her head off like this."

"Absolutely," Cab agreed. "Not only that, at least three of the abdominal injuries penetrated right through the victim's body from front to back, which indicates that the weapon was at least two feet long. But—whatever it was—we didn't find it in the immediate locality of the body."

"You've been through the whole property?"

Hicks said, "I organized a quick room-to-room. But Gerald Maitland was absolutely smothered in blood, head to foot—his wife's blood and his own—and he couldn't have disposed of the weapon anyplace else in the house without leaving any footprints or handprints.

"There are some traces of blood on the wall staircase, but Maitland was hanging wallpaper immediately prior to the killing and it looks as if he might have cut himself with his craft knife. We found the knife on the floor in the nursery, but it only has a two-inch blade, and although it does have a few drops of blood on it it obviously wasn't the murder weapon."

"Kitchen knives?"

"All of them clean except a small cook's knife used for cutting a chicken sandwich."

Decker said, "Hicks—we need to do another search and we need to do it now. I want this whole house taken apart. Look outside in the yard. Take up the floorboards. Look in the toilet cisterns and the water tanks. For Christ's sake, a weapon that size—it has to be somewhere."

Hicks raised his eyebrows at Cab in a mute appeal, but Cab nodded his assent. "Let's just find this sucker, shall we?"

While Hicks called in five uniformed officers for another search, Decker and Cab stepped outside the front door, onto the porch. It was stiflingly hot out there, but at least it didn't reek of blood. One or two reporters shouted at Cab for a statement, but he waved his hand and shouted back, "Five minutes! Okay? Give me five minutes!"

He dragged out a large white handkerchief and loudly blew his nose. "Goddamned allergy. It's the myrtle. I'm a martyr to myrtle."

Decker said, "Maitland was frisked, I hope? I mean he couldn't have smuggled the weapon out of the house down the leg of his pants or anything?"

"Not a chance. Wekelo subjected him to a full body search before the paramedics carried him out of the house."

Decker brushed back his breeze-blown pompadour. "I don't know . . . I'm beginning to smell something wrong with this already."

"So we haven't located the murder weapon. We probably will, but even if we don't we can still get a conviction. Who else could have done it?"

"You're probably right. But it kind of reminds me of the Behrens case. Like, Jim Behrens obviously garroted his entire family, but there was no apparent motive, and we never found the garrote, and Behrens claimed that some invisible force had come into his house and done it. The whole thing was so goddamned far out that the jury wouldn't convict." He put on his black-lense Police sunglasses. "Juries watch too much *X-Files*."

Cab sneezed and blew his nose again.

"I bet you'll shake that off, once you're out on the lake," Decker reassured him.

Cab frowned at him. "What are you talking about, lake?"

"You're going fishing this weekend, aren't you?"

"Who told you that?"

"Er—*you* told me."

"*When* did I tell you?"

"I don't know . . . couple of days ago."

"I only decided last night."

"Well, you must've mentioned that you were thinking about it, that's all."

Cab narrowed his eyes suspiciously. "I'm going fishing with Bill and Alfredick, if you must know, out to the Falling Creek reservoir."

"That's great, Cab. You deserve a break."

"You think so?" Then—even more suspiciously, "Since when did you give a fuck?"

Decker was tempted to say, "Every time you're on duty," but all he did was shrug and say, "I care about my fellow officers, Cab."

Cab still looked unimpressed, and blew his nose again.

CHAPTER THREE

Decker went back to headquarters. The first thing he wanted to do was listen to Alison Maitland's 911 call. Down in the basement, Jimmy Freedman, their sound technician, played it back for him, his chair tilted back, chewing gum and sniffing and tappety-tapping his pencil against the recording console.

"There's definitely a fault on the line, Sergeant, but it's not like any regular fault. The regular faults are usually opens, which give you white noise, or shorts, which gives you, like, static, or else you get intermittents, which are usually caused by earth shifting or water ingress. But you listen to this."

He switched on the tape, and Decker heard the 911 operator responding to Alison's call. "Emergency, which service?" This was followed by a crackling sound, and a very faraway voice, screaming. "Yes, ambulance"—more screaming, more crackling—"urgent—bleeding so bad!"

"What the hell?" Decker said. "Sounds like she's got the TV on."

"Uh-huh," Jimmy said. "It's not background noise. It's actually breaking into her call from another location."

"Crossed line, then?"

Jimmy shook his head. "It could be some kind of resistive fault, like an earth or a contact. But it's very strange, the way it just switches off and on. Listen."

"It's my husband—blood everywhere!"

Decker blew out his cheeks. "That's when he must have been stabbing her. Jesus."

But then there was shouting. It sounded like a crowd, panicking, but it was impossible to make out what they were saying.

"For God's sake—Alison—4140 Davis Street—my husband!"

"Ma'am, can you repeat that address please? I can hardly hear you."

Screaming, and then a crunching noise.

"Forty-one forty Davis Street! You have to help me—so much blood—you hear me?"

Decker listened to the tape to the end. Then he said, "Any ideas? That sounds like a goddamned battle."

"Who knows? Somebody else could have had their phone off the hook, and, like you say, there could have been a war movie playing on television. But it would have had to be a recording, because I checked the TV listings and there were no war movies playing on any channel when this call was being made.

"Like I say, though, it wasn't like a normal fault. I'll have to talk to Bill Duggan at the telephone company, see what he has to say about it. Meanwhile I'll do what I can to clean it up. Maybe we can hear what those guys are yowling about."

At 9:00 P.M. that evening, Decker received a call from the Medical College Hospital that Gerald Maitland had recovered sufficiently to be questioned. Decker called Hicks to see if he could join him, but Hicks was still taking 4140 Davis Street to pieces in his efforts to find the murder weapon.

He sounded exhausted.

"I was wondering whether we ought to cut open the couch. I mean it's real genuine leather, and it must have been pretty damned expensive."

"This is a homicide investigation, Hicks, not a furniture sale. Did you check up the chimneys?"

"I called in Vacu-Stack. They vacuum-cleaned all five of them, but all they found was dead birds."

"Tried the bedding? I found a shotgun sewn up in a mattress once."

"We tore up the mattresses, the comforters, the pillows. We pulled down the drapes—you know, in case the murder weapon was hidden in the hem. We even tore their clothes to pieces."

"Looked in the kitchen? Cereal boxes, packets of spaghetti, rolls of foil?"

"You name it, Lieutenant, we've looked in it."

"Okay . . . keep at it. I'll call you when I'm done at the hospital."

He was walking out through the shiny new lobby when a girl's voice called out, "Decker!"

He skidded to a reluctant stop and turned around. It was Officer Mayzie Shifflett, from traffic. She had a dimpled, kittenish face that made her look five years younger than she really was, with a little tipped-up nose and freckles and big brown eyes. Her khaki shirt was stretched tight over her small, rounded breasts, and her skirt was stretched tight over her firm, rounded bottom. Her blond hair was fastened in a tight French pleat.

"Are you *avoiding* me, Decker?"

"Of course not. Caseload, that's all."

"You weren't working Tuesday night, were you?"

"Tuesday? Ah—when was Tuesday?"

"Tuesday was the day before yesterday, and Tuesday was the day when you were supposed to be taking me to Awful Arthur's."

He kicked the heel of his hand against the side of his head. "Jesus—you're right, I was. Oh, Mayzie, I'm so sorry. Tuesday, my God. Do you know what happened?"

"Of course I know what happened. I put on my killer blouse and I pinned up my hair and I sprayed myself with Giorgio and then I waited for two and a half hours watching *Star Trek* until I finally decided that you weren't going to show."

"My mom had a fall. Her hip, you know? I had to go see her. I'm truly sorry. I was so worried about her that I totally forgot we had a date."

"Your mom had a fall. Decker—can't you even lie to me without bring your mother into it?"

"I'm telling you the truth, Mayzie. Do you think I would pass up on a date with you unless something really, really serious came up? Listen—I promise that I'll make it up to you."

"Like when?"

"I'm not sure. You've heard about this homicide on Davis Street—young woman had her head cut off. It's a shocker—I'm right in the middle of that."

"Decker, I have to talk to you."

He clasped her shoulders and gave her a kiss on the forehead. "Let's make it next Tuesday, then. Same place, same time."

"Decker, I have to talk to you sooner than that. I missed my period."

He snorted. "Can't you even lie to me without bringing my children into it?"

"I'm serious, Decker. I think I'm pregnant."

"Ah. Pregnant." He paused, and then he narrowed his eyes. "You're kidding me, right?"

She stared at him without blinking for a long, long time and gradually it dawned on him that maybe she wasn't kidding. He leaned closer and hissed, "How can you be *pregnant?* You're on the pill, aren't you?"

"I had to stop taking it because of my antibiotics. It was only for two weeks. I didn't think that—"

"You didn't think that if you made love without being on the pill that there might be some remote risk of motherhood? Or, even worse, *fatherhood?* I'm a detective, Mayzie, I'm not a daddy."

Mayzie's eyelashes sparkled with tears. "I'm sorry, Decker. I didn't mean it to happen. But we have to talk."

"What good is talking going to do?"

"I might be having your baby, Decker. It's not going to go away."

Decker took a deep breath. Detective George Rudisill was standing on the opposite side of the lobby, talking to a dithery old woman with her arm in a sling, and he gave Decker a slow, sly smile. Decker thought, *Shit, this is all I need.*

"All right, Mayzie," he said. "I have to go talk to my chief suspect right now. But I'll meet you at the Tobacco Company bar at, say—what time is it now? Eight o'clock, okay?"

"You'll be there, right? You won't let me down?"

"I swear on my mother's hip."

God, thought Decker. To look at, Mayzie was a peach. But whenever they had sex she let out a peculiar piping noise, like a wild goose flying south for the winter, and when they weren't having sex and she wasn't piping she never wanted to talk about anything but soap operas and nail polish and how she had once appeared in the audience in *Oprah!* (she had the videotape, if you wanted to see her, fifth row from the back, in the purple spotted dress).

Decker had invited her to Awful Arthur's for a last dinner to say, "Sorry, Mayzie, but I don't think this is really working out." It wasn't working out so much that he had totally forgotten to go.

"Eight o'clock," she insisted, and walked off back toward the traffic department.

Decker stood alone for a moment, slowly massaging the muscles at the back of his neck. Rudisill came up to him and grinned. "Hi, Lieutenant. Everything okay?"

"Sure, why shouldn't it be?"

"Shifflett didn't look too happy."

"Women are *always* happy, George. Especially when they're miserable."

Jerry Maitland was propped up in bed with the left side of his face and both of his arms thickly bandaged, so that he looked like a snowman. His pupils were dilated and he still smelled of the operating theater. The redheaded nurse said, "Ten minutes and no more, please, Lieutenant."

"You like Mexican food?" Decker asked her.

"I'm married."

"Being married affects your taste buds?"

"Nine minutes," the nurse said and closed the door behind her.

Decker approached the bed. Jerry stiffly turned his head to stare at him. Decker said nothing at first, but went over to the window and parted the slatted blinds with two fingers. Down below he could see the brightly lit sidewalks of Marshall Street, and the intersection with Fourteenth Street. After a while, he turned back and said, "How's tricks, Gerald?"

Jerry shook his head, but didn't say anything.

Decker drew up a chair and straddled it backward, shifting Jerry's plasma drip so that he could sit a little closer. "Is it Gerald or can I call you Jerry?"

"Jerry's okay," Jerry mumbled.

"Jerry it is, then. My name's Decker. Don't know what my parents were doing, giving me a goddamn outré name like that. It was something to do with my great-great-grandfather. Fought in the army of northern Virginia, in the Civil War."

Jerry tried to cough, but it obviously strained the stitches in his face, and he had to stifle it.

Decker said, "Hurts, huh?"

Jerry nodded. Decker nodded too, as if in sympathy. "You can have your lawyer present, you know that, don't you?"

"I don't need a lawyer. I haven't done anything."

"You're sure about that? It might be in your own best interest."

Jerry shook his head.

"Okay," Decker said. Then, quite casually, "What did you do with the knife?"

"I was putting up wallpaper and I cut myself. I don't know how. I dropped the knife on the floor."

"No, no. That's not the knife I mean, Jerry. That was a teensy weensy little craft knife. I'm talking about the *other* knife."

"The other knife?"

"That's right. I'm talking about the great big two-foot-long mother that you used to cut off Alison's head."

"You don't seriously believe that *I* killed her? How can you think—I *love* her. She's my wife. Why would *I* want to kill her?"

"Well, that's what I'm trying to find out, Jerry, and it

would make it a whole lot less complicated if you told me what you did with the knife."

"There *was* no knife. Don't you understand? There *was* no knife."

"So what did you cut her head off with? A pair of nail scissors? Come on, Jerry, there was nobody else in the house but you and Alison, and Alison wasn't just decapitated—she suffered more than seventeen deeply penetrative stab wounds and serious lacerations. I've been listening to her 911 call. The operator asks her what's wrong and she keeps saying, 'My husband.' "

Jerry's eyes filled up with tears. "She was calling because of me. I got cut first."

"Oh yes, by whom exactly?"

"By whatever it was that killed Alison. I didn't touch her. I love her. We were going to have a baby girl."

Decker was silent for a while. Then he reassuringly patted Jerry's arm. "All right, Jerry. You didn't touch her. But if you can tell me where the knife is, I can have the handle checked for fingerprints, and if it really wasn't you who did it, then we'll know for sure, won't we?"

"There *was* no knife. My arms got cut and then my face got cut, but I never saw a knife."

"You were alone, though? There was nobody else there except you and Alison? Is that what you're telling me?"

Jerry nodded, miserably.

Decker sat in thought for a minute or two, his hand covering his mouth. Then he said, "Okay, supposing that's what happened. How do *you* explain it?"

"I don't know. There was blood all over the kitchen. I was sure that I was going to die. Then Alison went to answer the door to the paramedics and she suddenly . . ."

"Go on. Take your time."

"I wasn't anywhere near her. She just collapsed. She kind of spun around, and—fell onto the floor and—her *head*—"

He turned his face away, rhythmically beating his bandaged arm against the blankets. All that he was capable of uttering were high, strangulated sobs.

"Okay," Decker said, after a while. "Let's leave it at that for now."

He stood up and placed the chair back against the wall. He had no doubt at all that Jerry had murdered his wife, simply because there was no other rational explanation. But there was little point in trying to question him until he came out of shock. Decker had seen it so many times before: mothers who couldn't admit that they had smothered their babies, husbands who genuinely believed that somebody else had shot their wives, even when they were standing over the body with a discharged revolver in their hand. Disassociation, they called it.

He left the room. A uniformed officer was sitting outside reading the sports pages. He put his paper down and started to stand up but Decker said, "That's okay, Greeley. Got any hot tips for Colonial Downs?"

"Mr. Invisible in the 3:45, twenty-five to one."

"Mr. Invisible, huh?" He glanced back at Jerry Maitland lying bandaged up in bed. *There was no knife. There was nobody there.*

He walked down to the nurses' station.

"That was quick," she remarked.

"I'm known for it. You're sure about that dinner invitation? I know a place where they do the world's most aphrodisiac tamales."

"I'm sorry, Lieutenant. I went to a palmist recently, and she made it quite clear that my future doesn't include Mexican meals with law enforcement officers."

"That's because she was predicting the wrong line. She was predicting your *head* line instead of your *heart* line."

"No, she wasn't. She was predicting your cheesy pickup line."

CHAPTER FOUR

Decker drove back to the Maitland house. Hicks was standing under a battery of floodlights outside with three uniformed officers and two more detectives from Customer Service Zone Central, John Banks and Newton Fry. The television trucks were still there, as well as scores of milling spectators. The evening was sticky and warm and smelled of live oaks and traffic fumes.

Decker ducked under the POLICE LINE tape. "So . . . no weapon yet?"

Hicks wiped a white smudge of plaster dust from the end of his nose. "I just don't get it. We've pretty much demolished the whole house and I'm damned if I can understand how Maitland got rid of it."

"I still think there must have been a third person present," Banks said. He was short and squat with a chest like a pit bull terrier. "I know Maitland insists that there wasn't, but what kind of mental state was he in? Or maybe he's covering for somebody."

Hicks shook his head. "We didn't find any footprints or handprints, apart from Mr. and Mrs. Maitland's. If there *was* a third person, how the hell did he or she get out of the house without leaving any tracks?"

"Maybe they got out before the blood started spraying around too much. Two-foot-long knives don't just disappear into thin air, do they?"

Decker checked his watch. It was 7:46 already and he was supposed to be meeting Mayzie at 8:00. "Look," he said, "let's call it a night and get back on to it in the morning. We need to question Maitland again before we can take this any further, and right now he's not exactly compos mentis."

He was just about to leave when a uniformed officer came up to him and said, "Excuse me, Lieutenant. There's a lady here wants to talk to you."

"Oh yes?"

"Says she was walking past here just after two o'clock this afternoon. Says her daughter saw somebody coming out of the house."

"Really?" Decker frowned shortsightedly at the crowd. "Bring her over, would you?"

The officer lifted the tapes and ushered over a middle-aged woman in a green flowery dress. She had fraying gray hair that even a dozen frantically crisscrossed bobby pins had failed to secure in a bun. She was accompanied by a plump teenage girl with Down's syndrome. The girl was dressed in a tight beige cardigan and a brown pleated skirt and she clung to her mother's arm.

"Hi," Decker said. "My name's Lieutenant Martin. My officer tells me that your daughter may have witnessed somebody coming out of this house this afternoon."

The woman gave an enthusiastic nod. "We didn't think anything about it until we saw it on the news, did we, Sandra?"

The girl covered her face with her hand so that only her milky blue eyes looked out. "Sandra can be very shy sometimes," the woman explained.

Decker said, "What time did you see this person exactly?"

"Just past two o'clock. I come to collect Sandra from her art class at two and we always walk back this way."

"Can you describe him?"

"Well, no. *I* didn't see him. Only Sandra did. She tugged my sleeve and said, 'Look at that man, Mom, don't you think he's so scary?' "

Decker frowned. "Sandra saw him but you didn't? How come?"

"Not *didn't*, Lieutenant. *Couldn't*."

"Exuse me, Mrs.—"

"Plummer, Eunice Plummer. And it's Ms."

"Okay, I'm sorry, Ms. Plummer. I don't think I'm quite following you here. Sandra said, 'Look at that scary man,' but you couldn't see him?"

"I can't always see the people that Sandra sees. I don't have her gift."

Decker thought, *Oh, shit. Another psychic.* He thought they ought to make it illegal for impressionable people to see movies like *The Others* and *The Sixth Sense*.

He took off his glasses and wiped the sweat from his forehead with the back of his hand. "Does Sandra see people very frequently, Ms. Plummer? I mean, people that you can't see?"

"Not often, no. She saw a preacher once, outside St. John's Church, in the graveyard. And then she saw a black woman in a funny hat, by Mason's Hall."

"I see. Has she talked to her doctor about this?"

Eunice Plummer looked puzzled. "Why should she talk to her doctor about it?"

"Well . . . it must be some kind of a symptom, right?"

"I'm sorry, Lieutenant. A symptom of what, exactly?"

Decker tried to put it diplomatically. "Seeing things, you know, having hallucinations . . ."

"Lieutenant, Sandra doesn't have hallucinations. She sees people that others can't, that's all. It's a facility, not a deficiency. It's like dogs hearing very high notes that are way beyond the range of the human ear. Not that I would ever compare Sandra to a dog."

"Of course. Well—I'd just like to thank you and Sandra for being so public-spirited."

"Don't you want to know what he looked like?"

"I'm sorry?"

"The *man*," Eunice Plummer insisted. "Don't you want to know what he looked like?"

"I, ah . . . I don't really think that a description is going to be necessary at this stage. Thanks all the same."

Sandra slowly lowered the hand that had been covering her face. Her cheeks were flushed and there was a large thumbprint on her glasses. "He was dressed all in *gray*," she blurted out.

Decker didn't know what to say, but Eunice Plummer coaxed her. "Go on, Sandra, tell Lieutenant Martin exactly what the man was wearing."

"He wore a gray hat like a *howboy* hat and a gray *hoat* with wings on. And he had a big black beard."

"I see," Decker said, with a tight, embarrassed smile. "That's very helpful, Sandra."

"And he had boots."

"Boots, terrific."

"Aren't you going to write this down?" Eunice Plummer asked. "She saw him, you know. She saw him as plain as day."

"Oh, sure," Decker said. He took out his notebook and a ballpoint pen that he had liberated from the Berkeley Hotel. While Eunice Plummer watched him, he jotted down *Gray. Hat. Coat. Wings?? Boots.*

"Big black beard," she added.

"Big black beard," Decker acknowledged.

"And a sword," Sandra put in.

Decker looked up. "*Sword?*"

"He had a sword. He wasn't *carrying* it. It was hanging down." She indicated with a little hand play that it had been suspended from his belt.

Decker closed his notebook. Sandra was staring at him and her expression was so fierce and unblinking that he almost believed her.

"When you first saw this man, where was he?" he asked.

Sandra pointed to the porch. "He walked through the door."

"So the door was actually open?"

She vigorously shook her head.

"Sandra—how did he walk through the door if it wasn't open?"

"He walked *through* the door," she repeated. She pronounced it, emphatically, *harooo.*

"All right . . . he walked through the door and then what?"

"He went down the steps and then he went that way." She pointed westward, toward North Twenty-sixth Street.

Eunice Plummer said, "She never lies, Lieutenant. She's incapable of telling any untruth, even if she knows she's going to get punished."

Decker said, "You go to art class, Sandra? Do you like to draw?"

Sandra nodded. "I like to draw and paint and I like pottery."

"That's good, because I'll tell you what I want you to do. I want you to draw me a picture of this man you saw walking through the door. Then when you're done, I want you to call this number and I'll send an officer around to your home tomorrow morning to collect it. Do you think you can do that for me?"

"She can do it," Eunice Plummer put in. "She's really very good."

"I'm sure she is."

The officer escorted Eunice Plummer and Sandra back to the police line. Before she ducked under the tape, Sandra turned around and gave Decker a shy little wave. Decker waved back.

"Who's your new girlfriend?" Hicks said.

"A very sweet young lady, that's all I can say."

"She really see anybody?"

"No, I don't think so. Her mother says she has some kind of extrasensory perception . . . sees people walking around that nobody else can see. Must be something to do with impaired brain function."

"So how did you leave it?"

"I've asked her to draw the man she saw, that's all. If nothing else, it might act as some kind of therapy."

"Since when did you become Bruce Willis?"

CHAPTER FIVE

It was ten after midnight by the time Decker let himself into his loft on Main Street and closed and chained the door behind him. He had been delayed for over fifteen minutes by a construction truck parked across the street while it was loaded with asbestos stripped out of Main Street Station. The station was being renovated and the trains were being brought back into the city center, but the Virginia Board of Health still had offices in what had once been the train shed, so asbestos stripping could only be done at night.

Decker tossed his crumpled black linen coat onto the couch and eased off his heavy shoulder holster, hanging it up on the old-style hat stand. He hadn't eaten since eleven this morning and he had bought two chicken breasts with the intention of making himself a Mexican chicken stir-fry, but he was well past hunger—and he was far too tired to cook anything now. He put the chicken into the fridge and walked back into the living area.

He switched on the television, although he kept the

sound turned off. On-screen, a witch was being burned at the stake in agonized silence. He went across to the mirrored drinks cabinet, took out a *caballitos* shot glass, and poured himself a slug of Herradura Silver tequila. He knocked it back in one and stood for a moment with his eyes watering before pouring himself another. It was made from 100 percent blue agave, one of the most expensive tequilas you could buy.

He could see that his answering machine was blinking red and he could guess who it was, but he didn't feel like answering it. He took his drink over to the window and looked out over Canal Walk and the James River, the water glistening as black as oil, with a thousand lights dancing in it, yellow and red and green.

He had moved to Canal Walk Lofts over a year ago, but in spite of all the pictures and personal clutter that he had brought with him he still felt as if he were a stranger, living without permission in somebody else's apartment. Come to that, he still felt as if he were living without permission in somebody else's life.

The walls were all painted gunmetal gray and the floor was shiny red hardwood, although it was badly scuffed in front of the chair that faced the television. The couch and the armchairs were upholstered in soft black leather, and there was a glass-and-chrome coffee table with dozens of overlapping rings on it where glasses and coffee mugs had stood. Amongst the rings stood a bronze statuette of an ecstatic naked dancer, her hair flying out behind her; as well as an enamel-plated shield from the Metro Richmond Police for marksmanship; heaps of *TV Guides* and *Guns & Ammo* and *Playboy* and newspapers; an ashtray from the Jefferson Hotel; and a well-thumbed copy of *Your Year in the Stars: Capricorn*.

Along one wall ran a long black mahogany bookcase,

crammed with a mixture of John Grisham novels and technical manuals for dismantling guns and rebuilding automobiles and step-by-step guides to Mexican and southern cookery. At the far end were ten or eleven books on mysticism and life after death, including the biography of Edgar Cayce, the famous clairvoyant, and Zora Hurston, the anthropologist who had investigated the zombie cult in Haiti.

On the wall above the bookcase hung a huge brightly colored print of a Dutch girl sitting in a field of scarlet tulips, wearing a snow-white bonnet and bright yellow clogs. Her stripy skirt was lifted and her legs were wide apart, her vulva as scarlet as the tulips. Next to it were more nudes, darker and moodier, and three etchings of a couple entwined together. But on the other side of the room, close to the window, there was a gallery of more than twenty photographs framed in black, some of them color and some of them black-and-white. All of them showed the same dreamy-looking blonde with dark brown eyes and very long fine hair.

Decker, as he always did, raised his glass to her.

"Another day in paradise, baby."

He drew the loosely woven drapes, and then he went through to the bedroom where his king-size bed remained exactly as he had left it that morning, the sheets twisted like the Indian rope trick and the pillows all punched out of shape. He had always been a restless sleeper, prone to nightmares, and the state of the bed was a silent but eloquent record of last night's journeys through the country of shadows—a country where faceless people murmured in his ears and strange white shapes fled ahead of him through endless arcades.

Beside the bed stood more photographs of the dreamy-looking blonde, one of them showing her arm in arm with

Decker on the pedestrian walkway under the Robert E. Lee Bridge, her right hand raised to keep the sun out of her eyes.

Decker stripped off his clothes, dropping them onto the bed, and went through to the white-tiled bathroom. He stepped into the shower and turned it on full-blast. For some reason the Maitland case had left him feeling very tired and discouraged. All homicides were messy and disgusting, and there were always loose ends and blind alleys and confusing evidence. On its own, the disappearance of the murder weapon wouldn't have worried him unduly. The circumstantial evidence against Jerry Maitland was overwhelming. But it was hard to imagine *why* he should have attacked his wife so frenziedly, and killed their unborn baby. He had a great job, an idyllic house, and everything in the world to look forward to. Unless he had violent schizophrenic tendencies that nobody had guessed at, there didn't seem to be any motive for his actions at all.

And then there was Sandra's So-Scary Man in gray. Gray hat, gray coat, and *wings*, whatever that meant. Decker didn't believe in ghosts and he didn't believe in reincarnation. After Cathy's death, he had wanted to, desperately, almost to the point of madness. He had talked to dozens of mediums and clairvoyants and read everything he could about "psychic phenomena." Anything to touch Cathy again, anything to talk to her and smell her and wake up in the morning with her hair spread out on the pillow. Anything to tell her how sorry he was.

But after three months of sick leave and nearly a thousand dollars of savings wasted on séances and "spirit empathy sessions," he had come to accept that she was truly gone. He didn't quite know how it had happened. He had been walking through Hollywood Cemetery one afternoon, where Confederate President Jefferson Davis was buried, along with eighteen thousand Confederate soldiers, and he had realized how silent it was, apart from the traffic on Route 1 and the endless rushing of the James River rapids. There was nobody there. No spirits, no whispers. The dead were dead and they never came back.

One thing he had learned from his research into clairvoyance, however, was that some people were capable of faking occult phenomena. They could throw their voices, or make themselves temporarily invisible to those around them, or at least *unnoticed.* It was nothing supernatural, it was simply a trick, like stage magic, or hypnotism, or an optical illusion. Because of her mental disability, it was conceivable that Sandra had been unaffected by whatever gimmick the man in gray had employed to distract the attention of passersby. That was why—the more Decker thought about it—the more interested he was in seeing the figure that Sandra might draw.

He shampooed his hair with Fix and felt the suds sliding down his back. He was beginning to relax now. One more shot of tequila as a nightcap, and he was going to bed, and to sleep, and tonight with any luck he wouldn't have quite so many nightmares. He reached for his towel and climbed out of the shower.

As he did so, he thought he heard a clicking sound coming from the living area. He stood still and listened. Nothing. It must have been the air-conditioning. He dried himself and went back into the bedroom. He was opening his drawer to take out a clean pair of boxer shorts when he heard it again. *Click—click—click.*

He stepped into his shorts and then stood perfectly still and listened. Almost half a minute passed. Then *click—click—click.* And then a rattle.

It sounded as if there were somebody in the kitchen,

rather than the living area. Decker opened his closet door and took out his baseball bat. He just hoped that if it *was* an intruder, he hadn't noticed that a fully loaded Colt Anaconda was hanging from the hat stand right outside the kitchen doorway.

Click—click. Decker eased the bedroom door open a little wider and then stepped out into the living area, keeping his back close to the wall. His holster was still where he had hung it up, thank God. But the odd thing was that the front door was still locked, and the security chain was still fastened.

He made his way across the wooden floor, trying not to make sticky noises with his warm feet. He reached the opposite wall and flattened himself against it, breathing deeply to steady himself.

The clicking continued, intermittently. Then he heard something else, and his back prickled as if cockroaches were rushing down it. *Singing. High-pitched, breathy singing*. Quite tuneless, and the words were barely distinguishable. But it was singing and it was Cathy. She had always sung like that.

Decker felt as if the entire world were tilting underneath his feet. Cathy was dead. He had seen Cathy dead. He had convinced himself that ghosts didn't exist and spirits couldn't be summoned back and yet here she was, singing in his kitchen in the middle of the night. It gave him a feeling of dread far greater than any intruder could have inspired. He lifted the baseball bat and his hands were shaking so much that he had to lower it again. Besides, what was he going to do, if it really *was* her? Hit her?

Decker took a sharp breath and stepped into the kitchen doorway. The singing abruptly stopped and there was nobody there. He stood there for a while, not knowing what to do. He cleared his throat and said, "Cathy? Are you here,

Cathy?" but of course there was no reply. He took another step forward, and sniffed, in the hope that he might be able to smell her, that distinctive flowery perfume she always wore, but there was no trace of it.

He peered around the corner of the kitchen toward the brightly lit countertop next to the sink. On top of his seasoned-oak chopping board there was a pattern of pale, glistening lumps. At first Decker couldn't understand what he was looking at, but with a growing sense of eeriness he realized that it was a *face*, with staring eyes and jagged teeth—not a real face, but a face that had been fashioned out of slices of raw chicken, with a pointed breastbone for a nose, two slices of banana for eyes, and teeth made from diced-up apple.

It was unsettlingly lifelike, and the way it was looking at him made him feel as if it were just about to speak. But who had created it, and why, and *how?* A small sharp knife lay beside the chopping board, but whoever had used it had completely vanished.

Decker paced slowly up and down the kitchen, waving his baseball bat from side to side, as if it might come into contact with somebody invisible. Again, he whispered, "Cathy? Are you here, sweetheart? Talk to me, Cathy." But there was still no reply, only the mournful hooting of a ship on the river.

He went back into the living area and checked behind the drapes. The windows were closed and locked, so nobody could have escaped by climbing out that way. Besides, it was a sixty-foot drop to the street. He went back to the bedroom and opened all of the closet doors. Nobody. He frowned down at the photo of Cathy beside the bed. "Was that you? Or am I going out of my mind?"

He returned to the kitchen. He stared at the chicken-meat face for a while but he had no idea what significance it had, if it had any significance at all. He thought of Jerry Maitland, saying, "There was nobody there . . . there was cutting and cutting but there was nobody there."

He wondered if he ought to call Hicks to take a look, but he decided against it. Hicks needed his sleep and—besides—Decker didn't want to give the impression that he was losing his grip. He had seen it happen too many times before, detectives subtly falling apart. Their breakdowns were mostly caused by the steady erosion of suppressed grief, after one of their partners had been killed; or after their marriages had broken up, and they had lost custody of their children; or after they had been called out to one too many grotesquely mutilated bodies. They always *thought* that they were keeping their emotions under control, while all of their fellow officers could see that they were as brittle as an automobile whose bodywork had rusted right through to the paint.

Decker took his Polaroid camera out of the bookcase, loaded it with film, and took six or seven pictures of the kitchen counter. Then he cleared all the meat and fruit into the sink, and pushed them into the waste disposal. The knife he picked up by the tip and dropped into a plastic food bag.

He looked around the kitchen one more time. He cleared his throat and said, "Cathy, sweetheart, if what I heard was really you, why don't you give me a sign? Why don't you tell me why you're here? Why don't you let me see you for a minute? Why don't you let me touch you?"

He waited but there was no answer and no sign. Maybe he *was* going crazy. Maybe he was simply overtired.

In the end he switched the lights off and went to bed.

* * *

As soon as he fell asleep the nightmares began. Nightmares more frightening than any he had ever had before.

He dreamed that he was struggling through thick, lacerating underbrush. It was nearly dark and he knew that he had to hurry. Off to his left he could see fires burning, and he could hear men shouting to each other.

The branches caught in his clothing and lashed against his face. His feet were bare and every step was prickly with briars. The fires began to leap up higher, and he could smell smoke on the wind, and hear the crackling of burning bushes.

He was shaking with exhaustion, but he knew that if he stopped for even a minute the fires would cut him off, and he also knew that there was somebody close behind him, somebody who wanted to do him serious harm. He looked over his shoulder. He couldn't see anybody, but he was sure that they were very close behind.

Somewhere ahead of him, in the gathering darkness, a hoarse voice called out, "Muster at the road, boys! Muster at the road or we're finished!"

He heard a rattling that sounded like rifle shots, and a man screaming. How could he muster at the road when he didn't even know where the road was? He couldn't see anything but densely tangled undergrowth and thornbushes.

He tried to go faster by leaping over the bushes in awkward galumphing bounds, but his face was ripped by the branches and he was terrified of having an eye torn out. He lifted one arm in front of his face to protect himself. His woolen mittens were snared by briars, and his fingers were scratched, but it was preferable to being blinded.

The fires were coming closer, and he felt gusts of furnace-like heat. Another man was screaming, and then another. Then he heard something else: a thick rustling noise, very close behind him, very close. Somebody was catching up with him fast.

He turned around, and a huge figure in a dark cloak was almost on top of him. It came rushing toward him and it didn't stop, so that it collided with him. He found himself struggling in a cage of bones, trapped, unable to get free. The cloak closed around him and he was imprisoned in airless darkness, desperately trying to disentangle himself from ribs and shoulder blades and knobbly vertebrae.

"*Can't breathe!*" he screamed. "*Can't breathe!*"

He twisted around and realized that he was lying on his bed with his sheet over his face, thrashing his arms and kicking his legs.

Panting, sweating, he sat up. He switched on the bedside light and he could see himself in the mirror that faced the end of the bed, pale-faced, with his hair sticking up like a cockerel. His throat was dry—almost as dry as if he really *had* been running away from a brushfire. He reached for the glass of water that he usually left on his nightstand, but tonight he had forgotten it. He said, "Shit," and swung his legs out of bed. It was then that he realized that his feet were lacerated. They were covered in dozens of small scratches, all the way up to his calves, and his sheets were spotted with blood.

More than that, there were several briars still sticking in his ankles.

Whoa, he thought. *This is getting dangerously close to insanity*. You can't catch briars in your feet from running through underbrush in a nightmare, no matter how vivid that nightmare might have been.

He put on his glasses and went through to the bathroom, hobbling a little. He switched on the light over the bathroom mirror. His face was scratched, too. There was a nasty little cut on the side of his nose, and the skin on his right cheek had been torn in three diagonal stripes.

Pulling out a Kleenex, he carefully dabbed the scratches on his face. Then he sat down on the toilet seat and plucked the briars from out of his feet. He sprayed aftershave on the wounds because he didn't have any antiseptic, sucking in his breath when it stung.

He stayed in the bathroom for almost five minutes, wondering if he ought to go back to bed. Like, what if he went back into the same nightmare and the brushfire caught up with him? He could be burned to death in his own bed. He had read about religious fanatics who had identified so strongly with the suffering of Christ that stigmata had opened in their feet and the palms of their hands, and their foreheads had appeared to be scratched by a crown of thorns. Maybe this was a similar kind of phenomenon.

At last he stood up and went back into the bedroom. He had to take control of this situation. He desperately needed to sleep, and he couldn't let his subconscious fears start ruling his life. "I'm not going crazy," he announced. "I'm probably suffering from delayed grief and work-related stress, but I am definitely not going crazy." He paused, and then he said, "Shit, I'm talking to myself. How crazy is that?"

He eased himself back into bed, but this time he left the light on. It made him feel as if he were a child again, terrified of what might be hiding in the dark. When he was five or six, he had imagined that the parchment-colored lining of his bedroom drapes was the skin of a tall, thin, mummified man, and that as soon as the light was switched off, the mummy would unfold itself and stalk across the room, stilt-legged, to take out his eyes.

At about 3:30, he fell asleep again. He dreamed that he and Cathy were walking together through the Hollywood Cemetery. It was late evening and the sky was a grainy crimson color. The crosses and urns and headstones looked like chess pieces in a complicated board game, and Decker was sure that when his back was turned they kept shifting their position. He kept trying to look at Cathy, but for some reason her face was always blurred and out of focus.

"What were you doing in the kitchen?" he asked her. His voice sounded oddly muffled.

"I was protecting you," she replied.

"Protecting me? Protecting me from what?"

"From Saint Barbara. Saint Barbara wants her revenge."

"Saint Barbara? What the hell are you talking about? What I have ever done to upset Saint Barbara?"

"I don't want you to know. I don't want you to find out."

"Cathy, listen to me. Tell me that I'm not going crazy."

She said nothing, but turned away from him. He reached out to take hold of her shoulder, but she collapsed, like an empty bedsheet, and when he opened his eyes, that was all he had in his hand.

CHAPTER SIX

The next morning was sweltering and off to the east the sky was a dark coppery color, as if an electric storm were brewing off to the east, over the Richmond Battlefield. Decker went to Sausalito's Café on East Grace Street for coffee and scrambled eggs and sat facing the window, watching the passersby. For some reason that he couldn't explain, the world seemed to be altered, as if the streets downtown had been hurriedly dismantled and reconstructed during the night and some of the details hadn't been put back exactly as they should be. He had always thought that mailbox was on the opposite side of the intersection, yet here it was, right in front of the window. Even the passersby looked unnatural, walking in a hurried, self-conscious way like extras on a movie set. Decker could have believed that he was still in a nightmare.

"More coffee, Decker?" Amy called, from behind the counter. As she did so, a young woman in an oddly shaped black beret looked in through the window and gave him a knowing smile. He gave her a questioning look in return and mouthed, *What?*—but she turned away and disappeared into the crowds, as quickly and completely as if she had been made of nothing more than jigsaw pieces.

Jesus, Decker, you're definitely losing it.

Mayzie was waiting for him at headquarters.

"You rat, you didn't show," she complained, bustling after him into the elevator. "I waited for over a half hour and you didn't show. Ha! As if I believed that you really would."

"I told you, sweetheart, I'm all tied up with the Maitland case. We had witnesses to interview, evidence to look at. Things dragged on much later than I thought they would."

"You could at least have called me."

"I'm sorry. I'm truly sorry."

"Oh, you're sorry. Look at your face, all scratches. Who gave you those?"

"I tripped over. I fell in a bush."

"Really? *Whose* bush? I'd like to know."

"Mayzie, I'm sorry-sorry-sorry. How about lunch? I'll meet you right here in the lobby at twelve."

"You're a rat, do you know that? I don't even know if I *want* a child if it's going to have you as a father."

"Well, that makes two of us."

"Rat."

"I'll meet you here at twelve, okay? Don't be late, will you?"

He left her in the elevator and walked along the corridor to his office. Hicks was already there, talking on the telephone. Hicks jabbed his finger toward the waiting room. Through the glass division Decker could see Eunice Plummer and Sandra sitting side by side. Eunice was reading an old copy of *The Carytown Guide* while Sandra was playing some sort of game with her fingers.

Decker took off his sandy-colored coat and dropped it over the back of his chair. His desk was heaped with papers and files and scribbled memos, as well as crumpled-up paper napkins and three Styrofoam cups of cold coffee. But there was also a brass-framed photograph of Cathy. He had taken it the day before she was killed, in a corn field out on Route 5, in Charles County. She was wearing a frayed straw hat that cast a ragged shadow over her face, and she was chewing a stalk of grass. My *beautiful hayseed.*

"What were you doing in my nightmares last night?" he asked her, out loud.

Hicks put down the phone and said, "You okay, Lieutenant?"

"Sure, I'm fine. Didn't sleep too good, that's all."

"Your face is all scratched up."

Decker touched the scab on his nose. "Yeah . . . kind of an altercation with the neighbor's pet cat."

"You should get shots for that. You don't want to get, what is it, rabies?"

Decker didn't answer. He didn't want to have to tell Hicks that it hadn't been a cat, but a briar, and not only that, an *imaginary* briar.

Hicks said, "I was just talking to the ME. She's pretty sure that Mrs. Maitland's injuries were caused by a double-edged swordlike weapon, approximately two and a half feet long. She suggested a bayonet, something like that."

"A bayonet? Jesus."

"I was thinking of drawing up a list of all the places in Richmond that sell bayonets. Like gun shops and military curio stores. Antique markets, too. If we can establish that Maitland actually *owned* a bayonet, then it won't matter so much that we haven't been able to find it."

"That's good thinking, Hicks. Why don't you start with Billy Joe Bennett at the Rebel Yell on West Cary Street? Believe me—if Robert E. Lee had ever had *half* as much ordnance as Billy Joe Bennett, he would have won the Civil War in a week."

"Okay, Lieutenant. Right on it." Hicks lifted his coat off the peg beside his desk and picked up his notebook.

"Hey, hey, slow down, sport," Decker said. "You don't need to take this weapon thing so personal. You conducted a thorough search, you couldn't find it, ergo it wasn't there. Obviously it's going to help us if we can produce the weapon in court, and prove that Maitland used it to kill his wife, but it's not the end of the world if we can't."

"I just like to have things neatly wrapped up," Hicks admitted. "I mean—how could a two-foot bayonet totally disappear? It isn't logical."

"All right, Mr. Spock," Decker said. But even as he said it, he thought about the face carved out of slices of raw chicken and banana, lying on his chopping board, and what was logical about that, or even sane?

He ran his hand through his hair, prinking up his pompadour. "I guess I'd best go see what my visitors want. By the way, how's your wife liking it here in the city?"

"Good, fine. She's okay."

"She doesn't miss Fredericksburg?"

"Some. I think she misses her friends most."

"Well, that's natural. You ought to bring her out one evening. . . . I know a couple of girls she'll really get on with. Does she like Mexican food? We could go to La Siesta."

Hicks shrugged. "I'll ask her. She's never been much for socializing."

"In that case, I insist that she comes. I can't have my partner's wife feeling lost and abandoned in the big city."

Hicks gave him a tight, unappreciative smile. "I guess not. Thanks. I'll talk to her about it."

* * *

He rapped loose-knuckled on the door of the waiting room. Eunice Plummer looked up and beamed at him, and so did Sandra.

"Sorry I kept you waiting so long."

"That's quite all right. Sandra finished her drawing at seven o'clock last night and she's been dying to show it to you ever since. She was up at six, all dressed up in her best frock and ready to go."

"I could have sent somebody to collect it. Saved you a journey."

"I wanted to show you myself," put in Sandra.

"Well, Sandra, I really appreciate that. It's people like you who make our job a whole lot more satisfying."

"I want to help you find that So-Scary Man. He looked like this." With that, Sandra lowered her chin and frowned, and then she made her eyes roll up into her head, so that only the whites showed.

"*Sandra!*" Eunice Plummer protested. "You mustn't make faces! If the wind changes, you'll stay like that!"

Sandra clapped her hands in excitement. "He looked just like that! Look at my drawing—*look!*"

She handed Decker a rolled-up piece of art paper. Decker sat down next to her and unrolled it. He had expected a stick person in a hat. What she had actually drawn was a highly detailed pencil rendition of the front of 4140 Davis Street, with its iron railings and its Doric-pillared porch and even its carriage lamp. She had included every single brick, and shaded everything. She had even included the decorative lace curtains behind the front parlor window.

"She has a wonderful memory," Eunice Plummer said, proudly.

Decker shook his head in admiration. "Not just that, she's

very talented. I know some professional artists who can't draw anything like as good as this."

Sandra pointed to the tall figure standing on the porch. "That's him. That's the scary man."

Her impersonation of the So-Scary Man's face had been disturbingly close to the face she had drawn. He was very tall. He was wearing what looked like a wide-brimmed slouch hat, with straggly black feathers around it, and his beard was black and wild. But it was his eyes that made him look so terrifying. They had no pupils, only whites, like the eyes of a boiled codfish, and yet they had a stare of concentrated fury, as if he were calling down every curse in the world on whoever he was looking at.

"You're right." Decker nodded. "He *is* pretty scary, isn't he?"

The So-Scary Man was wearing a long gray overcoat with a cape, and now Decker understood what Sandra had meant by "wings." The overcoat was unbuttoned at the front to reveal a long scabbard hanging from the man's belt. He wore dark britches and knee-length leather boots.

Decker studied the drawing for a long time. Then he asked Sandra, "You saw the So-Scary Man—but do you think he saw *you?*"

Sandra thought about that and then said, "Yes . . . I think so. He was looking right at me."

"Could that be dangerous?" Eunice Plummer asked, realizing what Decker was asking.

"I don't know. This is a very weird situation. This drawing—this likeness—it's totally amazing. I wish all of our witnesses could draw like this, we wouldn't need computer composites. But the fact remains that Sandra was the only person who saw this guy, nobody else. We've interviewed over thirty people who were walking along Davis Street at the same time you were, and not *one* of them reported seeing anybody who looked like this . . . and, let's face it, he's pretty darn distinctive, isn't he?"

Eunice Plummer took hold of Sandra's hand and gave it a protective squeeze. "What are you going to do?" she asked, worriedly.

"I'm going to assume for now that he *was* real. I have to say that it's very unlikely that anybody was able to walk out of the Maitland house without being seen by any other passersby, but it's not one hundred percent impossible. I'm going to assign an officer to keep an eye on Sandra for the next few days, just to be on the safe side."

"You don't think that this man would try to hurt her?"

"I don't think she's in any real danger, Ms. Plummer, to tell you the truth. But I'm going to issue this drawing to the media this afternoon, so that if he *does* exist he's pretty soon going to find out that he's a suspect. If he's innocent, he'll most likely come forward so that we can eliminate him from our inquiries. If he's guilty of any involvement in Mrs. Maitland's murder, the chances are that he'll shave off his beard and go on the lam, if he hasn't done it already. But if he's aware that Sandra was the only person who actually saw him . . . well, like I say, there's no harm in being careful."

He turned to Sandra and said, "You turn on your TV tonight, Sandra, and you'll see your drawing on the news."

Sandra smiled and gave him an unexpected high five.

Decker took them down to the lobby. "I want to thank you again, Sandra. I'll make sure that you get a special police badge for this."

"Thank you," Sandra said. "I hope you catch the So-Scary Man."

"Sure, well, me too."

Outside, there was a deafening collision of thunder. Sandra raised her head and said, "Something's going wrong, isn't it?"

"No, no. That's just an electric storm. Nothing to be afraid of."

Sandra shook her head. "I don't mean that. Something's going wrong."

"I don't understand what you mean. What's going wrong?"

"I don't know. Not yet."

"She gets feelings sometimes," Eunice Plummer explained. "Premonitions, I suppose you'd call them. She had a very bad feeling the night before her father died."

Decker put his arm around Sandra's rounded shoulders. "Don't you worry, Sandra. Everything's going to be fine. Come through to the garage and I'll have a squad car take you and your mommy home."

CHAPTER SEVEN

As he came jogging along the street, his new Nike sneakers slapping on the sidewalk, George Drewry saw lightning flicker in the distance, over the city center. He turned into his driveway and bent over double, his hands on his knees, gasping for breath. He was still bent double when the thunder reached him, and he thought that it sounded like distant cannon fire. This is what it must have sounded like here in Highland Springs in 1864, when Sherman was advancing from Williamsburg.

The front door opened and Jean came out, in a bright green tracksuit, her white hair wound up in rollers. "George? Are you all right?"

George slowly straightened his back. He was a big man, six feet three inches, and since his retirement from the army last August he had put on at least twenty pounds. His balding, sunburned head was tied with a red bandanna and he was wearing a khaki T-shirt and a drooping pair of gray jogging pants, both drenched in sweat. He limped toward the house, wiping his forehead with his hairy forearm. "All this exercise is going to be the death of me, do you know that?"

"Dr. Gassman told you to keep in shape, didn't he?"

"I know, but he didn't actually specify *what* shape, did he? I mean, pear-shaped is a shape, isn't it?"

George limped inside, with Jean following him. He was sixty-two years old, with a long face and wobbly jowls, and very large ears, like a mournful dog. He went into the kitchen, opened up the icebox and took out a large bottle of mineral water.

"How about a Caesar salad?" Jean asked, watching him gulp.

"How about some fried chicken and gravy?"

"You know what Dr. Gassman said about your arteries."

"Dr. Gassman is a miserable bastard who is doing everything possible to make me as miserable as him. Why can't I enjoy my life once in a while?"

"What's the point in enjoying your life if you're dead?"

George put the water bottle back and wiped his mouth with the back of his hand. "All right, Caesar salad, but don't be stingy with the ham."

He walked along the corridor to the bathroom. The walls were covered with military memorabilia—framed photographs of Wofford's brigade during the Civil War, engravings of Stonewall Jackson and Robert E. Lee, as well as three muskets and pennants and badges from TRADOC—the Training and Doctrine Command at Fort Monroe. George had been a soldier since the age of nineteen, ending his career as a major at the Office of the Command Historian, which kept records of U.S. Army history dating back to the earliest colonial militia. He had even written a short history book himself—*The Boys In Gray*, about the Regulars who fought the British at Chippewa and Lundy's Lane.

In the bathroom he stripped off his bandanna and his

T-shirt and jogging pants and voluminous Bugs Bunny boxer shorts. He was damned if all this galloping around the neighborhood was doing anything more than making him look like a prize asshole. He always felt like shit when he came back from a run, and he wasn't even allowed to have a beer. He looked at himself in the mirror and his face was crimson.

"Look at you," he told himself. "You're no damn good to anyone. Not even you."

He climbed into the shower and turned on the faucets. He knew that Jean was only trying to take care of him, but her endless fussing was like nettle rash. It was bad enough, not having an office to go to anymore, and no staff to order around. He had always imagined that he would relish his retirement, reading and fishing and giving occasional well-received lectures on military campaigns. But when he had opened his eyes on that very first morning and realized that he wasn't going to be dressing in uniform anymore, and that he wouldn't be saluted by everyone he met, he had felt as if he were rendered impotent during the night.

Now he spent his days moping around the house, while Jean pursued him from room to room with the Hoover.

"You should take up golf."

"Golf is for people who don't have anything else to do."

"But you *don't* have anything else to do."

"I know, but I'm damned if I'm going to advertise it."

Far from bringing him peace and self-fulfillment, retirement had taken away the only thing that had made him proud of himself. He felt so useless sometimes that it made him gasp for breath, as if he were going to start sobbing.

He was soaping his chest when he felt something cold sliding down his left inside leg. Looking down, he saw that he was bleeding from a long thin cut that ran all the way from his testicles to the side of his knee. Blood was already running down his calf, mingled with foam and water, and swirling into the shower tray.

How the hell . . . ?

George reached out of the shower cubicle for his towel. He could tell that the cut must be deep as well as long, because the blood was a rich arterial color, and it was flowing out in thick, warm surges.

"Jean!" he shouted. "Jean, I need some help here!"

He tugged his towel off the rail and wound it around his thigh as tightly as he could. All the same, it was soaked scarlet in a matter of seconds. "Jean!" he called. "Jean, I've cut myself!"

He lifted his right hand toward the faucets to turn off the water, but as he did so he felt an intense slice across his knuckles, and another cut appeared, so vicious that it almost severed his little finger. He cried out in bewilderment more than pain, and thrust his hand into his mouth, so that it was filled up with the metallic taste of fresh blood.

Then, with terrible swiftness, his left hand was cut, too, so that he dropped the towel that he was holding against his thigh. The towel blocked up the drain, and it took only a few seconds before the shower tray was brimming with blood and water.

George staggered sideways. He felt giddy already, as if he had just climbed off a carnival roundabout. The inside of the shower cubicle suddenly went dark, with swarming pinpricks of light. "*Jean, I need you!*" he shouted, but his voice sounded as if it were coming from the end of a very long pipe.

He felt a cut across the bridge of his nose, and then three more cuts on his shoulders. He slid down the wall until he was on his knees, leaving a wide streak of blood on the pale green tiles. The water pelted into his face and almost blinded him.

His back was cut in a series of diagonal slices that went right through to his shoulder blades and his ribs. He actually felt the blade sliding against the bone. He flailed around with his bleeding hands, trying to stop his invisible assailant from cutting him anymore, but there was nobody there, and all he succeeded in doing was decorating the shower cubicle in a ghastly scarlet parody of an action painting.

"*Jean*," he whispered.

With a soft *pop*, the point of a blade broke his skin just above his pubic hair. There was a moment's hesitation, and then the blade itself was pushed in deep through the layers of subcutaneous fat and into his stomach muscles. He cried out, "*No-no-no-no-no!*" because the blade was so cold and the pain was too much for him to bear. He tried to climb to his feet, his bloody hands sliding frantically against the tiles, and he almost succeeded. But then he slipped and fell down onto his knees again, and as he did so the blade cut his belly wide open all the way to his breastbone, where it stuck for a second before it was pulled out.

His intestines slithered out of his stomach cavity and piled up into a sloppy heap in the overflowing shower tray. He looked down at them, all yellowish and glistening and streaked with blood, and wondered if he should try to gather them up and stow them back in. He had seen a marine try to do it in Dong Ha. But his large intestine was sliced in half, and maybe it wasn't worth it.

He leaned one shoulder against the side of the shower. The best thing to do was sleep for a while, and *then* try. All that jogging around the block had made him feel so tired. That goddamn Dr. Gassman would be the death of him. He closed his eyes for a while, while the warm shower water poured into his face and filled his opened-up belly with a hollow gurgling noise. It reminded him of summer rain, gurgling down the gutters.

CHAPTER EIGHT

A different nurse was on duty when Decker and Hicks arrived at the hospital to question Jerry Maitland—a severe fortyish woman with a World War Two helmet of iron-gray hair. "I don't want my patient agitated," she warned them. "He's in a very depressed state, and we wouldn't like to exacerbate his condition, would we?"

Decker laid his hand on her shoulder and smiled. "Do you like Mexican food?" he asked her.

Jerry was sitting up watching the news channel with an untouched lunch tray in front of him, pale chicken salad with watery tomatoes and lime-green Jell-O. Decker sat on the end of the bed and helped himself to one of Jerry's saltines. "How's it going, Jerry?" he said, snapping the cracker in half. "I brought my partner, Sergeant Hicks, to see you."

Jerry glanced at them both but said nothing. His eyes were bloodshot and swollen and it was obvious that he had been crying.

"Had any more thoughts about the knife, Jerry?" Decker asked.

"I told you. There *was* no knife."

"Okay . . . how about this? Did you ever see a guy with a beard skulking around your neighborhood?"

"A beard?"

"That's it. Tall guy, wearing a wide-brimmed hat and one of those coats with a cape over the shoulders? Ever see anybody who looked like that?"

Jerry shook his head.

"Show him the picture, Hicks," Decker said. Hicks produced a folded-up copy of Sandra's drawing and held it up in front of Jerry's face.

"Not the kind of guy you'd forget in a hurry, huh?" Decker asked him.

"That's the front of our house," Jerry said, perplexed.

"That's right. And the person who drew this picture says that she saw this guy coming out of your front door round about the time that your wife was killed."

"I never saw him before in my life."

"He couldn't have been hiding in your house without you knowing it?"

"How could he? I mean, look at him. Besides that, Alison was killed right in front of my eyes and there was nobody there."

"You're totally sure about that?" Hicks asked. "You couldn't have suffered a blackout or nothing like that?"

"I was losing a lot of blood and I was feeling pretty faint. But I'm sure I didn't lose consciousness. I saw Alison fall down, but I swear to God there was nobody there."

"You realize you're not exactly helping your own defense?"

"I don't need a defense. I know that I was the only other person in the house but I didn't do it. It was like she was attacked by somebody invisible."

Hicks took out his notebook. "You interested in military memorabilia at all, Mr. Maitland?"

"What do you mean?"

"You know . . . guns, knives, battle flags, that kind of stuff."

Jerry shook his head.

"You've never owned, like, a sword, or a bayonet?"

"No, of course not. But this man in this picture . . . he's carrying some kind of a sword, isn't he?"

"That's right," Decker said. "It's a bayonet, as a matter of fact, and our medical examiner is of the opinion that your Alison was killed by a very similar weapon."

Jerry stared at him. "So it's possible that *he* might have done it? Even though I didn't see him?"

"That's what we're trying to establish. The only problem is, there were more than forty people in the immediate vicinity of your house when this guy was walking out of the front door, and only one of them saw him."

"Maybe they just didn't notice him."

"Dressed like that? In broad daylight?"

"I guess so," Jerry admitted. "But it doesn't make any sense at all, does it?"

Decker stood up. "You're right. It doesn't. So we're still left with the circumstantial evidence that *you* killed Alison. You realize that if you admit it, the DA will go much easier on you."

"Especially if you remember what you did with the weapon," Hicks put in.

Jerry shook his head even more emphatically. "I can't admit it, because I didn't do it. I never owned a bayonet and I never touched a hair of Alison's head."

"Okay," Decker said. "The doctors say that you'll be fit enough to go in front of the judge on Tuesday. In the meantime, you know how to get in touch with me if you have a sudden revelation."

"You're going to look for this man, though?"

"Oh, sure. We have to. Elimination of suspects, no matter how unlikely."

Jerry frowned at the drawing again. "He reminds me of somebody. I can't think who."

"You think you might have seen him before?"

"I don't know . . . there's just something familiar about him. I can't think what it is."

"Well, if it comes to mind . . ."

"Sure," Jerry said.

They left the room. "What do you think?" Decker asked Hicks.

"I think he did it. I'm *sure* he did it."

"What about the So-Scary Man?"

"Didn't exist. Come on, Lieutenant, Sandra's mentally challenged. I know she draws good, but a good drawing isn't evidence, is it?"

"Yeah, you're right," Decker agreed. "It's just that—why the hell did he do it?"

As they walked past the nurses' station, the helmet-haired nurse called out, "Lieutenant!"

"Yes? Oh, I'm sorry, nurse. We're through with Mr. Maitland for now."

"Oh, that's all right. I just wanted you to know that I *do* like Mexican food. In fact, I like it very much."

Decker looked at Hicks in desperation but all Hicks could do was grin.

"What's your name?" Decker asked her.

"Marion."

"Okay, Marion. Next time I call by, I'll bring you my recipe for cheese *empanadas*."

CHAPTER NINE

They were driving back to headquarters when Decker's cell phone played Beethoven.

"Martin."

"Decker? It's Rudisill. The captain wants you over at 2024 Laburnum Street, just off Nine Mile Road. Like, you know, instantly."

"Want to tell me why?"

"It looks like your invisible guy has been at it again. Some old coot's been gutted like a salmon."

Decker said, "On our way," and switched on his siren and flashing lights.

"Whoo," Hicks said, slapping his armrest.

Decker U-turned the Mercury in the middle of Broad Street, its tires squittering, and headed east. "Did I tell you that I was going to be a father?" he asked Hicks.

They stepped cautiously into the bathroom where the forensic team were already at work, waddling around in white Tyvek suits and taking tissue samples and footprints and measuring the smears of blood on the walls of George Drewry's shower cubicle.

Decker took a long look inside the shower. George Drewry's eyes were still half open, as if he were right on the point of nodding off to sleep. A fly settled on his heaped-up intestines and one of the forensic team flapped it away.

Decker turned back to Hicks and Hicks had his hand pressed over his nose and mouth. There was nothing guaranteed to bring up your breakfast more than the sweet smell of human insides.

Decker looked around the white-tiled floor, which was decorated with blood, like blotchy crimson roses. "How many sets of footprints?" he asked Lieutenant Bryce, who was kneeling on the floor beside the toilet bowl, painstakingly dipping Q-tips into one of the gradually congealing petals.

"Only one, as far as I can tell," she said. "Major Drewry's wife."

"*Major* Drewry?"

"That's right. Fort Monroe, TRADOC, retired."

They left the bathroom and went back to the living room, where Cab was talking to the medical examiner, Erin Malkman. She was a handsome blond woman with a strong chin, deep-set eyes, and lips that were so full and glossy that they always looked to Decker as if she were halfway through eating an overripe apricot. Her Tyvek suit was half unzipped and she was tugging off her protective gloves.

"Hi, Erin. How's the meat trade these days?"

"Hello, Martin. Haven't seen you in a while."

"Oh, I've been around."

"I'm sure you have."

He gave her a tight, humorless smile. "So what's the picture here?"

"I was just telling Captain Jackson that Major Drewry's

wounds are distinctly different from those that were inflicted on Alison Maitland. They're triangular, and they were probably caused by a large blade that was sharp on one side and serrated on the other."

"Bowie knife?"

"Something of that order. I've prepared some profiles of Alison Maitland's entry wounds and of course I'll be doing the same for Major Drewry."

"Bryce said there was only one set of footprints in the bathroom—Mrs. Drewry's."

"That's right," Cab said. "Major Drewry had been out jogging . . . he came in and went directly to the bathroom to take a shower. When he didn't reappear after ten minutes, Mrs. Drewry went in to see why he was taking so long, and that's when she found him."

"She didn't see anybody?"

"Nope. We have some similarities with the Maitland killing here . . . no evidence of any intruder, no murder weapon, no witnesses. But, I don't know . . . with Gerald Maitland in custody, my opinion is that we're probably looking at a copycat."

"What about Mrs. Drewry? Is she a suspect?"

"Are you kidding me? You should see her. She had blood on her hands and feet, but that was only consistent with going into the bathroom and finding Major Drewry's body."

"Where is she now?"

"Next door, with her neighbor."

"We'd better go talk to her then."

Erin said, "I'll start on the autopsy as soon as I get the body into the lab. I should be able to give you a preliminary report by midday tomorrow."

"Well, I thank you, kind medical examiner."

Erin didn't say anything, but then she didn't have to, because she and Decker understood each other only too well.

Eighteen months ago they had both used each other—Decker to recover from his grief for Cathy, and Erin to get over a protracted and nasty affair with a city official called Simon who used to beat her. After two and a half months together Decker had turned up at her apartment one afternoon to find her with two black eyes. She had spent the previous night with her city official, and her city official had made doubly sure that Decker knew about it.

As they left the Drewry house, Cab said, "This case gives me dyspepsia."

"Relax, Captain, there has to be some explanation. Somebody killed Major Drewry whether that somebody was seen by anybody or not."

"It still makes my stomach hurt. Listen—I've called a news conference for four o'clock and I want you back at headquarters by two-thirty to give me an update. We can't let this one get out of hand, public-relations-wise. You see that headline about the Maitland killing? *Homicide Squad Chase Their Own Shadows*. I don't want no more b.s. like that."

They crossed the lawn toward the next-door neighbors' house. There was a clamor of shouted questions from the gathered reporters, and a blizzard of flash photography, but Cab gave them nothing more than a dismissive wave of his hand. "Goddamn media. They give me a pain in the ass."

"Have we released that drawing yet?"

"No, I had a talk with Major Greaves and we decided against it."

"What? What do you mean you decided against it?"

Cab dragged out his handkerchief and blew his nose. "Think about it, Decker. The only person who saw this character was mentally challenged. Nobody else saw him, not even her own mother, who was standing right next to her, and to whom she actually pointed this imaginary character out. Even if we *could* find a guy who looked like her drawing, Sandra's evidence would never stand up in court.

"Major Greaves agrees with me that it's in everybody's best interests if we quietly forget about it. Ours, and Sandra's."

"So we're not even going to look for this guy?"

"He walked through the door without opening it? A door that was locked and chained on the inside, and the paramedics had to kick down? The house was a bloodbath but he didn't leave a single footprint or fingerprint? Come on, Decker."

"What happened here then, at the Drewrys' house? Don't tell me that Major Drewry committed suicide. What with? A bowie knife, which we can't find, any more than we could find the bayonet that killed Alison Maitland?"

"I don't know, Decker, for Christ's sake. Don't make me irritable. Like you say, there has to be an explanation and it's your job to find it."

"I want that drawing released."

"No, Decker. We have a watertight case against Gerald Maitland and I'm not going to jeopardize it by making it look as if we're searching for another suspect. This ain't *The Fugitive*."

They found Jean Drewry on the shady verandah at the back of the house, sitting with her neighbor on a flowery-cushioned couch. The electric storm had passed over now, although it was still grumbling and complaining out over Powhatan County. In spite of the humidity, Jean Drewry was wrapped in a thick maroon shawl. Her neighbor was a plump woman in pink ski pants. She looked up sharply as Decker and Hicks came out of the house.

"Can't this wait?"

"I'm sorry, ma'am. But I have to ask Mrs. Drewry one or two questions just to help us get a handle on this thing."

Jean Drewry was very white, as if her face were powdered with flour. "Is George gone yet?" she asked. "Have they taken him away?"

"The forensic people are going to need a couple more hours. But they'll move him as soon as they can."

"It's his *pride*, you see?" Jean Drewry said. "He wouldn't like people to see him like that."

"Mrs. Drewry, I can assure you that your George will be treated with the very greatest of respect," Decker assured her, thinking of Erin Malkman taking out her circular saw and cutting off the top of Major Drewry's skull, so that she could weigh his brain. He sat down on a wickerwork chair close to her, while Hicks perched on the verandah railing behind him. At the end of the garden there was a row of beehives and the afternoon hummed with steamy heat and bees.

"You were in the house when George came back from his run?"

"Yes. I was making us a salad. He's supposed to have salad, because of his arteries."

"You were in the house the whole time he was out?"

"Yes, except when I went out into the yard to take down my washing."

"Was the back door unlocked?"

"Yes, it was. But I was in the kitchen the whole time, and I can see right down the corridor. Nobody could have gotten into the bathroom. It's just not possible."

"When George arrived home, did you open the front door for him?"

"Of course."

"So for a very short time, you *couldn't* see down the corridor?"

"Only for one or two minutes."

Hicks jotted that down. "One or two minutes is a long time, ma'am."

"Yes, but you see, nobody came *out* of the bathroom."

That afternoon, Hicks and Banks and six uniformed officers went knocking on doors all around the Drewrys' house, asking their neighbors if they had seen anybody or anything suspicious. They were greeted at every door by "sorry, Officer, no," and shaken heads. Decker went back to headquarters and sent an e-mail of Sandra's drawing to every police division in the city, as well as the state police in Chesterfield. He also asked the duty secretary to print out two hundred photocopies.

He met Officer Wekelo in the corridor. "Show this around. Anybody's seen a guy looking like this, there's a fifty in it."

"What's with the Ping-Pong ball eyes?" Wekelo asked.

"How should I know, grasshopper? Just find him for me."

He pushed aside all the clutter on his desk and started to make comparative notes about the Maitland killing and the Drewry murder. The assailant in both cases had been completely invisible. He had entered his victims' houses unseen, and in the case of the Maitlands, without even opening a locked door or window. He had killed without a visible weapon and left without leaving a single physical trace of his having been there. However eager Cab was to bring Jerry Maitland to trial, Decker thought it much more likely that there was only one assailant, and that he had carried out both killings, and that he wasn't Jerry Maitland. Maybe he had used a bayonet for one and a bowie knife for the other, but most gun and knife fanatics owned a wide assortment of weapons. He had once arrested a Vietnam vet for holding up a convenience store with a switchblade knife in one hand and a scimitar in the other. Couldn't make up his mind if he was James Dean or Sinbad the Sailor.

No—unlike Cab, Decker was more interested in finding out what was similar between Maitland and Drewry, rather than what was different. As yet, there was no apparent motive for either murder, and no apparent connection between the two victims. But Decker had been in the business long enough to know that there was no such thing as a random killing. "Random" was a term that senior officers used when they really meant "We already have one reasonably likely suspect in custody and I don't want to spend any more of my overtime budget looking for somebody else."

He was sketching out a floor plan of George Drewry's house when Cab came in. "Where are we at?" he wanted to know. "I've got this goddamn media conference in ten minutes."

Decker scratched his ear with his pencil. "We're at square zilch, that's where we're at. But I guess you could tell the media that we're actively pursuing several promising leads and we're confident of an early arrest."

"We are? What promising leads?"

"You're the captain, you tell me."

Cab suddenly lifted up a crumpled sheet of paper he was clutching in his hand. "By the way, what the Sam Hill is this? I thought I made it clear that we weren't going to release this drawing. They're all over the building. They're even pinned up on the notice boards. This guy is a figment of a mentally retarded girl's imagination and we are officially not looking for him."

"I just thought the team ought to know who it is we're not officially looking for. You know—in case they see him, and officially try to arrest him."

"You and myrtle. You both make my nose run."

"You'll be out on the lake tomorrow."

"I wish. Weekend leave is canceled, because of this."

Decker said, "Oh?" Then, "Oh." *No dessert, then. Not this weekend, anyhow.*

CHAPTER TEN

He was on his way to the men's room when Mayzie came strutting along the corridor toward him.

"Don't be late?" she demanded. "Don't be *late?* It's nearly four and you were supposed to meet me at twelve."

"Mayzie, for Christ's sake, I'm dealing with two very complicated homicides here."

"I know. I know you're busy. But all I'm asking for is five minutes. This is my life we're talking about here. This is your baby's life."

"Mayzie . . . I know I've let you down but I really don't have time for this."

"Well, make time for it."

"Do you mind if I freshen up first?"

He pushed open the door of the men's room but Mayzie followed him.

"Hey, this is the men's room."

"Don't be sexist. I just want to know where I stand with you, how serious you are."

"How serious I am? About what?"

"About us. About you and me. Come on, Decker, we've been seeing each other for three and a half months now. I could be carrying your child. I think I deserve to know where I stand, don't you?"

Decker raised both hands in surrender. "Mayzie, I can't tell a lie. I like you, I think you're a gorgeous girl. But you know what I'm like. I've got a very short span of attention when it comes to emotional relationships. I'm not looking for anything long-term. And I'm certainly not looking for fatherhood."

Mayzie wrapped her arms around his neck, and pushed him back against the door of one of the stalls. "That's your defense mechanism talking, that's all. You lost Cathy, you're scared to commit to anybody else in case you lose them, too. Well, let me tell you, Decker, I love you and you won't lose me, ever. I promise."

Decker tried to pry himself free, but Mayzie forced him right back into the stall, so that he stumbled and sat down on the toilet seat. "Come on, Mayzie, for Christ's sake."

She gripped his shoulders and stared intently into his eyes. "Tell me you don't love me, go on. Tell me you don't think I'm the sexiest girl you ever went out with. Remember that afternoon at the Brandermill Inn? Remember what I did for you then?"

"Mayzie—"

She kissed his forehead. Then she kissed his nose and his cheeks and his eyes and his lips. He tried to stand up but she pushed him back down, kissing his ears and his neck and pulling at the buttons of his shirt.

"Mayzie—"

But at that moment, they heard the men's room door open, and voices. Mayzie pushed the door shut behind her and shot the catch. Decker tried to stand up again, but she pressed her finger over her lips and said, "*Shh!*"

Decker was about to protest when he heard Major Bruscow say, "I'm sorry, I can't agree with that operational study at all. We just don't have the manpower to have all of those locations under surveillance at one time."

"Okay . . . I'll talk to the chief about it. But I have to warn you that she's pretty set on making changes." That was Acting Deputy Chief Prescott.

Shit, Decker thought. With two senior officers standing at the urinals with their zippers open, there was no way that he could come barging out of the toilet stall with Mayzie Shifflett in tow.

Mayzie kissed him again and again and he tried to push her away, but her hands seemed to be everywhere. She took hold of his zipper and tugged it open in three sharp tugs, and then wriggled her hand inside his pants.

"No," he whispered. "I'll meet you later, I promise. We'll talk. We'll go to bed. We'll make love."

"I don't believe you," she whispered back.

She levered his penis out of his shorts and in spite of his annoyance it began to stiffen. She rubbed it slowly up and down, digging her square-tipped artificial fingernails into it, and kept on kissing his nose and his eyes and his lips.

"You cannot do this," he hissed, but she wouldn't stop.

Acting Deputy Chief Prescott let out a grunting noise, as if he were shaking himself. "The real problem we're facing is recruitment. We're still getting plenty of applications but sixty-five percent of them we can't accept. They can hardly read, some of them, and they have no idea of public service. I saw one application last week that said 'I want to be a cop because I can't afford my own car.'"

Decker heard the faucets running. Mayzie slowly went

down on her knees, even though he struggled to stop her. She took the plum-colored head of his penis into her mouth, and licked it around and around. Then she lowered her head and took it deep down into her throat. He gripped her shoulders and it took all his self-control not to groan.

Mayzie sucked and sucked, and as she did so she reached around with one hand and unclipped the tortoiseshell barrette that held her French pleat in place. She gave a quick shake of her head and her blond hair tumbled free. She started to suck even more forcefully, and to bite him with every suck.

"*Mayzie*—" he hissed, but she was determined to prove that he wanted her. Determined.

Major Bruscow started washing his hands, too. "I need to go over our vacation arrangements. It looks as if we're going to have to do some juggling, what with these latest two homicides."

"Who have you got on those?"

"Martin."

"Too many hunches and not enough homework, that's what I always think about him."

"I don't know . . . he's a lateral thinker, and that's what we need on cases like these."

"Lateral, huh! More like prone."

Mayzie struggled one hand into Decker's pants and started to tug at his scrotum. Once or twice she made him wince, and he was forced to bite his lip. How much longer were Bruscow and Prescott going to spend preening themselves? Mayzie was probing the opening in his penis with the stiffened tip of her tongue and he wasn't far away from a climax.

"*Mayzie, please*—"

Mayzie lifted her head up and swept the hair away from her face.

Only it wasn't Mayzie. It was Cathy, with her eyes closed.

Decker jerked back in shock, so that he was jabbed in the shoulder blade by the cistern handle.

Cathy opened her eyes and gave him a wide, slow smile, the same languid smile that she always used to give him when she opened her eyes in the morning. She continued to massage his glistening penis, but it was diminishing already. Decker opened and closed his mouth, unable to say anything coherent, and his heart was banging so hard that it hurt.

"You're not—no, no—tell me you're not."

Cathy kept on smiling and kept on massaging him. She looked the same as she always had, but her skin was the color of a clouded sky, and her irises were pale yellow, like a snake. Her fingers felt as cold as ice, which made his penis shrink even more.

"Listen, I have to—" Decker blurted, and made a clumsy attempt to struggle to his feet.

"Hey, everything all right in there?" Major Bruscow called out.

Decker took hold of Cathy's chilly wrists, trying to force her to stand up, so that he could stand up too, but as he did so the top of her head exploded and the stall was plastered in brains and blood and fragments of bone. Immediately, there was a second explosion, which made her bloody blond hair flap up, and blew away her left eye and half of her cheek. Decker screamed out, "*No! No!*" and twisted around on the toilet seat. His shirtfront was drenched in blood and a jellyish lump of Cathy's brain was sliding down the lens of his glasses.

"*Cathy! For Christ's sake! We've got to—*"

But Cathy fiercely gripped his hands and wouldn't let go. And even though most of the top of her head was missing, she kept on smiling, and her yellow right eye kept on staring at him, unblinking, as if she still trusted him to save her.

There was a third explosion and the whole of her head burst apart. A blizzard of bone and flesh flew into Decker's face, knocking off his spectacles and blinding him. He wrenched his hands free from her and threw himself sideways off the toilet seat onto the floor.

Major Bruscow shouted, "Okay! Okay! I'm going to kick the door down! Stand clear!"

Mayzie shouted back, "No! It's all right! I can open it! Everything's all right!"

Decker picked up his glasses and put them back on. When he looked up, he saw that it *was* Mayzie, not Cathy, and that there was no blood anywhere, nor lumps of flesh. He grabbed hold of the toilet-roll holder and heaved himself onto his feet, while Mayzie drew back the bolt and opened the door. Major Bruscow and Acting Deputy Chief Prescott were standing outside, both of them looking baffled and angry.

"What the hell is all this yelling about, Martin? And what are *you* doing in here, Officer Shifflett? This is the men's facility."

Mayzie tossed back her hair and shot Decker a look of total exasperation. Decker said, "I, ah—I wasn't feeling too good. Something I ate. Officer Shifflett saw me out in the corridor and she—ah—offered to give me a hand."

Major Bruscow looked down at Decker's open zipper. "She gave you a hand, huh? I hope you realize this is a serious disciplinary matter."

"I ate sashimi at Yamamoto. I guess the tuna must've been off."

"Very well. But I don't want anything like this happening again, and *you*, Shifflett, stay out of the men's room in the future."

"Yes, *sir*," Mayzie said, and left.

Decker went to the washbasin and splashed his face with cold water. Then he combed his hair and straightened his bright red necktie. He felt as shocked as if Mayzie really *had* turned into Cathy, and her head really *had* exploded.

Acting Deputy Chief Prescott left the men's room, but Major Bruscow stayed. "You okay, Martin? You're not having another of those stress-related things you went through last year?"

"I'm fine. Really."

"All right. I'll go along with that. But we can't afford to have a single detective in this division who can't give me 110 percent."

"I know that, Major. I'm okay. I shouldn't eat sashimi, that's all."

CHAPTER ELEVEN

Hicks came back just after five o'clock. His forehead was beaded in sweat, his coat was slung over his shoulder, and he was carrying a can of Diet 7-Up.

"Anything?" Decker asked.

"Nobody *saw* nothing. Nobody *heard* nothing. Nobody *knows* nothing." Hicks popped open the soda and took four thirsty swallows, wiping his mouth with the back of his hand.

Decker swung his feet off the desk. "Can't blame people for seeing nothing if there was nothing there to see."

"I don't know, Lieutenant. I just can't figure it. It's the lack of footprints and fingerprints and fiber evidence that bugs me the most."

"The perpetrator is a human being, Hicks. No human being can walk through life without leaving some kind of a trail behind him. We'll get him, believe me."

Hicks looked at his watch. "I need to be going."

"How's that list of military memorabilia stores?"

"Seven, so far, and seventeen online, although only one of the Internet stores is in the Richmond area."

"Right! No point in sitting on our asses. Let's start doing the rounds."

Hicks looked uncomfortable. "I was kind of hoping to call it a day. It's my little girl's birthday party this afternoon."

"Oh yeah? How old is she?"

"Three."

"That's okay, then. She'll never remember that you didn't show."

They parked outside the Rebel Yell on West Cary Street and climbed out of the car. An old-fashioned red-painted frontage was hung with Confederate battle flags. The windows were crowded with sepia photographs of whiskery Confederate officers and tarnished military buttons and replica Colt revolvers and cavalry swords.

A bell jangled as they opened the door. Inside, there was a scrubbed oak floor and rows of glass display cabinets containing rifles and musketoons and cutlasses and all the paraphernalia of war, from dented cooking pots to inkstands to cartridge-rolling papers. The store smelled of wood, and musty old clothes, and wax.

Billy Joe Bennett was standing behind the counter—a huge, big-bellied man, with a gingery gray beard and circular glasses, dressed in a gray artillery coat with epaulets and original eagle buttons on it. He was talking to a round-shouldered middle-aged customer in one of those floppy Woody Allen hats that looks like a wilted cabbage. Billy Joe suddenly picked up a heavy saber and slashed it crisscross in the air, so that it whistled, and the customer said, "Wow," and backed away.

"Know what they used to call this?" Billy Joe said, in a voice as rich as fruitcake. "The wrist breaker. But it could whop a fellow's head off with one blow."

"Real neat sword," the customer said. "How much do you want for it?"

"Couldn't take less than 3,500."

"Mind if I have a try?"

"Okay . . . but be careful. Wouldn't want you to do yourself a mischief."

The customer took the saber and jabbed it in the air a few times. Then he lifted it high over his head and whirled it about like a helicopter rotor. He let out a whoop and a "yee-haaa!" and promptly dropped it with a clatter onto the floor.

"Jee-zus! What are you trying to do, cut your damn feet off?" Billy Joe came bustling around the counter and picked up the saber as tenderly as if it were an infant.

The customer rubbed his wrist and said, goofily, "Guess I misjudged how heavy it is."

"Let me tell you something, this saber was carried at First Manassas by Captain Tom Hartley of the First Virginia Cavalry, one of the bravest Southern officers as was. He had his left arm blown off below the elbow by a minié ball but he never dropped it, not once."

"Really? That really gives it some provenance, doesn't it? It's going to look terrific hanging over my fireplace back in Madison. Do you take MasterCard?"

Billy Joe carefully laid the saber back down on the counter, polishing its blade with a soft yellow duster. He thought for a while, and then he said, "MasterCard? Uh-huh."

"How about American Express?"

"I can't exactly tell you that we take that either. Besides, this saber ain't for sale no more."

The customer blinked. "What do you mean it's not for sale anymore?"

"Exactly that."

"Well, how about that sword over there?"

"That's not for sale, neither."

"It doesn't have a 'sold' ticket on it."

"I know. But nothing is for sale. In fact, I've suddenly remembered that we're closed. Good-bye."

The customer hesitated for a moment, but when Billy Joe resolutely turned his back on him and noisily started counting out boxes full of military buttons, he looked around at Decker and Hicks and said, "Craziest store I ever heard of, won't sell you anything."

He hesitated a little longer and then he left. Billy Joe carried on counting buttons, but after a while, with his back still turned, he said, "What can I do for you today, Lieutenant?"

"I don't know. You're closed, aren't you?"

Billy Joe turned to face them, and picked up the saber again. "This isn't just a saber, Lieutenant. This is the glory of the South. And I'm damned if I'm going to sell it to some pigeon-chested nitwit who can't handle it with due respect."

"Pretty selective way to do business."

"Well, maybe it was just that particular guy. I hated his hat."

Decker peered into one of the display cabinets. "What I'm interested in is bayonets and bowie knives."

"Bayonets? I don't have too many of those. I have a good Kentucky bowie knife, though, with an ivory handle, dated 1863."

"I don't want to buy anything. I want to know if you've sold any bayonets and bowie knives recently, and to whom."

Billy Joe scratched his bearded chin. "Last bayonet I sold was a socket bayonet made by Cook and Brother, New Orleans, 1861 or 1862. Very good condition, double-edged, twenty-one inches long. Last bowie knife . . . I couldn't tell you."

Hicks took out a photograph of Jerry Maitland. "Ever see this guy before? Ever sold him a bayonet?"

Billy Joe lifted his glasses so that he could focus. "No . . . sorry."

Hicks handed him a copy of Sandra's drawing of the So-Scary Man. "How about this character? Ever see him?"

Billy Joe studied the drawing carefully, and then he said, "When was this drawing made?"

"What difference does that make?"

"You don't very often see pictures of these fellows, if at all."

"These fellows? What do you mean by that?"

Billy Joe pointed to the man's hat. "See them feathers, in his hatband? They're crow feathers."

"I didn't really take too much notice of them, to tell you the truth."

"Well, you shoulda, because they tell you a story. And the story is that this fellow is a member of what they called the Devil's Brigade."

"The Devil's Brigade? Who were they?"

"It's one of those Civil War legends, you know. Half truth and half legend. There was supposed to be thirteen men in all, twelve white and one colored, and they was specially recruited by Lieutenant General James Longstreet in April, 1864, just before the Battle of the Wilderness."

"Can't say I've ever heard of them."

Billy Joe handed the drawing back. "You never heard of them because they was like special forces, you know, the Civil War equivalent of Delta Force, and the whole operation was a close secret. Nobody knows who the individual men was, or what exactly they was assigned to do, but the story goes that they was charged with creating all kinds of hell regardless of the usual rules and conduct of war."

He carefully sheathed the saber and hung it up in one of the display cabinets.

Hicks said, "One of them was colored? That was pretty unusual, wasn't it, for the Confederate army? I didn't think they had any colored troops."

"Nor did they. The only coloreds who got involved in the war were personal servants that some of the officers took to the front line. I don't know why they made an exception in this particular case."

"Do you have any idea what this Devil's Brigade actually did?" Decker asked.

"Only stories and rumors. The situation was that the Confederates was being very hard-pressed by the Federals up by the Rapidan River. The Federals had more men and much more equipment. Grant was on the verge of breaking through the Confederate lines, and I guess Longstreet decided that he needed something to tip the balance back in his favor. I don't know if he recruited the Devil's Brigade with Lee's approval or not, but even if the stories and rumors are only half correct, those thirteen fellows wreaked some terrible havoc up there in the Wilderness. There were tales of men being turned inside out, and men catching fire spontaneous, and men being chopped into so many pieces that nobody could tell which piece belonged to who.

"On the night of May seven to eight, the horrors was supposed to have gotten so dreadful that there was wholesale panic in the Federal forces, and Grant had to order their immediate withdrawal, before it became a rout. Both armies left the Wilderness and eventually wound up at the battle of Spotsylvania."

"What happened to the Devil's Brigade? Didn't they go to Spotsylvania too?"

"The Battle of the Wilderness was the first and last time they was heard of. The stories and rumors say that Longstreet himself was so appalled by what they had done that he ordered them disbanded and gave special orders that they wasn't to be mentioned again. So the only accounts we have are those of eyewitnesses on both sides, and as you probably know the Wilderness was not a place where the common soldier could see much of what was going on, because the woods was so dense, and the underbrush was almost impossible to penetrate."

He looked again at Sandra's drawing. "I only ever saw one other drawing of the Devil's Brigade, and that was done by an artist lieutenant from Kershaw's division, who sketched all thirteen of them when they was gathered at Parker's Store, just before the battle. So I'd very much like to know who did this, and where they got their reference from, especially if they're in actual possession of the uniform. That would be worth thousands, and I'd be willing to make them an offer."

Hicks checked his notebook. "You say the Battle of the Wilderness was in May?"

"That's correct."

"Must have been pretty warm then, in May. So why did the Devil's Brigade wear greatcoats?"

"Good question," Billy Joe said. "By that stage of the war, you wouldn't have recognized what most of the Southern soldiers was wearing as uniforms at all. They threw away everything that hindered their marching—their greatcoats, their hats, their spare blankets, even their boots, sometimes. They didn't have much use for their bayonets, either, so they stuck them in the ground for the quartermasters to pick up afterward.

"All I can say is that the Devil's Brigade must have been privileged not to march with the main multitude; but why they wore greatcoats I can't imagine. I've got two greatcoats right back here . . . you try putting one on and see how damn heavy it is."

* * *

As they drove eastward, back to the city center, Decker said, "This is getting weirder by the minute. Even supposing Sandra *didn't* see the So-Scary Man, even if she only imagined him, how come she managed to draw such an accurate picture? If Billy Joe Bennett has only seen one other drawing of the Devil's Brigade, and he's an expert in Civil War memorabilia, where the hell did Sandra ever see one?"

"Maybe you should try asking her," Hicks suggested.

"I don't know. I think we're looking at this all the wrong way. There's a key to this somewhere, but it's like in *Alice in Wonderland*. It's way up on top of the table and we're trying to find it on the floor."

He took a left on Belvidere Street and headed toward Monroe Park. Hicks looked up from his notebook and frowned. "Where are we going?"

"Back to your house, sport. You have a birthday party to go to, remember?"

CHAPTER TWELVE

He dropped off Hicks at his small rented house off Valley Road. There were twenty or thirty small children playing in the front yard, and colored balloons tied to the porch. As Hicks walked up the path, a young, pretty woman in a pink dress came out onto the front steps. Hicks obviously told her who Decker was, and she gave him a smile and a wave. Decker waved back. Very tasty, he thought. Some guys have all the luck.

His cell phone played Beethoven. "Martin."

"It's Maggie. I just wanted to tell you that I'm thinking of you."

"You're a bad woman, Maggie. Thank God."

"Listen, Cab has to go to Charlottesville on Tuesday afternoon. How about calling by for some of that sweet, sweet stuff you're going to be missing this weekend?"

"Sounds tempting."

"I'll hold you to it," she said, with a thick, dirty laugh.

* * *

His shirt was sticking to his back and he felt like going home and taking a shower. He could use a couple of shots of tequila, too. But he couldn't stop thinking about what had happened in the men's room with Mayzie. He saw it over and over in his mind's eye, an endless video loop. Instead of Mayzie, Cathy lifting her face and smiling at him, her face as white as clouds and her eyes yellow. Then her head silently exploding, in a welter of blood and bone fragments and flesh. Then lifting her face again, and opening her eyes, and smiling again, and exploding again.

When he reached the intersection with Franklin Street he hesitated. A driver behind him blasted his horn and Decker mouthed *asshole* at him and gave him the finger. Then he turned right and drove back to headquarters. He collected a cup of strong black coffee from the vending machine at the end of his corridor, and walked along to his office, sipping it. He switched on his computer and hung his coat over the back of his chair while it booted up.

And she lifted her face, and smiled at him. And then her head slowly burst apart like a pumpkin, so that he was lacerated by flying teeth and splattered in blood.

He had looked up this file so many times before, but it still baffled him and it still hurt. Case number CZS/448/3251, Catherine Meredith Meade, aged twenty-nine years and two months. Right at the top of the report were several color photographs of the crime scene. That familiar bedroom at 318 West Broad Street, with its pale duck-egg walls. The dark blue woven throw, dragged to one side, and the cream-colored pillows that looked as if somebody had splashed a bucket of dark red dye all over them. Cathy's body, on the floor, one leg twisted behind her, her white nightshirt speckled all over.

It had happened at 1:30 on the morning of February 7. Decker had been called out to a suspicious drowning on

Brown's Island. While he was away, somebody had entered his apartment either by picking the lock or using a passkey. There was no sign of any forced entry. The perpetrator had gone directly to the bedroom, approached the bed, and fired three soft-nosed slugs that blew Cathy's head to pieces.

Cathy had been all smiles and sunshine. Even her previous boyfriend—although he had been desperately upset to lose her—still adored her. The only possible explanation for the killing had been that somebody had been gunning for Decker, and had mistakenly shot Cathy in the darkness—or else they had shot her to teach him a lesson that he would never forget.

The time that it happened, Decker had been involved in a complicated series of homicide investigations in the Jackson Ward. He had suspected that the murders were connected with a vicious power struggle between two of the ward's most ruthless criminal organizations, the Strutters and the Egun. He had persuaded three witnesses to give material evidence against Queen Aché, the leader of the Egun. But when Cathy was killed, Decker had been so grief-stricken that he had been forced to take six months' sick leave, and his witnesses had all contracted irreversible amnesia.

So why were all these thoughts of Cathy coming back to him now? He couldn't understand what they meant—the nightmares, the waking hallucinations, that bizarre business of the fruit-and-chicken face on the chopping board? He scrolled down through the incident report. Maybe he had been reminded of Cathy's death because Cathy's killer had left absolutely no evidence—just like the killer of Alison Maitland and George Drewry. Cathy's killer had even avoided detection on the video monitors in the lobby, in the elevators, and in the corridor right outside their apartment door. No suspects were ever arrested, and the case was still open, though inactive.

Decker was almost ready to leave when Cab came in. "How's it going?" Cab asked him.

Decker smeared his hands down his cheeks. "No place, fast. I think I'm going to call it a night."

Cab walked around his desk and looked at his computer screen. "You should let that lie. No point in picking your scabs."

"I don't know. I keep having these weird thoughts about Cathy and I'm wondering if my brain's trying to tell me something. Like, maybe there's some kind of connection between what happened to her and what happened to Alison Maitland and George Drewry."

Cab laid a hand on his shoulder. "You're a good cop, Martin, but don't start getting all inspirational on me. Don't lose sight of what matters, and that's the evidence."

"Maybe you're right. It's just that, in this case, I think the most important evidence is that there *is* no evidence."

Cab turned his head away and let out a violent sneeze. As he was stentoriously blowing his nose, Decker's phone rang. He picked it up and said, "Mackenzie?"

"Hi, Lieutenant. It's Jimmy Freedman, down in the sound lab. Listen, I cleaned up that 911 call from the Maitland case. Thought you might be interested in hearing it."

"Sure. Give me a couple of minutes."

From behind his handkerchief, Cab gave him a wave, which indicated that he could go.

Jimmy was furiously chewing gum. "I went through it with Bill Duggan from the phone company. He's the Stephen Hawking of line faults. He even *talks* like Stephen Hawking. He said that Alison Maitland's 911 call was interrupted by an EMP."

"A what?"

"An EMP—electromagnetic pulse. This induces kilovolt potentials that can burn out integrated circuits, interfere with telephone systems, or randomize computer data."

"I get it," Decker said, trying to sound as if he did. "So what causes it, this EMP?"

"Usually a flux compression generator, which is an explosive used to compress a magnetic field."

"Explosive? Ah, you mean like a bomb?"

"Exactly. They even call them 'pulse bombs.' They're pretty simple to build if you have a basic knowledge of electronics and demolition. The military have developed even more powerful ones, which use high-power microwaves. They dropped them in Iraq to take out Saddam's communications systems."

Decker said, "That's very interesting. The only trouble is, there was no explosion that day in the immediate vicinity of the Maitland house. In fact—so far as I know—there was no explosion that day anywhere in the Metro Richmond area."

"Well, that's right."

"So what caused this particular EMP, if it wasn't a bomb?"

"Bill was puzzled by that, too. But he reckons that it must have been some kind of natural phenomenon. A sunspot, maybe."

"So, actually, we're none the wiser?"

Jimmy looked upward for a moment, as if there were an answer printed on the ceiling. Then he looked down again and said, "No, you're quite correct. We're not."

"You said you managed to clean the tape up. Is it any clearer?"

"Hear it for yourself."

He hooked on his earphones and flicked a row of switches. Decker heard the first blurt of noise, and then the emergency operator saying, "Emergency? Which service?" This was immediately followed by a deafening crackle, and a man's voice screaming, "Help me! Oh, God, help me!"

Decker looked at Jimmy and Jimmy raised an eyebrow. "You hear that? That sounds distinctly like a fire burning. A bonfire, or brushwood, maybe. Maybe the guy's screaming because he's going to be burned."

Decker said nothing, but he felt a deep sense of foreboding, as if the floor were slowly creeping away from him, beneath his feet.

"Yes, ambulance—" That was Alison Maitland. "Urgent—bleeding so bad!"

Then more crackling—closer, sharper, and a man's voice calling, "Muster at the road, boys! Muster at the road!"

More crackling, more screaming, and then a heavy crunch like a falling tree. Decker raised his hand and said, "Thanks, Jimmy. That's enough. That's very helpful."

Jimmy blinked at him in surprise. "You don't want to hear the rest?"

"That's okay. I don't have to."

"What? It makes some kind of sense?"

"I don't know. Maybe."

Jimmy stared at him. "Are you *okay*, Lieutenant? You look kind of—"

"Fine, Jimmy. I'm fine. I'm absolutely fine."

As soon as he opened his apartment door, he became aware of a smoky, perfumed aroma, like incense. He hefted his revolver out of its holster, cocked it, and cautiously pushed the door a little wider. The smell could have been coming from the apartment below, where a young married couple regularly burned incense (they were either potheads or Buddhists, or both). But it seemed too intense for that.

Sliding his back against the wall, he made his way along the corridor to the kitchen. He jabbed his revolver into the open doorway, but the kitchen was empty. He crossed to the other side of the corridor and carried on sliding toward the living area.

There was nobody there, but three sticks of incense were smoldering in a small sand-filled urn that he usually used as an ashtray. And on the wall behind them, in jagged blood-red letters that were over two feet high, somebody had scrawled SAINT BARBARA.

Decker slowly approached the lettering and touched it with his fingertips. It was still wet. It had the consistency of blood, but he couldn't be sure that it actually was, and he certainly wasn't going to taste it. He walked crabwise across the living area until he reached his bedroom door. It was about two inches ajar. He stopped, and listened, but all he could hear was the muffled sound of traffic outside, and the burbling of a television in the next apartment.

He took a deep breath and kicked the door wide open. His bedroom appeared to be empty, although he ducked down and checked under the bed, and then threw open his closet doors. Nobody there.

It was then that he heard a trickling sound coming from the bathroom. He edged his way toward the door and pressed his ear against it. It was a small, steady trickle, more like a faucet left running than anybody washing their hands. He carefully grasped the doorknob, and then, when he was ready, he flung the door open.

The bathroom was empty, too, except for his own reflection in the mirror. But the hot faucet hadn't been turned off properly, and the washbasin was streaked with scarlet. It looked as if somebody had quickly rinsed their hands and then left.

But where had this somebody gone? The bathroom window didn't open, apart from a small louvered skylight, and nobody could have passed him on the way in. He dragged back the shower curtain, just to make sure, but there was nobody there, either.

He turned off the faucet, holding it with only two fingers, in case there were fingerprints on it. He put the plug in, too, to prevent any more of the gory-looking contents of the basin from draining away.

He looked at himself in the mirror. *You're not losing it, Martin. You're as sane as everybody else, and you can prove it.* But apart from the incense and the scrawling on the wall, there was an almost palpable sense that somebody had been here, going from room to room, disturbing the air.

He went back to the living area and snuffed out the incense. Then he stood and stared at the lettering. SAINT BARBARA. What the hell was the significance of Saint Barbara? Cathy had whispered her name in his nightmare, and now here it was again, in letters that could have been blood.

He searched the room again, prodding his revolver into the drapes, even though he knew that he wouldn't find anybody. Then he locked his front door, fastened the security chain, and holstered his Anaconda. He picked up the phone and dialed directly through to Lieutenant Bryce in forensics.

"Helen?"

"Lieutenant Bryce went home about an hour ago. Can I help?"

"I hope so. This is Lieutenant Martin. Do you have anybody free to take some fluid samples at Nineteenth and Main?"

"What kind of fluid samples?"

"Blood, it looks like."

"Is this a crime scene?"

"I don't know. To tell you the truth, I have no idea *what* happened here."

CHAPTER THIRTEEN

He dreamed that he was running through the briars again, barefoot. The fires were much closer now, and he could feel the heat on his back, like an open furnace. Sparks were showering over his head and dropping onto the underbrush up ahead of him, so that he had to fight his way through bushes that were already blazing.

"Muster at the plank road, boys!" somebody was shouting, his voice hoarse with smoke. "Muster at the plank road!"

He kept his left elbow raised to protect his eyes from thorns and branches and to shield his cheek from the heat. A spark settled on his shoulder, eating through his shirt. He swatted it off, but it was still painful, and he could smell scorched cotton and burned skin.

He had a rough idea that the plank road was off to his left, about a quarter of a mile, but the woods in that direction were burning fiercely and he could hear men screaming as they were overtaken by the flames. Instead, he headed off to the right, hoping to be able to circle around the fires and reach the road a little farther up. He tried to hurry, but the underbrush was even thicker here, and he had to leap and scramble like a hare.

What was even more frightening than the approaching fire was the feeling that somebody was catching up with him, hurrying through the thickets as black and fluid as a shadow. And he knew that this somebody was intent on killing him—not angrily, but cold-bloodedly, and gruesomely, inflicting more pain than anybody could imagine.

He quickly turned his head. He could see a silhouette only a few yards behind him. A tall silhouette, with flapping wings. Its coattails were snagged by the briars, but that didn't seem to slow it down at all, and he could hear its boots crackling through the bracken. *Oh, Jesus.* He simply didn't have the strength to jump any farther. His clothes were tangled in the bushes and his hands and feet were ablaze with thorns.

He stopped, gasping, and the silhouette rushed into him, knocking the breath out of him. He found himself in suffocating darkness, in a cage of bones, struggling desperately to get himself free.

"*Can't breathe!*" he screamed. "*Can't breathe!*"

He found Father Thomas in the diocesan garden at the back of the Cathedral of the Sacred Heart, his sleeves rolled up, weeding. Father Thomas stood up as he approached, a plump, pink-faced man with a bow wave of white hair.

"Lieutenant Martin! My goodness! It's been quite a while since we saw *you!*"

Decker looked around. "This is some garden, isn't it?" The flower bed that Father Thomas was tending was bursting with cream and yellow roses, and their fragrance was so heady that it was almost erotic.

"We do our best. . . . I always think that to keep a beautiful garden is like saying a thank-you to God, for granting us such earthly delights."

Decker had come to the Cathedral of the Sacred Heart at least twice a week in the days after Cathy had been killed. He had knelt for hours inside its cool, echoing interior, under its high gold-relief ceilings, and tightly closed his eyes and prayed that it was still January, and that her murder had never happened. *Oh, God, can't you just wind back the clock?*

The cathedral was unusual in that it had been financed and built entirely by one man, Thomas Fortune Ryan, the founder of the American Tobacco Company. Richmond had very few Catholics, but it was here that they could turn for hope and encouragement, a grand Romanesque building that proudly proclaimed the Church Militant—the Lord God and His angels in their eternal struggle against Satan and his devils.

Decker said, "I guess I got disillusioned with God. My fault. I asked Him for something impossible."

"Don't worry." Father Thomas smiled. "I can assure you that God isn't disillusioned with *you*. And who's to say what's impossible and what isn't?"

He propped his hoe against his wheelbarrow and said, "Why don't you come inside and have a drink?"

"Sure. It's hot enough, isn't it? There's a couple of questions I need to ask you."

"Of course. Always pleased to help the forces of law and order."

He led Decker through to a brown-and-white-tiled kitchen with a large oak table and windows that were glazed with muted yellow glass. He opened up the icebox and took out a frosted jug of lemonade. "Sorry we don't have any tequila."

"You remembered," Decker said, taking off his sunglasses.

"Well . . . let's say there was more than one occasion

when the condition in which you came here to pray owed more to the cactus spirit than the Holy Spirit."

He poured them each a tumbler of lemonade, making sure that there were plenty of lemon slices floating in them. Decker said, "What can you tell me about Saint Barbara?"

"Saint Barbara? Is there any specific reason for this?"

"I don't know yet. That's why I came to see you. I mean, you're the expert on patron saints, aren't you?"

"I like to think so. Saint Barbara, well . . . Saint Barbara was removed from the Roman calendar sometime in the late 1960s and her cultus was suppressed. But there are still many who are devoted to her, especially in the military, and those who work with explosives, such as armorers and gunners and bomb technicians.

"She's the patron saint of fire, you see, and lightning."

Decker said, "I've been having this nightmare . . . I'm running away from a brushfire. The first time I had it, I had another dream right afterward. I saw Cathy, and Cathy said that she wants to protect me from Saint Barbara."

Father Thomas raised his eyebrows. "I can't think why you need *protection* from her, particularly if you were trying to escape from a fire. Saint Barbara is honored by firefighters and by anybody working with fireworks or explosives. That's always assuming that your dream has any real significance, of course, and that it isn't just a fragment of something that you accidentally picked up during the course of your day's work."

"Cathy said, 'Saint Barbara wants her revenge.' She said it as clear as if she were standing right next to me."

"That's very strange. Saint Barbara was supposed to have been very beautiful and gentle and forgiving. It was said that she lived in Thrace, in the third century, and the story is that she was locked in a high tower by her father,

Dioscorus, for disobedience. While she was imprisoned she was tutored by a whole variety of philosophers and orators and poets. From them, she learned that the worship of many gods was nonsense, and she converted to Christianity.

"Her not-so-loving father denounced her to the local authorities, and they ordered him to kill her. She escaped, but her father caught her, dragged her home by her hair, tortured her, and cut her head off. But he got his just desserts. He was instantly struck by fire from heaven, and killed.

"Because of this, people used to ask Saint Barbara to protect them against fire and lightning and any other kind of death from the sky. You often used to see her image on fire stations and powder magazines and military arsenals, in a white robe, holding the palm of martyrdom in one hand and the chalice of happy death in the other.

"However, the official view today is that Saint Barbara is only a legend, and that somewhere along the line a pious fiction was mistakenly interpreted as history. So the likelihood is that your dream was nothing more than a dream."

Decker said, "The trouble is, it didn't stop at a dream. Saint Barbara's name was written on the wall of my apartment last night, in what looked like blood, and underneath it somebody had left incense burning. Don't ask me who. There was nobody there, and nobody in my apartment building saw any strangers entering or leaving."

"I have to admit that I'm baffled," Father Thomas said. "Although it's academically interesting that the name Barbara means 'stranger.'"

"I just wanted to know if you had any theories. Doesn't matter how wild they are. I'm investigating the Maitland homicide and the Drewry homicide, and as you've probably seen on the news, we don't have a single credible eyewitness and we don't have any evidence whatsoever. I mean, not even a single fiber, or a speck of saliva, or a microscopic sample of dirt. There's so much nothing that it's unreal.

"We had exactly the same dearth of evidence when Cathy was killed, and I've been trying to figure out if there's any kind of connection."

Father Thomas picked a lemon slice out of his tumbler and thoughtfully sucked it. "Sour," he said, when he caught the expression on Decker's face. "For some reason, I've always liked sour. Mortification of the palate, I suppose."

"So . . . you don't have any ideas?"

"Not really, Lieutenant. But I've always been a strong believer in the divine messages that are brought to us in dreams. They may not make a whole lot of sense to us at first, but when we think back on them later, they can often give us striking insights into what is really happening to us. Sometimes I think that we're much more in touch with the meaning of our existence when we're asleep than we are when we're supposedly awake."

He leaned forward and said, very quietly, as if he were imparting the greatest secret in the universe, "Let me put it this way . . . if *you* were God, and you wanted to talk to your dearest creations, when would you choose to do it? By day, when their minds were filled with noise and work and family and worry? Or by night, when everything is quiet, and your words could be heard in all their perception and their clarity? And their strangeness, too.

"I may well be wrong, but my feeling is that when you understand what that means, 'Saint Barbara wants her revenge,' then you will understand everything."

"Okay," Decker said. "But what am I supposed to think of *this?*"

He unbuttoned his shirt and tugged it sideways to expose his left shoulder. There was an angry blister about an inch above his collarbone, like a cigarette burn, and it was weeping.

"In my nightmare last night, in that brushfire, a hot spark fell on me. When I woke up, my T-shirt was burned, and so was my skin."

He held out his hands to show Father Thomas that they were crisscrossed in small red scratches. "I was fighting my way through a briar patch, and this is what happened. My feet are the same."

Father Thomas took hold of his hands and examined them closely. Then he looked up at Decker with his china-blue eyes and said, "If what you are telling me is true, this is very disturbing. When nightmares begin to cause physical harm, that is a sign that something truly terrible is about to happen."

"Father, I think it's already begun."

He was sitting with Hicks in the Third Street Diner when Beethoven summoned him on his cellphone. *Da-da-da-DAH!*

"Can't you change that?" Hicks complained. "Even Strauss hated Beethoven. Do you know what he said? He said, 'Beethoven is a shit.' He actually used those actual words."

"What would you prefer? 'The Camptown Races'?"

A woman's voice said, "Lieutenant Martin? This is Lily Messenger from forensics?" She had a way of lifting her words at the end of every sentence so they sounded like questions.

"Sure. How are you, Officer Messenger?"

"I'm good, thanks. I have the preliminary analysis from those fluid samples I took from your apartment yesterday evening?"

"That was quick."

"You're right, the lettering on your wall was drawn in human blood? Type-A, Rh-negative?"

"I see. Right . . . I appreciate that." He put the cell phone back on the table and said, "*Saint Barbara* was written in blood."

"You're kidding me. You think somebody's trying to warn you off?"

"Warn me off what? And *why*? It's not like we're breathing down anybody's neck."

Hicks cut a pancake with the edge of his fork. "Maybe we need to go through this whole thing right from the beginning again. Search the crime scenes again, reinterview the neighbors and the passersby. Like you say, nobody can go through life without leaving *some* evidence behind them. We've just missed seeing it, that's all."

Decker shook his head, unconvinced. "How's it going with the military memorabilia stores?"

"Only one more to check out, Wippler's Sutlery on Fifth Street, and one online."

Decker took one more bite of donut, grimaced, and dropped it back on his plate. "Let's try looking at this thing another way. We don't have any evidence, okay? But what else don't we have? We don't have motive. Alison Maitland was a very popular person and so was Major Drewry. All right, he was supposed to have been a bit of a grouch. But you don't normally disembowel people just because they complain about dogs messing on their front lawn.

"Whatever the captain thinks, I don't believe that *two* perpetrators could both be able to enter a house completely unseen and leave no forensic evidence whatsoever. I mean, that took some kind of skill that's practically supernatural. So we only have one perpetrator and we have to work out why this one perpetrator wanted to kill both Alison Maitland and George Drewry. They don't appear to have had anything in common. Different age, different sex, different background, different religion. But there must be *something* that connects them."

Hicks wiped his mouth with his napkin and crumpled it up. "How about we check up on their personal histories, as far back as we can go?"

"Well . . . it'll make us look as if we're doing something, if nothing else."

As they paid the check, Hicks suddenly said, "Did we pick up anything off that 911 call? I meant to ask you."

Decker shook his head. "Nothing conclusive. Jimmy reckons there was some kind of electronic glitch, that's all, but he's still working on it." What else was he going to say? That the screaming that had interrupted Alison Maitland's cries for help were the very same screams that he was hearing in his nightmares?

They stepped out into the street. Hicks said, "You know that invitation to go out for a Mexican meal? Does that still stand?"

"Of course it does. How about Wednesday?"

"The thing is . . . I don't know . . . Rhoda doesn't seem to have settled down here at all."

"Give her some time, sport. She'll get used to it."

"She says that Richmond gives her a bad feeling, she doesn't know why."

"I told you, she's probably missing her friends. Don't worry, we'll find her some new ones."

"Well, I hope so. We had a pretty bad fight last night, and we never used to fight."

Decker put on his sunglasses. "She wants attention, Hicks, that's all. All women need attention." To prove his point, he grinned at a ponytailed blonde in a red baseball cap. The blonde turned to smile back at him and almost collided with a streetlight.

* * *

Back at the office, his answering machine was flashing. Somebody had called him only two minutes ago. He pressed the *play* button, and there was some crackling and shuffling before he heard "Lieutenant Martin? This is Eunice Plummer. I thought you ought to know that Sandra's seen him again. The So-Scary Man."

CHAPTER FOURTEEN

He called back immediately. "Ms. Plummer? Yes, thanks for your message. When was this?"

"Only about fifteen minutes ago. We were walking along Marshall Street window-shopping when Sandra saw him walking toward us."

"Did *you* see him?"

"I'm afraid not. But Sandra was very frightened in case he recognized her, and she hid in a doorway."

"Where exactly was this?"

"Between Eleventh and Twelfth. Sandra says he went into the hospital."

"He did *what?*"

"She peeked out from the doorway to see how close he was, but he didn't cross over Twelfth Street—he went into the Medical College Hospital."

"Where's your close-protection officer? Can you put her on the phone?"

"She didn't show. I thought maybe you'd decided we didn't need her anymore."

Shit, thought Decker. *Cab and his goddamned cost-cutting.* "Where are you now?" he asked Eunice, and then he covered the mouthpiece with his hand and shouted out, "*Hicks!*"

"We're at McDonald's, on Eighth Street. Sandra was upset so I bought her a milkshake."

"Stay there. We're coming to pick you up. *Hicks!*"

Hicks appeared, carrying a heap of folders. "What's the problem?"

"Sandra's seen him again. The So-Scary Man. Let's get going. This could be just what we've been waiting for."

Jerry Maitland was sitting up in bed watching a program about Antarctic exploration in the 1900s—jerky black-and-white movies of men in furs and sealskins, standing in the snow.

"Of this American expedition in 1908, only one man, Clement Pearson, managed to return to base camp alive. He attributed his survival to a mysterious figure who led him through three days of relentless blizzards. The figure always walked twenty yards ahead of him always on his left, and never once spoke to him. On the morning that Pearson reached McMurdo Sound, the figure disappeared."

As he watched, Jerry became aware of a faint disturbance in the air, as if the door had been opened, even though it hadn't. He also had the unaccountable feeling that he wasn't alone anymore. He pressed the *mute* button on the TV remote and listened, frowning. On the screen, in utter silence, he saw Clement Pearson's charcoal sketch of the figure that was supposed to have saved him from freezing to death. Tall and hunched, a dark blur seen only through a teeming blizzard.

While he listened, and watched, the figure on the screen appeared to swell and distort, as if Clement Pearson's sketch were actually *moving*. Then the window next to the television rippled and distorted, too. Jerry felt as if he were seeing his room through languidly wallowing water.

He blinked, trying to clear his vision. He was still on antibiotics and painkillers, and he expected that this was one of the side effects. Yet the flowers beside his bed suddenly melted and flowed, and he felt sure that there was somebody standing very close to him, only inches away. He could even hear *breathing*—tight, suppressed breathing—and another sound, which he couldn't identify. It was a thick, unpleasant *rustling* noise. It reminded him of the swarm of cockroaches that he had discovered when he was seven, rushing in their hundreds through the crawl space of his parents' old house. And had screaming nightmares about, for years afterward.

Hesitantly, he reached out with his thickly bandaged right hand for the *panic* button that lay on top of his blanket. He didn't want to look like a fool, calling the nurse because he suspected there was somebody else in the room, when there obviously wasn't. But if this was a side effect of some of his medication, he thought that the nurse ought to know. He had never taken LSD or any other hallucinogenic, but he could imagine that this was what a trip was like. You could see, like, invisible people.

Just as he was about to press the button, the rustling noise abruptly changed into a sharp rush of air. Jerry felt something hit his wrist, something as hard as an iron bar. He said, "*Jesus!*" and jerked up his arm and he was sprayed in the face with blood. He stared at his wrist in disbelief. His hand had been cut off, and it was lying on the green cotton blanket with its fingers curled tightly in convulsion.

He said, "Jesus" again, and then "Jesus." His wrist didn't

even hurt, but blood was jetting all over the bed and spattering his pajamas. He thought: *This hasn't happened. This can't be real.* He could still *feel* his right hand, even though it was separated from his wrist, and he tried to make it reach for the *panic* button.

It was then that somebody grabbed his lapels and heaved him bodily out of bed. He lost his balance and rolled across the floor, knocking over his IV drip. Panting with fear, he tried to scramble toward the door on his knees and his remaining hand, leaving a zigzag trail of blood on the vinyl, but he was pulled onto his feet with such force that he heard his spine crackle.

"*Help me!*" he screamed. "*Help me!*"

Somebody crooked an arm around his neck, so that he could scarcely breathe. Somebody very tall, and very powerful. Somebody dressed in coarse woolen clothing. Somebody who breathed against the back of his neck in harsh, staccato bursts, *hah! hah! hah!* like the breath of a hungry wolf.

"*Help me!*" he choked. "*For God's sake, help me!*" But he could only manage the hoarsest of desperate whispers.

His pajama top was ripped open at the front, scattering buttons. Then—without hesitation—a knife blade was plunged into his stomach, an inch below his navel. The shock was intense, like being punched, and there was a high-pitched whistle of body gases. Jerry tried to struggle free, but his invisible attacker was so strong that he couldn't even buckle his knees and drop in submission onto the floor.

There was a moment's hesitation, and then his stomach was slit open, upward, with one measured stroke, as if his attacker were relishing every moment of terror that he was inflicting. Jerry stared down at himself in utter dread. He could see no knife, and nobody holding it. Yet his skin parted in front of his eyes, revealing glistening red muscle and thick white fat, and then the first bulge of stomach, with a tracery of scarlet veins.

At first he felt completely numb. But as he was opened up wider, he was suddenly gripped by an agony that made him cry out, "Mama!" like a terrified child.

Decker opened the Mercury's rear door and grabbed Sandra's hand. "Come on!" he urged her. "We have to be quick!"

Eunice said, "What about me? Do you want me to come, too?"

"Please, yes. Hicks—can you take care of Ms. Plummer?"

He ran up the hospital steps, tugging Sandra behind him.

"What if he *sees* me?" Sandra asked.

"You don't have to worry about that. I'll take care of him. All you have to do is tell me where he is."

They pushed their way through the revolving doors. A security guard approached them with his hand raised and said, "Hey, slow down! You have to report to reception first!"

Decker showed him his badge. "We're kind of pushed for time, okay?"

"Who's the little lady?"

"Acting Officer Sandra Plummer. Now—if you don't mind."

They hurried to the elevator bank. Hicks and Eunice were close behind, but Decker said, "Take the next one!" and hit the button for the fifth floor.

On the way up, Sandra gave him a nervous smile. "This is exciting. I'd like to join the police."

"You already have," Decker assured her.

The bell chimed and the elevator doors opened. Decker took hold of Sandra's hand again and said, "We're going to go see Gerald Maitland first. He's the guy who lives in the house where you first saw the So-Scary Man, okay?"

"Why are we going to see him?"

"Well . . . if my feeling about this is correct, I think the reason the So-Scary Man came here to the hospital was to look for him."

They ran along the corridor until they reached Gerald Maitland's room. There was no police guard outside, only an empty chair, an untidy newspaper, and two empty coffee cups. Decker tried to open Gerald Maitland's door, but it was jammed. It felt as if a chair had been wedged underneath the handle, but he couldn't tell for sure because the blind was pulled down.

"Jerry!" Decker shouted. "Jerry, are you okay?"

He banged on the door with the flat of his hand. "Can you hear me, Jerry? Are you all right in there? Can you get out of bed and let me in?"

Sandra looked up at Decker worriedly, biting her lip. "Do you think something's happened to him? You don't think he's hurt him, do you, the So-Scary Man?"

"Let's hope not," Decker said. He grasped the door frame with both hands and gave the door a kick, and then another. "Jerry! Can you hear me, Jerry? Open up, Jerry, come on!"

Sandra pressed her index fingers against her forehead, as if she were concentrating very hard. "It's that wrong feeling again," she said. "*It's that wrong feeling!*"

Decker kicked the door again and again, but it still wouldn't budge. At that moment Hicks and Eunice came running along the corridor—and, from the opposite direction, the cop who was supposed to be guarding Jerry Maitland's door.

"Where the hell have you been?" Decker shouted at him.

By way of explanation the cop lifted up a bag of donuts

and said, "I'm sorry, sir, I was only a couple of minutes. What's wrong?"

"Help me get this goddamn door open. It's jammed, and Maitland's not answering."

Hicks and the cop both put their shoulders to the door, while Decker kicked it.

Eunice protectively put her arm around Sandra's shoulders, while Sandra herself stood with her eyes wide and her hands over her mouth, making a thin mewling sound under her breath.

Inside the room, Jerry was still being held upright, although his head had fallen back onto his invisible attacker's shoulder so that he was staring blindly at the ceiling. He was suffering such waves of pain that he could hardly think, and there was a high-pitched singing in his ears. He was still trying to keep his intestines inside his sliced-open stomach, his left hand desperately gripping the slippery sides of his wound like a man in a storm trying to hold a thick rubber raincoat together.

"Now who's the martyr?" whispered a thick voice, close to his ear.

He didn't answer, couldn't. He just wanted it to be over with. Anything to stop the pain. Anything to end the horror of what was happening to him.

"Now who's making the ultimate sacrifice?" the voice demanded. "Now who's giving everything for honor and glory?"

He let out a gargle. He wanted to beg for mercy, but his attacker's arm was pressing too hard against his larynx. He thought he could hear knocking and somebody calling his name, but it seemed to be coming from very far away.

The room began to darken, as if a cloud had passed over

the sun. As it did so, he felt a dreadful tugging sensation in his abdomen. His head dropped forward and he saw that an unseen hand was pulling his small intestine out of his stomach cavity. It rose up in front of him in spasmodic jerks, like a huge white worm.

It rose higher and higher, and then it started to slide around the bedrail, around and around, and coil itself into a knot. "*No*," choked Jerry. He couldn't bear any more agony.

There was a moment's pause, and then he was lifted clear of the floor, and heaved up onto a shoulder that he couldn't see. He screamed, and coughed up blood, and the knocking grew more and more frantic.

"Jerry! What's happening? Open the door, Jerry, for Christ's sake!"

But Jerry was helpless. He feebly tried to struggle but he was carried across the room, toward the window, and as he did so his intestines were dragged out of his body, yard by bloody yard, even though he scrabbled wildly to keep them in.

He reached the window. He was lifted even higher into the air, with his arms and legs flailing, and then he was flung through the glass. There was an explosive smash, and he felt himself tumbling through the air, colliding with the side of the building as he did so. But then there was a hideous, agonizing jolt, and he spun around and found himself hanging in midair, suspended by his own guts.

He didn't scream. He was too shocked and winded to scream. But he gripped his large intestine with his left hand and tried to pull himself upward. The peritoneal coating was far too greasy, and he had no more strength, but he kept thinking, *I'm alive, I'm still alive, and as long as I'm still alive I can survive*. He saw horrified faces staring at him and he thought he could hear people shouting. He thought: *They've seen me, that's good, they'll send somebody to help*. He twisted his intestine around his hand to give himself some more purchase, but he was much too weak to pull himself any higher.

"Alison?" he said. Then darkness flooded into his head and he died, dangling, slowly spinning around and around in front of the third-story windows, on the end of twenty-eight feet of bloody, stretched entrails.

As the window smashed, Decker gave the door another kick and it flew open as if it had never been jammed. He yanked out his revolver and stepped into the room. The first thing he saw was the grisly scarlet rope that was tied to the end of the bed, although he didn't understand what he was looking at.

"What the fuck?" the uniformed cop said.

"Looks like Maitland's escaped," Hicks said. "Tied some sheets together and broken the window."

Decker looked across at the blood-spattered bed, and then down to the zigzag pattern of blood on the vinyl floor. "Cut himself real bad, by the look of it."

He cautiously approached the window. As he did so, he became aware of an odd distortion in the air. The buildings opposite the hospital appeared to ripple and melt, as if he were looking at them through the rising heat from a corrugated iron roof. Even the window frame wavered, which gave him an unexpected sense of vertigo.

He took one more step forward, and then he was violently pushed in the chest. He was thrown sideways against the end of the bed, hitting his shoulder. Hicks, bewildered, said, "*Lieutenant?*" but then he was pushed, too, and promptly sat down in the armchair in the corner. The uniformed cop was turning around to help Decker when he, in turn, was slammed against the doorjamb. "Holy *shit*," he said, as blood burst out of his nose.

Decker shouted, "The door! Shut the door!" but it was already too late. From the corridor outside, Sandra shrieked, "*It's him! It's him!*"

Decker pushed his way past the uniformed cop, his revolver raised in both hands. Sandra was clinging on to her mother and pointing along the corridor. "*There he goes! Look! Can't you see him? There he goes! He's there!*"

All that Decker could see was a fluid, transparent wobble at the very end of the corridor. He was about to shoot at it when a side door opened and two nurses stepped into his line of fire, laughing. "*Get back!*" Decker yelled at them. "*Get out of the way!*" but before they could react one of them was thrown to the floor and the other was pushed on top of her.

Decker ran down the corridor and kicked open the door that led to the elevator bank. An elevator opened, and he lifted his revolver and shouted, "*Freeze!*" but it was only an orderly pushing an elderly woman in a wheelchair. There were three other elevators, but two were at lobby level and the third was on seven. Not only that, the stairs were right at the other end of the hospital.

He said, "Shit," under his breath and holstered his revolver. There was no point in putting out an APB on somebody who couldn't be seen. He walked back toward Jerry Maitland's room, stopping to help up one of the nurses.

"I felt like somebody really *shoved* me," she said, straightening her cap. "Somebody shoved me but there was nobody there."

"I know," Decker said. "The same thing happened to all of us."

"But what was it?"

"We don't know yet. It's some kind of trick. Don't worry, we're on top of it. I'll need to talk to you later, if you could give me your names."

"*Lieutenant!*" Hicks called out, and Decker could hear the

distress in his voice. "Lieutenant, you'd better come take a look at this!"

At that moment, the door to the elevator bank was flung open and two of the hospital security guards came running toward them, followed by three male paramedics and a nurse.

CHAPTER FIFTEEN

Cab said, "This is getting very unfunny."

Decker took off his glasses and polished them with his garish red and yellow necktie. "At least we have a clear idea of what we're up against."

"Oh, you think so? We're up against some kind of invisible guy who can only be seen by a young girl with Down's syndrome? What's clear about that? I can't even give any details to the press."

"I don't see why not. Maybe there are some other people out there who have the ability to see him. You know, maybe Sandra isn't the only one."

"You really think I'm going to announce that we're looking for somebody we can't see? You must think I'm desperate for early retirement."

Decker put his glasses back on and shrugged. "I still think it might help. If what this guy can do is a trick, or some kind of mass hypnosis, then there could be somebody out there who can tell us how it's done. Then again—if he's a genuine supernatural phenomenon, there could be somebody out there who knows how to track him down and do whatever it is you have to do to supernatural phenomena to stop them from disemboweling people."

"Who? Father Karras?"

Hicks said, "No—I agree with Lieutenant Martin. I think people are pretty open-minded about weird stuff these days. Like, you know, poltergeists and demonic possession and shit."

Cab dragged out his handkerchief and loudly blew his nose. "I can't do it. The chief will go nuclear. The city manager's daughter went missing a couple of years ago and I called in a psychic detective. And then I made the mistake of mentioning it to Roger Barrett at WRVA."

"*Kaboom!*" Detective Rudisill remembered, with relish.

"Exactly. *Kaboom*. Can you imagine what the chief would do if I put out a public appeal for hypnotists and mentally challenged children and exorcists? She'd have my balls for her Sunday-best earrings."

"Okay, Captain," Decker conceded. "We still have a couple of orthodox lines of inquiry to follow up—like we're looking into the Maitlands' family histories, and Major Drewry's, too."

Cab said, "All right . . . see how far you get with your regular inquiries. After that—if you still think we need to involve the media—come back and talk to me first. Don't give me any nasty surprises."

"I wouldn't dream of it, Captain. But—one more thing. We need to reinstate Sandra Plummer's close protection."

"All right. I think I can find a way to justify that."

"Oh—and one more thing. Are you still planning to go to Charlottesville on Tuesday afternoon?"

"Why are you always so interested in my movements, Martin?"

"No particular reason. I just like to know where you are, you know—in case things get exciting."

Outside in the parking lot, he met Mayzie. It was early evening now, and the sky was golden.

"Hi, Mayzie," he said, putting his arm around her shoulders. "I've been meaning to call you. You're right. We really have to talk."

Mayzie twisted herself free of him. "I've decided I don't want a baby after all," she retorted.

"*You've* decided? Don't you think *I* have any say in this?"

"You told me you didn't want to be a father."

"I know . . . but I don't know. I'm kind of warming to it. I could take him fishing. I could teach him how to play five-card stud."

"How do you know we would have a boy?"

"He *must* be a boy. Do I look like the kind of guy who'd have *girls?*"

"Decker, you're a head case. What happened in the men's room . . . you were like a mad person. I don't want to have children fathered by a mad person."

"I had a—*thing*, that's all. Kind of, like, a hallucination. Overwork. Not enough sleep. Too much coffee."

"Decker, you can't change my mind."

He had reached his car. He caught hold of her arm and stopped her. "Have you been to a clinic yet? Talked about it? I mean the medical implications?"

"Why should I go to a clinic?"

He frowned at her. "You're not going to try and do it yourself, are you?"

"I don't know what you mean."

"The abortion. It could be really dangerous, doing it yourself."

"I'm not pregnant, Decker."

"You mean you lost it?"

Mayzie shook her head. "I'm sorry. I was stupid. I thought it might bring us closer together, if you thought that I was going to have your baby. You don't know what I feel about you, do you? You don't care, either. I see you flirting and sleeping around with any girl you can get your hands on, and that hurts. That really, really hurts."

Decker lowered his head and ran his hand through his hair. "I'm sorry, Mayzie. The last thing I ever wanted to do was hurt you. I've been hurting so much myself that I—well, I guess I got into the habit of it. I totally forgot that other people have feelings. That *you* have feelings."

He took hold of her and held her close, but they both knew that their affair was finished. After a while she wiped her eyes with her fingers and attempted a smile.

"He would have been a great little guy," Decker said. He punched his fists in the air as if he were having a playful fight with a five-year-old. "I would've called him Decker Martin Junior. Have to carry on the great family name."

Mayzie kissed his cheek and then walked away across the parking lot. Quite unexpectedly, Decker found it difficult to swallow.

He collected Hicks by the front entrance and they drove to 4140 Davis Street, where the Maitland house was cordoned off by yellow police tape wound around the front railings. They let themselves in and walked into the gradually darkening hallway. The floors and walls were still stained with Alison Maitland's blood, and the air was filled with a thick, sweet stench like rotten chicken. Blowflies were crawling up the windows and buzzing around the ceiling, and Hicks had to bat one away from his mouth.

"Jesus," he spat. "When are they going to clean this place up?"

"When we've found what we're looking for," Decker said. He went through to the breakfast area and looked around. "I don't know what the hell we're trying to find, but let's try to think backward."

Hicks covered his nose and his mouth with his hand. "Wish I hadn't eaten those breakfast links this morning. After seeing that poor guy hanging by his guts . . ."

"I never knew that intestines were so strong, did you?" Decker remarked. He opened the glass doors in the hutch and looked inside. "Then again, when you think about it, you have to boil tripe for hours."

"For Christ's sake, Lieutenant."

Decker opened all the kitchen drawers and closed them again. He even peered into the ovens.

"We looked there," Hicks said, his voice muffled behind his hand. "We looked *everywhere*."

"I know, sport. And you couldn't find the evidence that you were looking for. But maybe you were looking for the wrong kind of evidence."

"What do you mean?"

"Well . . . Mayzie just gave me a hard time, you know? She made me understand how bad I was making her feel . . . when all the time I was only worried about *me*, and the way *I* felt. Maybe we ought to be thinking about our perpetrator, and what it was about the Maitlands that annoyed him enough to murder them."

"Come on, they were two ordinary, harmless people."

"That's the way *we* see them. But maybe the perpetrator saw them different."

He went back into the hallway, still looking around. A large oil-painted landscape in a heavy gilt frame was hanging by the front door. He lifted it away from the wall so that he could check behind it.

"Already did that," Hicks said.

Decker mounted the stairs. Over a dozen paintings were arranged on the wall—views of Richmond and Mechanicsville and Newport News, as well as portraits of smiling children and dogs. There were some photographs, too: sepia pictures of houses and gardens, and group portraits of the Maitland family in the nineteenth century, all in their frock coats and stovepipe hats and crinolines.

Decker reached a group portrait on the turn of the stairs. He examined it very closely, and then he unhooked it and took it down from the wall. "Look at this," he told Hicks. "First Army Corps at Richard's Shop on Catharpin Road, May fifth, 1864, Major General M.L. Maitland commanding."

He took the picture up to the landing and switched on the light so that he could see it more clearly. It showed about twenty-five Confederate officers and men, stiffly posed on a plank road, with a wooden store in the background and overhanging trees. Two of the officers were holding horses, one of which had moved while the photograph was being taken, so that it appeared blurred and ghostly. One of the officers had moved, too: a tall man who was standing a little apart from the others on the right-hand side, at the back of the group. Unlike the others, who were dressed in tunics, he wore a greatcoat. He also wore a slouch hat, which appeared to have a black and ragged cloth knotted around it. Decker could see that he was heavily bearded, but because he had turned his head away during the exposure, it looked as if his face had melted.

"Jerry Maitland told me that Sandra's drawing of the So-Scary Man reminded him of somebody, but he couldn't think who. But look at this guy . . . what do you think?"

Hicks frowned at the photograph with his hand still clamped over his nose and his mouth. "I see what you mean. But this picture was taken over 140 years ago."

"Of course it was. I'm not suggesting that any of these people are still alive. But something lives on, doesn't it? The spirit of the Old South."

"I don't follow."

"Maybe the So-Scary Man has been dressing up as an officer in the First Army Corps and killing people who were connected with the Civil War in some way."

"Why would he do that?"

"How the hell should I know? But it's possible that he's deluded himself into believing that he *is* an officer in the First Army Corps. Some of these Civil War nuts—well, they're nuts. Look at Billy Joe Bennett. I was talking to him once and he was getting all worked up about different sorts of frogs."

"Frogs?"

"No, I didn't know either. Frogs are those loops they use to hang their bayonets from their belts. I mean, we're talking about *obsession* here. These people dress up in uniform and they stage mock battles, with carbines and everything. They trade cap badges and medals and cooking pots and all kinds of junk. We're only talking about one step away from full-blown lunacy."

"Well . . . I guess you could have something there. After all, George Drewry was an army man. *He* might have had ancestors in the Civil War, too. But what about *Alison* Maitland?"

"Let's see if we can check her family tree, too. Meanwhile, let's get this photograph back to the lab. I want it blown up and enhanced. And let's put a couple of guys on the Internet . . . let's see if they can log on to any Civil War Web sites and chat rooms. Maybe they can come up with some kind of pattern of behavior, or even some names."

They searched the rest of the house, but after an hour

Decker concluded that they weren't going to find anything else of any interest. He stood in the Maitlands' bedroom while the last light of the day gradually faded, and thought that there was nothing so sad as a once-happy house where people had been violently killed. Even Alison Maitland's pink satin nightdress was still there, neatly folded on her pillow.

"Come on, Hicks," he said. "Only ghosts here now."

They went out and closed the front door behind them. Hicks stood on the porch, held onto the railings, and took in three deep breaths. "That smell . . . I don't think I'll ever get used to it."

Decker slapped him on the back. "The day you get used to it is the day you're ready to quit."

On the way home, Decker called in to see Eunice and Sandra Plummer. They lived downtown on Twenty-seventh Street, at the top of a shabby old brown-brick apartment block that was scheduled for redevelopment. Inside the lobby the building smelled strongly of wax polish and dead flowers. The elevator clanked and rattled like a medieval instrument of torture.

Eunice let him in. "Thank you for stopping by, Lieutenant," she said, tightly, although it was clear that she wasn't very pleased to see him. "Sandra's having her supper right now."

She led him through to the living room, which was crowded with antique furniture. The mustard-colored wallpaper was fading, and the rugs were worn through to the strings, but the apartment had high ceilings and original cast-iron fireplaces and there was a view over the neighboring rooftops toward the sparkling lights along the waterfront. The window was ajar so that Decker could hear the traffic and the chugging of a tugboat.

Sandra was in the kitchen in a pink robe and slippers, eating cereal. Decker gave her a finger wave through the open door and she waved back at him and flushed in embarrassment.

"How is she?" Decker asked Eunice.

"She's fine. She didn't see anything, thank God, and she didn't realize that poor man was killed."

"I came to apologize for involving her, and you too. Believe me, if I'd had any idea what was going to happen—"

"Well, fortunately no harm was done. But don't expect us to help you again. Sandra is far too precious to me."

"There's no question of it," Decker reassured her. "I've arranged to have your close protection reinstated. I just hope it won't be necessary for very much longer."

"Do you think you're going to be able to catch this man?"

"I don't know. I hope so. This is the first time I've ever gone looking for somebody I couldn't see."

"He does have a physical presence, though, doesn't he?"

"Oh, you bet. He threw Gerald Maitland out of the window, and I felt him myself when he pushed me over. And if he has physical presence, that means we can restrain him. Theoretically, anyhow."

"It's a trick, isn't it? Like conjurors do."

"Yes, I think it is. All we have to do now is find out what *kind* of a trick."

Sandra called out from the kitchen and Eunice said, "Excuse me, Lieutenant," and went to see what she wanted. Decker looked around the room, picking up a silver-framed photograph of Sandra when she was a baby, and another photograph of a brown-haired man with a rather baffled-looking George W. Bush–type squint. Sandra's father, maybe.

Seven or eight of Sandra's sketches and watercolors were arranged on either side of the fireplace. Decker found her work unexpectedly moving—every drawing done with such atmosphere, and such attention to detail—and what a sadness it was that she probably wouldn't live beyond her twenties. Her most striking picture was a fine colored-crayon drawing of Main Street Station, with its Beaux Arts balconies, its orange roof tiles and its fairy-tale dormer windows.

Oddly, though, Sandra had drawn a heavily shaded cloud over its clock tower, more like a mass of writhing black serpents than a cloud.

"Interesting picture," he remarked, as Eunice came back into the living room.

"Yes. For some reason she calls it the Fun House."

"The Fun House, huh? What's that cloud hanging over it?"

"I'm not sure. I remember her drawing it and the weather was perfect."

"Strange, isn't it? Very, very good. But definitely strange."

CHAPTER SIXTEEN

The next morning Decker drove the ninety miles southeastward to Fort Monroe, headquarters of the U.S. Army Training and Doctrine Command, where Major Drewry had served in the military history section. It was a sunny day, but a fine warm rain was falling, so that the Mercury's windshield glittered and its tires sizzled on the highway.

Fort Monroe was situated on a spit of land in Chesapeake Bay. When Decker opened his car window to show his badge to the sentry at the gate, he could smell the ocean, like freshly opened oysters.

"I have a twelve o'clock meeting with Captain Tony Morello. Want to tell me where I can find him?"

"That's Toni with an *i*, sir. She's over in archives, right across there."

Decker parked his car in the visitors' space and walked across the parade ground. A squad of pink-faced cadets in full dress uniform were practicing formation marching, their shiny boots splashing in the puddles. Decker climbed the steps, pushed his way through the double swing doors and followed the signs that said OFFICE OF THE COMMAND HISTORIAN.

He found Captain Morello in the library, leaning over a desk with a computer in front of her. She was almost as tall as he was, with short black hair that was slashed straight back from her forehead. When she turned around, Decker saw that she was also strikingly attractive, in a 1960s Italian-actress way, with a heart-shaped face and vixenish eyes. Her immaculately pressed uniform only emphasized her very full breasts, and even in a midlength skirt her legs looked unnervingly long.

"Lieutenant Martin," Decker said, showing his badge. "But, you know, don't let's stand on ceremony. All my friends call me Decker."

"Captain Morello," Toni Morello said, with a tight little smile. "All my friends call me sir."

Decker looked around at the floor-to-ceiling shelving. Each shelf was filled with hundreds of gray-backed files, and each file was identified by a neat white label—*Armored Maneuvers in Italy, Spring 1945*; *Airborne Assault Forces in Cambodia, 1971*; *Logistical Operations in Bosnia-Herzegovina, 1994*. The library was more than 150 feet long, with a yellow-tinted clerestory window to filter the sunlight.

"Hell of a library," Decker remarked, although he was really thinking, *Hell of a librarian.*

"I won't keep you a moment, Lieutenant." Toni Morello tapped out a few more lines on her computer and then switched it off. "I understand you wanted to talk to me about Major Drewry. We were all deeply distressed about that."

"Well, yes. It was a pretty goddamned horrible way to go. I'm going to be talking to Mrs. Drewry again, but I don't want to upset her more than I have to and I was wondering if you could help me at all."

"I'll do my best."

"What I need to know is, were any of Major Drewry's ancestors connected with the army?"

"Oh *yes*. George was very proud of his family history. His great-great-grandfather fought with Robert E. Lee, and his grandfather was out in the Philippines with Teddy Roosevelt. He was always bitterly sorry that he never saw active service himself."

"Would you have any information here about his great-great-grandfather?"

"Of course. George used our archives to research his family tree, and he managed to find a whole lot more original material besides. Diaries, letters, that kind of thing. I don't think he'd even gotten around to cataloguing everything. Do you want to take a look?"

Decker followed her along the lines of shelving. She had a fluid way of walking that reminded him of a wildlife documentary that he had been watching on television that morning, nyala gazelles loping across the African bush. They reached a section at the far end of the library marked ARMY OF NORTHERN VIRGINIA, 1861–1865, and Toni Morello took out a box file with a label that said *Battle of the Wilderness, May 5–May 7, 1864: Maj. Gen. Maitland's brigade.*

She carried the file over to a reading table and opened it. Inside it was packed with original letters, dispatches, maps, and photographs. "Here," she said. "This is a picture of Major General Maitland's brigade at dawn on the morning of May sixth, just before they were sent up the Orange Plank Road to attack the advancing Federal army."

The photograph was remarkably similar to the one that Decker had taken from 4140 Davis Street. About a dozen bearded men in slouch hats and képis, some of them in tunics and others in nothing more than dirty shirts and muddied pants. A typed caption underneath identified the third mounted officer on the left as Lieutenant Colonel Henry Drewry.

Toni Morello was about to tuck the photograph back in the file when Decker said, "Wait up a moment. Let me look at that again."

He took off his glasses and studied the group as closely as he could. At the back of the group stood three men, well apart from the rest, and although they were deep in shadow, Decker could see that at least two of them were wearing greatcoats. All three of them had slouch hats, and their hats were all decorated with black ragged plumes.

"Have you ever heard of the Devil's Brigade?" he asked.

"I've heard it mentioned, of course. It was a myth, as far as I know. Propaganda, put out by the Federal generals to excuse themselves for being driven back by an army that had forty thousand fewer men than they did—not to mention being much more tired and hungry and very short on ammunition."

"Do you have any records about it?"

"I don't know offhand, but I could check for you."

Decker put his glasses back on. "I'd really appreciate it. Meanwhile—what time do you break for lunch?"

As he drove back toward Richmond with the steering wheel in one hand and a double cheeseburger in the other, his cell phone rang.

"Lieutenant? Hicks here. It looks like we've got ourselves another one."

CHAPTER SEVENTEEN

He turned into Sixth Street and was waved through the crowds of sightseers. The entire front window of Jimmy the Rib's Soul Food Restaurant had been smashed and the sidewalk was strewn with sun-glittering glass. Seven squad cars were parked higgledy-piggledy across the street with flashing lights, as well as an ambulance and two khaki station wagons from the coroner's department.

As he pushed his way past the crowd, Decker saw somebody he recognized—a lanky young man with a straight-nosed profile like a pharaoh from one of the pyramids. He wore a jazzy red and white shirt and huge hoop earrings and a sharks' tooth necklace, as well as a floppy red crochet beret that was decorated with feathers and antique keys and fishing flies.

"Hi, Jonah. What's happening?"

"Deck-ah! How should I know, man? I only just got here."

"Junior Abraham's been wasted, that's what I hear."

"Had it coming, man. Junior Abraham was a liar and a

blowhard and if anybody needs financial reimbursement for the bullet they bought to give him a premature funeral, then all they have to do is pass the hat around and I'll be the first to contribute."

"You have any idea who did it?"

"Uh-huh."

"Come on, Jonah, give me a clue. You know this termites' nest better than anybody."

"Deck-ah, even if I knew something I wouldn't tell you."

"What? This is African-American *omerta*, is it?"

"No, this is Jonah Jones thinking about his self-preservation. Whoever whacked a heavy-duty dude like Junior Abraham wouldn't have no compunction about swatting a mosquito like me. I'll tell you something, Deck-ah, even if I knew for sure who done this deed, which I don't, I wouldn't tell you who done it even if you rubbed my nuts with marrowbone and let two hungry Dobermans loose in the room."

Decker rubbed his forehead with the tips of his fingers, as if he were thinking seriously. "You know something, Jonah? *There's* an idea."

Decker crunched across the shattered glass into the restaurant, already crowded with scene-of-crime investigators and photographers and uniformed officers and bewildered looking witnesses. The interior was pungent with soul-food spices and fried chicken, and the walls were covered with sepia photographs of slave cabins and cotton fields and dozens of framed photographs of famous people of color, everybody from Maggie L. Walker, the first woman in America to found a bank, to Denzel Washington and Arthur Ashe Jr.

Cab and Hicks were talking to witnesses. Decker went to join them. Plastic grapevines hung down from the ceilings in such profusion that he had to push them away from his face. "Jesus," he said, "it's a jungle in here."

Cab said, "It sure is. Take a look at this."

Decker followed him to a booth at the very back of the restaurant, partly enclosed by a carved mahogany screen. In the corner hung a slanty-eyed African voodoo mask with an electric lightbulb shining through its eyes. Underneath the mask sat a skinny man in a shiny black satin shirt and shiny black satin pants, and black alligator moccasins with no socks. Above the man's collar, all that remained was his lower jaw, like a dental cast. The rest of his head was sprayed up the wall in an ever-widening fan shape of dark red blood and pink glistening lumps. Even as Decker was examining him, one of the lumps started to creep its way surreptitiously down the wallpaper like a garden slug.

"Heck—he was *right* in the middle of eating," Hicks said, in disgust. "If you look into his neck, you can still see chewed-up ham and potatoes. Didn't even have time to swallow them."

"I'll take your word for it, sport," Decker said. "What went down here, Cab? This doesn't look anything at all like the other two killings."

"It doesn't but it does. The story is that Junior Abraham comes here for lunch every Monday regular at one o'clock. Always sits at the same table and always orders the same thing, ham hocks and mixed greens, with candied sweet potatoes. He's sitting in the first booth right here with his brother Treasure and two of his heavies. A guy in a waiter's apron comes out of the kitchen door carrying a tray with four bowls of fish chowder."

Cab took out his handkerchief and slapped it open. "We got *nine* eyewitnesses, would you believe? They all say that the waiter guy goes up to the booth and throws the chowder into Junior's lap. Junior jumps up, hands clutching his crotch, natural reaction, and that's when the waiter guy pulls out a pump-action shotgun from under his apron and blows a respectable part of Junior's head off. There's another of Junior's heavies on the door but the waiter guy doesn't bother to exit via the door—he simply shoots out the window."

"Anybody recognize this waiter guy?"

"Nobody *says* they do. What do you expect? They all want to keep their heads intact."

"So it was a hit. What makes it anything like the other two killings?"

"The waiter guy was out *here*, right? In the restaurant. But—and this is the weird bit—he was never in the kitchen."

Decker blinked. "What do you mean he was never in the kitchen?"

Hicks said, "All the eyewitnesses in the restaurant say that he came out of the kitchen door, but the cooks insist that he was never in there. He just, like, *appeared*."

"Ah, come on. The cooks weren't concentrating, that's all. They were cooking, they were filling out orders, they were stacking plates. They weren't going to notice some guy in a waiter's apron."

"I'm telling you, Lieutenant. They all swear blind there was nobody there."

"*Blind* is probably the right word. Listen—I'll talk to the cooks in a minute, but I want to have a word with Treasure first. He still here?"

"There—over in the corner," Hicks said. "But I took a statement already . . . he doesn't know from squat."

Decker went over to a chunky young man with dreadlocks and a sweat-stained Michael Jordan T-shirt. He kept sniffing and blinking and jerking his head, as if he needed a snort of something.

"Hi, Treasure. Sorry about your brother."

"Yeah," Treasure said.

"Did you recognize the guy who did it?"

Treasure sniffed and blinked and shook his head. "Never saw him before."

"Want to tell me what he looked like?"

"I just told the other guy," Treasure said, jerking his head toward Tim.

"Well, do me a favor, and tell me, too."

"He was a brother."

"I see. How tall was he?"

"Kind of like normal height."

"I see. What about weight?"

"Not too skinny, not too fat."

Decker nodded. "Any distinguishing marks? Hair? Scars? Moustache? False nose?"

"Nothing. It all happened so quick. Sploosh with the soup, then bang."

"I see. Sploosh with the soup and then bang."

"Listen, man," Treasure said, with a thumping sniff. "If I knew who it was, I'd personally kill him myself."

Decker turned back to Cab. "Black, average build and height. That sure narrows it down."

"Yeah, we could hold an identity parade twenty-three miles long."

Decker pushed his way through the swing door to the kitchen, with Hicks right behind him. Standing by the stove were two anxious cooks and a dim-looking dishwasher with long red rubber gloves and his cap on sideways. The burners were crowded with huge simmering pots of corn chowder and crawfish stew and thick brown gravy going *blibble-blobble* like a swamp. The senior cook was even fatter than Cab, with a red bandana around his sweat-beaded forehead.

"I'm Lieutenant Martin," Decker said.

"Louis," the senior cook said, wiping his hand on a dish-cloth and holding it out. "This here is Roy and this here is Toussaint."

"My partner tells me you didn't see anybody in the kitchen immediately prior to the shooting."

"That's perfectly correct, sir. There was only us and nobody else. Anyhow there's only two servers, Gina and May, and Gina and May is both women."

"Really? Gina and May? Women?" Decker circled the kitchen, picking up spoons and spatulas and frowning at them as if he thought they might be circumstantial evidence. "You didn't see the door open? I mean, *nine* people saw this guy come out of the kitchen door with a tray of soup. How did he get the soup out of the kitchen if he didn't open the door? Where'd he get the soup from?"

"I don't know, sir. I truly can't say. But I can testify to you on my mother's life there was no waiter in here."

The other two men nodded in furious agreement. Decker lifted the lid of one of the pots and sniffed the ham hocks that were nestling in it. "Smells pretty damn good." Then he looked up and said, "You're not saying this just to protect your ass, are you, Louis? Because this is a homicide inquiry, and anybody who obstructs such an inquiry by professing, for instance, that nobody was there when they *were* there—well, they're almost equally as guilty as whoever pulled the trigger. Junior Abraham's brains are spattered all over *his* hands, too."

Louis quickly looked down at his hands and gave them another wipe with his twisted cloth. "It's the truth, sir. The absolute truth. There was nobody here in this here kitchen but us."

"So how do you think he did it? Come out of a door that he hadn't gone into?"

Louis hesitated for a moment, and then he said, very emphatically, "It was a spell."

"A spell?" Decker's eyebrows went up.

"A magic spell, sir. I can't think of no other explanation."

"I see. A spell. But that shotgun shell sure wasn't a spell, was it?"

"Ah, no. But that was a message. *Okana obbara.*"

"*Okana obbara?* What does that mean?"

"That means, like, don't lose your head just because you're going to die."

"Pretty sick sense of humor in that case."

"No other explanation, sir."

"This is all to do with Santería, right? All this magic spells and *obba-wobbas?*"

Louis crossed himself. "Yes, sir. Santería, sir."

"Well, who knows? You may be right. Listen—stick around, will you, Louis? And you, Roy. You too, Toussaint. We may have to talk to you again."

"Yes, sir."

Decker pushed his way back out through to the restaurant. Hicks said, "You really think this could have had something to do with Santería?"

"Too soon to say. But it wouldn't surprise me. Some of the major gangs here are Santeríans, especially the Egun. They think it gives them supernatural power, you know, and protects them from their enemies. Apart from that, it's very secretive, close-knit. Keeps the outsiders out and the insiders in."

"Rhoda's grandmother was all into that. You know, the herbs and the eggs and the seashells. I didn't think many people practiced it anymore. I mean, not these days."

"Oh, you'd be surprised what we have here in Richmond. Santería, voodoo, hoodoo. We even have some Episcopalians."

"You don't seriously believe that this waiter guy appeared by *magic?*"

"I don't seriously believe anything just yet. But I've heard stories about *santeros* who can materialize out of thin air. Don't ask me how they do it, but who knows? It might have happened here. Maybe Cab's right, and it happened in the Maitland case and the Drewry case, too—or something similar. Mass hypnotism, a trick of the light. What you might scientifically define as a spell."

Cab was talking to the two waitresses. One was plump and plain, with bunches, but the other was small and curvy with a lick of a fringe and a criminally short black skirt. "Which one are you?" Decker asked her. "Gina or May?"

"I'm May. This is Gina."

"Did you see the waiter guy in the kitchen, May?"

"I surely didn't."

"You ever see him before, ever?"

"I never did."

"Okay . . . look, why don't you give me your phone number? I might have to ask you some more questions later."

When the girls had gone, Cab said, "You are seriously incorrigible, Decker. I know what kind of questions *you* want to ask her."

"You misjudge me, Captain."

"Oh yeah? So how come you didn't ask the homely one?"

"You want me to enjoy my work or not?"

Cab sniffed, and then violently sneezed. "Goddam hay fever. How did you get on with the cooks?"

"They wouldn't qualify for Mensa, but the funny thing is I think I believe them."

"So where did the waiter guy come from?"

"The cook thinks it's a Santería spell."

"You're pulling my leg."

"Waiter guy apparently appears from nowhere at all. How else did he do it?"

"Oh, shit, Santería. You know what this means."

"Let me have one inspired guess, Captain. Queen Aché."

Cab nodded and wiped his nose at the same time. "Funny, though. I thought Junior was running most of Queen Aché's dope business, through the docks."

"Maybe Junior was helping himself to some unauthorized commission."

"Well, Martin, I know how much you like to get it on with Queen Aché."

"Uh-huh. No way. This one's for somebody else. Give it to Rudisill. Or better yet, Watkins. At least he's black."

"Martin, I don't have any choice. Who else has your experience? You *know* these people."

"Oh, sure. And look what happened the last time I got myself involved with Queen Aché."

Cab laid his hand on Decker's shoulder. "I'm aware of that, Martin. But it was never proved that Queen Aché was connected with Cathy being killed, and you're simply the best man I've got for the job."

"I'm not happy with this, Captain. You'd be much better off sending Watkins."

"Come on. Queen Aché *likes* honkies."

"Sure, with barbecue sauce and a side order of curly fries."

"Be a man, Decker. Besides, it's high time that young Hicks here met Richmond's most distinguished Afro-American citizen."

CHAPTER EIGHTEEN

Queen Aché lived in the Jackson Ward, in a fancy red-painted town house with white cast-iron balconies and elaborate white cast-iron railings. The house used to belong to Booker Morrison, the famous turn-of-the-century preacher, who said that "those who are bondsmen on earth will have eternal freedom in heaven; and those who enslaved them will themselves suffer slavery for ever and a day." For that observation, he was kidnapped by Klansmen, hung up by his heels from a lamppost on the corner of Franklin and Fifth Streets, soaked in paraffin, and set alight.

It was a grillingly hot afternoon, with only a few mares' tails streaked across a dark blue sky. Two bodyguards were standing on the redbrick sidewalk outside Queen Aché's front steps, both of them wearing jazzy African shirts, capacious shorts, knee-length socks, and mirror sunglasses. Decker parked directly outside and climbed out of his car, squinting up at the house as if he were interested in buying it.

"Hi, George. Hi, Newton. How's it going in the heavy business?"

"We generally axes folks not to park in that particular spot, Lieutenant, on account of security."

"Quite right, too. Is Her Ladyship at home?"

"She expecting you?"

"Oh, I should think so. You know that Junior Abraham has left the building."

"Junior Abraham? Didn't hear nothing about that, Lieutenant."

"Didn't think you would have, what with this deaf-and-blind epidemic going around. Now, how about telling Madame that I'd like to ask her a couple of questions?"

Newton took out his cell phone. "Mikey? We got Martin out here. *Lieutenant* Martin. He says he wants to talk to Queen Aché."

He waited, and then eventually he said, "Okay," and dropped his cell phone back into his shirt pocket.

"Well?" Decker asked.

"Queen Aché says the *ase* isn't favorable today."

"The *ase?* The *ase* my ass. Get back onto her. Tell her this is a multiple homicide investigation and if she doesn't want to answer questions here I can arrange for her to come down to Madison and Grace and inspect our nice new shiny headquarters."

Newton took out his cell phone again. "Mikey? Martin says he needs to talk to Queen Aché about Junior Abraham getting creamed. Yes. That's right. Okay. That's right."

He dropped his cell phone back in his pocket. "Queen Aché says okay but don't blame her if something seriously untoward happens."

Newton led Decker and Hicks up the front steps and the door was opened by a loose-jointed young man with protruding ears and an incipient black moustache. Before he went inside, Decker turned back and called, "George! There's a buck in it if nobody steals my hubcaps!" George flapped his fat hand in disgust.

The young man took them across a wide hallway with gilt antique mirrors and a dark mahogany floor. In the back of the house somebody was playing a Charles Mingus improvization, badly.

"Hey—you're not Michael, are you?" Decker asked the young man. "Queen Aché's youngest kid?"

The young man nodded.

"I don't believe it. You were only knee high to a high knee the last time I saw you. What have they been feeding you on? Giraffe food?"

"I'm fifteen," Michael said, defensively.

"Fifteen? How about that? Fifteen. God . . . I was fifteen when I was your age, too. Can you imagine it?"

Decker and Hicks followed Michael through an archway into the living room. Most of the white wooden blinds were closed, so that the sunlight was very subdued in here, and the room was filled with lazy loops of marijuana smoke.

Queen Aché seriously regarded herself as royalty, and this was her throne room. The drapes were crimson velvet, with swags and ties and gilded tassels. The chairs and couches were all gilded and upholstered in the same fabric, and a sparkling cut-glass chandelier hung from the ceiling. Yet the room wasn't all Versailles. On the walls hung dark oil paintings of mythical African beasts, and jungles; and inscrutable ebony figures stood guard on either side of the fireplace, with spears, and attenuated faces like praying mantises. In the far corner of the room there was an elaborate Santería shrine, crowded with statuettes and lighted candles and cowrie shells and painted masks and chicken feathers.

Three men were sprawled in armchairs, all of them wearing black shirts and flappy black Armani pants and carrying half of Schwarzschild's Jewelry Store around their wrists. Queen Aché herself was reclining next to them on a golden-striped divan. She was smoking a small ivory pipe with a face carved on it.

"What do you expect me to say to you?" she demanded, as Decker and Hicks approached her. "The *ase* isn't favorable . . . how do you expect me to have good *aba?*"

"It's up to you. Maybe you'd have better *aba* downtown."

"Hey," warned one of the men, and began to stand up, but Queen Aché waved her hand at him and he sat down again.

She was a remarkable-looking woman. Decker had known her father, King Special, and like King Special she was very tall, over six feet three inches, with long arms and long legs and wide shoulders. But there was no doubt that she had inherited the beauty of her Cuban mother. A high forehead, wide-apart eyes, and a look of sleepy aloofness. Her skin was almost pale enough to pass as white, but her hair was braided and beaded, and she spoke with African-American intonations.

She was wearing a filmy dress of white linen, through which Decker thought he could *almost* see the heavy curves of her breasts, and dozens of thin gold bangles. Her feet were bare, and she had gold rings on her toes, too.

"So what is all this you say about Junior Abraham?" she asked.

"Well . . . I was kind of hoping that you knew more about that than I do."

She shook her beaded hair. "This is the first I've heard of it. I'm very sorry. Junior wasn't such a bad man. A boaster, maybe. And not to be trusted. But he didn't deserve to die a violent death."

"Maybe you found out that poor old Junior wasn't being entirely honest with you. You know, like dipping his hand in the cash register."

"Why must we complain that the moon is slanting?" Queen Aché said. "Can't anyone reach the skies to straighten it?"

"Well, I don't know about the moon, but somebody sure straightened Junior."

Queen Aché smiled. Decker thought she really did have the most erotic smile. It made you think that something very sexy and very dangerous was going to happen next. But all Queen Aché said was, "He who has a head has no cap to wear on it; and he who has a cap has no head to wear it on."

"You said it, Your Majesty."

She kept on smiling. "There is nothing I can help you with, Lieutenant. If Junior was cheating me, I didn't know about it, and if I *had* found out about it, I would have made him pay me back, no more than that."

"You expect me to believe that? If there's one thing I know about you, it's that you don't forgive anybody anything, ever."

Queen Aché drew on her pipe and blew out a long thin stream of smoke. "You know nothing about me at all, Lieutenant. To you my soul is a closed book. And you have no evidence whatsoever that I was involved in any way in the killing of Junior Abraham."

"Oh, really? This was a little bit more than a straightforward hit. It happened in Jimmy the Rib's, in case you're interested, which you don't seem to be, because you probably knew that already. The killer came out of the kitchen and blew Junior's head off, which seems to happen to everybody who gets in your way. But the interesting thing is that nobody saw the killer in the kitchen beforehand."

"I don't understand why that should be any concern of mine."

"Well . . . there are only two possible explanations," Decker said. "One is that the kitchen staff simply failed to notice him."

"And the other?"

"It was a Santería spell. And who is the only person in town who would arrange for a hit using a Santería spell?"

"I might make an *ebbó* to protect me from my enemies, but nothing more than that."

"An *ebbó?*"

"An *ebbó* is more of a sacrifice than a spell, Lieutenant. An offering to our *orishas* so that they will give us the things we crave the most. Love, for instance, or money, or good luck; or protection from evil spirits."

"How about being invisible? What's the *ebbó* for that?"

Queen Aché shook her head and again her beads made a soft rattling sound. "There is no such *ebbó* and no such spell. All that one would ask is that one's misdeeds went unnoticed."

Hicks said, "That would be quite a request, though, wouldn't it? Like, even more all-inclusive than just being invisible."

"What do you mean?" Queen Aché asked, without looking at him.

"Well, if your misdeeds went unnoticed, nobody would ever know that it was you, whether you were invisible or not. Like, you might leave evidence, but nobody would ever be able to see it."

Queen Aché said nothing, but slowly turned her head and gave Hicks a hair-raising look, with slightly narrowed eyes, as if she were trying to remember not only his face, but his soul, too.

Decker said, "I want to ask you one more question, Queen Aché. Do you know of any reason why anybody should have wanted to kill Junior Abraham?"

"No. Absolutely not."

"Well, thank you for your time. When I've had the chance to check out Junior's bank account, I may ask to take a look at some of your books. You know, for comparison. It would be very educational to know how much he was taking you for."

"If I hadn't noticed, it couldn't have been very much. You know how careful I am with my business affairs."

"Oh yes."

"Still, one can't know everything. Some great scholars of Ifa cannot tell the way to Ofa. Others know the way to Ofa, but not one line of Ifa."

"Some detectives don't know who shot Junior Abraham, but they never fail to recognize bullshit, even when it's metaphorical bullshit."

"Good-bye, Lieutenant. Michael will show you out."

CHAPTER NINETEEN

They worked until 8:15 P.M., and then Decker took off his glasses and dry-washed his face with his hands. "That's it, let's call it a night."

Hicks came over and dropped a list of names on his desk. "Those are all the known members of the Eguns who could have been in the vicinity of Jimmy the Rib's at lunchtime today. I'll start tracking them down tomorrow and checking their alibis."

Decker picked up the list, scanned it quickly, and sniffed. "You can forget about Wendell Brown. The Strutters cut his balls off last February for messing with one of their women. *And* made him eat them. Otherwise—fine. You're doing good work."

Hicks checked his watch. "Listen, I know we were all supposed to be going out for a Mexican meal, but why don't you come round to our place for supper tonight? Rhoda always makes plenty."

"Ahh, I wouldn't want to put her to any trouble. Besides,

don't you want to leave your work behind you for a few hours?"

"No, I'd really appreciate it if you'd come. Maybe you can give Rhoda some idea of how important this is. How much the city needs us, you know—people like us."

"She's still hankering for Fredericksburg, huh?"

"If you could maybe just talk to her."

"All right, then," Decker agreed. He stood up and shrugged on his coat. "So long as you bear in mind that I'm not a marriage guidance counselor. My whole life has been one dysfunctional relationship after another, with a lot of floozies in between."

"Except for Cathy," Hicks said.

Decker glanced down at the photograph of Cathy in her straw hat and then he looked back at Hicks. "I think you're speaking out of turn," he said, coldly.

"I'm sorry. I didn't mean to—"

Decker closed his eyes for a moment and then he said, "No. I know. I'm the one who should be saying sorry. It's just that—I've been feeling her presence lately, very close. Almost like she's still alive."

Hicks looked embarrassed, so Decker patted him reassuringly on the back and the two of them left the office.

In the elevator they met Detective Bill Watkins, a broad-shouldered shaven-headed man with a broken nose. He looked like a linebacker for the Richmond Speed.

"Hear you talked to Queen Aché today, Lieutenant."

"Yeah, for what it was worth."

"She didn't admit to nothing, then? That woman . . . *whewf*, if she wasn't so evil, she'd be *bad*. Give me twelve hours and a king-size bed and I'd have her confessing to anything."

"She'd eat you alive, Detective, and then she'd suck your bones."

* * *

Hicks opened the front door. "Where the elite meet to eat." He grinned. The house was small, with a narrow hallway and a steep flight of stairs. Decker could smell frying chicken in the kitchen, and he suddenly realized how hungry he was. He hadn't eaten anything since Captain Morello had courteously but very firmly turned down his lunch invitation and he had been forced to resort to that soggy double cheeseburger.

"Tim, is that you?" Rhoda called. She came out of the kitchen in her apron, her hair tied up in a scarf, and immediately flushed in embarrassment.

Hicks said, "Hey—I know I should have called, but I thought I'd surprise you."

"Lieutenant, I'm so sorry . . . I must really look a mess."

Decker smiled and held out his hand. "You look great. I told Tim to ask you but he was afraid you'd say no."

Rhoda wiped her hand on her apron. "Of course I wouldn't have said no. This is an honor."

"Let me take your coat," Hicks said. "How about a beer?"

"Do you want a hand in the kitchen?" Decker asked Rhoda. "I make a chili-tomato salad dressing that some people would sell their kidneys for."

"No, no, I'm fine. Go into the living room, take the weight off."

Rhoda went back into the kitchen and Decker could hear her arguing with Hicks. "—could have let me *know*, I would have cooked something special—"

He went into the living room. It was wallpapered with a pale brown bamboo pattern, and furnished with big beige leather chairs. A crowd of Barbie dolls sat in one corner of the couch, where Hicks's daughter had obviously been playing before she went to bed. On top of the huge wide-screen television were at least a dozen family photographs, as well as a vase of artificial lilies in artificial water, a china church, and a painted-plaster figure of Jesus with His hands covering His eyes.

Hicks came in with two cans of Budweiser and a plate of tortilla chips. "Rhoda okay about this?" Decker asked him.

"Sure, you know what women are like."

"I'm beginning to wonder."

They sat down and Hicks eased his shoes off. "That Queen Aché's something, isn't she?"

"Oh, for sure. She's a *very* astute lady. If there's any racket in Richmond that she doesn't have some kind of a finger in, I'd like to know what it is. She calls her organization the Eguns, which is the Santería word for ancestors. Santeros worship their ancestors and she always worshiped her father. I mean, anybody who *dares* to insult King Special's sacred memory is lucky to end up with no teeth. But she's outdone her old man a hundred times over."

He popped the top of his beer can. "King Special started out as a fire-raiser . . . he burned down businesses when their owners were going bankrupt so that they could claim the insurance. Then it occurred to him that if he lifted some of their stock before he torched the place, he could use the stolen stock to set up his own businesses and burn them down himself.

"After that he got into extortion, money lending, dope dealing, property scams, you name it. His real name was Rufus Douglas but nobody ever called him anything but King Special."

"When did he die?"

"About three years ago. Liver cancer. I'll tell you, the funeral cortege stretched along Second Street from Jackson to Cary, eight blocks. Forty-eight Cadillacs, covered in flowers."

"And Queen Aché took over?"

"Not only took over but expanded—and expanded fast. King Special might have had a reputation for crushing anybody who crossed him, but believe me, he was *nothing* compared to his daughter. A guy from D.C. tried to muscle in on her dope trade. Charles Noone, his name was, and he always wore a yellow Derby hat, that was his trademark, that yellow Derby hat. Usually Queen Aché arranges for her victims to have their heads blown off, that's part of the Santería thing, so they can't be recognized when they try to be reunited with their ancestors. But when Queen Aché had Charles Noone offed, she had it done the other way around. A street cleaner found his severed head right in the middle of Main Street, still with his yellow Derby hat on. Never found the rest of him."

"Shit. I seem to remember reading about that."

Decker helped himself to a tortilla chip and dipped it into a saucer of homemade salsa. "I just want you to realize what we're up against when we're dealing with Queen Aché. She has everybody around here under her thumb, one hundred percent. She does it partly by violence but mostly by Santería. She uses their secret rituals to discourage her people from betraying her . . . if you betray Queen Aché, that's the same as betraying your religion. And she controls all the most powerful *santeros*. Everybody knows that if you offend Queen Aché, even a little, some *santero* is going to be casting a very nasty spell on you, and you're going to get the stomachache, or your hair's going to fall out, or your goldfish are all going to die."

"In that case, I'll remember to keep on her good side."

Decker said, "I think we ought to look into this Santería

thing a little deeper. Like, we have three homicides in less than a week and in each homicide the perpetrator is invisible or partly invisible? What you said to Queen Aché about evidence going unnoticed, Hicks—that was very sharp thinking. I think the evidence is right in front of our noses but for some reason we just can't focus on it. Like Sherlock Holmes said, we're looking, but we can't see."

"Supper's on the table!" Rhoda called.

Rhoda had brushed her hair into shiny flick-ups and put on some bright red lip color. She looked almost too young to be a wife and a mother, with a round face and a little bobbed nose. She had spread the kitchen table with a red-checkered cloth, and served up fried chicken, sweet corn, flowering broccoli, candied potatoes and gravy, with a salad on the side.

"It's pretty simple Monday-night eating, I'm afraid," she apologized.

"It looks great to me. I keep planning on cooking myself all these fancy meals like *pollo à la vinagreta* and the trouble is I'm always too tired to get around to it. And even when I *do* get around to it, I'm too tired to eat it."

He sat down and unfolded his napkin. He was suddenly aware that Rhoda was staring at him.

"Is everything all right?" he asked her. "I don't have salsa on my chin, do I?"

"No, no, everything's fine." Although she still looked as if she had seen something that disturbed her.

"I could eat an elephant," Hicks said, rubbing his hands in relish.

Rhoda said, "Would you like to say grace, Lieutenant?"

"Hey, please. Call me Decker."

Rhoda gave him the tightest of smiles. "*Decker*," she repeated.

"Are you sure everything's okay?" he asked her. She definitely looked uneasy.

"Yes. Great. I've had a busy day with Daisy, that's all."

Decker clasped his hands together and closed his eyes. He hesitated for a moment and then he said, "Oh, Lord, thank You for this food, and thank You for bringing us together to share it. We pray for Your guidance and Your protection, and most of all we pray that You open our eyes so that we can see our way to bring justice to those who cry out for it."

"A*men*," Hicks said, looking at him in surprise.

"What?" Decker said.

"It was just that—well, that was quite some prayer."

Decker helped himself to a chicken thigh. "I'm not embarrassed to call on the Almighty for extra assistance. Just like I'm not embarrassed to call on the FBI."

"Wine?" Hicks asked. "It's only Wal-Mart Red, I'm afraid."

"Sure, why not? This chicken is great, Rhoda. Just like my mother can't make. She can never get the fried to stay on the chicken."

They ate and drank in silence for a while. Decker noticed that Rhoda didn't seem to have much of an appetite. She prodded at her potatoes but never actually ate any of them.

"Not hungry?" he asked her.

She looked up and said, "How's it going? This investigation?"

"Well, I don't usually like to talk shop at the supper table, but we're following up one or two interesting leads. Hicks here—Tim—he's had some very creative ideas."

Rhoda put down her fork. "It's just that—ever since Tim came home last week and said that you'd been assigned to the Maitland homicide, I've had a really strange feeling."

"Rhoda?" Hicks said, with his mouth full. "You never told me nothing about this."

"I didn't want to upset you, that's all."

"I know you've been under the weather, but I thought that was just because you were homesick."

"What kind of a feeling?" Decker asked.

"Maybe it's stupid, but I keep thinking that something really terrible is going to happen."

"Something terrible like what?" Hicks asked her, frowning.

"It's hard to describe. I've had a feeling that lots more people are going to die, and that Tim's in danger. I didn't want to tell him, because I know it's his job and I didn't want him to be looking over his shoulder all the time just because of me and some fool premonition."

Hicks said, "Honey . . . you should have said something. Nothing's going to happen to me, you know that."

"I keep trying to tell myself that, but the feeling won't go away. It's like—I don't know—it's like when you're lying in the dark and you think there's something in the room with you. Something that wants to do you harm."

Decker took hold of her hand. "Rhoda—these homicides we're investigating, they're very unusual and they're very scary. You're bound to feel frightened, it's only natural. You think that *I'm* not frightened? But we're well trained and we're well armed and we believe that we could be making some progress. Tim and me, we're going to catch this guy, whoever he is, and then you won't have anything more to be frightened about."

Rhoda shook her head. "It's not like any feeling I've ever had before. It's like a real *dread*. And when we sat down tonight I had it again, only much, much stronger, and I still have it now. I can't ignore it, Lieutenant. It's like a kind of darkness, all around us, and I'm scared."

"When you say *darkness*—"

"It's real. I can *see* it. It isn't my imagination. I can see it now, all around us, and it's especially dark around *you*. It's like there's a shadow falling across you."

Hicks put down the chicken leg he had been eating and sat back in his chair. He said, as if he were admitting that there was hereditary weak-mindedness in the family, "Rhoda's grandmother, Rhoda's mother, Rhoda . . . they all claim to be sensitives."

"Sensitives? You mean like mediums?"

"Kind of like that, yes. They say they can sense a storm coming, or when somebody's going to die. They say they can hear voices from the spirit world."

"And this is what you're feeling now?" Decker asked her.

Rhoda nodded. "It's so strong it's like standing in the ocean when the tide's pulling out and you think that you're going to get dragged away."

"Do you have any idea what could be causing it?"

"I don't know. But I started to feel it on the day that Alison Maitland was killed. I felt it even before Tim came home and told me about it."

She hesitated, twisting her napkin, and then she said, "I heard a noise in the nursery and I went up to make sure that Daisy was okay. There's a long mirror on the landing and as I came up the stairs I *saw* somebody. Only for a split second. But it was like the mirror was an open doorway instead of a mirror and somebody walked across it, so quick that I couldn't see who it was."

Hicks said, "Honey . . . the lieutenant's right. This is a really gruesome case and you're letting your imagination run away with you."

"But this happened before I even knew about it."

"Come on, honey, what you saw in the mirror, it was a trick of the light." Hicks stood up and put his arm around her. "There was nobody there, was there?"

"I saw somebody, I swear it."

"And how about this darkness that's falling on me?" Decker asked. "Can you still see that?"

"It's not just the Maitland case. It's something that happened to you a long time ago. Something that you never allow yourself to remember."

"What, specifically? Do you have any idea?"

"I'm not sure. I'd have to do a reading to find that out."

"Oh, come on," Hicks protested. "The lieutenant came here for supper, not for mumbo jumbo."

"No, I'm interested," Decker said. "What kind of a reading?"

"I can use an *okuele*."

"An *okuele?*"

"Jesus," Hicks said, burying his head in his hands.

Rhoda got up from the table and went across to a small side table. She took out a carefully wrapped package of purple tissue paper. She laid it on the table and opened it up. Inside lay what looked like a necklace, eight tortoiseshell medallions connected together by a dull metal chain.

"My grandmother taught me to use it. It's like the tarot except that it explains the past as well as the future, and it's much more personal than the tarot. Through the *okuele*, the spirits prompt you to tell them what's troubling you, instead of the other way around."

Hicks sat down and stared at his half-eaten supper. "I don't believe this. All I wanted was fried chicken and what do I get? *Ghostbusters*."

CHAPTER TWENTY

Rhoda cleared the table and spread a plain white cloth on it. Hicks stood on the opposite side of the kitchen with his arms folded, looking deeply unhappy. Decker said, "I'm sorry . . . I didn't mean to spoil your supper. I'm not sure that I believe in this dark shadow any more than you do, but there must be some reason that Rhoda feels so strongly about it."

"I guess."

"There's another thing . . . *Sandra* said she had a premonition, too. She said she really believed that something bad's about to happen."

Hicks watched as Rhoda placed a silver-plated candlestick in the center of the table, with a tall white candle, and lit it, and arranged a sheet of paper and a pencil beside her chair. "I really don't like this, Lieutenant. I don't like Rhoda getting involved in my work. Especially when we're dealing with some kind of total freaking psychopath."

"If she's got some kind of intuitive feeling about it, sport, I think we need to know what it is."

Rhoda said, "You can sit down now. This is only a very simple reading, so that we can find out why Decker is walking in darkness."

Rhoda switched off all the lights so that the only illumination came from the candle, and then they sat down. "Do we have to hold hands or anything?" Decker asked.

"No. It's enough that we're sitting here together."

Rhoda closed her eyes and said nothing for what seemed like forever, although it was probably no more than two or three minutes. Hicks glanced at Decker in discomfort, but neither of them spoke in case they disturbed Rhoda's concentration. There was no draft in the room, and the candle flame burned steady and bright, without wavering.

At last, Rhoda tossed the *okuele* onto the table. Some of the medallions fell with their shiny side upward, others with their dull side upward. All of the medallions were marked on their shiny side with the sign of the cross. Rhoda picked up her pencil and marked a line of crosses and zeroes.

She picked up the *okuele* and threw it again, and again she marked down the way that the medallions had fallen. She repeated this process four times.

At last she said, "Something terrible happened and you won't allow yourself to remember it. Your mind has closed its eyes and it refuses to open them."

Decker said nothing. He didn't know what she meant. What had he ever refused to remember?

Rhoda hesitated a moment more, and then she said, "It's raining, and you're standing outside a black door. Do you remember that?"

"I don't know. I don't think so. I mean, I must have stood outside hundreds of black doors."

"It's dark. The number on the black door has two fours and a seven."

Decker uneasily sat back. "I remember, 1447 Duval Street, five years ago. We were on a drug bust."

"You're not alone. You have a partner with you."

"That's right. Jim Stuart. Just made detective first grade."

Rhoda touched her fingertips to her ears. "You say something about the back of the house."

" 'Cover the back of the house. Anyone runs out into the alley, shoot first and worry about who it is afterward.' "

Decker recited the words as if he were giving evidence. He looked at Hicks and Hicks was staring at him apprehensively, as if he were seeing a side of Decker's personality that he had never been aware of before.

Rhoda said, "You open the black door. You walk into the hallway. It's very dark inside the house."

"I can't see my hand in front of my face, that's how dark it is."

"You feel a door handle on your left. You open it."

Decker didn't say anything. He could remember opening that door because he had opened it time and time again, and wished that he hadn't.

"You enter the room. It's just as dark in here. You can smell people sleeping. You raise your gun in your right hand and your flashlight in your left. Just as you switch on your flashlight, you hear the click of a gun being cocked, right behind you. You turn round. You fire."

"It was dark," Decker said, hoarsely. "I told him to cover the back of the house. 'Anybody runs out into the alley, shoot first and worry about who it is afterward.' I specifically told him not to come inside. Specifically. A specific order."

Rhoda closed her eyes again and picked up the *okuele*, passing it through her fingers like a rosary, and gently rubbing every one of its tortoiseshell medallions.

When she spoke, her voice was unnervingly whispery, as if she were making a guilty confession to a priest. She didn't even sound like Rhoda. "*Saint Barbara knows what you saw.*"

"Saint Barbara? What are you talking about?"

"Saint Barbara is the shadow who is following you everywhere. She knows everything about you. She knows who your father's father was, and what sign you were born under, because she wants her revenge. She knows every bone in your body and she knows what you saw when you shot Jim Stuart."

"What do you know about Saint Barbara? Hicks—did you ever tell Rhoda about Saint Barbara, that thing on my wall?"

Hicks shook his head. "Come on, Rhoda. Enough of this shit."

But Rhoda stared at Decker and whispered, "Saint Barbara wants you, Decker. She knows what you saw when you shot Jim Stuart. She knows everything about you."

For a fraction of a second, Decker saw his flashlight jump across Jim Stuart's startled face. Wide-eyed, because of the dark. A little blondish moustache. But his finger had already pulled the trigger and it was *bang!* and Jim Stuart went down.

"It was dark. I couldn't see who it was. He had a specific order not to enter the house."

Another long silence. Rhoda's eyes were open, but it looked to Decker as if she were focusing right past him, and listening to somebody else, because she gave occasional nods of her head.

"Saint Barbara can see right into your soul," she whispered, and then, in her own voice, "Not yet." Then she turned directly to Decker and said, "There's a spirit here . . . a spirit who's trying to warn you."

Decker became aware that the kitchen was gradually

growing colder, and he had the strangest sensation that the floor was slowly sinking beneath them, and the walls stretching, like the elevator in the haunted house in Disney World. Hicks must have experienced it, too, because he looked up toward the ceiling and then down at the floor, and then back up at the ceiling again.

"I wish to speak to you," Rhoda said. "I need you to tell me more about Saint Barbara."

The kitchen was now so cold that Decker could see his own breath. He could faintly hear a high-pitched sound, like a steel wire being drawn across the back of a saw. It grew louder and louder and higher and higher, until he could feel it in the fillings in his teeth, and his saliva started to taste salty.

"Was it *you?*" Rhoda asked.

The candle flame burned brighter. It began to burn so intensely that it hissed, and wax begun to run down it faster and faster, pouring over the candlestick and onto the tablecloth.

"Was it *you?*" Rhoda repeated.

The flame widened, and swelled out, and right in front of Decker's eyes it formed itself into a fiery face, with hollow eyes and a mouth that was open in a silent scream.

"Jesus," Hicks said.

"Speak to me," Rhoda said. "Tell me what you want to say."

The face said nothing, even though its mouth was stretched wide open. But as it burned brighter, it increased in definition, so that Decker could begin to see that it was a young woman, with furiously waving hair.

"Speak to me," Rhoda encouraged her. "Tell me more about Saint Barbara."

At that instant, the young woman's eyes opened, and she stared directly at Decker with a look of utter wildness and agony. It was Cathy. Her face was made of fire but there was no doubt about it at all. It was Cathy, and she was screaming at him soundlessly from the other side of sudden death.

"Tell me about Saint Barbara," Rhoda insisted.

But then—with a soft *whoomph*—the face flared up into a fireball, and rolled up to the ceiling, and was gone. Decker and Rhoda and Hicks were left facing each other with only a small flickering stub of a candle between them, the shadows moving on their faces as if they were alternately smiling and scowling.

Hicks switched on the light. "What the hell was *that?*" he wanted to know. "Static? St. Elmo's fire? What?"

Decker said, "I take it back . . . about not believing in ghosts. Or spirits, or whatever. That was my girlfriend Cathy."

"You mean—"

"Yes. My dead girlfriend, Cathy."

Rhoda said, "She couldn't say any more. It was like she was suffering too much to speak."

"She spoke to me the other night," Decker said. "She warned me about Saint Barbara. Somebody painted the words *Saint Barbara* on my wall, too, the other night, in human blood. It wouldn't surprise me if it was her. Or her ghost. Or whatever that was."

"She's *dead*, Lieutenant," Hicks put in.

"That makes no difference," Rhoda said, gently. "Our spirit lives on, even after we die. Sometimes, if someone died a violent death, that makes their spirit even stronger . . . even more determined to protect the loved ones that they left behind. Your Cathy, Lieutenant, is trying very hard to warn you of a coming danger. That is why you carry the shadow with you. You've been marked already, for some kind of revenge, and Cathy knows it."

"*Rhoda*," Hicks protested, "this is my superior officer. You can't go telling him he's doomed or nothing."

"I'm sorry, but I have to. Would you stand by and say nothing if you saw that a man was going to be hit by a car?"

Decker said, "You don't have any idea what this 'coming danger' might be?"

"Your Cathy started to appear to you when you took on the Maitland homicide, so I guess it must be connected in some way. She senses that something very bad is going to happen to you, but I don't think that it's an accident or illness or anything like that. I think she believes that something terrible is after you, something that goes by the name of Saint Barbara."

"Santería," Decker said.

"What?" Hicks said.

"A saint's name, Saint Barbara. That's the whole thing about Santería, isn't it? When the slaves were brought over from Africa, the slave owners wouldn't allow them to worship their own gods, so they disguised what they were doing by calling their gods by the names of Catholic saints."

"That's right," Rhoda said. "'Saint Barbara' may not be Saint Barbara at all, but some god worshiped by the Santerians."

"Santería?" Hicks said. "That could mean Queen Aché."

"Makes sense," Decker agreed. "We definitely need to investigate that lady a whole lot closer. Although I don't see why *she* should have been interested in killing the Maitlands, or Major Drewry. What the hell did *they* ever do to upset her?"

"I'll check if either of them had any business dealings with the Eguns. Gerald Maitland was into real estate, wasn't he? It's possible that he might have done some property deal that ruffled Queen Aché's feathers."

"Okay. Look, it's getting late. Tim—Rhoda—I feel really bad for messing up your meal."

Rhoda said, "Don't. I couldn't let you sit there with that shadow on you, and not say a word. Would you like some coffee before you go?"

"No, thanks. I think me and my shadow will just take ourselves home. See you tomorrow, Tim."

That night, Decker was back in the blazing bushes, his face and his feet lacerated, and even more exhausted than before. He knew that the tall dark figure was very close behind him. He could hear him surging through the underbrush in his ankle-length greatcoat. But the heat and the smoke were searing his throat and his clothes were snarled by briars at every step and he was almost past caring.

"Muster at the plank road, boys! Muster at the plank road!"

He thought that he must have almost reached the plank road by now. Over the crackling and the popping of burning branches he could hear men shouting and screaming for help, and every now and then there was a brisk rattle of rifle fire. Minié balls came moaning and snapping through the scrub, and from a mile or so in the distance came the distinctive thudding of artillery.

He turned around to see how close the tall dark figure was, but he couldn't see it, only the fiery latticework of burning briars. Then, however, he heard a heavy rustling sound off to his left, and saw a shadowy shape moving swiftly behind the trees. The figure was outflanking him, and that meant that it would reach the plank road before he did, and cut off any hope of escape. Not only that, God alone knew what it would do to his friends and his fellows.

"*It's coming!*" he shouted out, even though his throat was raw. "*Keep away from the road! It's coming!*"

The figure stopped, and listened, and then it turned toward him. *Oh, Christ*, he thought. *It's heading straight for me. It'll have my guts*. He tore his tunic free from the thorns, and tried to run in the opposite direction, but already he could hear the figure coming closer and closer.

He twisted around, spraining his ankle. As he did so, the figure was on top of him, tangling him up in knobbly bones and suffocating cloth. "*Can't breathe!*" he screamed. "*Can't breathe!*"

He jolted upright. *Jesus*. He switched on the light and he could see himself in the mirror on the opposite side of the bedroom, his hair sticking up and his T-shirt dark with sweat.

He eased himself out of bed. His feet were scratched and bleeding, like before, and when he tried to stand up he found that his ankle was swollen. He hobbled into the bathroom, stripped off his T-shirt, and splashed his face with cold water.

He no longer believed that he was hallucinating, or suffering from stress. Rhoda had shown him Cathy's fiery face, and for Decker that was proof enough that something malevolent was after him, and that Cathy was trying to protect him from it. He had a pee and flushed the toilet, and then he went back into the bedroom to take a fresh white T-shirt out of the drawer.

As he pulled the T-shirt over his head, he suddenly realized that his top bedsheet was missing. He ducked down and looked on the floor. He looked around the other side of the bed, but the sheet was definitely gone. "The hell," he said, and stood perplexed in the middle of the room, trying to work out what could have happened to it.

Keep calm, he told himself. *Maybe you never had a top sheet.*

He went to the linen closet to take out another sheet. As he did so, however, he heard somebody chanting in the living area. Somebody was singing in a high, breathless voice, like Cathy's—*up*, down, *up*, down, plangently, yet he didn't recognize the song. It certainly wasn't Bob Dylan, or Joan Armatrading, or any of those other singers that Cathy used to like. He limped to the bedroom door and pressed his ear against it.

"*—ko gbamu mi re oro niglati wa obinu ki kigbo ni na orin oti gbogbo—*"

He listened for a moment, and then he opened the door.

"Cathy?" he called, and his heart was thumping hard against his ribs. "Cathy? Is that you?" The living area was totally dark. All he could hear now was the sound of traffic in the street below, and the faint whirring of the air conditioner.

"Cathy, if that's you, let me see you. I love you, sweetheart, and I know that you're trying to help me."

There was no answer. But as Decker's eyes became more accustomed to the darkness, he thought he could see a whitish figure standing close to the kitchen archway. He said, "*Cathy?*" and he was sure that he saw the figure sway from side to side. He edged across to the nearest wall, wincing on his twisted ankle, and reached for the light switches and flicked them on.

He said, "*Ah!*" out loud.

The figure was draped in his bedsheet, at least five and a half feet tall, with its arms outspread. Its hands were as white as alabaster, and so were its feet, and it appeared to be floating about a half inch above the floor.

Decker was so frightened by this apparition that he didn't know what to do. He stood by the light switches, rubbing his right arm, feeling terrified and miserable and helpless. This might be Cathy, covered by a sheet, but what if it wasn't? What if it was something terrible? How could it be Cathy? She was dead, with her head blown apart.

"Listen," he said, and his voice was very dry, as if he really had been running through burning scrub. "I need to know what you want. I need to know who you actually are."

The sheet-covered figure swayed a little more, but remained silent.

"If I was to drag that sheet off of you—I mean, who would you be underneath?"

Still the figure didn't respond.

Decker thought, *Shit, what am I going to do? I'm not dreaming, am I? I know I'm not drunk.* He took one step toward the figure and then another.

"I'm scared of you, right? Hiding under that sheet like that. But I'll bet you're scared of me, too. Otherwise, why don't you show yourself?"

"Saint Barbara," the figure whispered, although its voice seemed to come from behind him, and he wasn't at all sure it was Cathy's voice. "Saint Barbara wants her revenge."

Decker said, "Saint Barbara is a saint, that's all. A good saint, from what I've been told. She protects people from fire and explosions and stuff like that. Why should she want to hurt me?"

"Come closer," the apparition said.

"I don't think so," Decker said. "Not until I know who you are."

"Come closer, my darling."

Decker didn't know what to do. He was frightened that this figure wasn't Cathy, but in a way he was even more frightened that it *was*. He looked over at the hat stand, where his Colt Anaconda was hanging in its holster, and wished that he had learned the lesson and taken it into the bedroom with him.

"Are you Cathy?" he asked the sheeted figure.

"Don't you trust me?" it whispered, and it sounded as if it were speaking down a hollow pipe.

"I don't know. Aren't you going to show me who you are?"

"I am many things. I have many different faces."

"Are you trying to warn me about something bad?"

"Something bad is happening to you already."

Decker circled cautiously around the figure toward the hat stand. It didn't turn around to follow him, but stayed where it was, with its arms outspread, more like a statue than a human being, a statue that was waiting to be unveiled. Decker's throat was so dry that he had to cough, and cough again, but still the figure didn't move.

"Tell me about Saint Barbara," Decker said, without taking his eyes off it. He reached up for his holster and unfastened the clasp.

"Saint Barbara wants her revenge for what you did. For what you all did."

"Was it something that happened in the Wilderness? The Devil's Brigade?"

"Promises were made and promises were broken."

"What promises?"

"Promises of honor. Promises of war. Promises of just rewards."

Decker eased his revolver out of its holster and cocked it. He approached the figure until he was almost close enough to reach out his hand and touch it. He could see the indistinct outline of a face under the sheet, and the cotton was being drawn in and out, in and out, as if the figure were breathing.

"Are you afraid of me?" the figure whispered.

"Should I be?"

"Are you afraid of Saint Barbara?"

"I don't know. Are we really talking about Saint Barbara, or are we talking about somebody else?"

"*Oche ofun*," the figure said. "*The saints rescue you from the dead.*"

Decker took hold of the edge of the sheet, close to the figure's wrist. His blood was pounding in his ears and he couldn't remember ever having felt as terrified as this, not in all of his years of police work.

"Are you sure you want to know what I am?" the figure asked him.

Decker didn't answer, but grasped the edge of the sheet even more firmly, in his fist. He was just about to drag it off the figure's head, however, when the figure let out a piercing screech—a screech of rage and pain and frustration, as if five voices were all screaming at once.

The screech went on and on, and Decker let go of the sheet and stepped awkwardly away, his revolver raised, not knowing what to do. But then there was a dull, wet *thud!* and the top of the sheet ballooned outward, and was drenched in blood. Instantly, it collapsed onto the floor.

Decker stood staring at it, panting for breath. It lay crumpled in front of the kitchen archway, massively soaked in blood, but it was obvious that there was nobody underneath it. After a while he kicked it sideways, and he could see that it was nothing but a sheet.

"Christ," he breathed.

Still holding his revolver, he went over to the drinks table and one-handedly poured himself a shot glass of Herradura Silver. He tipped it back in one, and then he poured himself another.

He glanced back at the bloodstained sheet. Now he knew for sure that this investigation wasn't just about facts and evidence and tracking down a perpetrator. This was about religion, and beliefs, and acts of betrayal. This was spiritual, and not only that, it was *personal.*

CHAPTER TWENTY-ONE

He found Jonah in back of the Mask Bar on Second and Main, talking to two of his friends. The Mask Bar was dark and smoky and the walls were decorated with scores of African masks, some of them ebony, some of them beaten out of copper, some of them fashioned from dry reeds. Batá drum music was tapping in the background.

Jonah's friends looked up uneasily as Decker came in. One of them was thin as a rail, with tiny dark sunglasses and a black beret. The other was enormous, wearing a billowing brown caftan with zigzag patterns on it, and a brown fez with a tassel.

"Talk to you for a minute?" Decker asked.

"About what, man?" Jonah was being aggressive for the sake of his friends.

"I don't know. This and that."

"I don't know nothing more about Junior Abraham, if that's what you're excavating for."

"I wanted to catch up on the local gossip, that's all."

"You want local gossip, go to the mother-and-baby club on Clay Street. They'll even give you recipes for black bean chili, too."

"Not that kind of gossip. I was more interested in Queen Aché."

Jonah looked at his friends and eventually the fat one shrugged, as if to say, anything that was bad news for Queen Aché was good news for him. Decker didn't know him, but he recognized the man in the beret as one of the Strutters, a petty drug dealer who called himself Dr. Welcome. There was no love lost between the Strutters and the Eguns, so he guessed that Dr. Welcome wouldn't object if Jonah answered a few questions, either.

"All right, then," Jonah said. "Five minutes, and that's it. But I don't know nothing, man. Nothing about nothing."

They went and sat at a table in the corner, underneath a scowling green mask with a mouth that was smothered in glistening red varnish, to represent blood.

"I need to talk to a *santero*," Decker said.

"Listen, Deck-ah," Jonah interrupted, leaning forward and speaking in a hoarse whisper. "I like you and you like me. You done me some prime favors. But you can't just come trucking in here and act like we best friends or nothing. Those two brothers, they're cool, but I don't need the whole of Jackson Ward to find out that I'm exchanging social pleasantries with the man."

"This is serious, Jonah. I need to talk to a *santero* and I need to do it now."

"What's in it for me?"

"My undying gratitude, of course."

"How about your undying gratitude and two hundred bucks?"

Decker took out his billfold and peeled off a hundred dollars. "I'll give you the rest when you do your stuff."

Jonah made the bill disappear as if he were performing a conjuring trick. Then he said, "Most of the *santeros* are tied up with Queen Aché. You don't want to go talking to those dudes, because the next thing you know they'll be putting the hex on you and your dick'll drop off or something. But there's one who might help you, if you ask him real respectful. His name's Moses Adebolu. He used to be a close friend of Junior Abraham, and I know he's pretty sore that Junior got offed."

"Can you take me to him?"

"Okay, but we have to go by way of the Afro market."

"What the hell for?"

"You have to bring Moses a live rooster and some cigars and maybe a bottle of rum. Also some *rompe zaraguey* root if you can find it, or some okra."

Decker said, "I'm conducting a homicide investigation here, not a shopping trip."

"You have to bring those things, Deck-ah. They're part of the *ebbó*, the sacrifice. Otherwise Moses won't help you a-tall."

A little before noon, Decker parked outside a scabby, narrow-shouldered house under the shadow of Route 95. He and Jonah climbed out, and they had to shout to each other because the noise of the overhead traffic was deafening. The morning was hot, with 85 percent humidity, and the air was blurred with exhaust fumes.

Decker opened the trunk and took out a wicker basket with a querulous, brassy-plumed rooster inside it. Jonah lifted out a brown paper sack containing two bottles of Mount Gay rum, a box of King Edward cigars, and an assortment of sugarcane, palm oil, cinnamon sticks, and toasted corn.

"This had better be worth it!" Decker yelled in Jonah's ear.

"I don't know, man! I can't guarantee nothing! These *santeros*, they can be highly uppity if they don't like the smell of you!"

They climbed the steps in front of the house where three young boys were playing a game of pick-up-sticks with what looked like rats' bones.

"Moses at home?" Jonah asked.

The rooster flapped and clucked inside its basket. The oldest boy frowned and said, "What's that you bringing him?"

Decker opened up the lid so that he could see. "Takeout. Kentucky Unfried Chicken."

They pushed open the peeling, brown-painted door and stepped into the hallway. The floor was covered with cracked, curled-up linoleum and the stair carpet was so worn out that it was impossible to tell what color it might have been. The whole house was pervaded by an eye-watering smell of frying garlic and cinnamon, and somebody was listlessly playing the bongo drums. At the top of the stairs was a stained-glass window showing a man in white robes standing next to a river, John the Baptist maybe, but the top part of the window had been broken so that he had no head, only plain glass.

"Second story," Jonah said, and up they trudged. They crossed the creaking landing, and Jonah knocked at a door that was decorated in lurid reds and blues and maroons, with a staring yellow eye painted on each of its panels. "Let's hope Moses is feeling amenable. Not stoned or got a sudden attack of unreasonable racial prejudice or nothing."

He knocked again, and a hoarse voice said, "Don't be so

impatient, my friend, I hear you, I hear you." The door was opened by a big-bellied, gray-haired man with enormous spectacles that looked like the screens of two 1960s TVs. He was wearing a black short-sleeved shirt and black pants and sandals, and around his neck hung necklaces of colored beads and silver chains and brightly dyed guinea-hen feathers.

"Jonah, ain't seen you in a while, what you want, man?"

"I brung you some stuff, man."

Moses squinted suspiciously at Decker. "Looks like you brung me some trouble, too."

Decker lifted up his basket. "One live rooster. I just wanted to talk to you, that's all."

"Talk about what? I'm a busy man, friend. Got to do this, got to do that."

"Decker's the *man*, man," Jonah explained. "He's trying to find out who offed Junior Abraham."

"How should I know who offed him? And even if I did I wouldn't tell the man. What you say your name was?"

"Decker—Decker Martin."

"That's kind of a slave-owning name, ain't it?"

"I wish. I don't even have a cleaner."

The rooster skittered impatiently, and Moses said, "All right then, guess you'd better come along in. What you got there, Jonah? Cigars, is that? And rum?"

"One hundred twenty proof, just the way you like it."

Moses shuffled ahead of them into a gloomy, airless living room. The room was permeated with an extraordinary smell, bitter and yet fragrant, which somehow gave Decker the feeling that he had stepped out of the real world and into another. It was crowded with heavy 1950s-style furniture—two immense armchairs and a couch, all upholstered in brown brocade, with antimacassars draped over the back.

The drapes were thick and brown and dusty and looked as if they hadn't been taken down and cleaned since the first run of *I Love Lucy*. A huge television dominated one corner of the room, while the other was taken up by a Santería shrine—less glittery than Queen Aché's, but crowded with coconuts, red and green beads, candles, flowers, pictures of saints, and a scowling head made of cement, with cowrie shells for eyes.

Moses eased himself down into one of the armchairs and said, "Don't know what I can do to help you, my friend. The rumor was going around that Junior Abraham was doing some sly business on the side when he was supposed to be working for Queen Aché, but that was only a rumor. He had some fancy new threads and a fancy new SUV, but that don't prove nothing."

Decker sat opposite him and set down the rooster's basket on the matted brown rug. "I need to know some more about Santería," he said. "In particular I need to know how a man can make himself unseen."

"Unseen? You're talking a seriously serious spell here. Only a *very* prestigious *santero* can work a spell like that, maybe even a *babalawo*. A *babalawo* is a high priest, in case you wasn't aware of it . . . somebody who conducts the sacrifices whenever *santeros* get theirselves initiated."

Decker said, "The guy who killed Junior Abraham made himself unseen . . . at least for long enough to walk right up to him and blow his head off at point-blank range. And I'm dealing with three other cases, too, where the perpetrator has somehow managed to remain invisible."

Moses nodded. "Well, this is interesting, friend. I haven't heard of magic as strong as this for many years. These days, very few priests have the total faith that you would need to walk amongst other folks unseen. You want tea?"

Behind Moses' back, Jonah nodded a frantic *yes*, to indicate that this was a matter of essential courtesy. Decker said, "Tea? Sure, I'd like that."

Moses reached over to a side table and rang a small brass bell. Almost immediately, a young woman in a red and green turban and a red and green sari came into the room. She was twenty-three or twenty-four, with high cheekbones and a long, almost Masai face. She was wearing a sweet musky perfume that Decker didn't recognize.

"My daughter, Aluya," Moses said. "Aluya takes care of me, don't you, Aluya? Bring us some tea, yes, Aluya? And some of them honey-nut cookies."

Decker looked up at Aluya, grinned, and said, "Hi," but Aluya bashfully turned her face away. Moses said, with undisguised satisfaction, "Aluya will have plenty of time for socializing with men when I'm gone off to associate with my ancestors. Right now she has enough on her plate, cooking my dinners and washing my drawers."

"Sounds like she has her hands full."

After Aluya had gone back to the kitchen, Moses leaned forward in his chair. "Listen—to understand the power it takes for a man to make himself invisible to other people, you have to know about more than the nature of one particular spell. You have to know what Santería *is*."

Decker said, "All I really know about it is that it's an African religion, and that it was brought to America by slaves. I know that the slaves changed the names of their gods to the names of Catholic saints, but that's about it."

"Well, pretty much right so far as it goes. Santería is the name we give to two belief systems that got themselves, like, all tangled up with each other. Its roots was in southwestern Nigeria, in all of the myths and the magic rituals of the Yoruba people, but when the Yorubas came to the New World, and they had to hide what they were doing, they borrowed a whole lot of fancy trappings from the Roman Catholic church.

"The Yorubas was very *smart* and they was very *cultured.* Back in Africa they had theirselves a very sophisticated social structure, and they created all kinds of amazing art in wood and bronze and ivory. They had kingdoms, like Benin, and they built the holy city of Ile-Ife, which is the place where everything that exists comes from. They also worshipped many gods. *Orishas*, they called them. That's the Yoruba name for a god. *Orisha.*

"Trouble was, round about sixteen hundred and something, Yorubaland was invaded by the Ewe tribes from the north, and the Yorubas was forced to migrate down to the Nigerian coast. That was why so many of them was captured by slave traders and shipped to America.

"Like you said, they carried on worshipping their old gods, but they gave them the names of Catholic saints. So when their owners thought that they was praying to Saint Anthony, they was actually paying their respects to Elegguá, the owner of the crossroads and the messenger of the *orishas*. Oggún, the god of metals, he became Saint Peter, and Orunla, who knows all the mysteries of the universe, was honored as Saint Francis of Assisi. We still give a sacrifice to Orunla on October the fourth, which is Saint Francis of Assisi Day for the Roman Catholics.

"Santería is an *earth* religion, if you understand what I mean. It's all about nature and the forces of nature, like the Native American beliefs. Changó is the god of fire, thunder, and lightning. Oshún is the god of river waters, and also of love, and marriage, and fertility. Oyá is the wind, and the keeper of the cemetery, the watcher of the doorway between life and death. She ain't death itself, but she's the *knowledge* that we all have to die."

Aluya came in with a tray of teacups and a plate of cookies. As she handed Decker his tea she raised her eyes just a fraction and gave him a barely perceptible smile. So she didn't have time for men? thought Decker. He sipped his tea and it was completely tasteless—scalding water with little green fragments of twigs in it.

Moses took a cookie and pushed it into his mouth, and before he had finished chewing it, another, and then another. When he carried on talking he sprayed crumbs on his pants and he had to keep brushing them with his hand.

"There are two kinds of *orishas*—the white *orishas* and the dark *orishas*. The white *orishas* have the power to heal, and give life, like Obatalá and Oshún and Osain, the god of herbs. The dark *orishas* are hot and their strength is greatest in wars and battles. These are Changó, Oggún, Oyá, and Babalu-Ayé.

"Santería has two basic concepts, right? The first concept is *aché*, which means divine power, the power that was used to create the universe. Then there's the concept of *ebbó*, which means sacrifice.

"In Santería we make sacrifices to the *orishas* and we propitiate them because we want them to give us *aché*. With *aché*, we can sort out anything that's bugging us, we can screw our enemies, we can find pretty women and happiness and money. *Aché* also means *authority*, which is why Queen Aché calls herself by that particular name."

"I see," Decker said. "So *ebbó*—sacrifice—will bring you *aché*—power?" He hesitated for a moment, and then he said, "What kind of a sacrifice would somebody have to make if he wanted the power to be invisible?"

"*Unseen* more than invisible," Moses corrected him, helping himself to another cookie. "An *ebbó* like that—well, that would call for blood. We never shed blood lightly, not even the blood of a chicken, because blood is the essence of life. Usually we offer fruit or flowers or candles or whatever the *orisha* likes to eat. But if somebody wanted the power to walk through the world without being seen—yes, blood, my friend. Possibly maybe human blood."

"Is there any way in which you could make a kind of a counter—*ebbó?*"

"What do you mean?"

"Well, could I ask the *orishas* to give me the *aché* so that I could *see* this invisible person?"

Moses thought about that, and then he shook his head. "I can't honestly say I know the answer to that. One spell *can* be cast to break another. It depends who cast it, and how strong it is. I heard of a man who asked a *santero* to cast a spell on his older brother to bring him ill luck, and the spell worked. In only two or three months, his brother's wife ran off with one of his best friends, his business went bankrupt, and he caught a skin rash all over his body."

"That's not just *ill* luck," Jonah said. "That's *shit* luck."

"Oh yes. But the older brother went to a *babalawo*, a high priest, and the *babalawo* realized at once that somebody had put a curse on him. The *babalawo* made a sacrifice to the *ajogun*, who are the opposite of the *orishas*. The *ajogun* are the evil forces in the world—*arun*, which is disease; *ofo*, which is loss; *egba*, which is paralysis; and *iku*, which is death.

"The *babalawo* cast a spell that every bad thing the older brother had suffered should happen to the person who had cursed him, only a hundred times worse. That same evening all of the younger brother's family were killed in car crash, including his newborn son. Within a week his furniture business had burned down, and he was badly burned trying to get out of the building. In the hospital, before his burns were healed, he was diagnosed with incurable leukemia. It was only then that he confessed to his older brother that he had arranged for a bad-luck spell, and his older brother discovered who it was that he had cursed in return."

He took the last cookie and bit into it. "A true story," he said. Then—realizing that he had emptied the plate all by himself—he held out the half-eaten cookie to Decker and said, "Want one?"

"No, thanks. I just need the ability to be able to see this guy. I also need to see the evidence he leaves behind him. I know the evidence is there. Fingerprints, fibers, DNA. It *must* be there. But in some way he's made it invisible. I need *eyes*, Mr. Alebodu. Eyes that can see through magic."

"Well . . . I'll have to give this some sober thinking."

"Okay . . . I really appreciate your talking to me. If you come up with any ideas, maybe you can give me a call on this number."

"You've forgotten something," Moses said, quietly, as Decker stood up. Decker looked around and saw his teacup, still full.

"Oh . . . I'm more of a coffee kind of guy. Sorry."

"There's another question in your mind, my friend, and you don't know how to put it into words."

Jonah looked across at Decker and made a face that meant "don't ask me."

Decker said, "How do you know that?"

"Because an unspoken question, what's that like? It's like a bird sitting on a wall. It won't fly away until you clap your hands."

"It's not important."

"I think it cuts close to your heart, and this is why you decided not to ask it."

"Forget it, it doesn't matter."

"I think it *do* matter. Because what would a police detective with a slave-owning name want to know from a *santero*? Let's ask ourselves that."

"All right," Decker said. "What about Saint Barbara? Were any of the *orishas* named for her?"

"And you ask me that because . . ."

"I ask because I've been having bad dreams. I've been hearing my girlfriend, who was killed two years ago. I hear her talking to me, in my sleep. Or maybe not in my sleep, I don't know. Maybe she's really there."

"And she talks to you about Saint Barbara?"

"That's right. She says that Saint Barbara wants her revenge. A couple of days ago, when I got home, I found the name Saint Barbara written on my wall, in human blood."

"And . . ."

"I saw her again, last night. She was standing in my apartment, covered in a sheet, like she was playing ghosts."

Moses took off his glasses. His eyes were bulgy and unfocused, but somehow Decker felt that he could see him better without them.

"Sit down," Moses said. "Let me tell you this. Saint Barbara is the name that we gave to Changó, who is the mighty and terrible *orisha* of fire, thunder, lightning, and war. The cult of Changó came from the city of Oyo-Ile, the ancient capital of the Oyo kingdom. Changó reigned over the city for seven years, but he was always interested in magic and he had *great* magical power.

"One day Changó caused a great thunderstorm that destroyed his palace and killed many of his wives and children. He was so remorseful that he hanged himself. His enemies rejoiced, but soon afterward a hundred thunderstorms destroyed most of the city of Oyo-Ile, along with Changó's enemies. Changó's followers made sacrifices in his honor and declared that he was an *orisha*, a god. '*Oba ko so*,' they sang. 'The king did not hang himself.'

"Changó is the most powerful and popular of all the *orishas*. He has millions of followers all around the world. His priests keep his power in 'thunderstones'—which are the bricks of buildings that have been struck by lightning, and kept in a wooden bowl. You can see that I have one over there, on my shrine. If you wish to make a sacrifice to Changó, to propitiate him, you have to wash the bowl in herbs and palm oil, and then sacrifice a rooster and sprinkle its blood over the thunderstones. This is one of the oldest ceremonies in Santería, and goes right back hundreds of years to Africa.

"You can also give Changó chicken meat and bananas, although his favorite food is a freshly killed ram."

"Chicken meat and bananas?" Decker suddenly thought of the face that he had seen in his kitchen.

"That means something to you?" Moses asked.

Decker told him. Moses listened, and nodded, seemingly unsurprised. "I think your dead girlfriend is doing everything she can to protect you."

"From what? From Changó? What have I ever done to Changó?"

"I don't know . . . but it's pretty clear to me that he's looking for revenge. And when Changó looks for revenge, he makes double sure that he gets it. I hate to tell you this, my friend, but you in *acute* trouble."

Jonah asked, "Is there any way to find out what this Changó's so mad about?"

"I'm not sure. But I could help you to make an *ebbó* to Changó, which might make him forgive you. Right now, the only thing that's standing between you and some very horrible consequence is the spirit of your girlfriend, and she's putting herself in very serious danger by daring to mess with such a seriously powerful *orisha*. Every time she appears to you, she's going to have to suffer the moment of her death over again, and if she upsets Changó too often, he'll give her to Oyá, the watcher of the doorway between life and death, so that she spends the whole of eternity *trapped* in that moment, and never being free."

In his mind's eye, Decker saw Cathy's head exploding, again and again, and the thought that she would have to experience that forever was more than he could bear. He had seen enough and heard enough to believe now that there *was* an afterlife, and that the spirits of the dead were still among us, even if they only made their presence known in times of crisis.

"This *ebbó*," he said. "Tell me what I have to do."

"You have to be cleansed. I sacrifice this rooster you brought me to Changó. Then tomorrow you must come back and I will give you a bowl with the rooster's blood in it, mixed with an *omiero* for Changó."

"An *omiero?*"

"An *omiero* is a sacred elixir, my friend, which we use for bathing and also for drinking. Changó's *omiero* is a mixture of blood, *rompe zaraguey*, *zarza parilla*, and *paraíso*. You will have to take the *omiero* home and bathe yourself with it. Then take a second bath to wash off the blood mixture. Into this second bath you will have to stir some *álamo* and some *prodigiosa*, some holy water and some honey. I will give you all of these things. While you are bathing, ask Changó for his forgiveness for whatever you have done to offend him, and ask for his protection."

"And you think that could work?"

"You will have to believe that it is going to work, or else it won't. You have to have faith. You still love your dead girlfriend, don't you? Think of her, and what you are doing to save her from Changó's anger."

He tinkled his bell again, and Aluya reappeared. Moses said, "Bring me my *cuchillo* and a white bowl. And maybe some more of those cookies."

"That's some perfume she's wearing," Decker remarked, as Aluya went to do what she had been asked.

"Esencia Pompeya, one of the three sacred perfumes of Santería."

Aluya reappeared with a white bowl, a white cloth, and a long sharp knife, as well as a brown paper bag of cookies. Moses stood up and indicated with a wave of his hand that Decker and Jonah should do the same. "I will be invoking Changó. We must show respect. Aluya, the candles."

He spread the cloth on the coffee table in front of him and placed the bowl in the center of it. Then he held up the knife and kissed its blade.

Aluya brought over two white candles in silver candlesticks and lit them. Moses then waved at her to leave the room. He stood in front of the candles for a while, with his eyes closed and his head tilted back. Then he began to chant. "*Babamo Changó ikawo ilemu fumi alaya tilanchani nitosi ki ko gbamu mi re oro niglati wa obinu ki kigbo ni na orin oti gbogbo omo nijin gbogbo . . .* "

After a while, he opened his eyes and said, "Please give me the rooster."

Decker pointed at himself. "Me?"

"Yes, you. You are the one who is seeking forgiveness from Changó."

Hesitantly, Decker knelt down and unfastened the catch on the lid of the basket. As soon as he opened it, the rooster exploded into feathery fury, flapping and squawking and pecking at him. He managed to grab one its legs, even though it was scratching him with its claws. Jonah came over and seized its wings and at last he got hold of the other leg, so that he could lift it upside down into the air, still struggling and clucking.

"This chicken sure ain't a chicken chicken," Jonah said.

"Hold him up good and high," Moses instructed. Decker did as he was told, and Moses took hold of the bird's head and stretched its neck. "*Changó, kabio kabio sile*," he intoned, and the cockerel gave one convulsive shudder and then remained strangely still, as if it knew what was going to happen next, and was prepared to accept it.

Moses sliced its throat with his knife and its dark blood dripped quickly into the bowl. He then took the bird's legs from Decker, and began to circle it around in the air. "*Changó alamu oba layo ni na ile ogbomi*," he breathed. "*Kabio kabio sile*."

When the bowl was almost filled with blood, he laid the cockerel down between the candles. "The words *kabio kabio sile* mean welcome to my house," he explained. "I was invoking Changó so that he knows that you are seeking his forgiveness and that you wish to wash away your transgression, whatever it is."

He looked slowly around the living room. "Do you feel anything?" he asked.

"Like what?"

"Like the presence of a great power."

Decker looked around, too. He couldn't be sure that it wasn't just the humidity, and the strange smell of herbs, but he thought he could detect a *tension* in the air, as if a thunderstorm were brewing. And Changó, after all, was the god of thunderstorms.

"Changó hears me," Moses said. "Changó speaks in my ear."

"What does he say?"

"He says he has been waiting many seasons."

"What for? To come looking for me?"

"You are only one among many."

"Can you ask him why he's so mad at me?"

"Changó answers no questions. There is only one way to tell what his wishes are."

He rang his bell again and Aluya came back in. "Aluya, bring me the coconut shells."

While they waited for her, Moses stood with his eyes closed and his hands pressed together as if he were praying. Jonah kept looking uneasily around the room as if he, too, could sense the presence of something dark and powerful.

Aluya returned with a red and green silk scarf. She waited patiently until Moses had opened his eyes again and then she handed it to him without a word. He took hold of one corner of the scarf and whipped it in the air. Four quarters of coconut shell fell out and scattered on the floor.

Moses said, "I was afraid of this."

"What is it?" Decker asked. "What's wrong?"

"You see how all four pieces of coconut have fallen with their brown side upward? This is one of five patterns. When two pieces fall with the brown side upward and two with the white side upward, this is a good sign, and means yes. But when all the pieces fall with the brown side upward, like this, this means no and predicts death."

"So what can I do?"

"You can only cleanse yourself, my friend, and pray that Changó decides that you are truly sorry for whatever it is that you have done. Come back tomorrow, and I will give you the blood and the *omiero*."

With that, he helped himself to another cookie and stood chewing it thoughtfully, staring at Decker with his bulgy eyes as if he had already given him up for dead.

CHAPTER TWENTY-TWO

That afternoon Decker drove around to see Maggie. He parked around the block from Cab's house, as he always did, and walked the rest of the way. Cab and Maggie lived in a single-story three-bedroom house on the south side of the river, opposite Forest Hill Park. It had an orange-tiled roof and a bright yellow door, and elaborately-tied-up nets at the windows. Maggie had a taste in interior décor that reminded Decker of the early editions of *The Cosby Show*.

The summer heat was still stifling and the sky was so dark that Decker took off his sunglasses. His shirt clung to his back and if he hadn't been wearing his shoulder holster he would have taken off his black linen coat.

Maggie was waiting for him and opened the door as he walked up the driveway. Her hair was braided and beaded and she was wearing a loose, flowing dress in diagonal stripes of purple and pink.

She glanced up and down the street and then she put her arms around his neck and gave him a kiss. "I missed you, lover man."

"Yeah, me too. Any chance of a beer?"

She closed the door and led him through to the kitchen. "Cab called and said that he may have to stay in Charlottesville until tomorrow . . . so, if you're interested in some all-night moving . . ."

He took off his coat and his holster while she took a bottle of Heineken out of the icebox, and opened it. "I don't know. We're pretty tied up with these homicides. I'll probably have to go back to headquarters later."

She came up close to him and pressed the cold bottle of beer against his cheek. "You look tired. Maybe you should take off those clothes and come to bed."

"I'm bushed, as a matter of fact."

"Not *too* bushed, I hope?"

"These killings, I think they're beginning to get to me. Every time I think we've got a handle on them, it turns out to be the handle on something so goddamned weird I can't even understand what we're supposed to be looking for, or who, or why."

"Cab was saying that Queen Aché might have something to do with them. Now, that's one evil woman."

"Queen Aché was probably involved in Junior Abraham getting whacked, but as for the other two . . . who knows? We don't have any evidence to connect one with the other, because we don't *have* any evidence."

Maggie kissed him. "You should come to bed. Ease your troubled mind. Exercise your booty."

"You're some red-hot lady, you know that? You're going to wear me out."

She took hold of his hand and tugged him toward the

bedroom. "You know what's on the menu today? The four-course special, with extra gravy."

She unbuttoned his shirt and pulled it off, kissing and nipping his nipples with her teeth. Then she unbuckled his belt and pushed him back into a sitting position on the side of the bed. "Let's get those shoes and socks off. Ain't nothing look more stupider than a bare-ass man in nothing but his shoes and his socks."

Decker swigged his beer. A large-framed photograph of Cab stood on the dressing table opposite him, smiling cheerily, and for the first time since he and Maggie had started fooling around together he felt guilty. He hadn't felt guilt in a long time, ever since Cathy was killed, and it came as a sour, unpleasant surprise, like the sudden taste of copper pennies in his mouth.

Maggie peeled off his socks. "Least your socks don't smell. Cab—whew!—you could use his socks to carry out the death penalty."

"Maggie—"

"You just relax, lover man. This is my time to take care of *you*. Hey—what happened to your *feet?* They're scratched all over."

"Oh, it's nothing. I was helping a friend clear some briars at the back of his property and I was stupid enough not to wear any shoes."

"They look *sore*," she said, giving them a flurry of lipsticky kisses.

"I'll live. Teach me to wear shoes next time."

Maggie tugged down his zipper and wrestled off his pants. Maggie took hold of him through his blue-and-white-striped shorts and gave him a hard squeeze. "And what do we have in here? Don't tell me we'll be having *boudin blanc* for starters?"

"Maggie—" he said, but she pressed her fingers to her lips.

"You hush up. I'm the one giving the orders today."

She took the bottle of beer out of his hand and set it down on the nightstand. Then she hooked her finger into the elastic of his shorts and pulled them down at the front so that his erection was exposed.

"You need refreshment, my man, that's what you need."

She poured cold beer over the swollen plum of his penis so that it ran down between his legs. He jolted upward and said, "Shit, Maggie!" but she laughed that famously dirty laugh and leaned over him and sucked it. Cold one second, hot the next.

Climbing onto the bed beside him, she crossed her arms and lifted her dress over her head. Her breasts were huge, and she had a rounded belly and thighs like an Olympic shot-putter. And then there were all the gold and silver beads that she had woven into her pubic hair, so that she looked as if she were wearing a glittering thong.

She sat astride him and pushed his shoulders down onto the bed. She swung her breasts from side to side so that her prune-black nipples grazed his chest. "I'm going to make you so excited you're going to forget what day of the week it is."

He tried to smile at her, but somehow his heart wasn't in it. He kept thinking of Cathy draped in that sheet, and the sudden burst of blood. He kept thinking of George Drewry, with his intestines piled up in front of him in heaps. He kept thinking of Jerry Maitland, swinging from the hospital window like a grisly parody of a bungee jumper.

"You got to switch yourself off, lover man," Maggie told him. "You got to think about nothing but me, and this bed, and this moment. I know you're off wandering inside your head, but I want you here and now."

Without another word, she took hold of his penis and

guided it inside her. She was very juicy, but all the same he could feel her vaginal muscles rhythmically gripping him, as firmly as fingers. She lifted herself slowly up and down on top of him, sometimes rising so high that he was right on the very edge of slipping out of her, but then lowering her hips again so that he felt as if he were penetrating her soul as well as her body.

She began to hum, as she often did when she was aroused. It was a low, hypnotic humming, like a spiritual, and Decker found that he was gradually calming down. Maggie was dreamily smiling and her breasts were dancing their own slow merengue and there was that persistent lascivious *shlup*, *shlup*, *shlup* as she rose up and down on top of him.

"Nobody knows . . . the feeling you give me. . . . Oh, Lord, nobody knows . . . how deep you go . . ."

Then something flickered across the room, just behind her. It was so fast that Decker couldn't see what it was. It was like a ripple in the air, momentarily distorting the pattern on the wallpaper. He gripped Maggie's thighs to stop her riding up and down, and lifted his head up.

"What's the matter, lover? What's wrong?"

"There's nobody else in the house, is there?"

"Why do you say that? Of course not. It's just me and you and your uncle Willy."

"I thought I saw something, that's all."

"Oh, come on, you're tired and you're stressed. All you need is some good home cooking."

With that, she slowly rotated her hips, around and around, and squashed her breasts in her hands as if she were weighing them and testing them for ripeness.

Decker tried to get back into the mood but he began to shrink. After a few minutes Maggie had to climb off him. She took hold of him and flopped him from side to side.

"What's this?" she demanded, playfully but obviously frustrated. "I didn't order no *eel*."

Decker didn't say anything but rolled off the bed and walked naked through to the kitchen where he had left his shoulder holster hanging on the back of a chair. He pulled out the Colt and went straight to the back door. He jiggled the handle but it was locked.

Maggie came out of the bedroom. "Decker, what's wrong with you, lover? There's nobody here but us adulterers."

He walked past her into the living room, with its white leather couch and its gilded coffee table and its enormous reproduction painting of an orange sunset. Nobody there. Nobody visible, anyhow.

"Come on," Maggie coaxed him. "Come back to bed and let's do some real loving."

Decker reluctantly followed her back to the bedroom. The house was silent, but he was sure that he could hear the faintest of *prickling* sounds, as if somebody or something were moving from room to room, disturbing the molecules in the air. He opened the doors to the second and third bedrooms, and the cleaning closet, too, but there was nobody there, either.

Nobody visible.

They climbed back onto the rumpled bed, and this time Maggie lay on her back. She took hold of Decker's penis and pulled it between her bosoms, stretching it as if it were saltwater taffy. Then she pressed her cleavage tightly together, and said, "Second course. Stuffed breasts of quail," and gave that deep, dirty laugh.

Decker moved up and down on her, and he began to stiffen again. Maggie looked up at him with that sexually luminous smile on her face, and counterrotated her breasts with her hands so that she was massaging him with warm, sweaty flesh.

"You are the lover of the century, Decker. No question. The feelings you give me."

Decker began to feel the clock spring tightening between his legs. Maggie lifted her head and every time his penis bobbed up between her breasts she stuck out her long red tongue and licked it. Decker went faster and faster and his thigh muscles quivered with effort. Maggie let out little squeals and gasps, but Decker could do nothing but pant. At last he could feel his climax rising, and with a sound that was halfway between a snort and a cough he ejaculated over her collarbone, decorating her with a glistening necklace of white pearls.

"*Ohhh*, Decker, you're so *bad*. . . ."

But at that moment Decker opened his eyes, and in the dressing-table mirror he glimpsed a dark gray triangular shape, which was instantly gone. It looked like part of a coat, or a cape, but it disappeared so quickly that it was impossible for him to tell. He scrambled off the bed, picked up his revolver, and ran back into the living room.

Again, nobody there. Not only that, all the doors were locked from the inside and all the windows were closed. Maggie came after him and stood watching as he ducked down to check under the couch, and under the beds in the two spare bedrooms.

"You don't have to worry, Decker," she said, as he opened the closet in the second bedroom. There was something in her voice that made him turn and frown at her. She didn't sound like Maggie at all. None of that throatiness. None of that suggestive banter.

He closed the closet doors. "I don't have to worry about *what?*"

"I'll protect you, I promise. I won't let Saint Barbara harm you."

He went up close to her. "What do you know about Saint Barbara?"

"I know that Saint Barbara is looking for revenge."

"Don't you mean Changó?"

She gave a small, evasive smile. "You can call a god by any name you like. It's still a god."

He stared at her intently. It was then that he realized that her irises were yellow, rather than brown—yellow like a reptile's. Or maybe gold. His mother had once told him that all angels have golden eyes.

"Cathy?" he said.

"You have to find Saint Barbara, Decker, before Saint Barbara finds you. He knows who you are now. He knows where you live. It's only a matter of time."

"Was it Changó who killed the Maitlands? Was it Changó who killed George Drewry?"

"Find Saint Barbara before Saint Barbara finds you."

Decker took hold of her arm. "Cathy, if there's any way that you can—"

Without warning, half of Maggie's head exploded, leaving her with only one eye and only half a face, and plastering Decker in blood and brains.

"*No!*" he screamed. But then her head exploded again, and she twisted around and collapsed onto the carpet. Decker was left with flesh and mucus all over his face, and fragments of bone stuck to his lips.

You bastard!" he shouted, pushing his way back into the living room. "Show yourself, you son of a bitch, where are you?"

He went back to the kitchen and the master bedroom but there was still nobody there. "I'm coming to get you!" he yelled. "I'm coming to get you and you're going to suffer for this!"

It was then that he saw himself in the mirror, naked, with his gun in his hand, but not bloodied at all. He looked at himself for a moment, and he was just about to go back to the second bedroom when Maggie reappeared, intact, unharmed, and still wearing his rapidly drying necklace.

"Decker," she said. She went up to him and put her arms around him and held him close. "I don't know what's wrong, Decker, but I think you need some help."

"I'm fine, I'm okay. I'm stressed, that's all."

She shushed him by kissing her fingertips and touching his lips. "This is not the right time for us, lover man. Maybe it never was. This is the time to say that it was fun while it lasted."

He looked into her eyes and they were darkest brown. "Yes," he admitted. "Maybe you're right. It was fun while it lasted."

She sat and watched him as he dressed, and then unloaded his revolver and kissed each of the bullets. "There's some kind of fire burning inside you, Decker Martin," she said. "I hope you find a way to put it out."

CHAPTER TWENTY-THREE

The storm broke just after eleven o'clock. Lightning walked up the James River like the Martian tripods in *The War of the Worlds*. Thunder bellowed all the way across the city from Mechanicsville to Bon Air, and the rain crashed down in such torrents that the storm drains all along Canal Street and Dock Street were gushing water and the Richmond Fire Department was called to pump out basements and cellars all along the waterfront.

John Mason left Appleby's Restaurant on East Main Street just two minutes shy of midnight, and it was still raining hard. He hadn't brought an umbrella to work that afternoon but he had looked in the lost-property closet and borrowed a ladies' umbrella with splashy red poppies on it and three broken spokes. It didn't do much to keep him dry. The rain was clattering down so fiercely that it bounced off the sidewalk and soaked the bottom of his pants.

John had celebrated his thirtieth birthday last week and the rest of the staff at Appleby's had arranged for a Strip-A-Gram. In the photographs, with a half-naked redhead perched on his knee, John looked as if he had just been electrocuted, his thin mousy hair standing up on end and his teeth clenched. The red eyes hadn't helped, either.

John liked girls, but he had always found it difficult to talk to them. Edmundo, who worked in the kitchens with him, had a gorgeous black-haired girlfriend called Rita, and the way Edmundo spoke to Rita always amazed him. Do this, Rita, do that, Rita, bring me this, bring me that, shut up your face, you za-za. And yet Rita adored Edmundo and was always nuzzling him and kissing him. John was sure that if he spoke to a girl like that he would have his face slapped, twice, once in each direction.

All the same, he was fixed to go on a date tomorrow with a girl called Stephanie, to the TheatreVirginia on Grove Avenue to see *I Love You, You're Perfect, Now Change*. In actual fact Stephanie was a friend of his sister Paula and the only reason he had been invited was to make a foursome with Paula's boyfriend, Carl. John hated Carl. He was a six-foot-four-inch loudmouth who sold paneling and who was forever slapping John on the back and calling him "chief." But he liked Stephanie. She was quiet, with large glasses, and lank brown hair, and she enjoyed walking and reading and all the other solitary activities that John did.

He hailed a taxi and it pulled into the curb and drenched him in filthy rainwater up to his knees. The cabbie looked like the late Scatman Crothers, from *The Shining*. "Hell of a night," he said, as John climbed into the backseat, struggling to fold his broken umbrella.

"Sure is. May Street, please. Corner of Grove."

As the cabbie drove off, John sniffed and realized that there was a strong acidic smell in the back of the taxi. What was more, the seat of his pants was soaked. He rubbed his hand on the vinyl seat and then he sniffed his fingers. Somebody had vomited in the taxi and he had sat in it.

"Stop!" he shouted, rapping on the partition.

The cabbie said, "What?"

"I said stop! Somebody's puked on the seat!"

"Somebody's what?"

At last the cabbie pulled into the curbside again. John climbed out and said, "Somebody's puked on the seat. For Pete's sake, look at my pants."

"Shit," the cabbie said. "Just started my shift, too. Why don't folks keep their previously enjoyed food to themselves?"

John had to walk the rest of the way home. The umbrella refused to open and in any case he didn't really care if he got any wetter than he already was. Every time he breathed in he caught the sharp smell of vomit—alcohol and seafood and tomatoes.

Home was a second-story apartment he shared with his widowed mother on May Street, at the back of an ugly, squarish, brown-brick building that had been built in the 1900s as a hostel for disturbed children. John let himself in and trudged up the steep dark stairs. He had to feel his way because the lightbulb on the landing had gone again. The building's super was a shriveled monkey of a man and probably the most argumentative person that John had ever known. He would refuse to change lightbulbs because the sun was going to come up in only a few hours, and they wouldn't be needed anymore.

John opened the door to his mother's apartment. The living room was gloomy and smelled of dead-flower water. The kitchen door was a few inches ajar and as usual John's mother had left the portable television flickering with the sound turned off. He took off his soaking-wet shoes and left them on the welcome mat behind the door. Then he tippy-toed across the carpet to the kitchen. His mother had left a plate of chocolate-chip cookies on the table and a note saying *Please take my yellow dress to the cleaners tomorrow.*

On the TV screen, Vincent Price was desperately trying to escape the fire in *House of Wax*. John switched it off and went along the corridor toward the bathroom.

"Johnsy?" his mother called. "You're home late."

"I couldn't get a cab."

"You're not wet, are you?"

He opened the door to his mother's bedroom. She was sitting up in bed with a white scarf on her head so that she looked as if she had been having chemotherapy. She was a very thin woman, with an almond-pale face and smudges of grief under her eyes. She always gave the impression that if anybody touched her they would cause her actual physical pain.

"You're *drenched*," she said. "Get out of those clothes and run yourself a nice hot bath."

Lightning flashed behind the brown floral drapes, and then almost immediately the house was shaken by deafening thunder, as if somebody had tipped a mahogany wardrobe down the stairs.

"Some storm, huh?" John said. "The whole of Dock Street was flooded."

"What did you have to eat tonight? You ate, didn't you?"

"Sure, I had fried chicken."

"You and your fried chicken. Your father loved his fried chicken, too."

"Right—I'd better take a bath." His pants were sticking to him and he didn't want to get into one of those long reminiscences about his father. He had only been seven when his father was killed, and he could barely remember him. He knew what he *looked* like, of course: There were photographs everywhere. But what he had *felt* like, and *smelled* like, and what his voice had actually sounded like, he couldn't bring to mind. His father didn't even visit him in dreams.

He always wore his father's Marine Corps ring, but it had never imparted any feeling of what kind of man his father had been.

"Can I bring you anything?" he asked his mother.

She smiled and shook her head. "I've taken my tablets already. You get yourself to bed."

John went to the bathroom and disgustedly pulled down his pants. The rain had washed off most of the half-digested food, but there were still flecks of crab and fragments of tomato on them and he put them in the basin and sluiced them in tepid water. At the same time he turned on the old-fashioned brass faucets to run a bath. He would have preferred a shower, but the washer had worn out and the super hadn't gotten around to fixing it. "You think washers grow on trees?"

While the bath was running, he went into his bedroom. It was a long, narrow room, with a single sawed-oak bed with a dark brown candlewick throw and his pajamas neatly folded on the pillow. All along the wall beside the bed were photographs of classic automobiles—Hudson Hornets and Chevrolet Bel Airs and Packard Hawks—as well as pennants for Richmond's soccer team, the Kickers. John had once stuck up a picture of Pamela Anderson in a wet T-shirt, but his mother had looked at it with such a disappointed expression that he had taken it down.

He looked out of the window. Rainwater was spouting from a broken gutter into the darkened yard below. There was a dazzling flash of lightning and another crash of thunder. It felt as if the storm were right above his head.

He went back into the bathroom and climbed cautiously into the bathtub. Apart from having to walk most of the way home he had worked a double shift today and he felt bone-tired. He lay back and stared at the ceiling. What would his father have thought of him, if he could see him now? A chef in a family diner, instead of a captain in the marines. Pecan pie instead of *semper fi*.

He soaped his hair and plunged himself under the water to rinse it, his eyes screwed tight shut and his fingers in his ears. As he came up for air, he saw that the bathroom door was wide open.

Odd, he thought. He never left the bathroom door open. His mother wasn't the kind of woman who would sit on the toilet talking to him while he had a bath. In fact she appeared to find sex and nudity not just embarrassing but deeply distasteful. She called it "that sort of thing." John occasionally wondered how he had managed to be conceived at all.

"Mom?" he called out, but there was no answer. She always took two Seconals when she went to bed, so she was probably dead to the world by now.

He stood up in the bath and reached over to the door to close it. But as he did so he was suddenly taken by the feeling that there was somebody standing in the doorway. He couldn't see anybody, but he thought he could hear steady, slightly harsh breathing. It was difficult to be sure, because the bathwater was still slopping from side to side, and thunder was still rumbling over the rooftop, but he could sense a tension in the air, a *nearness*.

He lowered his left hand to cover himself. "Who's there?" he said, half expecting his mother to appear.

No answer. But the sensation that somebody was standing very close to him was even stronger now. He moved his hand toward the door, waving it from side to side as if he were feeling his way in the dark.

There was an immense explosion of thunder, and at the same time something sharp and pointed jabbed him in the right eye, bursting his eyeball. He let out a high-pitched scream and fell backward into the bath with a loud slap of water, knocking his head against the tiles. He grabbed the handrail and tried to sit up, his hand cupping his eye, and he felt a large blob of optic jelly slither between his fingers and slide down his cheek. The pain was unbearable—as if somebody had stuck a red-hot poker into his eye socket.

"*God-oh-God-oh-God-oh-God,*" he babbled, trying to climb out of the bath. "*Mom! Mom! Help me! My eye!*"

He managed to twist himself around and get himself up on one knee, but then he was roughly pushed back down again, and he actually felt hands gripping him, hands in coarse leather gloves.

"*Get off me!*" he screamed. "*Jesus, get off me!*"

But one of the hands gripped his hair and his head was forced under the bathwater. He could hear the watery clonking of his knees against the side of the tub as he struggled to get free, and the crackling of his hair being wrenched out by the roots, but the hand wouldn't let him go. His whole head felt as if it were caving in.

Just when he thought he couldn't hold his breath for a second longer, the hand pulled him up again. He gasped and spluttered and opened his remaining eye, expecting to see who was trying to drown him, but there was still nobody there.

"*Let me go, let me go, let me go!*" he begged, and there was a moment's pause. He tried again to sit up, but then something sharp stuck into his left eye, too, and everything went black.

"*I'm blind!*" he screamed. "*You've blinded me!*"

He thrashed in the bath from side to side, kicking and

yammering and letting out whoops of agony. He clawed at the air, trying to find his assailant, trying to climb out, but every time he found the handrail his fingers were pried away from it and he was pushed back into the water.

"What do you want?" he gibbered, and then whooped again because his eyes hurt so much.

There was no answer. He tried one more time to get out of the bath, but when he was forced back yet again, he cowered in the water with his hands over his face and just prayed that this was all a nightmare and that he hadn't been blinded after all and that he would soon wake up and it would be morning.

He thought the water felt hotter than it had before, but that was probably because his injuries had made him more sensitive. Soon, however, he realized that it actually *was* hotter. Not only that, it was increasing in heat as quickly as the water in a kettle. He sat up and reached blindly for the faucets, but when he found them they were both turned off. The water was heating up spontaneously, and it was already scalding his buttocks and his legs.

"*What are you doing to me?*" he screeched. "*Let me get out, let me get out!*"

Again he struggled and kicked, but again he was pushed back into the water. It was so hot now that he felt as if his entire body was burning, and he could hear a deep, thick bubbling noise as it rapidly rose to boiling point.

His agony lasted for less than a minute, but during that minute he discovered hell. He went into total shock, his legs and his arms quivering, his fists gripped tight. He had never thought that pain like this was possible.

The bathwater came to a rolling boil and for the final few seconds of his life he was cooking alive.

CHAPTER TWENTY-FOUR

When Decker walked into his office the next morning, gripping a fifteen-slice pastrami sandwich between his teeth and carrying a cup of espresso and three thick folders under his arm, Sandra and Eunice Plummer were already waiting for him. Sandra was wearing a flowery green dress and a medicine-pink cardigan. Sitting in the corner in a triangle of bright sunlight, she looked simple but saintly. Eunice was wearing a beige pantsuit and a look of irritation.

Decker said, "Mmm, mmm," and jerked his head to indicate that they should follow him over to his desk. He took the sandwich out of his mouth and laid it on top of Erin Malkman's autopsy report on George Drewry. "Good to see you again, Sandra. How can I help?"

"I asked her not to come," Eunice said, her brown vinyl purse clutched firmly in her lap. "But she stamped her foot and said she was going to see you whether I liked it or not."

"I saw him again," Sandra said. "The So-Scary Man."

"You did? Where?"

"I saw him at the station. He was going through the door."

"You mean Main Street Station?"

"That's right," Eunice said. "She says he crossed East Main Street and walked straight across the sidewalk and into the entrance."

"Do you think he might have seen *you*?"

Sandra shook her head. "I don't think so. He looked like he was in a big hurry."

"What time was this?"

"About 4:45 yesterday afternoon," Eunice said. "Sandra wanted to call you right away but I tried to persuade her not to. I'm sorry, maybe I'm wrong, but I really don't want her to get mixed up in this."

Decker sat down and pried the lid off his coffee. "I don't blame you, Ms. Plummer. But this kind of information could be really helpful. It means that whoever he is—*whatever* he is—he's still in the downtown area. If we can work out his behavior patterns . . . well, maybe we can find him, and find out how he manages to make himself unnoticed."

Sandra nodded enthusiastically and said, "We should go look for him."

"No you shouldn't," Eunice said. "You should go back home and finish your schoolwork. You've told Lieutenant Martin what you wanted to tell him, and now we should leave him in peace."

"I think your mom's right," Decker told her. "This is a city with nearly a quarter of a million people living in it. Where are we going to start looking?"

"The *station*," Sandra insisted.

"Just because you saw him at the station yesterday that

doesn't mean he's going to be there now. And what would he be doing there? It's all building work and renovations. There wouldn't be any place for him to stay."

"That's where he comes from," Sandra insisted. "I just *know*."

Decker suddenly remembered the drawing of Main Street Station hanging by the fireplace in Eunice Plummer's apartment. The dark cloud over it, which looked more like tangled black snakes. And what had Eunice told him? "She calls it the Fun House."

"*How* do you know?" he asked her.

Sandra touched her fingertips to her forehead. "I can see it. I can see him going up the stairs."

"You did a drawing of the station, didn't you? A very good one. But it had some kind of a cloud hanging over it."

"I saw it. Only it wasn't a cloud. It was a bad thing."

"A bad thing? What do you mean by that?"

"When people do wrong. When people hate people. That's what it's like."

Eunice said, "I'm sorry, Lieutenant. I really think that this is enough."

"You wouldn't consider letting me take Sandra down to the station for a look around?"

"You've said yourself that this man could be vengeful, especially if he knows that Sandra can see him, and identify him."

"Well, you're right, of course. And the last thing I want to do is expose Sandra to any danger."

"I *want* to look for him," Sandra said, drumming her heels on the floor. "It would be like hide-and-go-seek."

Decker shook his head. "I'm sorry, Sandra. If Mom says no, then it's no. But I'll go check the station myself, and if I find anything I'll tell you."

* * *

Decker and Hicks climbed the dark stone stairway from East Main Street to the second-floor lobby of Main Street Station, deafened at every step by weird, distorted banging and hammering.

They reached the lobby itself, where workers in hard hats were digging up the flooring and chipping the walls back to the bare brick. In spite of the noise and the dust and the snaking hydraulic hoses, the lobby was still awesome, with its tall columns and its high arched windows and its coffered ceiling. From here, Virginia's soldiers had departed for two world wars and Vietnam, and vacationers boarded for Buckroe Beach, as well as students bound for northern colleges and salesmen heading to new territory out West.

A short sandy man in blue overalls came over to greet them, carrying two red hard hats. "Lieutenant Martin? How do you do. Mike Verdant, I'm the project engineer. Have to ask you to put these on, I'm afraid."

"Thanks," Decker said. "Quite an operation you've got going here."

"It's going pretty good. We should have trains running by December on the eastern side, on the old Chesapeake and Ohio tracks, and then we can open up the Seaboard Line."

"History, huh?"

"Oh, for sure. Amtrak closed this station down in 1975 and shifted all of their rail operations out to the suburbs, because they thought that the interstate was going to kill off rail travel. But . . . here we are again. Opening it all up. Here, let me show you something."

He led them across the echoing lobby to the western side of the station, where workmen in white overalls were drilling up the floor. He picked up a piece of flooring and crumbled it between finger and thumb.

"You see this flooring? Black cinder ash, from the old coal-burning locomotives. You add water and it holds up pretty well."

Decker sniffed and looked around. "Any place here that somebody could hide?"

Michael Verdant stood up, dusting his hands. "Not sure what you mean. We've had a couple of down-and-outs in here lately."

"No, I mean any place that somebody could actually *live* in."

"I don't see how. There's too much work going on. During the day we're renovating the walls and the flooring. Over there—you see over there?—we took down all of the terracotta sculptures and we're having them molded and recast. Then we're stripping out all of the asbestos, we have to do that during the night, because of safety regulations. Nobody could set up camp here, wouldn't be possible."

Decker breathed in the smell of old plaster and pulverized brick. The lobby echoed with hammer drills and pickaxes, but he was sure he could sense something else here too. The Old South, which had depended on tobacco and cotton and slavery and free opinion, breathing its defiant last.

Richmond had once been the Secessionist capital. Now it was a tourist attraction, with antique stores and teddy-bear shops and plantation cruises on riverboats, lunch and dinner included, and the only men in gray were the guides at the National Battlefield Park.

Michael Verdant said, "Come on, follow me." He led them upstairs, to the fourth and fifth levels, through sheets of dusty plastic and sanded-down doors, until they came to a metal ladder in the corner. He climbed it as swiftly as a big sandy ape, and Decker and Hicks followed. They found themselves out on the balcony of the clock tower, their hair blown by the warm midday wind. Below them, traffic streamed along the interstate, which curved beneath the station only twenty feet away. But off to their right, they could see all the way down the Shockoe Valley, where the James River glittered, and ships were moored, and the woody hills were hazed with summer blue.

"Finest view of the city there is."

Decker turned around. Above him the four clock faces were creeping closer to noon, and he could hear the stealthy creeping of their automated movement.

"How about the lower levels?" he asked. "Any chance that somebody could be hiding themselves there?"

Michael Verdant led them back down to the gloomy, echoing train shed, 530 feet long, the size of a zeppelin hangar, with a gable roof. "This is where the Greyhound buses are going to be coming in. Not sure about the second level, though. It's like three football fields put together."

They went back down the stairway to the East Main Street entrance, and Michael Verdant unclipped a flashlight from his belt and showed them a deep excavation of rubble and old brickwork. "We're putting in a ramp here, for wheelchair users, and people who lug their bags on wheels. We found this old brick foundation when we started to excavate, and at first we thought it could be a wharf, because the old Shockoe Creek used to come in here."

"You're kidding me."

"No, it used to be deep enough for fishing boats. But this wall is probably later than that, 1920s or thereabouts. A whole lot of different building work has gone on here, over the years, levels on top of levels. It's like opening up Tutankhamen's tomb."

Decker peered into the darkness. "Is that a basement?"

"No, there's no basement. I guess the original planners were too worried about floods, this close to the river. There's a crawl space, but that's it."

"You think anybody could hide in there?"

"Pretty unlikely. It's damp and it's dark and it's suffocating. And you never know when the tide's going to come pouring in."

"Okay," Decker said. "Thanks for showing us around."

Michael Verdant gave him a dry, strong handshake. "Glad I could help. Make sure you come back when we're open for business. You won't believe this place, I can promise you."

As they walked back to Decker's car, Hicks said, "You want to tell me why we came here?"

"I don't know. I was given a tip-off, that's all. I just wanted to check."

"What tip-off?"

Decker turned around and looked up at the clock tower and the dormer windows with their red terra-cotta tiles. The station looked more like a palace out of *Grimm's Fairy Tales* than a twentieth-century railroad terminus.

"Do you get any vibrations out of that place?" he asked.

"*Vibrations?* You mean apart from jackhammering? Like what?"

"Like—I don't know. Like something very bad is hiding there."

Hicks shook his head. "You should ask Rhoda. She's the one who's into vibrations. Me—well, you know me, Lieutenant. I prefer procedure to witchcraft, any day."

"In that case, you definitely won't be happy about where we're going next."

CHAPTER TWENTY-FIVE

He parked outside Moses Adebolu's building and shouted, "Come on, Hicks! You should find this very instructive. It'll take you back to your ethnic roots."

"What ethnic roots? I was born in Fairview Beach."

The same kids were playing with rat bones on the steps. Decker took out a pack of fresh-mint gum and gave them a stick each. "Watch my car, okay?"

"So who's this we're going to see?" Hicks asked, dubiously.

They climbed up the creaking stairs. Somebody on the floor above was having a shouting match, and there was a clatter like saucepans being thrown.

Decker said, "You're going to meet Moses. He's a *santero*. One of the best, according to Jonah. Yesterday we sacrificed a rooster and today he's going to give me my *omiero*."

"What the hell is an *omiero?*"

"It's my magic antidemon potion. Rooster blood and herbs. I have to take a bath in it and then the great god

Changó might forgive me for whatever it is I've done to piss him off."

They had reached the second-story landing, under the headless image of John the Baptist. Hicks stopped and said, "Wait up a second, Lieutenant. Are you *serious* about this?"

"Never more so. You saw that image of Cathy that Rhoda conjured up. Whatever's happening here, it's supernatural, whether we like it or not. Or at the very least it involves some pretty weird influences. So it's no good trying to hunt it down with procedure. It's Santería magic, and that means we're going to have to use Santería magic to find it."

"Have you talked to the captain about this?"

"Cab? Uh-huh. It'll only make him sneeze."

"Well . . . I know what I saw when Rhoda did that séance, and I'll agree with you that it was something extremely strange. But what are we really talking about here?"

Decker laid a hand on his shoulder. "If we can safely believe Moses Adebolu, which from all the evidence I believe we can, then all we are up against is the single most vengeful god in the whole of the Santería religion."

"And that's his name? Changó?"

"You got it."

"All right," Hicks said. "Supposing I go along with this. Supposing it's true. What's this goddamned god so goddamned vengeful about?"

"I have no idea, specifically. But the nightmares I've been having . . . and the way that the victims were killed . . . I think it has something to do with the Civil War, and with the Battle of the Wilderness in particular."

"You're talking about the Devil's Brigade?"

Decker nodded.

"But all that happened in 1864. Over 140 years ago."

"I know. But gods don't die, do they? Not so long as people

go on believing in them. Maybe they don't die even if people *don't* go on believing them. They're not fairies, after all. They're part of the earth, part of the sky, part of everything."

"I don't want to step out of line, Lieutenant, but you're beginning to sound, well—this is kind of *Lord of the Rings* here."

"Come talk to Moses, see if he doesn't change your mind."

Decker knocked on Moses Adebolu's multicolored door. He waited patiently, turning to Hicks and lifting his eyebrows. "You wait till you meet this guy. He's a character. And you should see his daughter. That's if she *is* his daughter, which I seriously question."

He knocked again. "All right," Moses called. "I can hear you, my friend. I just have to pull up my pants."

They could hear him shuffling toward the door. As the handle turned, however, there was an extraordinary *warping* sensation in the air, as if the whole of perception had been twisted. This was instantly followed by a sharp, intense sucking sound, like a high wind, which Decker instantly recognized—oxygen being dragged violently into Moses' apartment through every crack and crevice around the door.

"*Down!*" he shouted at Hicks, and football-tackled him across the landing.

Hicks, sprawling, said, "What? What is it?"

"*Down! Get downstairs!*"

He shoved Hicks square in the back and Hicks lost his balance and went tumbling and bumping down to the hallway. Decker himself seized hold of the banister rails and swung himself down, six stairs at a time, like an acrobat.

As they reached the front door, there was a shattering explosion, and the whole building seemed to jump sideways.

Chunks of plaster dropped from the ceiling, rails were ripped up like railroad tracks, and what was left of the John the Baptist window burst apart in a million sparkling fragments.

Hicks stared at Decker and his face was white with plaster dust and shock.

"Was that a *bomb?*"

Decker was busy jabbing out the fire department number on his cell phone. "God knows. Come on."

Up above them, doors were opening and people were shouting and screaming. A large section of the third-story staircase had collapsed, and lumps of plaster were still falling down the stairwell. Decker shouted, "Police! Don't panic! We're going to get you out of here!"

He approached Moses' door. All the paint on it was already blistered, and only one painted eye remained, staring at him with the serene knowledge that all things must pass. He cautiously touched the door handle but it was too hot for him to try turning it. There was no smoke coming out from underneath the door. Instead, the air from the landing was still being steadily sucked *inward*, with a soft whistling sound, which told him that the interior of the apartment must be incandescent.

"Hicks, come on, sport—let's get these people out of here. This building doesn't have long."

A woman with dreadlocks and a black leather minidress was leaning over from the landing above, screaming, "I got to get my clothes! I got to get my DVDs!"

"Lady, no chance. This house is going to be ashes in two minutes flat."

Hicks and Decker stood at the foot of the third-story stairs and helped the residents to jump over the gap. The woman with the dreadlocks; an elderly woman in a holey bathrobe, carrying a cat; a young man with a shaven head and muscles; a middle-aged woman with a head scarf and dangly earrings.

When the last of them was clambering down the stairs to safety, Hicks turned to Decker and nodded toward Moses' door. "What about him?"

"Don't even think about it. Whatever happened in there, he's toast. We try to get in there, we're toast, too. Let's go."

They followed the residents down to the hallway. Decker was only halfway down, however, when Moses' door burst open. A huge fireball roared out of it, and flames rolled across the ceiling, setting fire to the hanging lampshade and the banister. Decker felt the heat blasting against his face and he clamped his hand on top of his head to prevent his hair from being singed.

Moses Adebolu appeared at the top of the stairs, staggering like a zombie, and he was blazing from head to foot. His clothes had been burned off him and his skin was shriveling. The heat from the blast had been so intense that his glasses were welded to his face, and the TV-like lenses had turned milky white.

"*Changó!*" he screamed. "*Changó!*" His voice sounded as if it had been wrenched out of his lungs with red-hot pincers.

"Fire extinguisher!" Decker told Hicks, and Hicks jumped down the front steps and crossed the road to the car. Decker took off his coat and climbed the stairs again, holding the coat up in front of him to shield himself from the heat.

Moses swayed, and then he toppled down the stairs, still blazing. Decker had to jump out of the way as his burning body cartwheeled past him, all fiery arms and legs. He fell all the way down to the hallway where he lay with flames flickering down his back, more like a black, crunched-up insect than a man. Hicks came back with the fire extinguisher and squirted foam all over him, but it was obvious that he was dead.

Decker went back upstairs to see if there was any chance of saving Aluya, but Moses' apartment was so fiercely ablaze that he couldn't even make it up to the landing. The fire was actually *bellowing*, as if it were furiously angry. Decker went back outside and made sure that everybody was standing well back. A crowd was gathering and every time another window shattered they let out a strange, long-drawn-out moan.

"My DVDs," wailed the woman with the dreadlocks.

"Any sign of the girl?" Hicks asked.

Decker wiped the sweat and smudges from his face. "Couldn't get close enough. If she *is* in there, she wouldn't have stood a chance."

They watched the flames waving from the second-story window. One of the drapes blew out and flew off into the morning sky, like a burning ghost.

"Think it was a natural gas explosion?" Hicks asked.

"Who knows? Moses had all kinds of herbs and potions and stuff. Maybe he had something inflammable."

The first fire truck arrived, its siren wailing and its horn blasting. Then another, and another.

As the firefighters unrolled their hoses, Decker looked behind him, underneath the shadow of I-95. Aluya was standing there, in an orange Indian-style silk pantsuit, with an orange silk scarf on her head. She was holding a woven shopping bag filled with celery and other vegetables.

Decker went over to her. "I'm sorry . . . there was some kind of explosion. Your father didn't make it."

She stared at him with her huge brown eyes as if she couldn't understand what he was talking about.

"Is there any place you can go?" he coaxed her. "Any relatives?"

"My father is dead?"

"I'm really sorry. The whole place went up, just like that. Where have you been, shopping? You were lucky you weren't inside."

"It was Changó."

"What?"

"It was Changó. I told him not to defy Changó."

"I don't think that he was defying him. It was more like he was trying to appease him."

"Changó wants his revenge on you. If Changó wants his revenge, he will never rest until he has it. *Owani irosun*, the greatest vengeance. My father thought that he could be greater than Changó, and this was the price. Changó warned him, with the coconut shells, but he didn't listen."

"I'm sorry," Decker said. Behind him, he heard the fire pumps starting up. "What are you going to do now?"

"I will stay with my sister."

"Okay . . . but if there's anything I can do . . ."

She looked at him for a long time without saying anything. Then she turned and began to walk away.

"I'll need to get in touch with you!" Decker called after her. "I have to ask you some questions, and we'll probably need you to identify your father's body!"

"You will find me when you need me," Aluya called back.

Decker caught up with her and took hold of her arm. "Listen," he said.

She shook her head. "You're not the man you once were, Lieutenant. Changó has put his mark on you, and there is no more time for you to do the things you once did. You will scarcely have time to panic."

"Well, that's honest, even if it's not exactly reassuring."

"My father also used to read the cowrie shells, Lieutenant, as well as the coconuts. He read his own shells last night, and no matter how they fell, the pattern always brought *ossogbo*, which is not good. The last pattern was *oggunda oche*, which means that the dead are angry."

"I still need to know how to get in touch with you."

"No, you don't. You need to find Changó and discover what it is that he wants from you. Otherwise you will not live longer than two goings-down of the sun."

With that, she walked away, with her shopping bag swinging. Hicks came up to Decker and said, "What was *that* all about?"

"You want it in words of one syllable? I'm in shitsville."

"That's two syllables."

CHAPTER TWENTY-SIX

Soon after they returned to headquarters, Sergeant Novick came up to Decker's office with a large yellow envelope. Novick was tall and hesitant, with a chestnut cowlick and spectacles that you could have used to start a campfire, but he was one of the best photographic experts on the force.

"I had a piece of luck with this one, Lieutenant," he said, taking out a glossy black-and-white print.

"Jesus, I could use some luck. Tell me."

Novick laid the print down in front of him. It was a blown-up detail of the photograph that Decker had taken from the Maitland home: a Confederate soldier in a slouch hat decorated with black rags and a long gray greatcoat. It was surprisingly sharp and clear, and Decker could see that the man had a long, stern face with angular cheekbones and deep-set eyes. His nose was hooked as if it had been broken, and he was heavily bearded.

Novick said, "The image was not only out of focus, because this man was standing in the background, but it was blurred, too, because he'd moved during the exposure. But what I did was to make a digital image of the original photograph, and enlarge the pixels so that I could examine the picture in minute detail. Then I could filter out the blurred pixels and crisp up the image by making a computerized analysis of what the guy would have looked like if he'd kept still."

"What's it like to be incomprehensible, Novick? Does it interfere with your social life or anything?"

"I'll tell you something, Lieutenant, I'm proud of this piece of work. And I'm even prouder because I've found out who he is."

"You're not serious?"

"Oh yes." Novick rummaged in his envelope again and produced another print. "I went to the library this morning and looked through *The Confederate Army in Photographs*. All I was looking for were more pictures by the same photographer, but look what I found."

It was unmistakably the same man, photographed in a studio, with a painted landscape of trees and cliffs in the background. He was wearing a slouch hat, but without the rags, and a neatly buttoned tunic. He was thickly bearded, but his beard was much trimmer than it was in the photograph taken during the Battle of the Wilderness.

Underneath, the caption read CAPTAIN JOSEPH SHROUD, OF KERSHAW'S DIVISION OF THE FIRST ARMY CORPS, OCTOBER 17, 1863.

Decker opened his drawer and took out a copy of Sandra's drawing. "Look at this. Sandra's So-Scary Man. No doubt about it. It's the same guy."

Novick leaned over his shoulder and pointed to Shroud's hat. "You see these . . . they're not rags at all, even though they look like them. I blew them up even more and they're *feathers*."

"So the So-Scary Man was one of the Devil's Brigade," Hicks said. "And it looks like Maitland's great-great-grandfather was too."

Decker said, "We need to know more about this. Something happened during the Battle of the Wilderness—something so bad that it refuses to go away. I think I need to go back down to Fort Monroe—see if I can't dig something out of the archives."

Cab came into the office, with his necktie loose, looking sweaty and harassed, and holding up a dispatch note.

"Hi, Captain. How was Charlottesville?"

"Forget Charlottesville. Uniform just called in another homicide, 1881 May Street."

"Can't you give it to Rudisill? I think we've got ourselves a hook on the Maitland case."

"This could be connected to the Maitland case. The apartment was locked on the inside. Nobody saw nobody enter and nobody saw nobody leave. Besides that, the method of killing was bizarre, to say the least. The guy had his eyes poked out, and apparently he was scalded."

Decker stood up and put on his coat. "In that case, I think we'd better go take a look. Hicks?"

Erin Malkman was already there when they arrived, snapping on her latex gloves.

"We can't go on meeting like this," Decker said.

Erin gave him a humorless grimace. "You're going to have fun with this one."

Decker and Hicks went through to the bathroom. John Mason was still floating in the bathtub, facedown. His skin was lobster red and he was grossly swollen. Erin rolled him over so that Decker could see his bloodied eye sockets.

"What's that smell?"

Erin stirred the bathwater. "Meat stock, to put it bluntly. This man was boiled for at least twenty minutes."

"Boiled? How could he be boiled?"

"Whoever did this to him found a way to raise the water temperature to one hundred degrees Celsius and keep it there."

"How is that possible?"

"I have no idea. Maybe he had some kind of portable heating element with him, like an immersion heater."

"This gets crazier."

A uniform came in with a notebook. "Victim's name is John Ledger Mason, aged thirty. Single, domiciled here with his widowed mother, Ivy Mason."

"His mother didn't see anything?"

"She takes sleeping pills. In fact she couldn't sleep too well during the night so she took two more than usual, which totally knocked her out."

"When did she last see her son?"

"Late yesterday evening. He works as a chef at Appleby's Family Restaurant on East Main Street. He told her good night and went to take a bath. As I say, she woke up at about three in the morning and took more sleeping pills, and she eventually woke up well past eleven o'clock.

"She called the victim and when he didn't answer she looked into his bedroom. His bed was made and the drapes were open, so she assumed that he had gone out. She didn't go into the bathroom until nearly one o'clock, because she wanted to change the towels."

"Where is she now?"

"One of the neighbors is taking care of her. Apartment eight."

"Anybody else see anything?"

"Nope. No sign of forced entry, either. The victim's bedroom window was open a couple of inches, but there's no possible access from outside."

Erin said, "You notice the bruising on his shoulders? It looks as if somebody was holding him down."

Decker and Hicks went across to apartment 8, where John's mother was sitting at her neighbor's kitchen table, looking even more pallid than usual, especially since she was wearing a bright red dress. Her neighbor was a fat woman with greasy gray hair and slippers that made a flapping noise as she walked around the kitchen.

Decker showed his badge. "The officer downstairs tells me you didn't see anything or hear anything?"

"That's right," she whispered.

"Well, maybe God was taking care of you, ma'am. Whoever killed your son was a very ruthless individual indeed. Who knows what he might have done to you?"

"John was always such a gentle boy. Why would anybody want to kill anyone so gentle?"

"We're going to do our best to find that out. You can't think of anybody who might have harbored a grudge against him? Anybody who might have wanted to do him harm?"

"He always kept to himself. He never argued with anyone, even if they upset him. He always used to say 'grin and bear it.'"

"Mrs. Mason . . . I gather you're a widow. What did your late husband do?"

"He was a printer. He used to work for CadmusMack."

"His family didn't have any military connections?"

She frowned at him, and then she shook her head. "Not that I know of. Why?"

"You don't happen to have a Mason family tree, do you?"

"What would that have to do with somebody killing John?"

"I'm not sure. But it would help me if I knew something about your late husband's antecedents. Especially his great-great-grandfather."

"I'm sorry, I don't think I can help you. Bill didn't get on with his family at all well, especially his father."

"Was he a Richmond man?"

"Born in Petersburg. But his family moved to Richmond when he was very young."

"All right, then. Thanks anyhow."

On the way downstairs, Decker said to Hicks, "We need to check the Mason family history, right back to the Civil War. I want to know if any of John Mason's forefathers was assigned to the Devil's Brigade."

Hicks said, "Okay, Lieutenant, but—"

"But what? But you have a better idea? A guy just got poached to death back there and you have some procedural explanation?"

"I just think that we shouldn't lose sight of the possibility that there could be a logical, nonsupernatural solution to this."

"Don't try to get all Sherlock Holmesy on me, Hicks. Sherlock Holmes wasn't always right. All those things that happened to Jerry Maitland and George Drewry and this poor bastard weren't just improbable, they were impossible, but the only way we're going to crack this case is if we start believing that sometimes impossible things can actually happen. Things that *seem* to be impossible, anyhow."

"Like a Santería god, taking his revenge?"

"Why not? Millions of people all over the world believe in Santería. People in Africa and Haiti and Cuba and all across America. Maybe they believe in it because their gods really exist, and their gods answer their prayers, and reward them when they're good, and punish them when they're bad."

"I don't know," Hicks said. "It all sounds so *ethnic*."

"You're not ashamed of who you are, are you? You're not ashamed of being colored?"

Hicks looked away. When he turned back, there was an expression on his face that Decker had never seen before.

They were nearly back at Madison and Grace when Decker's cell phone played the opening bars of "The House of the Rising Sun."

"You changed it," Hicks said.

"Didn't want you to think that I wasn't responsive to criticism. Yes? Martin here, who is this?"

"Hi, Decker. Dan Carvey, from the fire department."

"How are you doing, Dan? Haven't seen you since you burned all those burgers at the charity cookout."

"I have a preliminary finding on that fire of yours."

"Any sign of arson?"

"No. There were a couple dozen bottles of 120-proof rum on the premises, some of them broken, but I couldn't detect any accelerant."

"So what caused it? Natural gas?"

"Gas pipes were all intact. Stove was turned off. No—all the early indications are that it was lightning."

"Lightning? There was no lightning around."

"Well, it can come out of a clear sky sometimes. The way the humidity's been building up lately. But there's all the signs. Scorch marks on the wallpaper, electrical appliances all blown out."

"You're sure about this?"

"I'll stake my reputation."

Decker turned right, down the ramp into the police parking lot. Hicks said, "What?"

"The fire department thinks that Moses' apartment was hit by lightning. His daughter said that she warned him not to mess with Changó. Changó, in Santería mythology, is the god of fire and thunder and lightning. So what do we conclude from that?"

He pulled into his parking space and killed the motor. He turned and looked at Hicks and he expected an answer.

Hicks said, "I don't know. You make me feel cornered."

"I make you feel cornered, do I? How do you think *I* feel, with this Changó breathing down my neck? You don't believe in it? You don't want to believe in any of this? You're a police officer, Hicks, you *have* to believe in it. Just because you want to deny your ethnicity, don't let that distort your judgment."

"I'm not denying my ethnicity. I just don't like all of this African magic stuff. It's primitive, and it's demeaning."

"And?"

"And nothing. I just don't like it, that's all."

"Then why do I get the feeling there's something more personal here?"

Hicks didn't answer. "I'll get on to that Mason family tree."

CHAPTER TWENTY-SEVEN

Cab held a media conference at 4:15 that afternoon. The press room was crowded and noisy and electronic flash flickered like summer lightning.

"All I can tell you so far is that John Mason was the victim of a suspicious drowning incident. We have some constructive leads and we'll report any developments . . . well, as soon as any developments develop."

Leo Waters from WRVA News Radio raised his pencil and asked, "I talked to the super at John Mason's building He said that the victim was deliberately blinded and then scalded to death. Is there any substance in that?"

"The super was not an eyewitness to the incident."

"With respect, Captain, that doesn't exactly answer the question."

Cab paused for a moment and then he said, heavily,

"There were some unusual circumstances attached to this incident, yes."

"So you're admitting it's true? The guy was blinded and drowned in boiling water?"

"Yes."

Decker heard the news bulletin as he drove back to his apartment. "A cook was himself cooked last night. Thirty-year-old John Mason was boiled to death in his bathtub at his apartment on the edge of the Fan District. An unknown assailant blinded him with a sharp instrument and then somehow raised the temperature of his bathwater until he was literally poached to death."

Decker said, "Shit," and switched the radio off. The last thing he needed right now was hysterical pressure from the media. He had a feeling that the killings were somehow connected to the Devil's Brigade, but no clear idea how, or why, and no hard evidence at all. Having the media chasing him around was only going to make these investigations ten times more difficult.

He went home and took his ritual shot of Herradura Silver. Then he took a hot shower and changed into a baggy pair of gray drawstring pants and a white T-shirt. He felt hungry but he didn't know what he felt like eating. He opened the icebox and stared into it for a long time before closing it again. He would have done anything for one of Cathy's spicy pork and guacamole burgers.

The phone rang. To Decker's surprise, it was Father Thomas, from the Cathedral of the Sacred Heart.

"Decker, I tried to call you at headquarters, but they told me you'd gone home."

"Even us detectives get a few hours off. How can I help you?"

"I'm not sure, but I think that I may be able to be of some assistance to you. I heard about this latest homicide on the radio this afternoon, while I was out pruning my roses."

"Sick business, Father. Very sick."

"The thing that struck me was the way in which he was killed. Blinded, and then boiled in a bath of hot water."

"Not a pretty way to die, was it? But I guess you can't accuse the perp of not being original."

"Actually, I can. I think his method was highly derivative."

"Derivative? What do you mean?"

"That was the exact same way in which Saint Cecilia was martyred by the Romans in 265. Her eyes were put out. Then she was seated in a bath of scalding water and boiled."

"Go on."

"It was then that I got to thinking about your other victims. Mrs. Maitland was beheaded, and her unborn child was killed. This happened to Saint Anne of Ephesus, who was supposed to have been pregnant with a virgin birth. Major Drewry had his stomach cut open, like Saint Cyril. Mr. Maitland was disemboweled, and this was very similar to the martyrdom of Saint Erasmus in the fifth century . . . a hole was pierced in his stomach and his intestines were wound out of him by means of a winch. There's a very famous altar piece of it by Nicolas Poussin in the Pinacoteca Vaticana."

"So what are you saying? All of these people were killed in the same way that saints were martyred?"

"I may be jumping to conclusions, but you have four very unusual homicides on your hands, don't you? And it does seem that there might be some kind of pattern emerging. You see, I discovered something else: your victims were killed in the same sequence as their saints' days, starting with Saint Anne on December fourth, Saint Cyril on January twelfth, and so on. Saint Cecilia's day is March ninth."

"What about Junior Abraham? He had his head blown off."

"It's difficult to tell if Junior Abraham fits into this pattern, because so many saints had their heads removed, in one way or another. You should read your *Foxe's Book of Martyrs*. One poor soul was tied to the tail of a mad bull, so that he was dragged down the temple steps and had his brains knocked out."

"Jesus. Gives me a migraine to think about it."

"Oh, there were far worse tortures than that. Some Christian converts had their stomachs cut open and filled with corn, so that pigs could be brought to feed off it and devour their intestines at the same time."

"Terrific. I'm glad I haven't eaten yet. But thanks, Father. This could be a very useful line of inquiry. We're pretty sure that these homicides are something to do with Santería, so maybe you're right, and there *is* a connection with saints."

"Santería? I'd advise you to be extremely cautious, in that case. The *santeros* guard their secrecy with great zeal."

"Thanks for the warning, Father, but I think I already have a good idea of what I'm up against."

"God be with you, Decker."

"You too, Father."

That night, he was struggling his way through the undergrowth again. He knew it was only midafternoon, but the smoke from the burning scrub was so thick that the sun appeared only as a pallid disk, paler than the moon. The crackling of the fire was deafening, and he could hear terrible screaming somewhere off to his left. Men were being burned alive.

He lurched down into an overgrown hollow, where his face was lashed by crisscross briars. For a few moments he thought he was going to be hopelessly entangled, but then he managed to break free and climb up a short, steep slope. The next thing he knew he was standing on the plank road, and he could see troops gathering up about a hundred yards ahead of him, both cavalry and infantry, their bridles clinking, their swords and bayonets shining in the smoky gloom.

He slowed down now and walked more steadily, feeling the rough-sawed boards beneath his lacerated feet. Somebody was shouting, "Muster together, boys! We have them on the run now! Make for the railroad track, we can outflank them!"

He was only thirty yards away from the assembly of troops when he came across a blackened shape sitting on the edge of the plank road. At first he couldn't think what it was, but as he came closer he realized it was a man, almost completely charred, yet obviously still alive, because he was trembling and uttering grunts of pain. Smoke was still trailing from his hair, and his ears were burned to tiny cinders.

"What's your name, fellow?" Decker asked him.

The figure didn't answer.

"What division are you with? Anderson's? Wofford's?"

At last the figure turned its head and stared at him. "Hancock's," he croaked. "We were all set afire."

Decker unscrewed his water bottle and poured some into the palm of his hand, touching it against the man's lips. They felt dry and crisp, like burned bacon rinds. The man managed to suck up a little before he started coughing, and when he coughed he sprayed shreds of bloodied lung into Decker's hand.

"Tell me your name," Decker repeated. "You may be a Yankee, but I'll get word to your family, if I can."

The man shook his head. He couldn't stop coughing and he couldn't find the breath to speak.

Decker was still kneeling next to him when he felt the

plank road shaking, as if horses were approaching. He turned around and he could see the tall dark figure storming toward him, its coattails flapping like wings. It was less than fifty yards away, and it seemed to *rumble* as it approached, more like a thunderstorm than a man.

Decker stood up and tried to run—an exhausted, sore-footed canter. He knew that it was probably hopeless, trying to escape. If this creature had set fire to whole divisions, God knows what it was going to do to him. But he kept stumbling forward, gasping with effort, waving every now and again to see if he could attract the attention of the troops up ahead of him.

"Hi! Hi there! Help me!"

But then he turned to see how close the creature was, and it was right on top of him. He was suddenly overwhelmed by the curtains of its coat, and again he found himself trapped in a knobbly cage of bones, unable to twist himself free, unable to breathe.

He shouted out, and sat up, and switched on the bedside light.

And Cathy was there.

She was standing beside the bed, quite still. She was dressed in one of her plain white nightdresses, and there were green leaves and purple herbs entwined around her wrists, like bracelets. Her face was intensely white, almost fluorescent, and her eyes were blurry, as if they were filled with tears, or as if she were blinking as fast as a hummingbird's wing.

He started to say, "Cathy—" but then his throat choked up. He simply couldn't find the words. He had tried to talk to her so many times through mediums and clairvoyants. He had searched for any trace that she hadn't left him forever, that her spirit was still somewhere close by. He had heard nothing, felt nothing, found nothing. No perfumes, no whispers, no shadows. But now she was here, unbidden, looking as real as if she were still alive.

"This will be the last time," she said. Her voice sounded high and resonant, like a tuning fork. "If I try to come again, Saint Barbara will have me trapped by Oyá for all eternity in the split second between life and death—dying and dying and dying forever."

Decker smeared the tears from his eyes. "I, ah—I know that you have to go, sweetheart. But I know what you've done for me, too. How much you've been protecting me. I know who Saint Barbara really is, too."

"I can't keep her away from you any longer. She wants her revenge, and it has to be your time next."

"You don't know how much I miss you. If it's my time next, then maybe that's something I can look forward to. We can be together again."

Cathy gave him a wan smile. "The afterlife is not what you think it is, my darling. It's lonely and silent. The dead grieve for their loved ones as much as the living. They grieve for their lost lives, too."

"So this is it, then? The very last good-bye."

"I've come to tell you more than good-bye. You can still save yourself from Saint Barbara. But you will have to make an ally of the one person you hate more than any other."

"I don't understand you."

"I saw who killed me, Decker."

"What?"

"I saw who shot me. I was asleep and I felt somebody shake my shoulder. I opened my eyes and then she appeared, out of thin air. She was smiling. She had come to kill me, and she was smiling."

"A *woman* shot you?" Decker said, dumbfounded.

"She was very tall and she had beads in her hair."

"Jesus. I don't believe this. Queen Aché shot you *herself?*"

"Nobody saw her but me. She said, '*Irosun oche*,' and then she fired."

"I'll kill her. I swear to God I'll tear her head off."

"You need her help, my darling."

"Her *help?* All I want to do is blow her brains out, the same she did to you."

"Saint Barbara wants your blood, Decker, and it's your time next. Queen Aché is the only one who has the power to save you."

"Why should she? She hates me as much as I hate her. Why do you think she shot you? To warn me off. To keep me from breaking her drug racket. And she was clever, wasn't she? She killed a cop without actually killing a cop."

"She will help you if she has to."

"I don't get it."

"She came close up to me to shoot me, so close that she pressed the gun against my forehead. I seized her hair, and pulled it, and some of her hair and some of her beads came out in my hand. They're still there now, under the bed.

"I was the only witness to my own killing, but those beads will give you proof of who did it. Then there's Junior Abraham. When Queen Aché shot him, there were many witnesses. They don't think that they saw her. They think that they saw somebody else. But they *did* see her, and if you can find a way to open their eyes, you will have all the evidence you need."

"Cathy—"

"I have to go now, Decker. I can't do any more."

"Can I touch you?"

"Of course."

He stood up and cautiously approached her. She looked up at him and he saw in her yellow eyes all of the years they could have had together, all of the summers and the winters and the walks along the waterfront, where the Confederate army lay dead, and where she lay dead, too.

He took her in his arms and closed his eyes and there was nothing there, no substance at all, only the briefest of chills.

"Good-bye," she whispered, inside his head. He opened his eyes and she was gone.

He knelt down and peered under the bed, but he couldn't see any beads. He knew that the forensic people had gone over the apartment after Cathy was shot, and if there had been any beads there, or pulled-out hair, surely they would have discovered them.

He took the flashlight out of the nightstand and flicked it around, but he still couldn't see anything. In the end, he heaved the bed to the other side of the room.

They really took some finding, but there they were. Three small ivory beads, almost the same color as the carpet, in the gap between the edge of the carpet and the skirting board. Decker went to the kitchen for a polythene food bag, carefully picking up each bead with tweezers and dropping it inside. When he inspected them closely, he saw that two of them had wisps of hair in them.

"Got you, Your Majesty," he breathed.

CHAPTER TWENTY-EIGHT

Back at headquarters, Decker found that Hicks had left a scribbled note for him.

I checked the historical records at City Hall. John Mason's great-great-grandfather was Hiram P. Mason, who was manager out on Cudahy's tobacco plantation out near Tuckahoe. He served as a captain in Heth's division in the First Army Corps during the Civil War, November 1863–May 1864.

Decker went over to the window and looked down at Grace Street. It was only a few minutes past noon and—unlike him—nobody had a shadow. The street looked bright and unreal, like a scene from *The Bodysnatchers*. For all he knew, the So-Scary Man was down there, too, walking right through the crowds, unseen, unnoticed, on his way to murder another victim. On his way to murder *him*, if Cathy was right.

He was driving slowly along St. James Street when he saw Junior Abraham's brother Treasure walking toward him, with three other young men and a girl with cornrow hair and the tightest white jeans that he had ever seen. She looked as if she were naked and her legs had simply been painted white. He pulled into the curb and put down the window.

"Hi, Treasure," he said, without taking his eyes off the girl. "How about you and me having a little friendly conversation?"

Treasure sniffed and jerked his head. He was wearing sloppy brown cargo pants and a green T-shirt with *The Big Gig* printed on it in red letters. "Kind of busy right now, Lieutenant."

"Listen . . . I'm working my butt off trying to find out who killed your brother. You can spare me a couple of minutes, can't you?"

"I don't know. Maybe it's better if we kind of forget about it, you know? People like that . . . you don't want to go upsetting people like that."

"People like what?"

"I don't know, man. People who come up to you when you're eating your lunch and blow your fucking head off."

Decker reached across and opened the passenger door. "Ten minutes tops. Come on. Junior deserves that much, doesn't he?"

The girl winked at Decker and said, "Go on, Treasure. Go talk to the nice policeman. You can catch up with us later."

Treasure reluctantly heaved himself into the car. Decker immediately pulled away from the curb with a brisk squeal of tires and headed north.

"Where are we going, man?" Treasure asked, after they had driven six blocks. "I thought you just wanted to talk."

"I do. But I want you to meet a friend of mine. Somebody who can help you remember what happened."

"Hey . . . you're not going to pull out my toenails or nothing?"

"Of course not. We want to have a little relaxing chin music, that's all."

"I told you . . . I don't remember what the guy looked like. He was just kind of, like, normal. Not too tall, not too short."

"We'll see." He picked up his cell phone and punched out Hicks's home number.

He drove out to Valley Road and parked in front of the Hicks house. As they climbed out, Rhoda opened the front door, wearing a flowery yellow sundress. "Tim not with you?" she asked, looking around.

"No, poor guy. He had a whole heap of paperwork to finish off. This is Treasure, the young man I was telling you about on the phone. Treasure, meet Rhoda."

Treasure sniffed and wiped his hands on his pants.

"Come along in," Rhoda said. "Do you want coffee or anything? Maybe a soda?"

"No, we're fine, thanks, Rhoda. I promised not to take up too much of Treasure's time."

"Treasure, that's an unusual name."

"My mom always used to call me Mama's Little Treasure. It stuck even when I grew big."

"That's so sweet."

"You think so? I think it's wholly embarrassing."

Rhoda had already spread a neatly pressed white tablecloth on the kitchen table and set up two white candles. She drew the blinds and lit the candles, and then she sat down, her hands pressed together as if she were praying. Treasure looked at Decker and said, "What?"

Rhoda said, "All you have to do is sit down and try to relax."

"Go on," Decker urged him, and so he dragged out a chair and sat down, sniffing again and jerking his head.

Rhoda took hold of his hand. "What we're trying to do today, Treasure, is to talk to Junior."

"Say *what?* Junior had his nut blown off. Junior can't *talk*."

"Junior's dead, for sure. He doesn't have a physical presence anymore. But his spirit lives on, and always will, just as *all* of our spirits live on. God creates us, Treasure, and you don't think that God would ever allow His precious creations to die?"

"Listen, Lieutenant, I thought you and me was going to talk. I didn't think you was bringing me to no prayer meeting."

"This isn't a prayer meeting, Treasure. This is to help you remember."

"I told you. How many times did I told you? I can't exactly remember what the guy looked like. It all happened so fast, it was like I couldn't focus my eyes."

Rhoda turned her head abruptly to the left and said, "Junior! Junior Abraham! Your brother Treasure's here."

Treasure bobbed up out of his seat and looked around, wide-eyed. When he realized that Junior wasn't standing right behind him, he blew out his cheeks and said, "Shit, you scared me then. You really scared me."

Rhoda closed her eyes. "Junior Abraham, your brother's here. Your brother wants you to tell him what happened to you."

Treasure said, "Come on, this is seriously nuts. I went to Junior's funeral, I laid a rose on top of his casket. He can't *talk* to me."

Decker pressed his finger to his lips. "Give it a chance, Treasure. I've seen this myself, and it works."

"Maybe I don't *want* to talk to Junior. I mean, maybe I'm crapping my pants here."

"Your brother wouldn't do anything to harm you. Besides, he deserves justice, doesn't he?"

"I don't know. I guess."

Treasure stayed quiet, but he still couldn't stop himself from twitching and flinching. Rhoda took out her *okuele* and dropped it onto the table. She made a note of how the medallions had fallen, and then she said, "Junior, listen to me. Your brother's here. He wants to know who hurt you."

Treasure looked more and more unhappy, but Rhoda kept on calling Junior, her voice curiously flat, as if she were speaking from another room.

"Junior, you haven't gone far, I know that. You're still very close to us. Speak to us, Junior."

She cast the *okuele* three more times. More than ten minutes had gone by, and even Decker was beginning to feel that this wasn't going to work. But then he began to notice that the kitchen appeared to be growing darker, as if clouds were sliding over the sun. One of the candle flames gave a nervous jump, and then the other, and then they both began to burn brighter.

"I can feel you, Junior. I know you're here. Talk to your brother, ask him to remember what really happened."

The candle flames rose higher and higher, and they began to burn so fiercely that they hissed, like oxyacetylene torches. The light was so dazzling that Treasure had to shield his eyes with his hand. In the very center of the light, Decker thought that he could make out a face, but it was so intense that it was impossible to say for sure.

It was only when Rhoda began to speak that he knew that she had contacted Junior Abraham, wherever he was, in heaven or hell, or some place in between. Her voice was very harsh and low, and it made Decker feel as if his scalp were being pricked by dozens of sewing needles.

"We was sitting together, man, and we was talking about the Down Home Family Reunion."

Treasure stared at Rhoda openmouthed.

"You was saying that we ought to be giving protection to the folks who run the food and the craft stalls, you know, in case their stalls got accidentally knocked over or set on fire or something or some kid threw dog shit into their pork'n'beans."

"That's Junior," Treasure said, in disbelief, turning to Decker with his hand still raised to shield his eyes. "That's *Junior* talking. That's her talking but that's Junior talking. How does she *do* that?"

"You think now, Treasure. You think good. We was sitting there talking about the Down Home Family Reunion and somebody comes walking right up to the table carrying a tray."

"I remember," Treasure said, wildly nodding his head. "I remember it exactly."

"Try to vis-alize it in your mind's eye. You see the tray, yes? You see them four bowls of soup?"

"I see them. I see them."

"Now I want you to look up. I want you to raise your eyes, brother, and look directly in the face of the person who's carrying the tray."

Treasure said, "I can't, Junior. It's like it's all blurry. I just can't see who it is."

"Yes, you can. It ain't going to be easy, because that particular memory has a spell on it. Like a kind of a trick, man, to stop you remembering what you really saw. But you can do it, Treasure. Come on, brother. Show me that you're not as dumb as people say you are."

"Hey—who says I'm dumb?"

"You ain't dumb, man. You can raise your eyes and tell me who's carrying that tray."

"I don't know, Junior. My eyes won't go up that far."

"You remember that tray flying in the air and the bowls of soup flying in the air and then what?"

"Bang! that's all. Bang, and your head got blown off."

"Think of that very instant when the gun went off. Think hard, Treasure. Who was holding that gun?"

Treasure squeezed his eyes tight shut and gritted his teeth in concentration. The candles hissed hotter and hotter and the wax was pouring down the candlesticks and onto the tablecloth.

Suddenly Treasure opened his eyes and stared at Rhoda with his mouth open. "Shee-it!" he exclaimed. "Shee-it, it weren't no waiter guy at all! Shee-it!"

"Who was it, Treasure? I want to hear you say the name."

"It was *her.* That Queen Aché ho, that's who it was! I *seen* her! I seen her as clear as daytime! She come up to the table and she throw the soup all over us and bang! I turn around and say, 'Junior, you been hurt?' but Junior ain't got no head no more. Queen Aché, shee-it. I'm going to *kill* that ho, I swear to God! I'm going to kill her!"

Almost at once, the hissing died down and the candle flames began to gutter. Rhoda stood up and leaned over the table and blew them out. Amidst the curls of acrid smoke, she reached over and took hold of Treasure's hand, and squeezed it, and smiled at him.

"Now you remember who killed your brother, don't you?"

"Absolutely. I can't understand how I couldn't remember it before."

"You couldn't remember it before because Queen Aché cast a Santería spell on everybody in the restaurant, including you. It was very powerful earth-magic. There's hardly anybody who can work that kind of spell these days, even a *babalawo*."

"But why did she have to *do* that?" Treasure asked. "She could have whacked him some place private, couldn't she? She didn't need no *spell*."

Decker shook his head. "That was Queen Aché all over. She wanted people to know that if you try to double-cross her, you can't escape from her *anywhere*, even in a public restaurant."

"I'm going to *waste* her, man, I swear to God."

"No, you're not. But you're going to go into court and testify against her. You and all the other witnesses, when I can get *them* to remember what you just remembered." They heard the key in the front door, and Daisy, from the living room, calling out, "Daddy! Daddy!"

Rhoda stood up and put up the blind. Hicks came into the kitchen, toting Daisy on his arm, but when he saw Decker and Treasure his smile immediately vanished.

"What's happening?" he demanded. "What's *he* doing here?"

Decker coughed and said, "Ah—I can explain."

Rhoda turned to Decker in bewilderment. "You mean to say that Tim didn't *know* you were coming here?" she asked him. "That's not what you told me on the phone."

"Actually, to be fair, I didn't tell you that he knew and I didn't tell you that he *didn't* know."

"You lied to me, Lieutenant. There's nothing fair about that!"

"Well, I truly apologize if you got the wrong impression, Rhoda. But to be honest I don't think that Tim would have been very happy about your holding another séance, do you? Especially with Treasure here."

"*I* ain't done nothing," Treasure said. "I just came along because I was axed."

Hicks put Daisy down on the floor. "Can I talk to you in private, please, Lieutenant?"

"Tim—" Rhoda said.

"Let me handle this, honey. I'm not going to say anything out of line."

"Too right you're not," Decker told him. "This is a multiple homicide investigation and I'm in charge of it and it was my decision that we needed Rhoda's assistance."

"Rhoda's my wife, Lieutenant."

"She's also the only person I know who could help Treasure to remember who killed his brother. And she has. He's remembered."

"If I'd known you were going to pull a stunt like this—"

"Exactly, that's why I didn't tell you."

"I'm going to have to make a formal complaint about this. You realize what you've done here? You've put my family in jeopardy."

"Don't overreact. Nobody has to know about this."

"Oh no? What are you going to say to the district attorney when he asks you how Treasure suddenly managed to remember what he saw?"

"I'm sure as hell not going to say that his dead brother told him, during a séance."

"I can't believe this. I can't believe you did this."

"It was Queen Aché herself," Decker said.

"What?"

"There was no waiter. Queen Aché used a Santería spell and shot Junior Abraham herself."

"Well, that makes me feel a whole lot better. My wife has been duped into providing incriminating evidence against the single most ruthless racketeer in Richmond. For Pete's sake, Lieutenant, think what happened to your Cathy!"

"Your family's going to be safe, Tim, I promise you. Think about it: We're never going to have any chance of catching our invisible killer unless we have somebody on our side who can see him, and knows what it takes to corner him."

"What are you saying?"

"We can use Treasure's evidence as a way of persuading Queen Aché to help us."

"You're prepared to do that? You're really prepared to do that? I thought you suspected that Queen Aché had your Cathy killed."

"I don't just suspect it, sport. I know it for certain. But there are times in this job when you have to work with people you would happily see dead, because that's the only way you're going to get a result. This guy has already killed four people and I'm pretty sure that he's going to kill a whole lot more. What do you suggest we do? Shrug our shoulders and let him carry on with it?"

Hicks put his arm around Rhoda and held her close. He was obviously finding it difficult to contain his anger, but Rhoda reached up and touched his lips with her fingertips to keep him silent.

Decker stood up. "I'm going to take Treasure back to the city. I'll see you back at headquarters."

CHAPTER TWENTY-NINE

He dropped off Treasure on Clay Street. "Listen—when Queen Aché finds out that we have eyewitnesses you're going to be in real jeopardy, you understand that?"

"You think I give a flying fuck about that? That woman blew my brother's head off."

"Is there some place you can go, somewhere safe? If not, I can arrange some protection for you."

"I got cousins in Chester."

"Okay, then. So long as you let me know where you are."

Treasure twitched his head. "That was something else, wasn't it? Junior talking to me just like he's still alive?"

"It surely was. Here's my number. Call me as soon as you get to Chester."

He watched Treasure lope off bandy-legged along the sidewalk, and as he did his cell phone rang.

"Lieutenant? This is Captain Toni Morello from the Office of the Command Historian. I've found something that I think will really interest you."

"You want me to come down to Fort Monroe? I can be with you by . . . say, five o'clock if that's okay."

"No . . . you don't have to do that. I have a social evening in Richmond tonight. I can meet you around nineteen hundred hours."

"Okay . . . you know where we are?"

Hicks said nothing when he returned to headquarters but went directly to his desk and started to sort through the material that he had amassed on the family backgrounds of Jerry and Alison Maitland, George Drewry, and John Mason. After a while Decker went over to him and said, "Listen, Hicks. My humblest apologies. Asking your wife to hold a séance . . . that was something I decided to do on the spur of the moment, and I just knew that you wouldn't go for it. But, come on, you have to admit that it worked. We made a serious breakthrough here . . . and if we can persuade all the other witnesses to remember what they saw—"

Hicks tossed his pen onto his desk and sat back, looking deeply unhappy.

Decker said, "If you want me to pull you off this investigation, I'll understand. Rudisill's pretty much up to speed on it."

Hicks furiously shook his head. "I want to find this sucker as much as you do, Lieutenant. I just don't want my family compromised. You really think that all of those other witnesses are going to stand up in open court and testify against Queen Aché?"

Decker said, "That isn't the point. The point is we need Queen Aché to help us find this So-Scary Guy. You think I want to work with her, after what she did to my Cathy? But life is all about priorities."

"My family is my priority, Lieutenant. My Rhoda. My Daisy."

"I don't think your family is in any danger at all. This guy is working to a very specific agenda. In fact I'm pretty sure that the next person on his list may be me."

"*You?* Why you?"

"He's not killing people at random. He has a list, and he's working his way through it one by one."

"You have evidence of that?"

"Nothing substantive. Only more nightmares, more voices, more illusions. I thought I saw Cathy in my bedroom last night and she warned me that Saint Barbara would be coming after me within forty-eight hours."

Hicks raised his eyebrows. "I don't know whether it's my place to say this, Lieutenant. I mean I'm not a psychoanalyst or nothing. But don't you think that maybe you're *imagining* all this crap? It could be just stress."

"Stress can't write on your apartment walls in blood, Hicks. Stress can't leave briar scratches on your feet when you're only *dreaming* about running through the underbrush. This investigation doesn't just have *connotations* of the supernatural, Hicks. It *is* supernatural. It's totally strange and abnormal and weird. Besides, Moses Adebolu's daughter warned me that Saint Barbara was coming for me, too, except that she used Saint Barbara's Santería name, Changó."

"So that's what she said to you. But why you?"

"I'm not one hundred percent certain, but I think it has something to do with my great-great-grandfather. Something he did when he served in the army of northern Virginia."

"You really think that these killings are connected with the Civil War?"

"The Devil's Brigade, yes. Something happened in the Battle of the Wilderness, Hicks. Something so goddamned awful that it never went away."

Captain Morello came into the office at 7:00 P.M. sharp. Decker glanced up when she appeared, but in that first instant he didn't recognize her. Her dark wavy hair was unpinned, and her lips were glistening scarlet. Instead of her neatly pressed military uniform, she wore a black-sequined bolero, with a short black dress that clung to her hips, and glossy black panty hose.

"Lieutenant?"

Decker looked up a second time, and then he jumped up and saluted. "Yes, *sir!*"

She smiled and said, "At ease, Lieutenant. I'm off duty now."

"You look—well, you certainly *look* off duty."

"Thank you." She lifted a brown leather briefcase and said, "I discovered these papers yesterday afternoon in one of Major Drewry's research files, and I've been reading them for most of the night."

"Oh yeah?" Decker said, dubiously.

"Major Drewry bought them in October last year, when he went to an auction of family effects from the Longstreet family, out in Hopewell. He hadn't even had the chance to read most of them, let alone categorize them."

She opened the briefcase and took out a sheaf of old discolored papers, tied together with gray string, which still had fragments of crusty yellow sealing wax clinging to it.

"Listen," Decker said, "do you think I can twist your arm and persuade you to do this some place more comfortable? I could really use a drink around now."

"All right," Captain Morello said. "Consider my arm twisted."

They left police headquarters and walked along East Grace Street to the Raven Bar, which was one of Decker's favorites. It was decorated to look like a turn-of-the-century library, with oak paneling and Tiffany lamps and deep leather banquettes. Decker guided Captain Morello to a corner booth, underneath a framed engraving of Edgar Allan Poe, his forehead like the full moon.

"Beer, please, Sandie," he asked the waitress, who was dressed in a mobcap and floor-length apron. "And what's it for you, Captain?"

"Old-fashioned, plenty of ice."

"Wouldn't have taken you for a whiskey drinker."

"Just goes to show that even hotshot detectives can misjudge people sometimes."

He rested his elbow on the table and stared at her narrowly for a full thirty seconds. She met his inspection with unflinching boldness, her eyes challenging him to tell her what kind of a woman she was.

"Daddy was something high-ranking. Mommy was a dancer."

"Wrong again. Daddy was in recycled paper products. Mommy was a paralegal."

"So why did you join the army?"

"My best friend, Marcia Halperin, wanted to sign up, so I did, too. After three weeks she decided that she hated it, and quit. But I loved every minute, and I still love it. I guess I'm the kind of woman who likes discipline and organization."

"And history?"

"Sure—but this is history with an up-to-date purpose. Most people think that the Office of the Command Historian does nothing but keep musty old archives, but the Pentagon always consults our records whenever they're planning to go into offensive military action. They can see how tactical problems were tackled in the past—what went right in the gulf and what went wrong in Somalia. An army that knows its history, Lieutenant, that's an army that knows its strength."

"Well, thanks for the lecture."

Their drinks arrived, along with a bowl of mixed nuts. Decker took a deep swallow of beer and wiped his mouth with the back of his hand. Captain Morello laid her briefcase on the table and flipped open the catches. "I kid you not, Lieutenant. These documents are real historical dynamite. These are the *personal* diaries that Lieutenant General James Longstreet kept while he was in the hospital after the Battle of the Wilderness.

"Of course he wrote an official report of the action, but he never admitted to the First Army Corps what really happened, and most of those men who had inside knowledge were killed that night, or at Spotsylvania, or Appomattox, or else they refused to discuss it and took what they knew to their graves."

She untied the papers and spread them out. They smelled vinegary, like all old papers, but they had another smell, too, which reminded Decker of dried lavender that has almost lost its fragrance. "Here it is, over ninety pages of it, a firsthand account of the Devil's Brigade. It's amazing. Over the years there must have been scores of rumors and myths about it."

She picked up a photocopy of the front page of a Civil War newspaper. "The *Memphis Daily Appeal*, June 1864. This is the first public mention of what could have been the Devil's Brigade. A young soldier named Josiah Billings was sent home after he lost his left forearm in the Battle of the Wilderness. He said that during the evening of May sixth he and his fellows had been trying to reach the unfinished railroad from Gordonsville to Fredericksburg when they became lost in the thick undergrowth behind enemy lines. All of a sudden they were surrounded by 'crackling bolts of lightning, not solid shot,' and he saw a Union soldier 'riven by a lightning flash from his head to his groin, so that he looked like a split-open side of beef.' He saw another Yankee turned inside out—'easy as a pulled-off glove.'

"Then he said that 'fires started all around us, spontaneous, and the woods were burning so fierce that hundreds of men were trapped and burned alive.' "

Decker nodded. "Billy Joe Bennett told me a similar story. You know Billy Joe Bennett? He runs a Civil War memorabilia store on Cary Street."

"Oh, sure, the Rebel Yell. Known Billy Joe for years. He's absolutely *obsessed* with the Civil War, isn't he? But he often turns up original maps and diaries and rare Civil War artifacts and he always brings them down to us to take a look. About a month ago he brought me a tiny square of silk . . . it was part of the battle flag of the Second Company Howitzers. After the Confederate army had surrendered at Appomattox Courthouse, the company's guidon cut it up into pieces and handed them out to the artillerymen as keepsakes. Only a tiny square of silk, but what *history* it represented. What emotion."

Decker scooped up a handful of nuts. "This stuff really means something to you, doesn't it?"

"Of course it does. It's real. And so are these documents. Think about it. The first account of the Devil's Brigade by the man who actually formed it."

Decker picked up the first page. The writing was in faded purple ink—a scratchy, sloping script he could barely decipher, except for one or two odd words.

"You can *read* this?" he asked.

"You get used to it. The trick is to tilt the page at an angle."

"Hmm," Decker said, trying it. "Still can't work out more than one word in ten. What's 'paffage'?"

" 'Passage.' His double Ss always look like Fs. Here . . . I've done a transcript for you."

Decker took the thick sheaf of double-spaced print. "Thanks. But why don't you tell me the bare bones of it yourself? You have the time, don't you?"

"Well, okay . . . I don't have to be at the Berkeley Hotel till eight."

"You really have to go? I don't often have the opportunity to go out with a woman who's dressed as fancy as you."

"It's an American Legion fund-raiser, and, yes, I do have to go. But thank you for the compliment anyhow."

She opened her purse and took out a pair of gold-framed half-glasses. She leafed quickly through the transcript of Lieutenant General Longstreet's diary, and then she said, "Here it is.

"On April eleventh, I received orders at Bristol from the adjutant and inspector general to report with the original portion of the First Corps (Kershaw's and Field's divisions and Alexander's battalion of artillery) to General R.E. Lee, commanding army of northern Virginia. On the twenty-second I marched my command to Mechanicsville, and encamped in the near neighborhood thereof. I was advised by the commanding general that a portion of the enemy was advancing swiftly and had reached the Culpeper Mine Ford on the Rapidan River and were preparing to cross into Orange County.

"During the night of June twenty-ninth I was unexpectedly approached by Colonel Frederick Meldrum from Heth's division, who was accompanied by his Negro servant, a man known only as John. Colonel Meldrum in civilian life was a wealthy tobacco planter and a man of considerable presence and intelligence. He said that he understood that our military situation was now parlous, and that General Grant was on the point of breaking through

our Confederate lines and driving us all the way back to Richmond herself.

"He asked if he could speak to me further in the conditions of greatest secrecy, to which I agreed. He informed me that his servant John was an adherent of a magical religion from West Africa called Lucumi, or Santería, or sometimes voodoo. Being a man with a greatly inquiring mind, Colonel Meldrum had taken the trouble to learn the religious beliefs of his servant, and had persuaded him to demonstrate some of its rituals and spells.

"You may understand that I was very tired and preoccupied with all manner of other considerations, in particular the late arrival of my reinforcements, which was occasioned by want of transportation on the railroad. Yet Colonel Meldrum asked me to witness one Santería spell to demonstrate its effectiveness. John produced some stones from the pockets of his vest, as well as strings of black and green beads, and proceeded to chant monotonously and at some length. I was beginning to grow impatient when before my eyes his skin appeared to melt away, like brown butter melting in a hot skillet, and he became a skeleton, *a man of bones, still dressed, still animated, but completely fleshless. To say that I was horrified and frightened would be an understatement. For a moment I doubted my sanity, and thought that the pressures and conditions of war must have turned my mind.*

"But the skeletal John rose from his chair, and approached the mockingbird which I always keep caged in my quarters as a mascot. He raised both of his bony hands and it was plain that the poor bird was highly agitated. It screamed and screeched and dashed itself wildly against the bars of its cage. John spoke no more than two words to it, and these were instantly followed by a sharp rapping sound not unlike a musketball hitting a cartwheel. The bird in-

stantly exploded into a tangle of feathers and bones and grisly intestines, and dropped dead to the floor of its cage.

"Gradually, John's flesh began to reappear, as if they were shadows collecting after the sun has gone down. Before half a minute had passed, he was fully clothed in his own skin again, and smiling at me with a knowing impudence that I found profoundly disturbing. I am a religious man, but to witness such a powerful manifestation of heathen magic shook my faith to their very core.

"Colonel Meldrum explained to me that in times of war the West Africans could call upon their various gods to possess them, and that John had been temporarily possessed by a fearsome god called Oggún, who represents war and death and the act of slaying. Even here in America, he informed me, our slaves continue to worship Oggún by pretending to their masters that they are worshipping Saint Peter. It was Oggún who had given him the ability to be able to kill the mockingbird through fear alone, because the poor creature had turned itself out rather than face the terror which Oggún inspired in it.

"I now began to grasp what Colonel Meldrum was suggesting to me. If we were to form a brigade of perhaps a dozen volunteers, he said, his servant John could perform the necessary summonings and incantations, so that these volunteers would be possessed by some of the most powerful and warlike of Santería's gods. They would wreak such havoc among the advancing Union forces, and spread such elemental terror, that our enemy would flee from the battlefield and never have the courage to return.

"I asked Colonel Meldrum to give me time to reflect on his suggestion. After all, we were Christian men, fighting a Christian cause, and to call on the forces of African darkness would be tantamount to admitting that we did not

ourselves have the strength or the moral courage to defeat our foe.

"In the morning, however, a dispatch rider came to my quarters to inform me that the Union forces had crossed the Rapidan River. Generals Hill and Ewell had been heavily engaged and were retreating in confusion. I knew now that the South was on the brink of being overrun, and that Richmond herself was in immediate peril.

"I considered sending a letter to General R.E. Lee, asking his permission to employ the magical forces of Santería, but I knew that he would never consent. Even if I had been able to spare the time to locate him, and to give him a demonstration of the powers that Colonel Meldum's servant had already displayed to me, I doubt very much if he would have agreed to it. He was a man of such unassailable honor and integrity, and his belief in the Gospel was so strong, that I believe he would rather have surrendered our army there and then rather than call upon the works of any devil.

"I prayed for forgiveness if the choice I was about to make flew in the face of everything that we in the South held to be glorious and dear. Having done so, I summoned Colonel Meldrum and his servant John and instructed Colonel Meldrum to select twelve of his most competent men, with my authority, for a special duty. He was to explain to them clearly what was expected of them, and to make it explicit that what he was asking of them was entirely voluntary.

"Only one of the officers and men he approached declined the assignment, even though it was clearly explained to them that they would be surrendering their minds and their bodies to un-Christian influences. The one who refused, Captain Hartnett, was the son of a fundamentalist preacher.

"Consequently—and in utmost secrecy—our brigade was prepared for their strange and terrible task. Colonel Meldrum himself said that he would be possessed by Oggún (Saint Peter). The remaining officers and men were as follows:

Major-General M.L. Maitland *(commanding) (Yegua, the bringer of death, often known in Santería as Saint Erasmus.)*

Lieutenant H.N. Stannard *(Oyá, the goddess of the cemetery, often syncretized in Santería with Saint Anne of Ephesus.)*

Lieutenant R.F. Mason *(Ochosi, or Osowusi, the night watchman, Saint Cecilia.)*

Sergeant W.B. Brossard *(Babalu-Ayé, the god of contagious diseases, Saint Lazarus.)*

Sergeant L. Taylor *(Orunla, the only god who tricked Death, Saint Francis.)*

Corporal C. Hutchinson *(Allaguna, one of the manifestations of Obtalá, a fierce fighter on horseback, Saint Luke.)*

Lieutenant Colonel H.K. Drewry *(Osain, who terrifies people in the woods at night, Saint Cyril.)*

Major F.D. Martin *(Osun, the messenger of imminent danger, Saint James Intercisus.)*

Corporal W. Cutler *(Elegguá, the trickster, Saint Martin of Porres.)*

Major J.H. Shroud *(Changó, god of lightning and fire, Saint Barbara.)*

Captain G.T. Brookes *(Orisha-Oko, the god of sacrificial blood, Saint Barnabas.)*

"In spite of the warm and humid weather, each of these volunteers was to be issued with a greatcoat, since during their period of possession by their respective gods, they

would appear as the Negro servant John had appeared, as an ambulant skeleton, or even invisible to the naked eye, and we were anxious not to put our own men in fear of them. They were also to be issued with slouch hats, with bands of crow feathers around them, which John insisted would enhance their magical power."

Decker laid his hand on top of the papers, and Captain Morello took off her reading glasses and looked up. "Who could have seen this diary?" Decker asked her. "Apart from Major Drewry and you? I mean, recently?"

"Nobody. It's been kept in the archives under lock and key."

"Do you think there could be another copy of it somewhere?"

"I doubt it. It was tied up and sealed, presumably by Lieutenant General Longstreet himself, and I'm pretty sure the sealing wax was original."

"So nobody could have seen this roster of names since 1864?"

"Not very likely, no."

"Yet three of our four homicide victims were descendants of one of these men. Maitland, Drewry, and Mason. And it's conceivable that Alison Maitland was descended from one of them, too."

He hesitated, and then he said, "For that matter, so am I. That was my great-great-grandaddy—Frederick Decker Martin."

"But why should anybody want to kill them?"

"Grudge, I guess." He didn't want to tell her anything about his nightmares, or the way in which Cathy had appeared in his apartment.

"Hell of a long time to bear a grudge."

"I don't know."

"Maybe your perpetrator is somebody whose great-great-grandfather was in the Union army, and got turned inside out, or struck by lightning, or whatever." She shrugged. "Just a wild guess. You know more about criminal motivation than I do."

"Well . . . you're right. People kill other people for the strangest reasons. Old guy in the Fan District strangled his wife last year for serving him spinach every day for thirty-eight years. But—go on—tell me more about the Devil's Brigade."

"Oh, for sure, because this is where it really gets interesting. Very early in the morning of May sixth, Longstreet marched his divisions up to Parker's Store on the Orange Plank Road, including the Devil's Brigade. They arrived about dawn. The whole line of the Union army was advancing through the woods, and up in front of them Heth's and Wilcox's divisions had broken, and they were running for their lives.

"It was at this point that Longstreet deployed Kershaw's division on the right of the plank road, and Field's on the left. They managed to check the enemy's advance, but it was impossible for them to make any real headway because the underbrush was so thick."

She started reading again from Longstreet's diary.

"The line of battle was pressed forward and we came in close proximity to the enemy. The dense and tangled undergrowth prevented a sight of the opposing forces, but every man felt they were near. Everything was hushed and still. No one dared to speak above a whisper. It was evening, and growing dark.

"Then a man coughed, and instantly the thicket was illu-

mined by the flash of a thousand muskets, the men leaped to their feet, the officers shouted, and the battle was recommenced. Neither side would yield, but I could see that some of the bravest officers and men of my corps were falling all around me, and I realized that our line was close to breaking point.

"I called for Major General Maitland and Colonel Meldrum and advised them that I wished to send forward one of their special brigade to see what assistance he could give to our divisions. Colonel Meldrum argued that we should send forward at least four or five of them, but I was reluctant enough to send any at all. The Negro servant John said that if I was adamant that we should send only one, we should call upon Major Shroud to be possessed by the god of fire and lightning, Changó, since the woods and the thickets were highly inflammable, and the wind was in our favor, from the southwest.

"Major Shroud came forward and, witnessed by only four or five of us, performed a ceremony involving stones which he called 'thunderstones,' and the crushing of a snail, whose juice he dropped upon the stones, and oil. Then he brought forward a rooster and cut its throat, dropping its blood upon the stones also.

"The fighting was very close now, and musket balls were snapping through the underbrush and striking the trees. John made one last incantation and hung a necklace of red and white beads around Major Shroud's neck, which he explained were the sacred colors of Changó.

"The transformation of Major Shroud was appalling to behold. Like the Negro servant John, his flesh appeared to melt from his face like candlewax, leaving him the appearance of a grinning eyeless skull. He furled his greatcoat, and as he did so I could see that his chest was nothing but a bare rib cage.

"John took a lighted cigar and blew a stream of smoke toward the enemy lines, uttering some words that were completely incomprehensible. Major Shroud turned and began to make his way in that direction. He appeared to be able to walk through the underbrush with no difficulty whatsoever, more like a terrible shadow than a man.

"Only a few minutes later, the woods were luridly lit by lightning, a hundred times brighter than the flashing of musketry. Lightning struck in eight or nine places all at once, and was followed by a peal of thunder that shook the very ground beneath our feet. Fires sprang up on every side, and in a very short time the woods were fiercely ablaze, here, there, and everywhere.

"Men scream in battle, when their bowels are penetrated by a musket ball, or their leg is torn off by solid shot, or their arms crushed by a minié round. I was familiar with such screams.

"But that night in the woods of the Wilderness I heard screams that sounded as if they had been uttered by souls being shoveled wholesale into the fires of hell. They were screams of such hopelessness that my very skin shrank, and when I turned to Major General Maitland and Colonel Meldrum to adjudge their reaction, I could see that they were similarly affected. Major General Maitland was so deathly white as to resemble a ghost of himself.

"The lightning continued to strike with a horrendous crackling and the thunder continued to split the skies. As the fires burned furiously northeastward, our divisions were able to make a general advance in their wake, since most of the entangling brush was burned away. At this time I gave orders to Lieutenant Colonel Sorrel to take the brigades of Generals Mahone, G.T. Anderson, and Wofford and to conduct a flanking movement behind the enemy's left and

rear. The movement was a complete surprise and a perfect success. With the woods afire all around them, and our volleys striking them on three sides, the Federals fell back in utter disarray.

"Major Shroud returned to our ranks, his flesh restored to him, but his face blackened by smoke, and in a very diffident mood. I ordered him to bathe and rest since his experience seemed to have put him into a very unpleasant humor indeed.

"By the light of dawn I was able to assess the extent of the carnage. We came across many of the enemy with their bodies indescribably mutilated, with their limbs twisted into impossible positions, and many of them had been turned completely inside out, like my unfortunate mockingbird, so that their intestines were bound around them like twisted ropes. Others had been cremated where they stood, and were nothing but columns of black charcoal. Although I did not see him myself, another was reportedly stretched out so long that until they discovered his distorted face the surgeons did not realize at first that he had once been a man.

"Despite the success of our action, I resolved that this was to be the first and only time that I would call upon the forces of Santería to assist us. War has no glamour, but it has honor, and codes of conduct, and should the Confederacy win this noble struggle, I want our victory tainted by nothing that could cause our sons and daughters to think of us with shame.

"The brigade was assembled, and I thanked them for their commitment to the cause, and informed them of my decision. However, Major Shroud flew immediately into the most incontinent of rages, and said that he still had much work left to do, and would never rest until the last of our enemies had been incinerated and their cities razed to the

ground. He held forth with such appalling curses and imprecations that I immediately ordered him to be put under guard.

"Colonel Meldrum's servant John informed me that while Major Shroud had returned to the appearance *of normality, it was plain that the spirit of Changó still exercised control over him. When I asked how this spirit might be exorcized, John said that Changó had obviously found Major Shroud to be such an amenable host that he would never be wholly free of this possession for as long as he lived. It was true that while Major Shroud was an excellent officer in the field, and discharged his military duties with courage and diligence, he did have a reputation for his evil temper and his unwillingness to forgive even the smallest of slights. He had also been demoted after First Manassas for cutting the ears off a living Union prisoner as a souvenir of victory, and it was said (although never proved) that he had cut the privates from two other prisoners while they were still alive and forced them into their own mouths.*

"John was of the opinion that Major Shroud would continue to pursue the enemy until every last one of them was dead, and any who tried to thwart him in this purpose would suffer a similar fate. Even after the cessation of hostilities, there was a real danger that he would pose a mortal threat to anybody who was unfortunate enough to cross him in any matter large or trifling.

"John said that the only way in which this threat could be contained would be to seal Major Shroud alive in a casket lined with solid lead, in which would be placed various propitiatory fruits and herbs, such as apples and sarsaparilla, and over which, once welded shut, a male sheep would be sacrificed.

"This casket, he said, should be taken to sea and sunk to

the bottom, since Changó's power was much circumscribed by water.

"Of course I was now faced with a truly appalling dilemma. Major Shroud had agreed voluntarily to be possessed of this spirit, and had turned the tide of battle most decisively in our favor. Almost single-handedly, he had prevented the rout of our divisions and the taking of Richmond. Yet it was clear that he had become a threat of unimaginable magnitude not only to our enemies but to ourselves. Even as I discussed this matter with Major General Maitland and other officers, a duty sergeant came to advise us that Major Shroud had become so uncontrollably furious and violent that his guards had been obliged to shackle him with the chains which were normally used to secure the cannon.

"John warned that Changó was one of the fiercest and most warlike of all Santería gods and that he would not easily be consigned to his casket. He therefore suggested that all of the remaining volunteers should go through the ceremony of possession, which would give them the combined strength to restrain Major Shroud while he was thus imprisoned.

"I was very reluctant to approve this course of action, since there was obviously a risk that the other eleven men would also *be possessed forever by their respective gods, and represent eleven times more danger to the Federal forces and to those around us as Major Shroud. John, however, assured me that this was unlikely. He said that Major Shroud had probably committed an act of vengeance sometime in his past life which had made him especially susceptible to Changó's possession. Evil, he said, would always give a home to evil."*

Decker finished his beer. "So that's what they did? They *all* got themselves possessed? And they buried him alive?"

Captain Morello nodded. "Lieutenant General Longstreet says that he fought against their influence like a devil out of hell. There was lightning, and thunder, and several officers and privates were killed or injured. But between them the eleven other volunteers were strong enough to overpower him and lift him into his casket. It was like 'eleven columns of dazzling light, with a billowing cloak of absolute darkness in the arms.' They filled up the casket with all the apples and herbs that were required to make an offering to Changó. Then the lid was welded shut by the same marine engineers who had worked on the *Hunsley*—the hand-powered submarine that the Confederacy had built in their attempt to break the Union blockade of Chesapeake Bay."

She read again from Lieutenant General Longstreet's diaries.

"That night, the casket was hurried by gun carriage to Richmond, and at midnight put aboard the frigate Nathan Cooper *to be taken as far out toward Chesapeake Bay as was possible, having regard to the Union blockade, and dropped at the greatest possible depth.*

"Unfortunately, the Richmond waterfront suffered that night a heavy barrage from the enemy's naval guns, and before she could even be untied from the dock at Shockoe Creek, the Nathan Cooper *was struck amidships by a cannonball which sank her immediately, along with eighteen of her crew. I am sad for their unfortunate demise, but at least I am safe now in the knowledge that Major Shroud will be incarcerated in his casket forever underwater, and will never again represent a threat to humankind.*

"I myself am overwhelmed with remorse for my misjudgment, and for having been tempted to take the wrong path, *because it is only through the will of the Lord God*

Almighty that righteousness may prevail; and if the Lord God Almighty considers that I was gravely mistaken in appealing to a heathen religion for assistance in our time of extreme trouble, then I can only beg Him for forgiveness, and hope that He will understand that I was looking only *to save the Confederacy, and its commitment to glory, and to honor, and to God."*

CHAPTER THIRTY

The telephone warbled right next to his ear and made him jerk. He was hunched on the couch with his coat over his shoulders. He had started off the night in bed, but as soon as he had fallen asleep he was overwhelmed by nightmares of fire and screaming and men made of nothing but bones, and so he had camped the night in the living room, with the lights on.

"Lieutenant?"

Decker stiffly sat up and rubbed the back of his neck. "Hicks? What the hell time is it?"

"Seven-twenty. I'm haven't left home yet, but I've been checking my e-mail."

"What do you want? A citation?"

"I had a message from public records in Charlottesville. Alison Maitland's maiden name was Alison Bell, but her mother was the great-granddaughter of Lieutenant Henry Stannard, of the Second Company, Richmond Howitzers."

Decker reached over to the coffee table and picked up the

transcript of Lieutenant General Longstreet's private diary. "Bingo. Lieutenant H.N. Stannard was one of the Devil's Brigade, too. He was possessed by Oyá, who was syncretized with Saint Anne of Ephesus. Father Thomas guessed right. Saint Anne was supposed to have been a virgin, but she became pregnant with a child whom she claimed was 'a gift from God.' Her child was killed in the womb and then she was beheaded.

"This is what our perpetrator is doing, sport, beyond any shadow of a doubt. For some reason he's taking his revenge on the descendants of every man who served in the Devil's Brigade, and he's killing them in the same way that their syncretized saints were martyred. Saint Anne, stabbed and beheaded; Saint Erasmus, disemboweled; and so on. And he's doing it in the same order as their saints' days."

"So what was your great-great-grandfather's saint, Lieutenant?"

"Hold on . . . here it is. He was Osun, the messenger of immediate danger, whatever that means. He was worshiped in Santería under the name of Saint James Intercisus."

"So whatever happened to Saint James what's-his-face . . . the same thing's going to happen to you?"

"I guess so. The trouble is, I don't know what happened to him."

"I'm still on the Internet . . . I can check it out for you. Want to give me that name again?"

"In-ter-cis-us. Listen, I'm urgently in need of some coffee. I'll see you at nine, okay? If Ayula Adebolu is right, Changó wants this to be my last day on earth. I'm just going to make damn sure that it isn't."

"Okay, Lieutenant. Be cool."

Decker took a shower. Then he brewed himself a double-strength espresso. He dressed in a dark gray shirt with a maroon silk necktie and black pants. As he flicked up his hair into his usual pompadour, he suddenly stopped and stared at himself. There were damson-colored circles under his eyes that matched his necktie, and the lines in his cheeks looked as if they had been engraved in his skin. What if this *was* his last day on earth? What if his visions and nightmares were all going to come true? There was no evidence yet that Moses Adebolu had been killed by anything other than a freak lightning strike, but supposing he *had* been incinerated by Changó, because Changó was angry at him for offering Decker his help?

Aluya had seemed to believe that was what had happened to him; and Cathy had warned him again and again, even at the risk of suffering her killing over and over again, for all eternity.

Up until now, in spite of everything he had witnessed, he hadn't been able to believe that he was in any real danger. Ghosts and visions were frightening, but after all they were only ghosts and visions. But he thought about Lieutenant General Longstreet's account of men being "shoveled wholesale into the fires of hell" and for the first time in his career he felt genuinely unsettled. He had coped in his career with attacks with broken bottles, knives, and shotguns. Once a half-ton block of concrete had been dropped onto the roof of his car. But there nothing so disturbing as knowing that somebody evil and angry was coming for him, somebody he might not even be able to *see*, and that he was helpless to stop him.

He walked back through to the living room to read through Toni Morello's transcript again, and to finish his coffee. As he did so, the long net curtains along the window appeared to ripple, as if they had been stirred by an early-morning breeze. The strange thing was, though, that all of the windows were closed.

He stared at the curtains for a while, but they didn't move again. For some reason he had the distinct feeling that he wasn't alone, that there was somebody else in his apartment, hiding. He didn't know why. He put down his coffee mug and went across to the kitchen. Nobody there. The front door was still locked and chained, although he knew from the way in which Cathy had manifested herself that spirits weren't deterred by walls or locked doors.

He took down his shoulder holster from the hat stand and buckled it on. Then he crossed the living room and went back into the bedroom.

"Anybody there?"

This was insane. Yet Jerry Maitland must have thought that he was insane, too, when his arms started to bleed all down his new wallpaper, and when his pregnant wife was stabbed and her head cut off in front of his eyes. And Major Drewry must have thought he had lost his reason, when he was gutted in the shower. And John Mason, too, when he was blinded and boiled.

There was somebody here, or some *thing*. Some deeply malevolent force, a force that wanted to do him serious harm. It had warned him right from the very beginning, on Alison Maitland's 911 call, and it had warned him in his dreams. It wasn't quite ready to take him yet, but time was hurrying away and it was very close.

He listened and listened but he couldn't hear anything. But that was what disturbed him so much. The interior of his apartment was utterly silent. No traffic from I-95; no steamboats hooting; no airplanes flying overhead from Richmond International. He felt as if the entire apartment had been swaddled in thick insulation, or his ears had been packed with cotton.

He took one step across the room, and then another. He stopped and turned around. For an instant, out of the corner of his eye, he thought he glimpsed a shadow flitting across his bedroom mirror, but *inside* it, as if it were another room.

He hefted out his gun and approached the mirror very slowly. He reached out and touched the glass with his fingertips. The man in the mirror stared back at him as if he had lost his way and didn't know where to turn next.

Hicks had his feet propped up on his desk and his mouth was full of apple donut.

"Oh, hi, Lieutenant. The captain was looking for you."

Decker went to his desk and quickly rifled through his memos and notes and letters. He sniffed and said, "Any idea what he wanted?"

"Uh-huh. But if you want to know what kind of a mood he was in, I would say 'warpath' just about sums it up."

Oh, God, thought Decker, *don't say that Maggie has had a fit of conscience, and confessed everything.* If Cab had found out about *that*, he wouldn't have to worry about Changó. His last day on earth would be over before lunch.

"By the way," Hicks added. "I found out all about this Saint James Intercisus dude."

"Oh yeah?"

"Oh yeah . . . and if that's what's going to happen to *you*, well, if I were in your shoes I'd be booking myself a plane ticket to some place very, very, *very* far away."

"Go on."

Hicks produced a printout from the Catholic Patron Saints Web site. "Says here that Saint James Intercisus was a military adviser and a courtier to King Yezdigerd the First of Persia, back in the fifth century. Seems like he was converted to Christianity, but he made the mistake of confessing his conversion to King Yezdigerd's successor, King Bahram. Apparently King Bahram really liked him, and didn't want to do nothing to hurt him, but, you know, he couldn't have people worshiping God when they were supposed to be worshiping *him*. King Bahram asked Saint James to give up on God, but when he wouldn't, he ordered him hung up from a wooden frame and subjected to the Nine Deaths."

"The Nine Deaths? Not too sure I like the sound of that."

"It means chopping bits off of you, one at a time, until you say uncle. First of all they cut off Saint James's fingers and thumbs, that was the First Death, but all he said was, 'Lord, I may not have any fingers to write my prayers, but I still worship you.' Then they cut off his toes, the Second Death, but he still wouldn't renounce God.

"The Third and Fourth Deaths meant cutting off his hands and the Fifth and Sixth Deaths meant cutting off his feet, but he still refused to deny God. They cut off his ears, the Seventh Death, and then they cut off his nose.

"He was given one last chance to recant, but all he said was, 'I am like a ruined house, but God still lives in me.' So that didn't leave King Bahram a whole lot of choice. He ordered his guards to whop Saint James's head off.

"All in all, they cut him into twenty-eight separate pieces, which is why they call him Intercisus, which I guess is Latin for 'cut up into twenty-eight separate pieces.' "

Decker sat staring at Hicks for a long time with his mouth open. Then he said, "Hicks, I think you just seriously spoiled my day."

"Only telling you what it says on the Web site, Lieutenant. By the way, Saint James Intercisus is the patron saint of torture victims and also of lost vocations."

"Lost vocations? That's me all right. I always wanted to be a country-and-western singer."

Cab's door was open but Decker knocked on it just the same. Cab was on the phone and he pointed to the chair on the other side of his desk. When he had finished talking he took out his handkerchief and loudly trumpeted his nose.

"I've had a complaint," he said.

"Sorry to hear it. Sounds like you still do."

"I don't mean *that* kind of a complaint, I mean I've had a complaint about the way that you're investigating these homicides. Ms. Honey Blackwell from the city council says your homicide team has been unjustifiably discriminating against people of color, especially those of the Santería religion. These *santeros*, they're very sensitive people. They don't like being rousted."

Decker lifted both hands in a gesture of innocence. "Captain—I'm not discriminating against anybody. I just happen to have a strong suspicion that the motive for *all* of these homicides is linked to Santería."

"Junior Abraham's okay. But the other victims were four white middle-class people. What makes you think that *they* could have any connection at all with Santería? Where's your evidence?"

"Ah. Well, it's only circumstantial, at the moment. More theoretical, really, than circumstantial."

"All right, then, tell me what your theoretical evidence is, so that I can get Ms. Blackwell off my tail."

"If it's all the same to you, I'd really like to wait until I can firm things up a little."

"Decker, I'm your superior officer and as such I am ultimately responsible for the progress of this investigation, which so far seems to be achieving nothing whatsoever, except to cause major irritation to the Afro-American community, whose trust and confidence it has taken me the best part of seven years to build up."

"With all respect, sir, Honey Blackwell isn't the Afro-

American community. Honey Blackwell is a racially motivated political opportunist, and a fat one, at that."

"Nutritionally challenged, I'll admit. But we still need her support. I've also had the interim chief on my tail, wanting to know what we can report to the media."

"You can tell them that we're very close to a major breakthrough. We have a prime suspect and we should be making an arrest within a matter of days."

"We have a prime suspect? Why the hell didn't you tell me? Who?"

"I don't want to go off at half-cock on this, sir. The prime suspect isn't aware that he's a prime suspect, so my strategy is to keep him believing that we're still floundering around in the dark."

"You still haven't told me who he is."

"No, sir. You're right. I haven't."

Cab was about to say something when his phone rang. He picked it up and demanded, "What the hell now? Oh, sorry, ma'am."

It was the interim chief again. While Cab flustered and blustered, Decker idly looked out of his open office door. He looked, and then he looked again, frowning. He couldn't be sure, but the wall of the corridor outside appeared to be slightly distorted, as if he were seeing it through a sheet of flawed glass. He moved his head from side to side, and as he did so, the distortion shifted and altered.

He took off his glasses, but the wall was still oddly curved. He stood up. Cab pressed his hand over the telephone receiver and said, "Lieutenant—I'm not done with you yet!" But Decker ignored him and stepped outside the office.

Halfway along the corridor he saw a tangled, transparent shape. It reminded him of a huge jellyfish that he had once seen in Cumtuck Sound—a glistening and deadly disturbance that was visible only for what it wasn't, rather than what it was. He didn't know if he ought to approach it or not. If it was Changó, cloaked by a Santería spell, then he could be in truly appalling danger.

He lifted out his gun, cocked it, and raised it in both hands. Then he edged his way carefully toward the transparency, trying to distinguish some kind of outline, some kind of distinguishing features. But it kept on rolling and unrolling, knotting and unknotting, and every time he thought he could make out a face, or an arm, or a shoulder, it unraveled itself into another shape altogether.

"Is that you, Major Shroud?" he said, with a phlegmy catch in his throat.

The distortion moved away from him, and now it became more geometrical, so that the wall behind it appeared to be broken up into irregular diamond patterns. He began to realize that he was witnessing an optical trick, a way of diverting his attention away from what he was really looking at, like a mirage, or a complicated arrangement of mirrors.

"I know you're there, Major, or Changó, or whatever you call yourself. I know you're there and I know where to find you and believe me, you bastard, I'm coming to get you."

He had no idea if this ripple in the air really was Changó, or Major Shroud, or if he was simply experiencing another illusion. Neither did he know if it possessed any intelligence, or if it could hear what he was saying—or, hell, if it could be stopped by a bullet, or stopped by anything. Maybe Hicks was right, and his mind was giving way.

At that moment, Cab came out of his office. "Lieutenant, what in the name of God are you doing?"

Decker didn't turn around. But as soon as Cab approached, the distortion in the air rolled away and disappeared. Decker waited for a moment to make sure that it had gone, and then he cautiously holstered his gun.

"Lieutenant?"

"Oh . . . I was practicing my grip, Captain. Sergeant Bliss down at the range said that my balance needed some work."

"Your balance? Too damn right it does. Listen—I have to go talk to the chief. Give me an update on what you've been doing and leave it on my desk. Like, immediately."

"Yes, sir, Captain. It's done already."

CHAPTER THIRTY-ONE

He swerved his Mercury into the curb outside Queen Aché's house and both he and Hicks rolled out of their seats like TV cops. Two squad cars followed close behind, with four uniformed officers, three of them black and two of them female. Decker knew his politics.

George and Newton, Queen Aché's bodyguards, stood shoulder to shoulder and blocked the front steps.

"Queen Aché ain't seeing nobody today."

"Says you. I have a warrant here for Queen Aché's arrest on suspicion of homicide in the first degree."

He held it up and George peered at it closely. "Like you can read," Decker said, and whipped it away again.

"She still ain't seeing nobody. She gave me orders. 'Tell everybody I ain't seeing nobody no matter what,' that's what she said."

"George Montgomery, you are under arrest for obstructing a police officer. You have the right to remain silent—"

"Okay, okay! Cool. I'll tell her you're here. She won't like it, though. She's holding an *asiento*."

"I don't care if she's holding her breath. Get her to open up."

George went to the intercom and buzzed it. "Mikey," he said. "It's trouble. We got Martin down here and half of the police department. He has a warrant."

After a while, Mikey opened the door. Decker turned around to the uniforms and said, "Give me a couple of minutes, will you? I'll whistle if I need you."

He and Hicks followed Mikey into Queen Aché's throne room. As before, the white wooden shutters were all closed, and the room was illuminated only by a few thin shafts of sunlight, like a chapel. Queen Aché wasn't there, but Mikey said, "Wait, okay? I'll go bring her." Scores of candles were steadily burning on Queen Aché's shrine, and there was a strong, bittersweet smell of herbs and spices and flowers in the air, *escoba amarga*, *prodigiosa*, *yerba luisa*, and cinnamon. The aroma heightened the sense of unreality in the house, as if he and Hicks were visiting a dream house together. Hicks nervously flexed his shoulders and tugged at his shirt collar.

After a few minutes Queen Aché appeared through the double doors, and she was like a tall ghost flowing into the room. She wore a headdress of blue flowers and silver stars and she was robed in flowing white muslin, with blue and white and crystal beads around her neck. Her makeup was ivory white, although her eyes were circled by crimson eye shadow and her lips were bloodred. Her face reminded Decker of a West African death mask.

"This intrusion is an *outrage*, Lieutenant! I am holding an *asiento* for my friend's cousin, an initiation. This is the *día del medio*, the day in the middle, when all his family and friends will be gathering to pay tribute to his *orisha*."

"Oh," Decker said. "Bummer."

"You can come back in two days. Make an appointment with Mikey."

"Sorry, Your Majesty, this can't wait. I'm here to arrest you on suspicion of the murder of Herbert 'Junior' Abraham."

Queen Aché flapped one hand in contempt, so that her bangles clashed. "You think I would soil my own hands with such a deed? In Santería we say *oddi oche*—absolved through lack of evidence."

"In the City of Richmond Police Department we say that maybe a perpetrator can make herself invisible but she always leaves some evidence behind her, no matter how smart an occult cookie she thinks she is."

Queen Aché sat down on the chaise longue. She could even make sitting down appear erotic, the way she slid sideways and crossed her thighs and looked at Decker from out of those bloodred eye circles around her eyes. "Nobody knows what is at the bottom of the sea, Lieutenant."

Decker cleared his throat. "I'm not worried about the bottom of the sea, Queen Aché. I'm concerned with what happened at Jimmy the Rib's."

"Pfff! I was here at home. How should I know what happened?"

"I have at least one eyewitness who is prepared to swear on oath that it was you who came into that restaurant, and that it was you who personally blew Junior Abraham's head off. I'm talking to other eyewitnesses, too."

"You're crazy. I saw it on the news. Everybody said that Junior was shot by a man—a man who looked like a waiter."

"Sure they did. But that was before I asked a very special somebody to jog their memory. A very special somebody who saw you clearer than anybody else."

"Is that so? I don't suppose you're going to tell me who that very special somebody is."

"For sure. The best witness of all. Junior Abraham himself. You tricked everybody else into thinking that they saw a waiter, didn't you? But there was one person you wanted to show yourself to, and that was Junior. Just so he was absolutely clear *why* his brains were going to be splattered all over the wall."

"Ha! Since when did the Richmond City police detectives confer with the dead?"

"Since we found out just how powerful your magic is, Queen Aché. Since we learned what tricks you can play with people's perception. I've learned a whole lot about Santería these past few days, and I have to say that I've developed a very healthy respect for it. A religion that can call on every force of nature. Wind, fire, lightning, you name it. You can walk through solid walls if you know how to do it. You can walk through a crowded room and nobody can see you. You can change the way that people look at you, so that they think you're somebody else."

"Do you seriously think that anybody is going to believe you?"

"Oh yes. Because me and Sergeant Hicks here, we've been prepared to approach this investigation with a very open mind. That means we've been talking to people that other detectives would never think of talking to. Like dead people. Like people who can tell us how you did what you did. Like *santeros*."

"You can't convict me with the words of a headless corpse. *Obbara osa*. You're crazy."

"You want to know how crazy I am? I'm also arresting you for the murder of Catherine Meredith Meade."

Queen Aché dismissively waved her hand. "Catherine *who*? I don't even know who this person is."

"Oh, I think you do, Your Majesty. Catherine Meredith Meade was my partner during that time a couple of years ago when I was investigating your various enterprises with illegal substances and property scams. I was called out in the middle of the night to investigate a suspicious drowning. As soon as I was gone, you came to my apartment—*you*, personally—and you blew that poor girl's brains out. Now do you know who she is?"

Queen Aché said, "I am not going to speak to you anymore. This is insanity."

Decker held up a small plastic evidence bag containing two beads. "Yours, I think. You left them at the crime scene."

"What do two beads amount to?"

"Murderers have been convicted on a damn sight less. We nailed one guy when we found a single grain of gunpowder in his coat pocket, practically invisible to the naked eye."

"I was never at your apartment and I can prove that I was never there. You're wasting my time."

"Ah, but somebody *saw* you there. Somebody heard you speak."

"I was never there. Never. You are a fool, Lieutenant."

Decker looked at her with his eyebrows raised, saying nothing. Then he turned to Hicks and said, "Sergeant . . . you want to give me a moment alone with Queen Aché here?"

Hicks didn't look very happy about it, but he said, "Whatever you say, sir," and left the room. Decker called out, "Close the doors, would you, sport?"

He went over to Queen Aché's shrine, with all its steadily burning candles. "Who's your personal *orisha*, Your Majesty?"

"Yemayá, the goddess of the sea waters, and of the moon."

"Powerful, is she, Yemayá? I would guess so."

"She is the mother to everyone. Her children are as numerous as the fish."

"Powerful as Changó, say?"

"Hmm. That shows how little you know of Santería, Lieutenant. I said that Yemayá is the mother to everyone. She is also Changó's adoptive mother, and perhaps more than that. When Changó returned home after many years away, he did not recognize Yemayá, and fell in love with her."

"So . . . Yemayá could have some influence over Changó? I mean, if Changó was causing trouble, Yemayá could tell him to, like, cool it?"

"Why are you asking me this? I thought you were more interested in proving that I am a killer."

"I *know* you're a killer, Queen Aché."

"Oh yes, I forgot your evidence. Your two beads, produced years after your girlfriend was murdered."

"Not just beads, but several small hairs, which I've sent for DNA matching. And something else. Another eyewitness account."

Queen Aché stood up. "I don't have the time for these fantasies, Lieutenant. I have to get back to my *asiento*."

"You just wait up," Decker cautioned her. "When Cathy's killer entered my apartment building that night in February, he or she left no footprints and no fingerprints and no image on the closed-circuit television cameras. There is nobody else I know of who could have done that, except you.

"The killer passed through a solid door and didn't materialize until he or she was actually standing in my bedroom. There is nobody else I know of who could have done that, except you.

"I know it was you, Queen Aché. You came up real close, so that you could shoot Cathy point-blank in the face.

Cathy grabbed your hair and pulled out some of your beads. You said, '*Irosun oche!*'"

Queen Aché stared at him, her eyes so wide that she looked as if she had gone mad, and actually *shuddered*. Her white dress was illuminated so brightly by a single shaft of sunlight that it looked like an incandescent gas mantle.

"So you *do* know," she said, at last.

Decker nodded.

"You will find these accusations impossible to prove in court."

"That doesn't matter, as far as I'm concerned. I'm satisfied that you killed both Cathy and Junior Abraham, and that's good enough for me."

"What are you talking about?"

Decker took his Colt Anaconda out of its shoulder holster, opened the cylinder, and ejected all of the shells into the palm of his hand. One by one, he kissed the tip of each shell and pressed it back in.

"I do this every day," he told her. "I bless these bullets. And do you want to know *why* I bless these bullets? I do it because once I accidentally shot a fellow officer because I was too jumpy and too quick and I didn't make absolutely sure that I was shooting at the right person. So I promised myself that I would never do that again. If I had to shoot anybody, each bullet would be blessed, and each bullet would be fired with forethought. Not out of fear, or panic, but because it was right, and because I had no other choice."

Queen Aché didn't say anything, but she didn't stop staring at him.

"I have a serious problem," he said. "You've heard about this recent spate of homicides, people getting beheaded, people having their guts cut out. I'm pretty certain that they're connected with Santería, and that the perpetrator is possessed by Changó. I'm also pretty certain that there are going to be more. Up to eight more, at least."

Queen Aché frowned. "Why should that be any concern of mine?"

"It isn't, not directly, but I'm going to make it your concern. You see, you're the only person in Richmond who has the power to deal with this joker, and in spite of the fact that you're a killer and a racketeer I'm going to ask you to help me to track him down and put him out of business for good."

Queen Aché closed her eyes and tilted her head back and said, "*Ha!*"

"Ha? Is that a no or a yes?"

She came up close to him. He was almost overwhelmed by the musky perfume of Esencia Pompeya. "You have wasted too much of my precious time, Lieutenant. If you are going to arrest me, then you had better arrest me. My lawyers will have me released before you can say 'insufficient evidence.' Don't think for a moment that you can play games with me."

Decker raised his revolver and pointed it straight between her eyes. "I wasn't really going to *arrest* you, Your Majesty. You see this warrant? This is only a search warrant to check through your accounts. But I wanted to tell you face-to-face that I am completely satisfied that it was you who killed my Cathy."

"And what?"

"And if you don't agree to help me I'm going to do to you, with two or three of my blessed bullets, the very same thing that you did to her. I don't give a shit for the consequences. You killed the only woman I ever loved and I'm going to blow your fucking brains all over this room."

Queen Aché stared at him, her eyes glittering, her bosom rising and falling as she breathed, as if she had just finished running, or making love.

"You'd actually do it, wouldn't you?" she said at last.

"Oh yes. You can be totally sure of that."

"And if I do agree to help you? What then?"

"Then my witnesses conveniently forget to remember that it was you who shot Junior Abraham."

"And you?"

"Me? I try to accept the fact that at least one good thing came out of Cathy's death."

Queen Aché touched her face with her fingertips as if she were making sure that, in the afterlife, she would always remember what it felt like. Decker pulled back the Anaconda's hammer.

"Aren't you going to count?" Queen Aché asked.

"You want me to? Okay, five."

"The death penalty is almost guaranteed in Virginia."

"I know that. But at least my ancestors will recognize me. If you don't have a head, how's King Special going to know that it's you?"

"Don't mock my religion, Lieutenant."

"Four."

Queen Aché stood up very straight and flared her nostrils. She wasn't used to dealing with people who weren't afraid of her, and Decker could sense her rising uncertainty.

"Three."

She was still staring at him as if she were trying to hypnotize him, but Decker knew without any doubt at all that if she didn't ask him to stop, then he was going to shoot her. The So-Scary Man was going to get him, anyhow, one way or another, and he was probably going to suffer the Nine Deaths, so what did it matter? From whatever limbo it was that her spirit still lived on, Cathy had done everything she possibly could to save him, but if she couldn't, she deserved avenging, at the very least.

"Two."

At that moment, the doors on the opposite side of the throne room were thrown open, and Hicks came back in. He held up his cell phone, and said, "Lieutenant—the captain wants a word with you. Like, you know, *now.*"

"One," Decker said, without blinking.

"Lieutenant? The captain says that—Lieutenant? *Lieutenant?* What the fuck are you doing, Lieutenant? Lieutenant!"

Hicks struggled to get his gun out, but Decker shouted, "Don't!"

"What's going on?" Hicks said, in a panicky voice. "You can't just—"

"You want to say a prayer?" Decker asked Queen Aché.

Queen Aché breathed in, breathed out, breathed in. Then she said, "I will say just one thing. *Yenya orisha obinrin dudukueke re maye avaya mi re oyu ayaba ano rigba iki mi iya mayele.* An invocation to Yemayá, to fill me with her strength, as I go to face Changó."

Decker lowered his revolver, eased the hammer forward, and slid it back in its holster.

"Where is this man who is possessed by Changó?" Queen Aché asked.

"Not far. Somewhere in Main Street Station."

"And when do you want me to help you?"

Decker checked his watch. "Sooner the better."

"Very well. But only because my *orisha* wills it, and because I wish to confront this man."

"Whatever you say."

Queen Aché said, "I have to change. You can wait for me."

"Just one thing, before you go. What does *irosun oche* mean?"

"It is one of the patterns of the cowrie shells. It means 'the dead are circling to see who they can seize.'"

CHAPTER THIRTY-TWO

Decker and Hicks waited nearly a half hour for Queen Aché to make herself ready. Decker and Hicks sat at the bottom of the stairs, sullenly watched over by George and Newton. People came and went: family members and friends who had been invited to the *asiento*, all dressed up in their best clothes and carrying baskets of fruit, jars of honey, rum, cigars, chickens, and flowers. When they learned that the *asiento* had been delayed, and why, they looked across at Decker and Hicks with restless hostility, and one elderly man came over and said, "You are not the law. The *orishas* are the law. You have ruined my grandson's *asiento*."

Decker said, "Sorry about that, sport. Nothing personal."

"Something bad will happen to you today because of what you have done here. You will know justice and blood."

"Thanks for the warning, but that's part of my job description."

Eventually Queen Aché descended the staircase, no

longer a crimson-eyed white-faced ghost in muslin, but a tall, athletic-looking black woman in skintight black leather pants and a dark brown sleeveless suede top, with six or seven silver armbands on each arm. Her head was covered by a dark brown silk scarf, tightly knotted, with a silver medallion dangling over her forehead. She carried a large leather bag over her shoulder, with fringes and beads.

One of her heavily bejeweled henchmen came down with her, a shaven-headed man with mirror sunglasses and a neck like a tree stump. "You listen to me, Mr. Detective. This is Queen Aché here and Queen Aché is the queen of all she survey. Any bad shit come to her, then a hundert times more bad shit is going to be happening to you."

"I'll take care of her," Decker assured him; although he knew that, in reality, Queen Aché was coming along to take care of *him*.

In the car, with the two squad cars following close behind them, Decker gave Queen Aché a brief outline of who they thought they were looking for, and why. He told her all about the Devil's Brigade, and Major Shroud, and all of his nightmares. She listened, and nodded once or twice, but said nothing.

"You don't seem particularly *surprised* by any of this," he told her, when he had finished.

"Nothing in Santería surprises me, Lieutenant. I have known people whose dead ancestors are still walking the streets after two hundred years. You forget that Yoruba beliefs not only gave birth to Santería, in America, but Candomble in Brazil and Shango in Trinidad; and in Haiti, Yoruba traditions were mixed with those of the Fon people from Dahomey, and resulted in the creation of voodoo."

"So you think that it's perfectly possible that the So-

Scary Man could be Major Shroud himself, risen from the dead?"

"Why not? A lead-lined coffin would preserve his body—as well as all the herbs and spices that were buried along with him. And if he was really possessed by Changó, that would preserve his soul. Changó, like all of the *orishas*, is immortal."

"You think you might be able to call him off? Like, appeal to his better nature or something?"

"Changó is Changó. He is the most popular of all orishas. But when he wants revenge, he will never rest until he gets it."

Hicks's cell phone rang. He said, "Yes—yes, Captain. I'm afraid he's driving right now."

"That Cab again?" Decker asked.

"He says he wants you back at headquarters, no arguments."

"How does he sound?"

"Enraged."

"Not apoplectic yet? That's good. Tell him to give me twenty minutes."

They parked on East Main Street, right outside the station entrance. Over to the west, the sky was growing gloomy, even though it was only a few minutes past midday, and the clouds had a strange bruised appearance, purple and red.

They pushed their way through the swing doors. Inside it was dark and unexpectedly chilly, and they all took off their sunglasses. The steep stairway was coated in concrete dust and the whole building echoed with hammering and drilling and shouting.

They climbed the stairs until they reached the arrivals' lobby.

Mike Verdant saw them and gave them a wave. He

crossed the floor of the lobby, stepping over hydraulic hoses and lengths of timber, and held out his hand.

"Come back for another look, Lieutenant? You're in luck—we're just about to reinstall the decorative railings."

"Actually we want to pay another visit to the crawl space."

"Really? I don't think there's anything down there, only debris."

"All the same."

Mike looked dubiously at Queen Aché. "You want to take this lady down there too?"

"That's the idea. She knows what we're looking for more than we do."

"Well . . . okay. But you have to wear hard hats, and I ought to lend you some coveralls. It's pretty slimy down there."

He came back with hard hats and three bright-yellow coveralls with CRDCD lettered in red on the back—City of Richmond Department of Community Development. They stepped into them—Hicks almost overbalancing as he caught his shoe in the leg hole—and buttoned them up.

Mike said to Queen Aché, "Pardon me . . . but do I *know* you?"

Queen Aché looked down at him haughtily. She was at least four inches taller than he was. "Give thanks to God that you don't."

Mike turned to Decker, pulling a face. Decker shrugged as if to say, *That's the way she is . . . don't push it.* Mike said, "Here . . . you're going to need these flashlights."

They went back down the staircase to the East Main Street entrance. As they did so, they heard a bellow of thunder, and through the dusty glass of the swing doors they could see spots of rain on the sidewalk outside.

Mike led them to the break in the wall that led to the lower level. "I'd come with you but I have to put in those railings. One half inch out of line and we're screwed."

"That's okay," Decker said. "I think we can manage from here."

When Mike had gone back up to the arrivals lobby, Hicks said, "Lieutenant—do you really think this is a good idea?"

"No, but what else are we going to do?"

"I don't know. But we know how powerful this So-Scary Man is. Think of the way he pushed us both over, in the hospital. Maybe we should try smoking him out of here with tear gas, or knocking him out with nitrous oxide."

"Hicks, we don't have the time, and I can't see Cab authorizing a SWAT team, can you? Besides that, I'm not sure whether tear gas or nitrous oxide would have any affect on this joker at all. For Christ's sake, he's dead, or the living dead, or whatever you call it in Santería."

Queen Aché said, "*Egun*, the ancestors, who are dead but still live. That is why I call my followers the Egun."

Hicks said, "I still think this is too risky. Either that, or we're wasting our time."

Queen Aché pointed her finger directly at Hicks, as if she were picking him out in a lineup. "You believe, don't you? You're a believer. You pretend that you're a skeptic, but you know that the dead can walk amongst us, and that spirits can talk to us from beyond the grave."

Hicks looked uncomfortable. "Let's just do it, shall we, if we're going to do it?"

"Why do you deny it?" Queen Aché persisted. "Why do you deny your roots? Do you really choose to spend the rest of your life in the soulless world of the white people? The dog has four legs but walks only one path."

"Come on," Decker said. He climbed into the hole in the wall, clambering over heaps of broken brick, shining his flashlight up ahead of him. "You next, Your Majesty. Hicks, you watch our rear ends."

Once they had negotiated the bricks, they found themselves in a low, vaulted cellar. The walls and the ceiling were black with damp and encrusted with salt. In the far corner, the salt had built up against the brickwork in a series of lumpy gray stalagmites, which looked like a gaggle of hideous dwarves, some of them with swollen heads and others with hugely hunched backs.

"Must have flooded here pretty often," Decker remarked.

Queen Aché said, "The city flooded on the day when I was born. My father always said that it was an omen from Yemayá, that I too would flood the city one day."

"Well, you certainly flooded it with second-rate smack."

They penetrated farther into the cellar, flicking their flashlights left and right, but there was no sign of a coffin, or a niche that the So-Scary Man might have used as a hiding place. No bunched-up blankets, no newspaper bedding, no discarded Coke cans. Over in the left-hand corner, however, it looked as if a large section of the floor had collapsed into the crawl space below.

"What makes you sure that he's here?" Queen Aché asked. Although she was standing still, and her face was serious, her shadow was dancing on the ceiling right above her, as if her spirit was mocking them.

"His coffin was sunk right here, in Shockoe Creek, and this is the first time that these lower foundations have been disturbed since the station was built. Apart from that, the little girl I was telling you about . . . the one who can see him . . . she saw him entering the station through the same doors that we came in. Another time she saw a kind of a twisted cloud over the station rooftops, which she thought was a cloud of evil. She even drew a picture of it. For some reason she said it was the House of Fun."

"The House of Fun?" Queen Aché thought about that and then she shook her head. "No . . . not the House of Fun."

"Excuse me?"

"She probably understood it wrong. She meant the House of *Ofun*. Ofun means 'the place where the curse is born.' "

"You're serious? 'The place where the curse is born?' Hear that, Hicks? What more proof do we need than that?"

Queen Aché stepped ahead of him, deeper into the cellars, occasionally ducking her head because the ceiling was so low. Thirty feet in, she stopped, and raised her hand to indicate that they should stay where they were, and stay silent.

"What is it?" Decker asked, after a while.

"I can smell something," she said.

"Me too. Dead rats and damp."

"No . . . there is something else. Close your eyes. Breathe in deeply and hold it."

Decker breathed in. Hicks did too, and whistled through one nostril. Decker couldn't be sure, but he thought he could detect the faintest aroma of stale herbs, like taking the lid off a jar of dried oregano.

"Smells like my grandma's larder," Hicks said.

"That's right," Queen Aché agreed. "Those are the herbs they would have used to seal Major Shroud in his casket."

She knelt down and opened up her leather satchel. Out of it she lifted a canvas pouch, tightly tied at the neck with black waxed string. She set this down on the floor in front of her, and then she took out four dried apples, a glass bottle of pale green liquid, and another bottle containing a dark red liquid.

While Decker kept his flashlight shining on her, she untied the canvas pouch and tipped out a handful of dull, blackened stones.

"What are you doing?" Decker asked her.

"These are thunderstones . . . stones from a building that was struck by lightning."

As if to emphasize their importance, there was a loud bang of thunder from outside, and even here in the cellar they could smell the fresh, ozone-laden draft that came with the following rain.

"I cast the stones, and then I pour this liquid over them. It is made from the leaves of the alamo tree, boiled in water. This will dispel evil. Then I say an invocation to Changó, *kabio, kabio, sile*, and anoint them with rooster's blood."

"Okay . . . and what will this do?"

"It will tell me if any manifestation of Changó is here. Just watch and wait."

Decker hunkered down beside her. She pulled the stopper out of the bottle of blood and sprayed it across the stones like a priest spraying holy water. "*Kabio, kabio, sile*," she repeated. "*Kabio, kabio, sile*."

They waited for over a minute. The thunder rumbled again, and this time it echoed through the cellar as if it had come from somewhere below the ground, rather than the sky.

"I guess he's not here after all," Decker said.

"Wait. This always takes a little time."

Another minute passed, but then Decker heard a faint sizzling sound. He sniffed, and he could not only smell damp, and dried-out herbs, but a burned smell, like meat stock burning on the side of a cooking pot. He shone his flashlight on the thunderstones and saw that the rooster blood was drying up and bubbling, and giving off smoke. The thunderstones themselves had turned gray, and one or two of them were beginning to glow red-hot.

"Changó is here," Queen Aché said, emphatically.

"You're sure about that?"

"Look for yourself. Look at the stones."

One by one, the stones turned to scarlet, and Decker could feel the heat they were giving off, the same dry heat as a sauna. "Changó's power is attracted to this *ebbó*. He is showing us that he is close by."

"Yes, but *where?*"

"You won't be able to see him, but I will. I will call on Yemayá to help me against my enemies, and to give me strength."

With that, she reached into her satchel again and brought out a plastic bag, neatly folded and tied with blue tape. She untied the tape and opened the bag, revealing a small silvery-scaled fish. She took out yet another bottle and poured a thin, sticky liquid over the fish. "Sugarcane syrup," she explained. Then she dropped seven shiny pennies onto it.

"*Yenya orisha obinrin dudukueke re maye avaya mi re oyu* . . ." she sang, closing her eyes and swaying her head from side to side.

Hicks looked at Decker uneasily. "I hope we're not getting ourselves into something we can't get out of."

"Like I said, sport, we don't have any choice."

Hicks's cell phone rang again, but when he took it out to answer it, Decker said, "Leave it. It's only Cab getting close to boiling point."

". . . *lojun oyina ni reta gbogbo okin nibe iwo ni re elewo nitosi re omo teiba modupue iya mi.*"

Queen Aché stopped swaying and opened her eyes. She arched her head back and stared at the ceiling for a moment. Then she said, flatly, "Yemayá is with me."

Decker looked at her, and then took off his glasses and looked at her even more closely, because there was no question at all that something had possessed her. It was difficult to pin down exactly what it was. But she seemed to radiate an extraordinary energy, and when he took a step closer to her he could feel the hairs on the back of his neck rising up, as if he were standing close to an electrical transformer. She turned to look at him, and although she was still Queen Aché, with that high forehead and those erotically drooping eyelids and those full, slightly parted lips, there was another face within her face, a face that was calm and stony-eyed and infinitely old.

Decker realized that, at secondhand, he was looking at the face of an *orisha*, a goddess from the earliest days of African civilization, a creator of dynasties and magic. He had been frightened before. His nightmares about the Battle of the Wilderness had frightened him. But nothing had ever frightened him like this: the realization that there *was* a world in which the dead could live forever, and that men could walk through walls, and that none of the laws of possibility meant anything at all.

He was suddenly reminded of Eduard Munch's painting of *The Scream*—the utter terror of finding out that life has no boundaries whatever.

"What now?" he asked Queen Aché.

"We find out where your So-Scary Man is concealing himself."

She picked up the apples one by one and placed them on the hot thunderstones. They sizzled and blistered, and gave off a thick, caramel-smelling smoke.

"Lead me now to Changó," Queen Aché said. "Lead me through the paths of Changó Ogodo, Alufina Crueco, Alafia, Larde, Obakoso, Ochongo, and Ogomo Oni. Lead me through all his various disguises: Saint Barbara and Saint Marcos de Leon and Saint Expeditus."

Up until now, the smoke had been billowing upward, but as Queen Aché continued her chanting it began to drift toward the opposite side of the cellars. It coiled its way past the stalagmite dwarfs, and then it seemed to disappear into the darkness, as if somebody were pulling a long gray chiffon scarf through a keyhole.

"He's there. Changó can't resist the smell of apples."

Decker unholstered his gun, but Queen Aché laid her hand on top of his. "You must understand that you cannot kill Changó. You can only kill Major Shroud."

"He'll do, for starters."

"But you cannot kill Major Shroud while Changó still possesses him."

"So how can we stop him?"

"In Santería, we believe that everybody has an *eleda*. It means their head, or their mind, but it also means their guardian angel. In Major Shroud's case, his guardian angel is Changó. While Changó is alert, he will protect Major Shroud against any attack. But *eledas* can grow hungry, and need feeding and entertainment. If you invoke Changó, and give him a *plaza*, an offering of fruit and candy, and light some candles for him, he should be distracted long enough for you to kill Major Shroud."

She dug farther into her satchel and pulled out another cotton bag, tied with red and white string. "I brought apples, and bananas, and herbs, too. *Rompe zaraguey* and *bledo punzó*."

"And candles?"

"Of course." She produced three church candles, tied together with red ribbon.

Decker took the bag and the candles and pushed them into his pockets. "You're not really doing this because I threatened to shoot you, are you?"

Queen Aché gave him a strange smile, and he was sure that he could see Yemayá smiling, too, behind the mask of Queen Aché's face.

"When there is no man who can stand up against you,

Lieutenant, what is left? You have to test your strength against the gods."

"Haven't you ever—"

"Relied on anyone? Yes. Once. But one morning we both woke up and knew that I had grown stronger than him, and so he packed his bag and left without saying a single word."

"Do you know how much I hate you for what you did?"

"No, Lieutenant, I don't. I never loved anybody as much as that."

Hicks was shining his flashlight in the far corner of the cellars, where the smoke was hurrying away. "There's an opening here, Lieutenant. Part of the wall's collapsed."

Decker came over to join him. Just past the dwarfish stalagmites was a narrow alcove, and most of the brickwork at the back of it had fallen inward. It looked like the wall in which the drunken Fortunato had been bricked up alive, in Edgar Allan Poe's story *The Cask of Amontillado*. *"For God's sake, Montresor!"*

When he probed his flashlight into the back of the alcove, Decker could see that it led to a cavity between the station walls. The cavity was only a little more than two feet wide, but in between the walls the rubble had fallen to form a kind of staircase, leading down. The smoke was steadily sliding in the same direction.

"Well . . . the smoke seems to think that he's hiding down here."

Hicks grimaced, as if this was all too much for him. "The *smoke* thinks he's down here? For Pete's sake."

Decker took an awkward step over the broken bricks and eased himself sideways through the opening. The smell of herbs was even stronger here, but there was another smell, too, and it was sickening. The smell of seawater and raw sewage, and bad fish, and half-decayed crabs.

He maneuvered himself around and offered his hand to

Queen Aché, but she managed to climb through the opening unaided. The "staircase" was only a steep slope of crumbled masonry, slippery with damp, and Decker had to keep one hand pressed against the right-hand wall to steady himself as he descended. Halfway down he lost his footing and landed on his backside, sliding down six or seven feet before he managed to catch hold of a protruding beam of rotten timber and stop himself.

At the bottom of the slope was the opening to a low, pitch-black crawl space. They shone their flashlights into the darkness, crisscrossing like light sabers. The floor of the crawl space was thick with streaky black mud, and the ceiling was buttressed with dripping brick. Decker reckoned that it ran more than two hundred feet, from one side of the station building to the other.

Hicks said, "If you get caught in here, Lieutenant, you won't stand a hope in hell."

"Has to be done, sport."

"But if you can't even *see* him—"

"*I* can," Queen Aché reassured him.

"Okay . . ." Hicks said, reluctantly, "so what's the plan?"

"I guess we'll just have to search the place on our hands and knees. Do it systematically, in squares."

"No, Lieutenant," Queen Aché said. "You won't have to do that. Look."

Decker turned around. The smoke from the burning apples was drifting steadily down the staircase and into the crawl space. When Decker shone his flashlight on it, he saw that it was hurrying toward the right-hand side, about three-quarters of the way under the station, where it abruptly disappeared downward This was where the ceiling had collapsed from the floor above.

"Looks like we've found him," Decker said.

"So what do we do now?" Hicks asked.

"We propitiate his *eleda*."

"I thought we were just going to blow his head off."

"Same thing, differently put."

CHAPTER THIRTY-THREE

Decker took the bundle of candles out of his pocket. Queen Aché untied the ribbon around them and lit them, handing one to Decker and one to Hicks.

"You will have to think respectful thoughts about Changó. Make him your offering of fruit and beg his forgiveness for the sins of your forefathers."

"And you really think that will work? Think what he did to Moses Adebolu."

"Changó saw Moses Adebolu as a traitor to his faith. You are only his blood enemy."

"Is that all? That's reassuring. But, well, we all have to die someday, don't we? Let's go do it."

He crouched down and entered the crawl space, the brick ceiling scraping against his back. The sewagey reek of river water was even more overpowering down here, and the greenish black mud squashed thickly into his brand-new Belvedere loafers.

As he approached the hole where Queen Aché's apple smoke was disappearing, he could see more clearly what had happened. A large section of the ceiling had collapsed, not enough to cause any structural damage to the station, but enough to cause the floor beneath it to collapse, too. He shone his flashlight on the bricks and rubble and saw that there was a gaping cavity beneath the foundations, black as a prehistoric cave. He could also see rotting wooden uprights, and part of an old brick wall, which he took to be remnants of the old fishing dock at Shockoe Creek.

Inside the cavity he saw greasy wet planks, blackened with age, which could have been a section of a ship's deck, although most of them had given way, and there was another cavity below them, where the ship's hold must have been.

Queen Aché and Hicks came crouching up to join him. Hicks knocked his head on the ceiling and said, "God *damn* it."

"You see that?" Decker said. "I'll bet you that was the ship that was carrying Major Shroud's casket—the *Nathan Cooper*, wasn't it? When they started renovating the station last year, all the drilling must have brought the ceiling down, and opened up the old Shockoe dock."

"You mean to say they built the station right over the ship, without even bothering to move it?"

"Maybe it wasn't practical to move it. Maybe the builders were too *scared* to move it. It looks like they filled in the creek and buried the ship, too."

Decker tried to penetrate the ship's hold with his flashlight, but the darkness seemed to swallow the beam of light completely, and absolutely nothing was reflected back. His jaw was trembling, not only because of the chilly damp down here in the crawl space, but because he could sense that something deeply malevolent was very close. It was the same feeling that he had experienced in his nightmares—the feeling that somebody was rushing toward him, somebody who wanted to do him terrible harm.

He paused for a moment and took a steadying breath, and then another, even though the air down here was so fetid. He had never suffered from claustrophobia before, but now he was conscious of the tons and tons of brick and masonry that were weighing down on him, and the fact that he would have to crouch like Quasimodo to escape anything that came after him.

"Lieutenant?" Hicks asked. "You okay, Lieutenant?"

"What? Never felt better."

"You really think there's something down here?"

"I'm sure of it. Let's get down there and check it out."

"That deck don't look none too safe."

"Well, we'll just have to tread easy, then, won't we?"

Queen Aché knelt down in the mud. Her candle flame was dancing in the draft, so her expression seemed to change from one second to the next—amused, indifferent, scornful, disturbed. "Changó is here, no question about it. Yemayá can sense his Changó's presence, very strong."

"In that case, we'd better go get him."

Queen Aché gripped his sleeve. "Don't forget. You must acknowledge Changó's greatness. You must beg him to forgive you for all of your misdeeds. Whatever Major Shroud looks like, however he talks to you, it is Changó to whom you are paying your respects, not him. When Changó is distracted—then and only then can you deal with Major Shroud."

"How will I know when that is?"

"Because I will tell you. You cannot see Changó, but Yemayá can."

"Okay, then. Hicks, you ready?"

"I guess so."

Decker turned around and cautiously climbed backward down the heaps of rubble. His shoes immediately dislodged broken bricks and crumbling mortar, creating a miniature landslide that rattled onto the planking of the ship below. As he climbed down lower, he saw that a rusted iron girder had fallen across the ship, preventing the rubble from dropping any farther, so that there was a gap of at least three feet between the rubble and the deck. Grunting with effort, he edged himself around so that he could jump down. More bricks suddenly slipped beneath his feet and before he could jump he fell awkwardly sideways and landed on his side, bruising his shoulder and his hip. He said, "Fuck!" His candle rolled away from him, into a pool of stagnant water, where it instantly fizzled out.

"Are you okay, sir?" Hicks called.

"Terrific, damn it."

"Your candle!" Queen Aché warned him. "You must light your candle!"

Decker climbed to his feet and retrieved his candle. He dried it on his sleeve and then lit it again with his cigarette lighter. "Queen Aché? You coming down next?"

Queen Aché slid down the debris and landed on the deck with a stumble that was almost graceful. Hicks came next, slithering and cursing, although he managed to jump over the gap and land on his feet.

Queen Aché brushed herself down. "Try to show no fear when Major Shroud appears. He is one of the walking dead, but like all *zombis* he doesn't know it. He believes that he is still the same man that he was when he was sealed in his coffin, so you must talk to him as if he is a normal person. While you are doing that, I will present your *plaza* to Changó and see if I can draw his attention away from protecting Major Shroud's head."

"Sounds like a plan to me."

"One thing, though . . . whatever you do, make no attempt to kill Major Shroud until I tell you that Changó has left him unprotected. Otherwise, you will be directly attacking Changó and Changó's anger will be terrible."

"You got it."

They walked along the deck to the fathomless hole where the planks had rotted away. Decker leaned forward and swept his flashlight from side to side. He could make out some of the timbers of the lower decks, and some coils of rope, and a bulging bundle of gray slime that must have been a bale of cotton, but no sign of a casket. "I guess I'll have to go down there and look for it."

"For Christ's sake, Lieutenant, be careful."

"Hicks, old man, this is part of the job."

Although most of the interior of the ship had been gutted by wood rot and boring beetle, there was still the skeleton of a corroded iron companionway clinging to the right-hand side. Decker inched his way toward it and managed to reach out and get a grip on the uppermost railing. The deck planking splintered wetly beneath his weight, but he paused and took a sharp breath, and then he managed to swing himself around and perch both feet on one of the steps.

"You stay there," he told Queen Aché and Hicks. "I'll shout out if I find anything."

He descended the companionway a step at a time, testing each step to make sure that it wouldn't give way. It was at least twenty feet down to the remains of the next deck, and it looked so rotten that—if he fell—he would probably fall right through it, and down to the next deck, and the keel, if the *Nathan Cooper* still had a keel.

It took him nearly five minutes to climb down to the bottom of the companionway. He looked around, trying to orient himself, and trying to work out which way the ship had been docked. The likelihood was that it had been sailed into Shockoe Creek prow-first, and since the sides of the ship tapered off to his right, the hold was probably amidships, to his left.

Holding up his candle in his left hand and his flashlight in his right, he crossed the deck toward a darkened, dripping passageway. The floor was heaped with dead crabs in various stages of decay, like the chopped-off hands of hundreds of massacred children, and the stench was so strong that he couldn't stop himself from letting out a loud, cackling retch. He carefully stepped his way aft, his shoes slipping and sliding, and the flickering flame from his candle made it look as if the crabs were still alive, and crawling on top of each other.

As he neared the end of the passageway he heard a loud, flat, clattering sound. He reached a wooden door with broken hinges, and wrenched it open. Beyond the door was more absolute darkness. He stepped out onto a rusted iron platform and found himself in the *Nathan Cooper*'s hold. Water was cascading down from the hatches above, and that was what was causing all the clatter. Rainwater probably, thought Decker, from the overflowing storm drains along East Main Street. The hold was hung with dozens of heavy-duty chains, which swung and clinked together as the water poured down them. Decker was uncomfortably reminded of the hold of the spaceship *Nostromo*, in *Alien*. Chains, and water.

He directed his flashlight downward, systematically sweeping the floor of the hold. At first he thought that it contained nothing more than some stoved-in barrels and a stack of packing cases, but then he shone it right over to the far side, deep into the shadows, and he saw a heap of timbers and rubble, and a large grayish green box, a quarter buried in bricks, tilted at an angle of forty-five degrees.

He transferred his candle to his flashlight hand, and hefted out his revolver. Then he carefully swung himself around and climbed down the iron ladder that led to the floor of the hold, testing each rung as he went. He had almost reached the bottom when he stepped right up to the top of his sock in stinking, freezing-cold river water. "Shit," he muttered. The hold was flooded more than a foot deep. Definitely no chance of salvaging his loafers now.

Holding his candle and his flashlight high, he waded across the hold toward the grayish green box. Ripples spread across the water and splashed against the broken barrels. Beneath the water, the deck was greasy with weed, and he was only a third of the way across when he slipped, and soaked the legs of his pants right up to his knees.

He stopped for a moment, but he didn't say anything. There was nobody to blame but himself. But if Hicks had been here, he would have been shouted at for ten minutes nonstop.

At last he reached the box. Now that he could see it close up, Decker didn't have any doubt that it was Major Shroud's casket. It was huge, more than eight feet long, hand-beaten out of thick lead. A face was embossed on the top of it—a slitty-eyed, almond-shaped face with a mailbox mouth. It looked like the tribal faces that hung on the wall in the Mask Bar.

At first, Decker thought that the casket was still intact, but when he waded his way around it, he saw that one side of it was heavily corroded, pitted and pustular like gangrenous flesh, and split wide open. He bent down and shone his flashlight inside. He could make out bunches of dried herbs and mummified apples and little wooden figures, but no sign of Major Shroud's body.

He looked around, but he couldn't see anything else apart from mounds of black sludge from the river bottom and more shoals of dead crabs. He paddled his way back toward the ladder, not knowing if he was relieved or disappointed. But he couldn't forget what Cathy had warned him about. If he didn't get Major Shroud first, then Major Shroud was going to get *him*.

He started to climb the ladder, but he was only halfway up when he felt a sharp, cold draft and his candle was suddenly snuffed out. Cursing, he holstered his revolver, and searched in his pockets for his cigarette lighter. He flicked it once, but it wouldn't light, so he flicked it again and again. It still refused to light.

He was still flicking it when he became aware that the cold draft was growing even chillier—so chilly that a curtain of icy vapor began to pour down from the edge of the iron platform above him, like dry ice off the edge of a stage in a rock concert. He looked up, but his glasses were fogging up and everything was blurred. He took them off and wiped them on his necktie, and looked up again.

At first he saw nothing but vapor, but when he lifted his flashlight he thought he could see the vapor forming a shadowy outline, as if somebody was standing in it. For an instant, as the vapor curled around, he even thought he could see the impression of a *face*—a face formed of nothing but frozen air. A living death mask.

"Major Shroud, is that you?" His voice sounded small and flat, barely audible over the promiscuous clattering of the water and the *clink-clink-clink* of the swaying chains.

"Major Shroud? I've come down here to help you. Do you understand that? Do you understand what I'm saying?"

He climbed one more step up the ladder, and then another. "Major Shroud? Or is it Changó I'm talking to? The great and all-powerful Changó, king of the city of Oyo? I greet you, Changó. The king hung himself, but the king did not die."

He climbed farther still, until he reached the edge of the platform. He shone his flashlight from side to side, and he was sure that he could see the transparent outline of a man's shoulders and the side of his head.

"Changó, listen to me. I've come down here to ask you to forgive me for what my great-great-grandfather did to you. He should never have helped to seal you up in that casket, and I'm sorry, okay? I didn't know anything about you before, but now I do and I want to tell you that you're the greatest. Like, *respect*."

He waited, while the freezing fog continued to pour down all around him. Changó—if it was Changó—didn't reply. Decker thought: *How the hell are you supposed to speak to an orisha? And what do you do if they refuse to answer you? Maybe orishas only understand Yoruba.*

But as he waited, the fog appeared to thicken and knot itself into shadows, like the clots of blood in a fertilized egg. Gradually, right in front of Decker's eyes, a shape began to resolve itself, the shape of a tall, dark, broad-shouldered man. In a little over a minute, he had solidified, although his image still appeared smudgy. He looked down at Decker with black, deep-set eyes. He was heavily bearded, and he wore a wide-brimmed hat with ragged black feathers all around it, and a long black overcoat.

"Major Shroud?" Decker said.

"You're a Martin," the figure replied. His voice made Decker feel as if his hair were infested with lice. It was hoarse, and thick, and he spoke with a curious saw-blade accent, which Decker supposed was how everybody must have spoken in Virginia in Civil War days. But more than that, it seemed to come from several different directions at once, as if he were standing on the other side of the ship's hold; and close beside him, too, right next to his ear.

"Your forefather was one of those eleven who betrayed me. Your forefather was one of those who condemned me to spend an eternity, imprisoned, unable to move, in absolute darkness, but always awake."

"Major Shroud, I've come here to settle our differences."

"Differences? You call what they did to me differences?"

"What the rest of the Devil's Brigade did to you, back in the Wilderness—look, I know they were wrong. But it was war, you know? It was right in the thick of a goddamned *battle*, for Christ's sake. Men were dying right, left and center. At the time they genuinely believed that they were doing right."

"They betrayed me, and they betrayed Changó. If it hadn't been for Changó's spirit, I would have suffocated and died. I won that battle for them single-handed, with Changós help. But did they reward me? No. Did they promote me? No. They sealed me in that casket with spells and spices and hoped that I would stay there forever."

"They were afraid of you, Major Shroud. Okay—it doesn't say much for their courage, does it, or their comradeship? But they panicked and they didn't know what else to do."

"All I wanted was the honor that was due to me. I gave up everything—my life, my home, my beloved family—so that Changó could possess me, and we could win the war. Honor? All I received in return was treachery."

"But murdering those men's descendants . . . what good can that do? That's not going to earn you any honor."

"It's not murder! It's revenge! And Changó has taught me all I need to know about exacting my revenge. I lay in that suffocating coffin, for all of those countless years, but

Changó spoke to me, and he nurtured me, and he gave me strength, and he promised me that I would have my day."

While Major Shroud was talking, Decker saw a quick, furtive shadow in the passageway behind him. After a few moments, Queen Aché appeared, her boots crunching over rotting crabs. She saw Major Shroud, and then she saw Decker, and she stopped where she was. Decker made a face at her and quickly shook his head to indicate that she shouldn't do anything hasty. Queen Aché gave him the thumbs-up.

"You've already killed four people," Decker told Major Shroud. "Don't you think that's revenge enough? They were innocent, all of them. None of them had any idea what their great-great-grandparents had done, all those years ago."

"Revenge is revenge. If you can't have revenge on the father, then you're entitled to take your dues from the son. And if not the son, the grandson, and the great-grandson, forever."

"Times have changed, Major Shroud. Years have gone by. The North and the South are one nation now, and what happened during the war—well, it's all forgotten now. It's history."

"Changó!" Queen Aché called out. "Listen to me, Changó! I bring Yemayá with me! *Babami Changó ikawo ilemu fumi alaya tilanchani nitosi.* I have fruit for you. I have honey. I can give you songs and laughter and love."

Major Shroud swung around, his coat billowing. "Who are you? How dare you call on my eleda?"

"I am Queen Aché, daughter of Yemayá, and Yemayá comes to make an offering to Changó."

Major Shroud's voice abruptly changed. When he spoke now, he spoke in a harsh, abrasive growl. "Changó refuses your offering. Changó sees you for what you are. Yemayá betrayed Changó in the Wilderness as surely if she had sealed the casket with her own hands. She allowed the eleven orishas to bind him and take him away—Yeggua and Oshún and Elegguá and all the others—and she didn't lift one finger to intervene. You might have been Changó's stepmother once, Yemayá—you might have been his lover—but that night you turned your back on him, and he has never forgiven you."

"I bring you a *plaza*, Changó. I bring you ram's blood, and *manteca de corojo*."

Major Shroud didn't appear to have heard her. He lowered his head and pressed his fingers to his forehead, as if he were thinking. Queen Aché caught Decker's attention, her eyes wide and alert. She raised her hand with her index finger pointing straight out and her thumb cocked like a revolver hammer. Decker got the message and lifted out his Anaconda. Any second now, Changó would be distracted by her offering, and Decker would be able to blast Major Shroud's head off.

"*Kabio, kabio, sile*," Queen Aché murmured, her voice soft and seductive. "Welcome, Changó, my darling one. Welcome, my child and my passionate lover. Take a moment's rest for apples and herbs. Refresh yourself with honey and blood."

Major Shroud remained as he was, his head bowed, apparently lost in thought. Suddenly, however, crackles of thin blue light began to dance around his hat, like electrified barbed wire. Queen Aché looked triumphantly at Decker. Changó was gradually making his appearance, and in a few seconds he would leave Major Shroud unprotected so that he could taste the food and drink that Queen Aché had brought him.

Decker lifted his revolver and pointed it directly at Major Shroud's head. From this angle, the bullet would enter the soft flesh underneath his jaw, penetrate his tongue and his palate, blow his sinuses apart, and exit through the top of his skull, carrying most of his frontal lobes along with it.

"Come on, Changó, my love," Queen Aché coaxed. She sounded distinctively different from the sophisticated southern lady of color that she usually was. Her intonation was much more African, with a lilting, knowing accent. "Honor my family by tasting my *plaza*. Eat your fill."

The blue electric crackling grew more and more agitated, and it began to form a cagelike structure around Major Shroud's head, like a fencing mask. Queen Aché opened the bag of offerings that she had brought with her and held it up and swung it from side to side.

"This is for you, O great one. My son and my lover, and the god of all fire."

There was a deafening *crackkkk!* and a bang like two cars colliding. For a split second Decker actually *saw* Changó—the *orisha* of thunder and lightning. Changó's hair flew up in all directions, showering thousands of glittering sparks. His eyes glowed like red-hot thunderstones. But what struck Decker more than anything else was his mouth, which seemed to have tier upon tier of jagged teeth, with caterpillars of lightning crawling on his tongue.

"Here!" Queen Aché said, taking out an apple and holding it up to him. "Take it, eat, my beloved Changó!"

But just as the crackling mask of Changó's head turned sideways, to take a bite of Queen Aché's apple, Major Shroud screamed out, "No! It's a trick! You can't leave my head, Changó! They'll kill me, and then you won't have anyplace left to hide!"

Queen Aché shrilled, "Lieutenant—*now!*"

Decker fired, and the Anaconda kicked in his hand. But

Major Shroud swayed backward at an impossible angle, more like a swiveling shadow than a man, and the bullet only clipped the brim of his hat. Black crow feathers burst in all directions, but the bullet thumped harmlessly into the wooden bulkhead. The blazing vision of Changó instantly vanished, like a firework dropped into a bucket of water.

Major Shroud screamed at Decker in hysterical fury.

"Damn you! Damn you to hell! A Martin betrayed me in the Wilderness and now a Martin has betrayed me again! I will cut you into pieces for this, I promise you!"

"Changó!" Queen Aché cried. "Listen to me, Changó!" But it was obvious from the desperate tone of her voice that she had very little hope of tempting him back out of Major Shroud's head.

"You will surely die, Martin," Major Shroud fumed. "Not tonight, because your appointed day is tomorrow, the feast of Saint James Intercisus, and I can happily wait one more night until I come to kill you. I've waited long enough, God knows."

But then he turned to Queen Aché. "This *santera*, on the other hand, is a very different matter. She has perverted her religion and sullied the names of the saints. Look at the way she tried to trick Yemayá into betraying her only son and her only real love! Those who try to deceive the orishas must pay for what they have done, and pay with their lives."

Decker said, "Let her alone, Shroud. This was my idea."

"Revenge is revenge, Martin. Nobody can go unpunished for their sins, ever. That is the law."

"The law? What law? The law of the African jungle? The law of Santería, and voodoo, and *zombis?* What *law* says that you can cut a pregnant woman's head off because her great-great-grandfather tried to stop you from committing a massacre?"

"The law of the earth, and of all things, and of natural

justice. The law of Changó, who protects his followers against their enemies."

Decker lifted his revolver again, and aimed it directly between Major Shroud's eyes. "I'm sorry to disappoint you, sport, but there's a greater law than Changó's law, and it's called the law of the State of Virginia."

Queen Aché said, "*No*, Lieutenant! Don't shoot him!"

"I don't think he's given me a whole lot of choice, do you?"

Major Shroud's vaporous image appeared to slide sideways, like smoke caught in an unexpected breeze. "There is nothing you can do to stop me, Martin. Tomorrow you will die in the same way that Saint James Intercisus died. But so that you will fully understand what your fate will be, I will punish this *santera* in the same way."

"What?"

Major Shroud turned around, and as he turned around he disappeared, leaving nothing in the darkness but a twist of vapor. He disappeared from Decker's sight, but it was plain that Queen Aché could still see him, because she suddenly screamed out, "Changó! This is the daughter of Yemayá! *Changó!*" But Major Shroud said nothing at all, and Changó didn't materialize. Queen Aché suddenly flung one arm up to protect her face and stumbled backward into the passageway.

"Queen Aché!" Decker yelled. "Get the hell out of here!"

He wildly waved his revolver from side to side but he couldn't see anything to fire at. He thrust it back into its holster and heaved himself up the last five rungs of the iron ladder. The jumbled light from his flashlight showed Queen Aché on her hands and knees, trying to scramble along the passageway over the mounds of crabs. She had dropped her candle and her bag of offerings to Changó, and she was whimpering like a beaten animal in terror.

"*Shroud!*" Decker yelled. He hauled out his revolver again and fired a warning shot into the ceiling. The explosion was deafening, and made his ears sing, and for a fleeting moment, in the gunsmoke, he saw the outline of Major Shroud's back, and an arm lifted. His flashlight caught something else, too—the long curved glint of a cavalry saber.

"Queen Aché! Get up! Get out of here!"

Queen Aché seized the wooden handrail at the side of the passageway, but the second she did so Decker heard a quick, sharp *chop!* and all of the fingers of her left hand were scattered onto the floor, still wearing her gold and silver rings. She screamed, and held up her bloody, fingerless hand. "*Yemayá! What has he done to me? What has he done to me? Yemayá! Help me! Yemayá!*"

Decker hurried into the passageway and knelt down beside her, his knees squelching and crunching into layers of putrescent crabs. He lifted up her hand and wound his handkerchief tightly around it, although it was immediately flooded dark red. She was juddering wildly, and staring at him in shock. "He took off all of my fingers. *He took off my fingers!*"

She gripped his shoulder with her right hand and begged, "Get me out of here, please! Get me out of here! He's going to kill me!"

Decker coughed and stood up and tried to lift Queen Aché from the floor. She clung to his shoulder with her good right hand, and was almost off her knees when Decker felt a violent blow against his back, as if he had been struck very hard with a walking stick. Queen Aché screamed again, and dropped onto her knees. "My fingers! My fingers! Yemayá, save me! My fingers!"

She held up her right hand—and that, too, was left with nothing but the stumps of all five fingers, and all of them squirting blood. *Christ almighty*—now Decker knew what Major Shroud was doing. He was attacking Queen Aché with the Nine Deaths that Saint James Intercisus had suffered, just to show Decker what *he* could expect.

He groped his left shoulder blade and found that his coat was soaked with blood. Major Shroud had chopped right through Queen Aché's fingers, right through his coat and shirt, and into his trapezius muscle.

"Get up!" he yelled at Queen Aché. He thrust his arms under her armpits and hoisted her onto her feet. She was a good three inches taller than he was, and at least as heavy, and he almost dropped her back onto the floor. But he managed to wind her bloody left arm around his neck and grip her wrist to stop her from falling, and together they managed to stagger back along the passageway, tilting from side to side as they went.

At last they reached the forward hold. Decker was momentarily dazzled by a beam of light, but then he looked up and saw Hicks kneeling on the deck above them.

"Hicks! For Christ's sake, Hicks, give me a fucking hand here, will you?"

"Lieutenant? What's happening? You look like you're hurt."

"Just shine your flashlight on the steps, will you?"

Decker guided Queen Aché to the foot of the companionway. She was keening under her breath like a mourner at a funeral, and her knees kept giving way. "You're going to have to climb," Decker told her.

"How can I climb with *these?*" she demanded, raising her mutilated hands like a pair of scarlet mittens.

"Listen to me," he told her, pointing the flashlight in his

own face so that she could see him clearly. "There's no other way to escape. I can't carry you up."

Queen Aché looked up at the companionway. Decker heard a scuffling noise close by, and turned around and fired two shots at nothing at all. "You have to climb, Your Majesty, otherwise you're going to die here."

Queen Aché miserably approached the rusty steps and tried to curl her right wrist around them.

"That's it. Now your foot. Now pull yourself up."

She managed to climb up one step, and then another, but then she had to stop. "My hands," she wept. "They hurt so much! Yemayá, please stop them from hurting!"

"Climb," Decker urged her.

"Oh, Yemayá, please take this pain away from me, please!"

"Fucking *climb*, will you!"

Queen Aché hooked her left wrist around the railing and pulled herself up a little farther. At last she was close enough to the top for Hicks to be able to lean over and take hold of her forearms and help her negotiate the last few steps. Decker scrambled up right behind her.

"Major Shroud?" Hicks asked, wiping his bloody hands on his pants.

"Oh, you bet your ass. He's here and he wants his pound of flesh and he's not listening to any apologies or any deals. We have to get Queen Aché out of here double quick. The Nine Deaths, remember? Fingers, toes, hands, feet."

Between them, they lifted Queen Aché up from the deck, and helped her over to the slope of rubble that led to the crawl space up above them. "How the hell we going to get her up here?" Hicks asked.

"Have you tried calling for backup?"

"No signal. Not down here."

"Shit. Okay, here's what we do. We climb up backward sitting on our butts, and we heave her up after us."

Decker guided Queen Aché to the fallen girder and made her stand with her back to it. Her face was pale gray, and her eyes were filmed over. "Queen Aché? Listen . . . stay there, just like that. Hicks and me, we're going to pull you up the slope. You got it? If you can, dig your heels in to stop yourself from sliding back down again, that'll help."

"Justice and blood," Queen Aché mumbled. "*Oggunda ofun*—justice and blood through a curse."

"Forget about the sayings, we have to get you out of here, and you're a big tall lady, and we need you to help us to do it."

"Yemayá, I pray to you, save me."

"Absolutely. And while you're at it, you can say three Hail Yemayás for me and Hicks, too."

Puffing with effort, Decker climbed up onto the girder, and then sat down on the slope of rubble, kicking a few bricks away to give himself a better foothold. Hicks climbed up beside him, and then the two of them leaned forward and lifted Queen Aché up so that she was sitting on the rubble, too.

"Leave me," she said, her bloodied hands hanging loose. "I can't take any more. Leave me. Yemayá will take care of me. Changó would never hurt Yemayá."

"It's not Changó I'm worried about, Your Majesty. It's Major Shroud. Changó has all of the elemental power, that's for sure. He's got all of the thunder, and all of the lightning, and he's truly frightening. But Major Shroud is the one who's in charge here."

Hicks frowned at him. "What do you mean?"

"I mean, sport, that this is a case of a possessed person taking control of the spirit that possesses him—because he's meaner, and more determined, and much more focused. Sure—the great god Changó had the power to set fire to those woods in the Wilderness, and to turn those Yankee soldiers inside out, but who was the one who was really salivating to do it?

"Changó isn't fundamentally evil. Changó takes revenge on people who do him wrong, but Changó doesn't murder innocent people for the sake of it. It's Major Shroud. Now, let's get this lady out of here before he comes after her again. One—two—three—*heave!*"

CHAPTER THIRTY-FOUR

In showers of sliding sand and broken bricks, they managed to manhandle Queen Aché up to the top of the slope and lay her down on the mud in the crawl space. Hicks prodded at his cell phone again but there was still no signal.

"Come on," Decker panted. "There's nothing else for it, we'll just have to pull her along behind us."

He hunkered down beside Queen Aché and said, "How are you feeling? Think you can stand being dragged a bit farther?"

She stared up at him and her face was expressionless, although he still had the feeling that he could see another face, a far older face, looking through her eyes. "I can't feel my hands anymore."

"Believe me, that's probably a blessing."

"Why didn't you leave me behind?"

"Are you kidding me? Shroud would have diced you and sliced you."

"But I killed the only woman you ever loved. If I had been in your place, *I* would have left me behind."

"You know what? That's because King Special never taught you the difference between justice and revenge."

"He took me to a *santero* once, when I was thirteen, to have my fortune told. The *santero* told me that I was going to be strong and tall and beautiful. But then he said, 'Remember one thing . . . even the saints in all their glory cannot save you from the living dead.' I never understood what he meant, not for years, but now I do."

"Let's just get you out of here. We can worry about the hocus-pocus later."

Decker took hold of one of Queen Aché's arms and Hicks took hold of the other, and together they dragged her across the crawl space, leaving a snakelike trail in the black, slimy mud. They were less than halfway toward the broken-brick staircase, however, when the beam of Decker's flashlight was suddenly refracted at an angle, bent sideways. He lifted it higher and pointed it back toward the cavity in the floor, and he was sure that he could see a distortion in the air, so that the brickwork shifted and rippled.

"Shit, he's following us! There, look! You see that?"

"What? Where? I don't see nothing."

"Over there, just left of that pillar. Like the air's dancing around."

"I still don't see nothing."

They started to drag Queen Aché farther, but they had only shifted her four or five feet when they heard a whipping sound, and Queen Aché let out a cry like a run-over dog. The toecap of her left boot had been sheared clean off, taking her toes with it.

Decker pulled out his gun and fired off a single shot, even though he knew that there wasn't even a cat-in-hell's chance of hitting anything. "Shroud! You fuck!" he shouted. "You cut her again, I swear to God, Shroud, I'll do the same to you!"

"*He's there!*" screamed Queen Aché. "*He's there! I can see him! He's there!*"

"Point!" Decker shouted, and she pointed wildly to her left. Decker fired again, and again. Chips of brick sprayed from one of the buttresses, and a ricochet sang from the opposite wall.

"Did I hit him? Is he hit? Where's he gone now?"

"I don't know, I don't know," Queen Aché moaned. "I can't see him anymore."

Decker seized her arm again. "Come on, Hicks, let's just get the two-toned hell out of here."

Crouching under the overbearing arches, they pulled Queen Aché out of the crawl space. All they had to do now was carry her up the rubble slope to the station's lower level. Decker lifted her up under her arms, while Hicks took her legs, and together they struggled upward, one bent-legged step at a time, sweating and grunting, while Queen Aché lolled lifelessly between them.

At last they reached the top, and managed to maneuver her through the narrow hole in the back of the alcove, into the basement. They laid her down gently on the floor, and Hicks sat down beside her, while Decker leaned against the wall, trying to get his breath back. His arms and legs were quivering from the effort.

"What's the plan, Lieutenant?" Hicks asked.

"First of all, we're going to take Queen Aché to the hospital. Then we're going to work out how we're going to deal with Major Shroud."

"How about a SWAT team? If they laid down, like, wall-to-wall machine-gun fire, somebody's bound to hit him."

"Oh, really? And how do you think he's going to retaliate? The same way he did in the Wilderness. He's going to incinerate the whole place and turn our guys inside out."

"So what are we going to do?"

"I know what *I'm* going to do. I'm going to *think*. I'm going to use my head, while I still have it."

He bent over Queen Aché. She had been unconscious while they carried her up the rubble staircase, but now her eyelids flickered open. "Am I really here?" she asked him. Her scarf had slipped off and one side of her tightly braided hair was caked in mud.

"You're here, yes. But not for much longer." He looked up. Hicks was already splashing across the flooded cellar floor, to call for an ambulance and backup.

Decker took off his coat, bundled it up, and propped up Queen Aché's head. "My rings," she said, with a small, regretful smile. "When he cut off my fingers, I lost all of my precious rings. My daddy gave me such a pretty gold ring when I went through my *ebbó de tres meses*."

"We'll find them for you," Decker reassured her.

"What good will they be, if I have no fingers to put them on?" She was so matter-of-fact that Decker knew that she was deeply in shock. He remembered a man in a serious car smash on the Midlothian Turnpike who had smiled and winked at him and said, "See that leg, my friend—over there—on the median strip—that's *my* leg."

Hicks came back. "Ambulance in five minutes, backup in three."

"Okay," Decker said, standing up straight. But at that moment, hell arrived. There was another *whippp*! and the toe of Queen Aché's right boot was whacked off at a sharp diagonal, and a fine spray of blood flew up Decker's cheek. Hicks said, "Jesus Christ!"

"*Where is he?*" Decker yelled at Queen Aché. "*Tell me where he is!*"

But Queen Aché was too stunned to answer him, and the next second her right arm was pulled straight up into the air, as if she were giving him a defiant salute. Decker seized her wrist and tried to pull it back down, but he was shoved in the chest so hard that he was thrown back against one of the hunchback stalagmites, jarring his spine. He was still struggling to get his balance when Queen Aché's fingerless hand was chopped from her wrist and sent flying across the basement floor.

"*Hicks—grab him!*" Decker shouted. Hicks came forward, crouching and feinting like a wrestler, but as soon as he tried to grapple with their invisible opponent, his legs were kicked out from under him and he fell heavily backward, knocking his head.

Queen Aché's left arm was yanked up in the same way as her right, and with a crunch of bone, a V-shaped cut half severed her hand, so that it flopped sideways on a skein of skin and tendons. Seconds later, another cut lopped it off completely.

"*Shroud!*" Decker roared at him. "*Show yourself, you bastard!*" He fired another two shots but he knew that he must have missed. He ejected his cartridge cases, but as he tried to reload he was violently slammed in the shoulder and sent flying against the stalagmites again.

He rolled over, winded. He was still on his hands and knees when Queen Aché's feet were chopped off at the ankles and thrown in different directions, with blood spinning out of them like Catherine wheels. Then her hair was suddenly tugged up, so that her head was lifted from the floor. Her left ear was sliced off, upward, and then her right. Then—with no hesitation, and with a gristly crunch—her nose was cut away, so that she had nothing left in the middle of her face but two triangular holes, bubbling with blood. Decker fired again, twice, as close to Queen Aché as he dared.

He waited, panting, straining his eyes to see the slightest deflection in the air.

"Shroud . . . I swear to God, I'm going to kill you for this."

"Changó protects me," Major Shroud said. His voice sounded so close to Decker's ear that he twisted around in alarm, his gun raised two-handed in front of his face.

"He has punished this *santera*. Tomorrow it will be my turn to take my revenge on you."

Decker could hear police and ambulance sirens, although he didn't know what possible use any backup could be. He tried to stand up, but the air suddenly warped in front of his eyes, and Major Shroud pushed him roughly back onto his side. "Why do you struggle, Martin? You might just as well fight against the wind."

He tried to get up yet again, but again Major Shroud thrust him back down. "If you defy me anymore, I will give you a Tenth Death tomorrow. I will cut off your manhood and push it down your throat."

"I bet you will, too. You did the same thing to those poor young kids after Manassas, didn't you? You're a fucking out-and-out sadist, Shroud."

"Sadist?" Shroud said, puzzled.

"Somebody who gets their kicks out of hurting people, asshole. This is nothing to do with Changó, is it? You're using Changó's power, for sure. But this is nothing to do with Santería, it's all about *you*. Eleven good men found out what a psycho you were, and sealed you up where you belonged, and that's the only reason you want your revenge. Believe me, you're not going to get it."

"You really think so? Believe me, Martin, I've waited far too long for this day."

Decker heard car doors slamming outside, and running feet. Hicks shouted, "This way! This way!"

The distortion in the air flickered away from Decker and moved around Queen Aché, who was lying on her back with a shiny balloon of blood where her nose had been.

"Don't," Decker said. But at the same time, he asked himself if Queen Aché would even want to go on living, without hands, without feet, grotesquely disfigured as she was.

Queen Aché was slowly lifted up. She rose like a puppet, her arms hanging loose, her knees half bent. Her head hung to one side with long strings of blood sliding from her nose. As she stood erect, on her chopped-off ankles, half a dozen uniforms came running into the basement with their guns drawn.

"Lieutenant! What's happening here? Lieutenant!"

Decker climbed to his feet and raised his hand. "Take it easy, guys. This is kind of a hostage situation."

The rest of the men stayed back but Sergeant Buchholz came waddling right up to him. He was a big-bellied man, with a moustache like a sweeping brush. "What's the story, Lieutenant?" He jerked his thumb toward Queen Aché. "What the hell happened to *her*?" She appeared to be standing on her own, but she was smothered in blood and she swayed improbably from side to side.

"You don't recognize her? Well, I can't blame you. That's Queen Aché."

"Queen Aché? Holy shit."

"She's being held hostage."

"Hostage? What do you mean? Who by?"

"He's right here, Buchholz, but he's not exactly one hundred percent visible."

"Excuse me?"

Decker laid a hand on his shoulder, more for support than anything else. "The hostage taker is holding her up. Look at her. She can't stand up on her own, because he cut her feet off."

Sergeant Buchholz was even more baffled. "He's holding her up? I don't understand what you mean, Lieutenant. There's nobody there."

"Tomorrow, Martin!" Major Shroud called. "This is what will happen to you!"

Sergeant Buchholz turned wildly around, first to the left and then to the right. "Who said that? Who the fuck said that?"

"Shroud," Decker said. "I'm begging you."

"Shroud? Who's Shroud? Come on, Lieutenant, for Christ's sake!"

"*Shroud!*" Decker repeated, but he knew that it was no use. He caught the faintest shine of a saber blade, and Queen Aché's head was struck from her shoulders and tumbled onto the floor. It rolled over and over and ended up close to his feet, noseless, earless, and staring at him. Her headless body stood upright for three countable seconds, *one, two, three*, with arterial blood jetting out of her severed neck like spray after spray of scarlet flowers, and then she twisted around and collapsed.

His eyes bulging, Sergeant Buchholz jabbed his revolver in every possible direction. "Who the hell did that? Who the hell *did* that?"

Decker lowered his Anaconda. "You witnessed that, right?"

"Of course I witnessed it. But who did it?"

"Sorry, Sergeant. It's a very long story."

"Somebody cut her head off, for Christ's sake. But there's nobody there."

"Like I told you, the hostage taker isn't exactly visible."

"Meaning *what*, Lieutenant, or am I missing something?"

"Meaning he's here but you can't see him, that's all."

"So where the hell's he gone now?"

"Your guess is as good as mine, Sergeant. He could be standing right behind you, for all I know."

"What?"

"Unlikely. I think he probably left the building already."

Hicks came over, circling as far away from Queen Aché's sprawled and bloodied body as he could. He glanced down at her head but then he looked away.

"You okay?" Decker asked him.

"What do you think? I've spent the whole of my life trying to get away from this voodoo stuff. My grandmother, my aunts, and my uncles, they all had their spells and their magic cures and their coconut shells. My friends at school got sick, their parents took them to the doctor. When I got sick, they rubbed me with egg yolks and blew cigar smoke all over me. It made me feel like I was some kind of savage.

"Why do you think I don't like Rhoda doing her séances? It's mumbo-jumbo. It's slave stuff. Why can't they leave it where it belongs, back in Africa, back in the past? I hate that stuff."

"Maybe you do, but it works."

Hicks said, "The Nine Deaths. Jesus. And that's what he's going to do to you."

Decker checked his watch. Three paramedics were coming through the basement, pushing a loudly rattling gurney. The police officers were milling around, wondering what to do. Decker said, "I still have five and a half hours till Saint James Day."

"How are you going to stop him?"

Decker looked down at Queen Aché's head. "I told you, I'm going to think."

"If I were you, I'd take the first flight out of here, as far away as possible."

"Uh-huh, that's not the way to do it. You got to face up to things, sport. No use in running away."

Hicks gave Queen Aché's head another disgusted look. "Something else, wasn't she? Really something else."

"Oh yes. But she didn't get any more than she deserved."

CHAPTER THIRTY-FIVE

Cab said, "I guess I can be thankful for *one* small mercy."

"Oh yes? And what's that?"

"The whole time you failed to report back to headquarters, I didn't sneeze once. It ain't myrtle I'm a martyr to, it's *you*."

Decker didn't know what to say to that. Cab opened the folder on his desk in front of him and studied it for a while, and then he said, "Queen Aché accompanied you voluntarily to Main Street Station?"

"Yes, Captain. No duress whatever."

"And she was mutilated and eventually decapitated by your prime suspect, whom you conveniently managed not to tell me the name of the last time we spoke? Right in front of you, and in front of Sergeant Hicks, and seven uniformed officers?"

"Yes, sir."

"Do you have any idea what the political repercussions of this killing are going to be? I mean, do you have any idea at *all?* We haven't informed the media yet, but I'll give it another hour before somebody from the Egun makes a public complaint. Ms. Honey Blackwell is going to accuse us of everything from willful endangerment to institutionalized racism.

"Apart from that, Decker, where the hell are you going with this investigation? The interim chief is screaming down the phone at me every five minutes and the *Times-Dispatch* has started calling us 'Richmond's Finest Fumblers.'"

"Well, Captain, you have to understand that this is a very unusual case. Even more complex than it appeared at first sight. It's going to take patience, and imagination, and even more patience."

"But you *do* have a prime suspect?"

"Absolutely."

"So . . . who is it?"

"I'd rather not give you his name, sir, not just yet."

"I am your captain, Decker."

"Yes, sir. But I seriously believe it would jeopardize my investigation if I were to tell you his identity before I made my final move."

"Oh yes. And why is that?"

"Because (a) you wouldn't believe me, and (b) you couldn't officially approve of what I'm planning to do in order to stop him."

"I don't like the sound of the word 'stop.'"

"All right, 'apprehend.'"

Cab heaved himself up from his chair and walked across to the window. "You're a good detective, Decker. Tell me that I can trust you on this."

"You can trust me, Captain. Really."

"So how much patience are you looking for?"

"Twelve hours' worth, maybe a whole lot less. It depends on the suspect."

"All right, then, much against my better judgment. But if I give you that much rope, it'll be your fault if you hang yourself with it."

"Hanging? That's the least of my worries."

Billy Joe Bennett was polishing a Civil War coffee boiler when Decker and Hicks came into the Rebel Yell.

"See this?" he said, holding it up. "This is a genuine rarity. When the army of northern Virginia went to war in 1861 they took along whole wagon trains of baking trays and sheet-iron stoves and cutlery and flour boxes and every convenience you could think of. But after six months of toting all that stuff around they threw away just about everything but a bucket and an ax and a frying pan."

Decker said, "I'm looking for a uniform."

"A uniform? Sure. Depends what you want. I've just bought a jacket from the Second Company, Richmond Howitzers, used to belong to Captain Lorraine F. Jones and it's still got his name in it. I've got pants from Cutshaw's battery, and any number of slouch hats and buck gloves and belts."

"I'm looking for a general's uniform. I want to dress up like Robert E. Lee."

Billy Joe raised his eyebrows. "Fancy-dress party?"

"Something like that."

It took almost a half hour of rummaging, but eventually Billy Joe came up with a double-breasted frock coat, a pair of gray pants with canvas suspenders, a broad-brimmed hat, a pair of long buck gloves, and a pair of high black riding boots. Decker tried on the hat and the frock coat, and Billy Joe stood back and nodded in approval. "All you need now is a white beard and Traveler. That was Lee's favorite horse. Oh, and how about this?"

He went over to the display cabinet and came back with

the same wrist breaker that he had refused to sell to the customer from Madison, with a decorative scabbard for Decker to hang it on his belt.

"Can't have Robert E. Lee without his sword, wouldn't be right. But don't go swinging it about, Lieutenant. You don't want to be taking anybody's bean off, by accident."

As they drove away from the store, Hicks said, "Are you going to give me any idea what this is all about?"

"You'll see." He picked up his cell phone and punched out Jonah's number. "Jonah . . . it's Decker Martin. No, don't worry about that. No. Listen, you remember that store you took me to, to buy all those gifts for Moses Adebolu? That's right. Can you do me a favor and go there and buy me everything it takes to make an offering to Changó? Bananas, spices, apples, and all those herbs, you know, like *rompe zaraguey* and *prodigiosa*. Oh yes, a live rooster, too. Why? You don't need to know why. Just drop it all off at police headquarters. Yes, of course I'll pay you."

When they reached Seventh Street he took a left and parked outside Stagestruck Theatrical Supplies. It was a small store with a window display of Shakespearean costumes—Romeo in doublet and hose, and Juliet in a long pearl-studded dress and a wimple. Decker went up to the diminutive old gnome behind the counter and said, "I'm looking for a beard."

"A beard, you say? Then you came to the right place. We have the finest selection of surrogate facial hair in all Virginia. What are you looking for? Goatee, Abe Lincoln, or Grizzly Adams?"

They collected Jonah's shopping from police headquarters. The sergeant on the desk handed over the basket containing the live rooster with obvious relief. "Damn thing wouldn't stop clucking. Worse than my wife."

Next, they stopped at the Bottom Line Restaurant on East Main Street for hamburgers and buffalo wings and beer. Decker could eat only two or three mouthfuls of his hamburger. "Shit—I feel like the condemned man, eating his last meal."

"You have a plan though, don't you?"

"Not much of one."

"You're going to dress up like Robert E. Lee?"

"That's the general idea."

"And you think—what? That Major Shroud is going to stop and salute you?"

"Maybe. The point is that Major Shroud feels deeply aggrieved because he expected to be treated like a hero instead of a war criminal. He spent nearly 150 years sealed up in that casket. Can you imagine it? Never able to sleep, never able to die. That's plenty of time to develop a raging homicidal obsession, wouldn't you say?"

"He's not going to believe that General Lee is still alive, though, is he?"

"I don't know. If he doesn't, then this isn't going to work. But he's not mentally stable, there's no question of that. Who would be, after being buried alive for so long? And if we can take him by surprise—"

"I still think we should call in the SWAT team."

Decker shook his head. "Waste of time. When Shroud's invisible he's not a solid physical presence in the same way as you or me. He has the kinetic energy to push us around, that's for sure, but I don't think we can hurt him with bullets. It's all part of the same Santería magic that allows him to walk through walls. God knows how it's done. I mean, it defies every law of physics you can think of. But maybe it's like ultraviolet light, which you can't see, or dog whistles, which you can't hear. Just because you can't see them and you can't hear them, that doesn't mean they're not there."

"Too heavy for me, Lieutenant."

Back at Decker's apartment, Hicks hung up his coat and angled one of the armchairs so that he was facing the door. He laid his gun on the coffee table beside him, for all the use that was going to be. Decker unloaded all of Jonah's shopping in the kitchen, including the fretfully clucking rooster, and then went through to the bedroom.

"Help yourself to a soda," he told Hicks. "I don't know how long we're going to have to wait for Major Shroud to make an appearance."

"Not too long, Lieutenant, if you want my opinion. The way he was talking, he's just champing at the bit to cut you into chitterlings."

"Sure. Thanks for the reassurance."

Decker laid out his Civil War uniform on the bed. He hoped to God that he hadn't misjudged Major Shroud's motives, or overestimated how much control Major Shroud was able to exert over the spirit of Changó. But when Major Shroud had ordered him to, Changó had immediately returned to protect him—in spite of Queen Aché's offer of apples and herbs. Why would Changó have done that, unless—in this unholy symbiosis of god and man—Major Shroud was the dominant partner? Men and their gods are inseparable, and sometimes the gods have to do what men bid them to do, for the sake of their own survival. When men don't believe in them any longer, gods die.

Decker picked up the photograph of Cathy on the Robert E. Lee footbridge. *If I get out of this, the first thing I'm going to do is visit your grave and lay camellias on it, heaps of camellias, your very favorite flower. Wherever you are now, I love you still, and I always will, just as much as you love me, and more.*

He pulled on the rough gray Civil War pants and fastened the withered suspenders to hold them up. The pants were two or three inches too short in the leg, but that wouldn't matter when he put his boots on. He picked a plain gray shirt out of his closet, and then he shrugged on the heavy frock coat and fastened it right up to the neck. It smelled of dry-cleaning, and age.

The boots were a size too tight, but he managed to force them onto his feet by repeatedly stamping his heels on the floor. He didn't know how he was going to get them off, but he could worry about that later. Finally, he went into the bathroom and painted his chin and his upper lip with the spirit gum that the gnome in Stagestruck had sold him. He took his bristly white beard out of its polythene bag and carefully pressed it on. In a few minutes, he looked twenty years older. A slightly sharp-faced version of General Lee, but not an unconvincing likeness, apart from his Italian designer glasses. He adjusted his wide-brimmed hat, hung his saber onto his belt, and then he stood in front of the full-length mirror and struck a pose.

He came out of the bedroom, stalked across to where Hicks was sitting, and stood in front of him. In a deep, sonorous voice, he said, "After four years of arduous service marked by unsurpassed courage and fortitude, the army of northern Virginia has been compelled to yield to overwhelming numbers and resources."

"Holy shit," Hicks said, rising to his feet.

"Think it'll work?" Decker asked.

"Well, you sure convinced *me*."

Decker took off his hat and sat down. "This is madness, isn't it?"

"I don't know. This whole thing is madness. Maybe the only way to fight madness is to act even madder."

"Well, sport, I hope you're right. I don't know what the media are going to make of it, if I get chopped into pieces while I'm all dressed up like Robert E. Lee."

All they could do now was sit and wait. Midnight passed, and Hicks checked his watch and said, "That's it, Saint James Day," but after twenty minutes there was still no sign of Major Shroud, and the only sound they heard from outside was the lonely hooting of a riverboat.

Decker said, "If this doesn't come to anything . . . you know, if Shroud doesn't show . . . you won't mention this to anybody, will you?"

"What, you dressing up like General Lee?" Hicks hesitated, and then he smiled and shook his head. "What kind of a partner do you think I am?"

"You're a good partner, Hicks. Hardworking, bright. I think you're going to go far."

"I don't know. This investigation, you know, it's thrown me completely. I keep asking myself, how would *I* have handled it, if *I'd* been in charge? You know what I mean?"

"Sure, I know what you mean. And what was your answer?"

"I wouldn't have dared to do anything that you did."

"Of course you would. Don't sell yourself short."

"You think I would have arranged a séance with my partner's wife, without even asking him?"

"I'm sorry about that, I told you."

"You don't have to be sorry. It was the right thing to do. Do you think I would have blackmailed Queen Aché into looking for Changó for me?"

"I don't know, maybe."

"That woman frightened three colors of shit out of me. I wouldn't have dared to do that."

"You can't say that. Maybe you would."

"I wouldn't, because I didn't want to believe in any of this

Santería stuff. You didn't want to believe it, either, but at least your mind was open, and you followed the clues where they led you."

The white-bearded Decker said, "That's where you're wrong, sport. I didn't follow any clues. I was shown the way, by a spirit who loves me more than I even realized. That was the only reason I believed in the Devil's Brigade, and Changó, and that was the only reason I went looking for Major Shroud."

Hicks looked at his watch. "How about a cup of coffee? Want me to make it?"

"Sure, sounds like a good idea."

Hicks went into the kitchen and switched on the light. As he did so, there was a ring at the doorbell. He turned and stared at Decker, and Decker pulled his Anaconda out of his holster and cocked it.

There was a long pause, and then the doorbell rang again.

"Think it's him?" Hicks asked, in a hoarse whisper.

"He'd just walk through the wall, wouldn't he? He wouldn't ring the bell."

"Yeah. But it *could* be him."

"Go take a look through the spyhole."

While Hicks went to the door to see who was there, Decker went from lamp to lamp, switching them off, so that the light was subdued, apart from a single bright desk lamp directly behind him. Then he stood in the center of the room, stiff-backed, bearded chin protruding, as if he were General Robert E. Lee himself, expecting an audience.

Hicks turned around and said, "It's not him."

"It's not? Then who is it?"

"Friends of yours. Sandra Plummer and her mother."

"*What?* What the hell are they doing here?"

"You want me to let them in?"

"Of course I want you to let them in."

Hicks opened the door and Sandra came in, blinking against the light. She was wearing a gray duffel coat and a maroon woolly hat. Eunice Plummer came in right behind her, her hair even wilder than usual, dressed in a long brown raincoat.

"Where's Lieutenant Martin?" she asked.

Decker took off his hat. "Right here, Ms. Plummer. Don't let the beard fool you."

Eunice Plummer peered at him closely. "My goodness, it *is* you. Why are you dressed up like that?"

"Because I'm expecting a visitor, Ms. Plummer. I'm expecting the man who killed Jerry and Alison Maitland, and George Drewry, and John Mason. Apparently I'm next on his list."

"But why do you have to look like Robert E. Lee?"

"I'm flattered—you guessed who I was supposed to be. It's called psychology, Ms. Plummer. Catching your suspect off guard. But what are you two doing here? It's past midnight."

"The So-Scary Man is coming," Sandra said, emphatically.

"How do you know that, Sandra?"

"She woke me up and said she could feel it," Eunice Plummer said, somewhat impatiently. "I told her she was imagining things, and to go back to bed, but she wouldn't. I'm afraid she threw a bit of a tantrum, so in the end there was nothing I could do but bring her here and show her. Otherwise she could have suffered an episode."

"An episode?"

"A fit, Lieutenant, and they can be very harmful."

Decker said, "Sit down, please. How about a cup of coffee? Sergeant Hicks here was just making some."

"No, thank you," Eunice Plummer said. "But Sandra might like a glass of warm milk."

Decker sat next to Sandra and took hold of her hands. "Sorry about the beard, Sandra. It's my disguise."

"You look like Santa Claus."

"Yes, you're right. Ho-ho-ho! Sorry I don't have any presents for you. But listen—tell me what you felt about the So-Scary Man."

"I was having a dream. I was dreaming about the House of Fun."

"Go on."

"I saw the twisty cloud over the rooftop and then I saw the So-Scary Man coming out of the door. He was wearing his long gray coat and he was wearing a hat like yours, and I knew that he was coming to find you."

She hesitated, and then she said, "He was carrying a sword, too. Just like yours."

Eunice Plummer looked at Decker keenly. "You're really expecting him, aren't you? What Sandra saw in her dream—that was real, wasn't it?"

Decker nodded. "The So-Scary Man is Major Joseph Shroud, who was possessed by a Santería god called Changó, back in 1864, during the Battle of the Wilderness. Changó gave him such power that he was able to massacre hundreds of Union soldiers, and I guess he could have turned the tide of the war, if Lieutenant General Longstreet had allowed it."

"I don't understand. How could he still be alive today?"

"I don't really understand it myself. But his fellow officers sealed him in a lead casket so that his body was preserved, and I guess that his life spark was kept alight by Changó."

"And he's coming here—tonight?"

"My great-great-grandfather was one of the men who sealed him up. He wants his revenge."

Sandra said, "I woke up and I looked out of my bedroom window and I saw the black twisty cloud over the House of Fun and I knew it was real."

"You're right, Sandra," Decker told her. "It *is* real." He turned to Eunice Plummer and said, "There's no doubt about it—Sandra has some extrasensory sensitivity, whatever you want call it. Otherwise she wouldn't know that Main Street Station is the House of Fun—or, actually, 'Ofun,' which means 'the place where the curse is born.'"

To Sandra, he said, "Sandra—I want to thank you for all of your concern. You've been amazing, and you've helped us to solve all these murders. But things could get dangerous here tonight, so I want you to take your mom home, okay? When all of this is finished with, and we've locked the So-Scary Man up in prison, I'll come around and take you and your mom out for lunch. How do you like fried chicken?"

"He's outside the door," Sandra said, in a matter-of-fact voice.

"Excuse me?"

"The So-Scary Man. He's standing right outside the door."

Decker immediately stood up and jammed on his hat. "*Hicks!*" he shouted. "Forget about the coffee! He's here! Bring in the fruit and everything! Bring in that rooster! And bring in that carving knife, too!"

Eunice looked flustered. "What shall *we* do?"

"You and Sandra go into the bedroom. Close the door and lock it. He won't try to hurt you unless you get in his way."

"I have to stay," Sandra said.

"You can't! This man is a homicidal maniac! Now get in the bedroom, please!"

"But you won't be able to see him!"

Hicks was coming out of the kitchen with a paper bag of groceries in one hand and the rooster in the other. The rooster was fluttering and flustering and trying to burst out of its basket. Hicks said, "She's right, Lieutenant. Think what happened to Queen Aché."

But Decker took Sandra's arm and started to propel her toward the bedroom. "I can't risk it. If the So-Scary Man sees that you've been helping me—God alone knows what he could do to you!"

"I have to stay!" Sandra protested. "Don't you understand? *It's what I was born for!*"

Decker stopped pushing her and stared at her. Sandra stared back at him, her pale blue eyes unblinking and determined.

Eunice Plummer came forward and put her arm around Sandra's shoulders. "She's right, Lieutenant. Don't you see? She was born with a handicap, but she was also born with a very great gift. This is her destiny, isn't it?"

Decker opened his mouth and then closed it again. He didn't know what to say.

Hicks lifted up the brown paper bag of fruit and herbs. "All ready, Lieutenant."

"Okay, then, sport." Decker turned back to Sandra and looked at her seriously. "If you really want to stay, Sandra—you can stay. But promise me you'll keep right behind me, and don't attract attention to yourself. If things start to go wrong, don't hesitate, don't try to help—you and your mom run into that bedroom as fast as you can and lock the door tight and call the police."

Sandra said, "I promise."

Decker turned around. Hicks was waiting in the kitchen doorway and gave him the thumbs-up. "Is the So-Scary Man still outside?" he asked Sandra.

Sandra nodded. "He's saying something, inside his head. Like a prayer."

"All right, then. Hold tight."

After a while, Sandra closed her eyes and began to mutter. Decker couldn't hear everything she was saying, but he recognized some of it. "*Babami Changó ikawo ilemu fumi alaya tilanchani nitosi . . .* "

He went back to the middle of the room, took off his glasses, and stood very stiff, in the same way that General Lee had posed for so many photographs and engravings. He tried to look calm and unafraid, even though his heart was galloping like a panicky horse and he kept seeing flashes of Queen Aché, hopelessly holding up the stumps of her fingerless hands, with sticks of bone showing above the flesh.

Sandra muttered, "*. . . Ni re elese ati wi Changó alamu oba layo ni na ile ogbomi.*" She paused for a while and then she opened her eyes.

"Is he moving yet?" Decker asked.

Sandra said nothing. Her eyes seemed to be focused on nothing at all.

"Sandra? Is he moving yet?"

"He's already inside," Sandra whispered. "He's standing by the door."

Decker narrowed his eyes, trying to see any disturbance in the air, but without his glasses the middle distance was a blur.

"He's coming nearer. He's walking past the kitchen. He's here. He's right in front of you. He's staring at you."

Decker cleared his throat. "Major Joseph Shroud?" he asked, gruffly.

"He's still staring at you," Sandra said. "He's got his hand resting on his sword handle."

Decker said, as grandly as he could, "I've received a dispatch about you, Major Shroud, from Lieutenant General Longstreet."

"He's taken his hand off his sword handle. He's lifting his arm. He's saluting you."

"General Lee, sir? Is that really General Lee?" Major Shroud's disembodied voice was husky with emotion.

"It seems that the army of northern Virginia owes you a considerable debt, Major Shroud."

"I only did what was required of me, General."

"No, Major Shroud, you did much more than that. You sacrificed yourself for your country. Single-handed, you drove back the enemy, and you safeguarded our capital and our cause. In recognition of your valor and your devotion, I am hereby promoting you to the rank of colonel."

"I'm honored, General."

"Yes, Major Shroud. You *are* honored. Not condemned, not reviled. But *honored*. Let me see you now, so that I can grasp your hand."

"He's giving you a funny look," Sandra warned.

"Come now, Major Shroud," Decker urged him. "Where is your hand?"

"You can't see me, General? How did you know I was here, if you couldn't see me?"

"I sensed you, Major. I can always sense bravery. I can smell it on the wind."

Seconds ticked by. For a long moment, Decker thought that Major Shroud had recognized him behind his disguise, and that there would be no way of stopping him from inflicting the Nine Deaths on him—or even, God forbid, the *Ten* Deaths.

But then Sandra whispered, "*Look*." And gradually, the air in front of Decker began to curdle and thicken. It formed in dark, shadowy lumps, and then veins and arteries began to wriggle from one lump to the next, and bones took shape, and in less than a minute Major Shroud had materialized, in his crow's-feather hat, and his long gray topcoat, and his boots.

"At your service, General," he declared.

Decker gave a grave, dignified smile. He stepped forward

and took hold of Major Shroud's hand and shook it. Even through his buck gloves it felt as if it were nothing but knuckles and finger bones.

"Major Joseph Shroud, I hereby promote you to the rank of full colonel in the army of northern Virginia. You have your country's unceasing admiration and thanks, and the name of Shroud will enter the annals of this mighty conflict as a name forever associated with valor and with duty faithfully performed."

It was then, while he was still gripping Major Shroud's hand, that he said, quite quietly, "*Now*, Hicks."

Hicks came out of the kitchen shaking the brown paper bag. "Changó! Changó, listen to me! I bring you an offering! I bring you fruit and and spices! I bring you rum!"

"What is this?" Major Shroud demanded. "Who is this nigger?" He tried to pull his hand away but Decker held it tight.

"Changó!" Hicks sang out. "Leave this host and refresh yourself! *Kabio, kabio, sile!*"

"General Lee! Release me!" Major Shroud shouted. He was powerful, and his bony hand was knobbly and awkward to hold on to, but Decker didn't loosen his grip.

"I honor you, Changó!" Hicks cried. "I give you everything you hunger for!"

He tore open the bag and scattered the fruit and the herbs across the floor. "*Kabio, kabio, sile!* Welcome, Changó!"

Oh, God, this is not going to work, thought Decker. Changó isn't going to leave him. And with a sudden twist that almost sprained Decker's wrist, Major Shroud tugged his hand free and immediately went for his saber. He drew it out of its scabbard with a metallic sliding sound that set Decker's teeth on edge.

"Changó! I welcome you! Changó!"

Decker shouted at Sandra and Eunice Plummer, "Back—both of you! Get into the bedroom!"

Major Shroud advanced on him, his eyes glittering, his teeth bared in the black briar thicket of his beard. "You're no more Robert E. Lee than I am, are you? You're that damned Martin! Well, now, Martin, you're going to see where downright treachery gets you!"

Decker knew that he couldn't shoot him, not while Changó still protected him. Changó's anger at being attacked would be a hundred times worse. But all the same he drew out his own sword, Billy Joe's wrist breaker, and he waved it defiantly from side to side.

"You want to cut me to pieces? Okay, you throwback, let's see you try!"

Major Shroud lunged forward and his sword clanged and clashed against Decker's saber and almost knocked it out of his hand. Decker swung his arm and managed to deflect another lunge, but then Major Shroud performed a quick flurry of movements and the point of his sword jabbed deep into Decker's left shoulder.

Decker hardly felt any pain, but now he was seriously worried. Major Shroud began to press him harder and harder, his sword flashing in crisscross patterns that Decker could hardly see. He kept clashing his saber from side to side, and he managed to parry most of Major Shroud's lunges, but he knew that he wouldn't be able to hold him off for very long.

Retreating, he fell backward over the arm of the couch. Major Shroud raised his sword high above his head and smacked it down on the seat cushions just as Decker rolled off them onto the floor. Multicolored sponge stuffing flew up like a snowstorm.

Decker tried to crawl away, but Major Shroud had him

now. He stabbed him in the back of his right thigh, and then his right shoulder, and then he straddled him and gripped him tight between his knees.

"The Nine Deaths, Martin," he grunted. He reeked of stale sweat and gunpowder and filthy clothes and herbs. His hair was seething with lice.

Decker twisted himself around and tried to seize Major Shroud's wrist, but Major Shroud sliced him across the palm of his hand, at least a quarter inch deep, and blood poured out between his fingers and down his sleeve.

"Now for the First Death," Major Shroud told him, and took hold of Decker's left arm. "I'll grant you a little respite, Martin, and take the fingers off your left hand first."

He raised his sword—but as he did so, Decker heard a furious clucking. Hicks came forward, and he was holding up the wildly flapping rooster by its legs.

"Changó!" Hicks shouted. "Come to me, Changó! This is your sacrifice! This is your blood! Come eat! Come drink! *Kabio, kabio, sile!* Welcome to our house!"

Major Shroud turned his head around and screamed back, "What are you doing, you damn fool nigger? Get away from here! Get away! By God, I'm going to have your head next!"

"Changó! Let us see you! Changó, master of fire! Changó, master of thunder and lightning! Changó—are you master of your own destiny?"

With that, Hicks slashed the carving knife across the rooster's neck, almost beheading it. He swung the bird around and around, high above his head, and blood flew everywhere, spattering the walls, spattering Decker's face, pattering onto Major Shroud's hat and coat.

"No!" Major Shroud roared. "No, Changó! I forbid it! *I forbid it!*"

But Decker could see the blue crackle of electricity

crawling around the outline of Major Shroud's face. Then—while Major Shroud still ranted in frustrated fury—a lattice of quivering light formed around his head.

"No! No! No! Changó! You have to protect me! If I die, you die!"

But Changó slowly rose out of Major Shroud like a ghost rising from a grave, his arms outstretched. His face was a mask, decorated with fire. His eyes burned red, his hair was like a hundred streamers of flame, and his mouth was filled with dancing, sizzling voltage. He wore a cloak of billowing brown smoke, in which Decker could glimpse intermittent flashes of lightning.

"*You can't leave me!*" shrieked Major Shroud. "*You can't leave me!*"

The whole apartment began to shake. Pictures dropped off the walls, lamps overturned and smashed on the floor, chairs tipped over. A double fork of lightning jumped from one side of the living room to the other, and Decker was almost blinded. Then—almost immediately—there was an earsplitting bellow of thunder. The couch burst into flames, and then the drapes.

One arm raised to protect his face from the heat, Hicks yelled, "Changó! You are indeed your own master! You are the master of the world!"

Major Shroud climbed off Decker and went for Hicks with his sword flailing. Decker scrambled to his feet, too, and pulled his Anaconda out of his Civil War holster. Hicks was retreating toward the kitchen, trying to parry Major Shroud's lunges by wildly waving the dead rooster from side to side. In the middle of the room, half hidden by thick, swirling smoke, Changó glittered and blazed.

Decker cocked his revolver and pointed it at Major Shroud's head. "*Major Shroud!*"

There was another flash of lightning, and then another

rumble of thunder, far longer than the first, a rumble that seemed to go on and on, as if it would never stop. Lumps of plaster dropped from the ceiling, and wide cracks appeared in the walls. The apartment was already fiercely hot, and one of the windows shattered. A hungry wind gusted in from the river, and the couch flared up like a Norse funeral pyre.

With the briarlike afterimage of the lightning strike still dancing in front of his eyes, Decker took aim at Major Shroud again, and fired. Major Shroud tilted his head to one side, and the bullet hit the picture of the Dutch girl and smashed the glass. Decker fired again, and again, but Major Shroud moved like a speeded-up film, and both of his shots went wide.

"You'll have to hit me to kill me!" he screamed, above the funneling noise of the fire. He hacked furiously at Hicks, and caught him a blow on the shoulder. Hicks said, "Shit!" and dropped to the floor, still clutching the bloody rooster. Now Major Shroud turned on Decker, and came striding toward him, with his sword whistling in ever more complicated figures-of-eight.

"Nine Deaths, Martin? Ten? I'll give you twenty!"

He lifted his sword right back behind his head, and there was a look on his face that Decker had never seen on a man before. It was triumph, and mockery, and an excitement that was almost orgasmic. But it was more than that. It was the look of a man who had undergone a physical and spiritual metamorphosis. He was no longer a man, nor a beast, but something altogether more terrible. He was viciousness incarnate, and vengefulness, and war.

Decker fired at him again, and again he missed. He was just about to fire again when there was a third flash of lightning, so bright that Decker was blinded. It struck the tip of Major Shroud's sword, and Major Shroud was hurled bodily across the living room, colliding with the opposite wall and tumbling onto the floor. He lay there, jerking and twitching, with smoke pouring out of his coat. His beard glowed with a thousand orange sparks, like a smoldering sweeping brush.

Decker looked around. The burning figure of Changó was standing in the smoke, with one arm still extended.

Decker said, "*You* did that?"

Changó opened his mouth and static electricity sparkled on his teeth. He didn't actually speak, but somehow Decker could hear him, inside his head, and in a strange way, more like pictures than words, he could understand what Changó was trying to tell him.

He kept my spirit prisoner for thousands of darknesses. He thought of nothing but bringing pain and death to those good men who harbored my brother and sister orishas. He deserved nothing but punishment. He killed those warriors who fought to set my people free.

Decker said nothing for a moment, but nodded, and coughed.

Changó said, *Your gift is well received. Your summons was welcome.*

With that, his fiery image began to fade. For a few seconds, through the smoke, Decker could make out an arrangement of twinkling stars, more like a distant constellation than a dwindling god. Then Changó was gone, and there was nothing but the burning couch and the blackened, burning drapes that flapped in the wind.

Major Shroud groaned. Decker walked over to the other side of the room and looked down at him. Major Shroud's face was blackened and his eyes were rimmed with red.

"—betrayed me," he complained. "Even my god betrayed me."

"Nobody betrayed anybody except you, Major Shroud."

"It was war. That's what you forget. It was war, and I was doing my duty. The only trouble was, I did it too well."

"Yes," Decker said. "You probably did."

With that, he cocked his Anaconda again and pointed it between Major Shroud's eyebrows. "Hicks," he said, "can you walk okay?"

"Yassuh, boss."

"Go get Sandra and her mom out of the bedroom, would you?"

Hicks limped across the living room and opened the bedroom door. "Come on out, it's safe now. But hurry."

He led them out of the door while Decker kept the muzzle of his Anaconda only an inch away from Major Shroud's forehead, unwavering.

"The South will rise again," Major Shroud said. "You'll see."

"Pity you won't," Decker replied, and pulled the trigger.

At that instant the apartment exploded. Decker was flung against the kitchen archway, knocking his head so hard that he saw nothing but a blinding white light. He managed to crawl to the door, and Hicks grabbed hold of his coat collar and dragged him out into the corridor.

"My hat!" he said. "Billy Joe will kill me if I lose my hat!"

They walked out of the apartment building together to find the street already crowded with fire trucks and squad cars and sightseers. When Decker looked back up to his apartment, he saw that flames were waving out of the window like a burning Confederate battle flag, fanned by the early-morning wind.

As he crossed the curb, holding hands with Sandra, a TV floodlight was suddenly switched on, and this was instantly followed by a barrage of camera flashes.

Somebody called out, "Hey—it's Robert E. Lee! I swear to God, it's Robert E. Lee!"

Hicks turned to him and grinned, even though his left shoulder was soaked in blood. "They still love you, General Lee."

As they were surrounded by reporters and police and paramedics, a woman's voice began to sing "Dixie," and one by one, others joined in, and as Decker stood in the middle of the crowd, there was nothing he could do but nod and smile and lift his hat in the same respectful way that Robert E. Lee had lifted his hat to his defeated army.

The crowd didn't sing the popular words about the cotton fields, but the rousing battle hymn written by Albert Pike.

Southrons, hear your country call you!
Up, lest worse than death befall you!
To arms! To arms! To arms! In Dixie!

Lo! All the beacon fires are lighted!
Let all hearts be now united!
To arms! To arms! To arms! In Dixie!

Advance the flag of Dixie!
Hurrah! Hurrah!
For Dixie's land we take our stand,
And live or die for Dixie!

Cab arrived and climbed out of his car. It was obvious by his stripy collar that he had hurriedly pulled his big red sweater over his pajamas. "What happened here, Decker? Why the hell are you dressed up like that?"

Decker gritted his teeth and slowly tugged off his beard. "Long story, Captain."

Cab looked up at the fire. A turntable ladder was being swiveled around toward the side of the apartment block, and there was a fine spray of water in the wind.

Decker said, "We got him, Captain. You can call up the chief and tell her it's a wrap."

Cab sniffed, and then he sneezed. He didn't have a handkerchief, so Eunice Plummer had to hand him a crumpled tissue. "You're a good detective, Decker, but don't ever tell me how you do it. I think I'd come out in hives."

Three days later, on his first day back to the office, Decker's phone rang.

"Decker? This is Captain Morello."

"Well, well, and a very good morning to you, sir."

"You're a general now, sir. You don't have to call *me* 'sir.' "

"You saw the news, then. I was going to call you and thank you for everything you did."

"Lunch would be a very welcome thank-you."

"So long as you don't mind making it a threesome. I have another young lady that I have to thank."

"Should I be jealous?"

Decker thought about it, and smiled, and looked across at Sandra, who was drawing a picture of Changó on the back of a crime-report sheet.

"Yes," he said. "I think you should."

Before he took Sandra and Toni Morello for lunch, he stopped off at the cemetery and stood in front of Cathy's grave, with an armful of white camellias. The breeze blew across the ruffled surface of the James River and made the trees whisper.

"I don't know where you are now," he told Cathy, as he laid the flowers on the red marble plaque. "But thanks, sweetheart. Thanks for everything."